The Adventures of Theagenes and Chariclea

The Adventures of Theagenes and Chariclea

Heliodorus of Emesa

MINT EDITIONS

The Adventures of Theagenes and Chariclea was first published in 1789.

This edition published by Mint Editions 2021.

ISBN 9781513269603 | E-ISBN 9781513274607

Published by Mint Editions®

 MINT
EDITIONS

minteditionbooks.com

Publishing Director: Jennifer Newens
Design & Production: Rachel Lopez Metzger
Project Manager: Micaela Clark
Translated by Rowland Smith
Typesetting: Westchester Publishing Services

Contents

Book I

The day had begun to smile cheerily, and the sun was already gilding the tops of the hills, when a band of men, in arms and appearance pirates, having ascended the summit of a mountain which stretches down towards the Heracleotic mouth of the Nile, paused and contemplated the sea which was expanded before them. When not a sail appeared on the water to give them hopes of a booty, they cast their eyes upon the neighbouring shore; where the scene was as follows: a ship was riding at anchor, abandoned by her crew; but to all appearance laden with merchandize, as she drew much water. The beach was strewn with bodies newly slaughtered; some quite dead, others dying, yet still breathing, gave signs of a combat recently ended. Yet it appeared not to have been a designed engagement; but there were mingled with these dreadful spectacles the fragments of an unlucky feast, which seemed to have concluded in this fatal manner. There were tables, some yet spread with eatables; others overturned upon those who had hoped to hide themselves under them; others grasped by hands which had snatched them up as weapons. Cups lay in disorder, half fallen out of the hands of those who had been drinking from them, or which had been flung instead of missiles; for the suddenness of the affray had converted goblets into weapons.

Here lay one wounded with an axe, another bruised by a shell picked up on the beach, a third had his limbs broken with a billet, a fourth was burnt with a torch, but the greater part were transfixed with arrows; in short, the strangest contrast was exhibited within the shortest compass; wine mingled by fate with blood, war with feasting, drinking and fighting, libations and slaughters. Such was the scene that presented itself to the eyes of the pirates.

They gazed some time, puzzled and astonished. The vanquished lay dead before them, but they nowhere saw the conquerors; the victory was plain enough, but the spoils were not taken away; the ship rode quietly at anchor, though with no one on board, yet unpillaged, as much as if it had been defended by a numerous crew, and as if all had been peace. They soon, however, gave up conjecturing, and began to think of plunder; and constituting themselves victors, advanced to seize the prey. But as they came near the ship, and the field of slaughter, a spectacle presented itself which perplexed them more than any which they had yet seen. A maiden of uncommon and almost heavenly beauty sat upon a rock; she seemed deeply afflicted at the scene before her, but amidst that affliction preserved an air of dignity. Her head was crowned with laurel; she had a quiver at her shoulder; under her left arm was a bow, the other hung negligently down; she rested her left elbow on her right knee, and leaning her cheek on her open hand looked earnestly down on a youth who lay upon the ground at some distance. He, wounded all over, seemed to be recovering a little from a deep and almost deadly trance; yet, even in this situation, he appeared of manly beauty, and the whiteness of his cheeks became more conspicuous from the blood which flowed upon them. Pain had depressed his eye-lids, yet with difficulty he raised them towards the maiden; and collecting his spirits, in a languid voice thus addressed her (while the pirates were still gazing upon both): "My love, are you indeed alive? or, has the rage of war involved you also in its miseries? But you cannot bear even in death to be entirely separated from me, for your spirit still hovers round me and my fortunes."—"My fate," replied the maiden, "depends on thee: dost thou see this (showing him a dagger which lay on her knee)? it has yet been idle because thou still breathedst;" and saying this, she sprang from the rock.

The pirates upon the mountain, struck with wonder and admiration, as by a sudden flash of lightning, began to hide themselves among the bushes; for at her rising she appeared still greater and more divine. Her "shafts rattled as she moved;" her gold-embroidered garments glittered in the sun; and her hair flowed, from under her laurel diadem, in dishevelled ringlets down her neck.

The pirates, alarmed and confused, were totally at a loss to account for this appearance, which puzzled them more than the previous spectacle; some said it was the goddess Diana, or Isis, the tutelary deity of the country; others, that it was some priestess, who, inspired by a divine frenzy from the gods, had caused the slaughter they beheld; this they said at random, still in ignorance and doubt. She, flying towards the youth and embracing him, wept, kissed him, wiped off the blood, fetched a deep sigh, and seemed as if she could yet scarcely believe she had him in her arms.

The Egyptians, observing this, began to change their opinion. These, said they, are not the actions of a deity; a goddess would not with so much affection kiss a dying body. They encouraged one another therefore to go nearer, and to inquire into the real state of things. Collecting themselves together, then, they ran down and reached the maiden, as she was busied about the wounds of the youth; and placing themselves behind her, made a stand, not daring to say or do any thing. But she, startled at the noise they made, and the shadow they cast, raised herself up; and just looking at them, again bent down, not in the least terrified at their unusual complexion and piratical appearance, but earnestly applied herself to the care of the wounded youth: so totally does vehement affection, and sincere love, overlook or disregard whatever happens from without, be it pleasing or terrifying; and confines and employs every faculty, both of soul and body, to the beloved object. But when the pirates advancing, stood in front, and seemed preparing to seize her, she raised herself again, and seeing their dark complexion and rugged looks,—"If you are the shades of the slain," said she, "why do you trouble me? Most of you fell by each other's hands; if any died by mine it was in just defence of my endangered chastity. But, if you are living men, it appears to me that you are pirates; you come very opportunely to free me from my misfortunes, and to finish my unhappy story by my death." Thus she spake in tragic strain.

They not understanding what she said, and from the weak condition of the youth, being under no apprehension of their escaping, left them as they were; and proceeding to the ship, began to unload it. It was full of various merchandize; but they cared for nothing but the gold, silver, precious stones, and silken garments, of all which articles they carried away as much as they were able. When they thought they had enough, (and they found sufficient even to satisfy the avidity of pirates,) placing their booty on the shore, they divided it into portions not according to value but to weight; intending to make what related to the maiden and the youth, matter of their next consideration. At this instant another band of plunderers appeared, led by two men on horseback; which as soon as the first party observed, they fled precipitately away, leaving their booty behind them, lest they should be pursued; for they were but ten, whereas those who came down upon them were at least twice as many. The maiden in this manner ran a second risk of being taken captive.

The pirates hastening to their prey, yet from surprise and ignorance of the facts stopt a little. They concluded the slaughter they saw to have been the work of the first robbers; but seeing the maid in a foreign and magnificent dress, little affected by the alarming circumstances which surrounded her, employing her whole attention about the wounded youth, and seeming to feel his pains as if they were her own, they were much struck with her beauty and greatness of mind: they viewed with wonder too the noble form and stature of the young man, who now began to recover himself a little, and to assume his usual countenance. After some time, the leader of the band advancing, laid hands upon the maiden, and ordered her to arise and follow him. She, not understanding his language, yet guessing at his meaning, drew the youth after her (who still kept hold of her); and pointing to a dagger at her bosom, made signs that she would stab herself, unless they took both away together.

The captain, comprehending what she meant, and promising himself a valuable addition to his troop in the youth, if he should recover, dismounted from his horse, and making his lieutenant dismount too, put the prisoners upon their horses, and ordered the rest to follow when they had collected the booty; he himself walked by their side, ready to support them, in case they should be in danger of falling. There was something noble in this; a commander appearing to serve, and a victor waiting upon his captives; such is the power of native dignity and beauty, that it can even impose upon the mind of a pirate, and subdue the fiercest of men.

They travelled about two furlongs along the shore; then, leaving the sea on their right hand, they turned towards the mountains, and with some difficulty ascending them, they arrived at a kind of morass, which extended on the other side. The features of the place were these: the whole tract is called *The Pasturage* by the Egyptians; in it there is a valley, which receives certain overflowings of the Nile, and forms a lake, the depth of which in the centre is unfathomable. On the sides it shoals into a marsh; for, as the shore is to the sea, such are marshes to lakes.

Here the Egyptian pirates have their quarters; one builds a sort of hut upon a bit of ground which appears above the water; another spends his life on board a vessel, which serves him at once for transport and habitation. Here their wives work for them and bring forth their children, who at first are nourished with their mother's milk, and afterwards with fish dried in the sun; when they begin to crawl about they tie a string to their ancles, and suffer them to go the length of the boat. Thus this inhabitant of the Pasturage is born upon the lake, is raised in this manner, and considers this morass as his country, affording as it does shelter and protection for his piracy. Men of this description therefore are continually flocking thither; the water serves them as a citadel, and the quantity of reeds as a fortification. Having cut oblique channels among these, with many windings, easy to themselves, but very difficult for others, they imagined themselves secure from any sudden invasion; such was the situation of the lake and its inhabitants.

Here, about sunset, the pirate-chief and his followers arrived; they made their prisoners dismount, and disposed of the booty in their boats. A crowd of others, who had remained at home, appearing out of the morass, ran to meet them, and received the chief as if he had been their king; and seeing the quantity of spoils, and almost divine beauty of the maiden, imagined that their companions had been pillaging some temple, and had brought away its priestess, or perhaps the *breathing image* of the deity herself. They praised the valour of their captain, and conducted him to his quarters; these were in a little island at a distance from the rest, set apart for himself and his few attendants. When they arrived he dismissed the greater part, ordering them to assemble there again on the morrow; and then taking a short repast with the few who remained, he delivered his captives to a young Greek (whom he had not long before taken to serve as an interpreter), assigning them a part of his own hut for their habitation; giving strict orders that the wounded youth should have all possible care taken of him, and the maiden be treated with the utmost respect; and then, fatigued with his expedition, and the weight of cares which lay upon him, he betook himself to rest.

Silence now prevailed throughout the morass, and it was the first watch of night, when the maiden, being freed from observers, seized this opportunity of bewailing her misfortunes; inclined to do so the rather, perhaps, by the stillness and solitude of the night, in which there was neither sound nor sight to direct her attention, and call off her mind from ruminating on its sorrows. She lay in a separate apartment on a little couch on the ground; and fetching a deep sigh, and shedding a flood of tears, "O Apollo," she cried, "how much more severely dost thou punish me than I have deserved! Is not what I have already suffered sufficient? Deprived of my friends, captured by pirates, exposed to a thousand dangers at sea, and now again in the power of buccaneers, am I still to expect something worse? Where are my woes to end? If in death, free from dishonour, I embrace it with joy; but if that is to be taken from me by force, which I have not yet granted even to Theagenes, my own hands shall anticipate my disgrace, shall preserve me pure in death, and shall leave behind me at least the praise of chastity. O Apollo, no judge will be more severe than thou art!"

Theagenes, who was lodged near, overheard her complaints, and interrupted them, saying, "Cease, my dear Chariclea; you have reason,

I own, to complain, but by so doing you irritate the deity: he is made propitious by prayers, more than by expostulations; you must appease the power above by prayers, not by accusations." "You are in the right," said she; "but how do you do yourself?"—"Better than I was yesterday," he replied, "owing to the care of this youth, who has been applying medicine to my wounds."—"You will be still better to-morrow," said the youth, "for I shall then be able to procure an herb which after three applications will cure them. I know this by experience; for since I was brought here a captive, if any of the pirates have returned wounded, by the application of this plant they have been healed in a few days. Wonder not that I pity your misfortunes; you seem to be sharing my own ill fate; and, as I am a Greek myself, I naturally compassionate Grecians."

"A Greek! O gods!" cried out both the strangers in transport, "a Greek indeed, both in language and appearance! Perhaps some relief to our misfortunes is at hand." "But what," said Theagenes, "shall we call you?"—"Cnemon." "Of what city?"—"An Athenian." "What have been your fortunes?"—"Cease," he replied; "why touch upon that subject; my adventures are matter for a tragedy. You seem to have had sorrows enough of your own; there is no need to increase them by a recital of mine; besides, what remains of the night would not be sufficient for the relation; and the fatigues you have gone through to-day demand sleep and rest." They would not admit his excuses, but pressed him to relate his story; saying, that to hear of misfortunes something like their own, would be the greatest consolation to them.

Cnemon then began in this manner:—"My father's name was Aristippus, an Athenian, a member of the Upper Council, and possessed of a decent fortune. After the death of my mother, as he had no child but me, he began to think of a second marriage, esteeming it hard that he should live an unsettled life solely on my account; he married therefore a woman of polished manners, but a mischiefmaker, called Demæneta. From the moment of their marriage she brought him entirely under her subjection, enticing him by her beauty and seeming attentions; for there never was a woman who possessed the arts of allurement in a greater degree: she would lament at his going out, run with joy to meet him at his return, blame him for his stay, and mingle kisses and embraces with the tenderest expostulations. My father, entangled in these wiles, was entirely wrapped up in her. At first she pretended to behave to me as if I had been her own son; this likewise helped to influence my father. She would sometimes kiss me, and constantly wished to enjoy my society. I readily complied, suspecting nothing, but was agreeably surprised at her behaving to me with so much maternal affection. When, however, she approached me with more wantonness; when her kisses became warmer than those of a relation ought to be, and her glances betrayed marks of passion, I began to entertain suspicions, to avoid her company, and repress her caresses. I need not enumerate what artifices she used, what promises she employed to gain me over, how she called me darling, sweetest, breath of her life; how she mingled blandishments with these soft words; how, in serious affairs, she behaved really as a mother, in less grave hours but too plainly as a mistress.

"At length, one evening, after I had been assisting at the solemn Panathenæan festival (when a ship is sent to Minerva by land), and had joined in the hymns and usual procession, I returned home in my dress of ceremony, with my robe and crown. She, as soon as she saw me, unable to contain herself, no longer dissembled her love, but, her eyes sparkling with desire, ran up to me, embraced me, and called me her dear Theseus, her young Hippolytus: How do you imagine I then felt, who now blush even at the recital?

"My father that night was to sup in the Prytanæum, and, as it was a grand and stated entertainment, was not expected to return home till the next day. I had not long retired to my apartment, when she followed me, and endeavoured to obtain the gratification of her wishes; but when she saw that I resisted with horror, regardless of her allurements, her promises, or her threats, fetching a deep-drawn sigh, she retired; and the very next day, with uncommon wickedness, began to put her machinations in force against me.

"She took to her bed; and, when my father returned and inquired the reason of it, she said she was indisposed, and at first would say no more. But when he insisted, with great tenderness, on knowing what had so disordered her, with seeming reluctance she thus addressed him:— 'This dainty youth, this son of yours, whom I call the gods to witness I loved as much as you could do yourself, suspecting me to be with child (which, till I was certain of it, I have yet concealed from you), taking the opportunity of your absence, while I was advising and exhorting him to temperance, and to avoid drunkenness and loose women (for I was not ignorant of his inclinations though I avoided dropping the least hint of them to you, lest it should appear the calumny of a step-mother)—while, I say, I took this opportunity of speaking to him alone, that I might spare his confusion, I am ashamed to tell how he abused both you and me; nor did he confine himself to words; but assaulting me both with hands and feet, kicked me at last upon the stomach, and left me in a dreadful condition, in which I have continued ever since.'

"When my father heard this, he made no reply, asked no questions, framed no excuse for me; but, believing that she who had appeared so fond of me, would not, without great reason, accuse me, the next time he met me in the house he gave me a tremendous blow; and calling his slaves, he commanded them to scourge me, without so much as telling me the cause of it. When he had wreaked his resentment, 'Now, at least,' said I, 'father, tell me the reason of this shameful treatment.' This enraged him the more. 'What hypocrisy!' cried he; 'he wants me to repeat the story of his own wickedness.' And, turning from me, he hastened to Demæneta. But this implacable woman, not yet satisfied, laid another plot against me.

"She had a young slave called Thisbe, handsome enough, and skilled in music. She, by her mistress's orders, put herself in my way; and though she had before frequently resisted solicitations, which, I own, I had made to her, she now made advances herself, in gestures, words, and behaviour. I, like a silly fellow as I was, began to be vain of my own attractions; and, in short, made an appointment with her to come to my apartment at night. We continued our commerce for some time, I always exhorting her to take the greatest care lest her mistress should detect her. When, one day, as I was repeating these cautions, she broke out, 'O Cnemon! how great is your simplicity, if you think it dangerous for a slave like me to be discovered with you. What would you think this very mistress deserves, who, calling herself of an honourable family, having a lawful husband, and knowing death to be the punishment of her crime, yet commits adultery?'—'Be silent,' I replied; 'I cannot give credit to what you say.'—'What if I show you the adulterer in the very fact?'—'If you can, do.'—'Most willingly will I,' says she, 'both on your account, who have been so abused by her, and on my own, who am the daily victim of her jealousy. If you are a man, therefore, seize her paramour.'—I promised I would, and she then left me.

"The third night after this she awakened me from sleep, and told me that the adulterer was in the house; that my father, on some sudden occasion, was gone into the country, and that the lover had taken this opportunity of secretly visiting Demæneta. Now was the time for me to punish him as he deserved; and that I should go in, sword in hand, lest he should escape.

"I did as Thisbe exhorted me; and taking my sword, she going before me with a torch, went towards my mother's bedchamber. When I arrived there, and perceived there was a light burning within, my passion rising, I burst open the door, and, rushing in, cried out, 'Where is the villain, the vile paramour of this paragon of virtue?' and thus exclaiming, I advanced, prepared to transfix them both, when my father, O ye gods! leaping from the bed, fell at my feet, and besought me, 'O my son! stay your hand, pity your father, and these grey hairs which have nourished you. I have used you ill, I confess, but not so as to deserve death from you. Let not passion transport you; do not imbrue your hands in a parent's blood!'

"He was going on in this supplicatory strain, while I stood thunderstruck, without power either to speak or stir. I looked about for Thisbe, but she had withdrawn. I cast my eyes in amaze round the chamber, confounded and stupified: the sword fell from my hand.

"Demæneta, running up, immediately took it away; and my father, now seeing himself out of danger, laid hands upon me, and ordered me to be bound, his wife stimulating him all the time, and exclaiming, 'This is what I foretold; I bid you guard yourself from the attempts of this youth; I observed his looks, and feared his designs.'—'You did,' he replied; 'but I could not have imagined he would carry his wickedness to such a pitch.' He then kept me bound; and though I made several attempts to explain the matter, he would not suffer me to speak.

"When the morning was come, he brought me out before the people, bound as I was; and flinging dust upon his head, thus addressed them: 'I entertained hopes, O Athenians, when the gods gave me this son, that he would have been the staff of my declining age. I brought him up genteelly; I gave him a first-rate education; I went through every step needful to procure him the full privileges of a citizen of Athens; in short, my whole life was a scene of solicitude on his account. But he, forgetting all this, abused me first with words, and assaulted my wife with blows; and at last broke in upon me in the night, brandishing a drawn sword, and was prevented from committing a parricide only by a sudden consternation which seized him, and made the weapon drop from his hand. I have recourse, therefore, to this assembly for my own defence and his punishment. I might, I know, lawfully have punished him even with death myself; but I had rather leave the whole matter to your judgment than stain my own hands with his blood:' and, having said this, he began to weep.

"Demæneta too accompanied him with her tears, lamenting the untimely but just death which I must soon suffer, whom my evil genius had armed against my parent; and thus seeming to confirm by her lamentations the truth of her husband's accusations.

"At length I desired to be heard in my turn, when the clerk arising put this pointed question to me: Did I attack my father with a sword? When I replied, 'I did indeed attack him, but hear how I came so to do'—the whole assembly exclaimed that, after this confession, there was no room for apology or defence. Some cried out I ought to be stoned; others, that I should be delivered to the executioner, and thrown headlong into the Barathrum. During this tumult, while they were disputing about my punishment, I cried out, 'All this I suffer on account of my mother-in-law; my step-mother makes me to be condemned unheard.' A few of the assembly appeared to take notice of what I said, and to have some suspicions of the truth of the case; yet even then I could not obtain an audience, so much were all minds possessed by the disturbance.

"At length they proceeded to ballot: one thousand seven hundred condemned me to death; some to be stoned, others to be thrown into the Barathrum. The remainder, to the number of about a thousand, having some suspicions of the machinations of my mother-in-law, adjudged me to perpetual banishment; and this sentence prevailed: for though a greater number had doomed me to death, yet there being a difference in their opinions as to the kind of death, they were so divided, that the numbers of neither party amounted to a thousand.

"Thus, therefore, was I driven from my father's house and my country: the wicked Demæneta, however, did not remain unpunished; in what manner you shall hear by-and-by.—But you ought now to take a little sleep; the night is far advanced, and some rest is necessary for you."

"It will be very annoying to us," replied Theagenes, "if you leave this wicked woman unpunished."—"Hear, then," said Cnemon, "since you will have it so.

"I went immediately from the assembly to the Piræus, and finding a ship ready to set sail for Ægina, I embarked in her, hearing there were some relations of my mother's there. I was fortunate enough to find them on my arrival, and passed the first days of my exile agreeably enough among them. After I had been there about three weeks, taking my accustomed solitary walk, I came down to the port; a vessel was standing in; I stopped to see from whence she came, and who were on board. The ladder was no sooner let down, when a person leapt on shore, ran up to me, and embraced me. He proved to be Charias, one of my former companions.—'O Cnemon!' he cried out, 'I bring you good news. You are revenged on your enemy: Demæneta is dead.'—'I am heartily glad to see you, Charias,' I replied; 'but why do you hurry over your good tidings as if they were bad ones? Tell me how all this has happened; I fear she has died a natural death, and escaped that which she deserved.'—'Justice,' said he, 'has not entirely deserted us (as Hesiod says); and though she sometimes seems to wink at crime for a time, protecting her vengeance, such wretches rarely escape at last: neither has Demæneta. From my connexion with Thisbe, I have been made acquainted with the whole affair.

"'After your unjust exile, your father, repenting of what he had done, retired from the sight of the world, into a lonely villa, and there lived; "gnawing his own heart," according to the poet. But the furies took possession of his wife, and her passion rose to a higher pitch in your absence than it had ever done before. She lamented your misfortunes and her own, calling day and night in a frantic manner upon Cnemon, her dear boy, her soul; insomuch that the women of her acquaintance, who visited her, wondered at and praised her; that, though a step-dame, she felt a mother's affection. They endeavoured to console and strengthen her; but she replied that her sorrows were past consolation, and that they were ignorant of the wound which rankled at her heart.

"'When she was alone she abused Thisbe for the share she had in the business. "How slow were you in assisting my love! How ready in administering to my revenge! You deprived me of him I loved above all the world, without giving me an instant to repent and be appeased." And she gave plain hints that she intended some mischief against her.

"'Thisbe seeing her disappointed, enraged, almost out of her senses with love and grief, and capable of undertaking anything, determined to be beforehand with her; and by laying a snare for her mistress, to provide for her own security. One day, therefore, she thus accosted her: "Why, O my mistress, do you wrongfully accuse your slave? It has always been my study to obey your will in the best manner I could; if anything unlucky has happened, fortune is to blame; I am ready now, if you command me, to endeavour to find a remedy for your distress."— "What remedy can you find?" cried she. "He who alone could ease my torments is far distant; the unexpected lenity of his judges has been my ruin: had he been stoned or otherwise put to death, my hopes and cares would have been buried with him. Impossibility of gratification extinguishes desire, and despair makes the heart callous. But now I seem to have him before my eyes: I hear, and blush at hearing him upbraid me with his injuries. Sometimes I flatter my fond heart that he will return again, and that I shall obtain my wishes; at other times I form schemes of seeking him myself, on whatever shore he wanders. These thoughts agitate, inflame, and drive me beside myself. Ye gods! I am justly served. Why, instead of laying schemes against his life, did I not persist in endeavouring to subdue him by kindness? He refused me at first, and it was but fitting he should do so; I was a stranger, and he reverenced his father's bed. Time and persuasion might have overcome his coldness; but I, unjust, and inhuman as I was, more like a tyrant, than his mistress, cruelly punished his first disobedience. Yet with how much justice might he slight Demæneta, whom he so infinitely surpassed in beauty! But, my dear Thisbe, what remedy is it you hint at?" The artful slave replied: "O Mistress, Cnemon, as most people think, in obedience to the sentence, has departed both from the city and from Attica; but I, who inquire anxiously into everything that you can have any concern in, have discovered that he is lurking somewhere about the town. You have heard perhaps of Arsinoë the singer: he has long been connected with her. After his misfortune, she promised to go into exile with him, and keeps him concealed at her house till she can prepare herself for setting out."—"Happy Arsinoë!" cried Demæneta; "happy at first in possessing the love of Cnemon, and now in being permitted to accompany him into banishment. But what is all this to me?"—"Attend, and you shall hear," said Thisbe. "I will pretend that I am in love with Cnemon. I will beg Arsinoë, with whom I am acquainted, to introduce me some night to him in her room; you may, if you please, represent Arsinoë, and receive his visit instead of me. I will take care that he shall have drunk a little freely when he goes to bed. If you obtain your wishes, perhaps you may be cured of your passion. The first gratification sometimes extinguishes the flame of desire. Love soon finds its end in satiety: but if yours (which I hope will not be the case) should still continue, we may perhaps find some other scheme to satisfy it; at present let us attend to this which I have proposed."

"'Demæneta eagerly embraced the proposal, and desired her to put it into immediate execution. Thisbe demanded a day only for preparation; and going directly to Arsinoë, asked her if she knew Teledemus. Arsinoë replying that she did, "Receive us then," says she, "this evening into your house; I have promised to sleep with him to-night: he will come first; I shall follow, when I have put my mistress to bed." Then hastening into the country to Aristippus, she thus addressed him: "I come, master, to accuse myself; punish me as you think fit. I have been the cause of your losing your son; not indeed willingly, but yet I was instrumental in his destruction: for when I perceived that my mistress led a dissolute life, and injured your bed, I began to fear for myself, lest I should suffer if she should be detected by anybody else. I pitied you too, who received such ill returns for all your affection; I was afraid, however, of mentioning the matter to you, but I discovered it to my young master; and coming to him by night, to avoid observation, I told him that an adulterer was sleeping with my mistress. He, hurried on by resentment, mistook my meaning, and thought I said that an adulterer was then with her. His passion rose; he snatched a sword, and ran madly on towards your bedchamber. It was in vain I endeavoured to detain him, and to assure him that no adulterer was then with my mistress; he regarded not what I said, either made deaf by rage, or imagining that I changed my purpose. The rest you know. You have it in your power at least to clear up the character of your banished son, and to punish her who has injured both of you; for I will shew you to-day Demæneta with an adulterer, in a strange house without the city, and in bed."

""If you can do that," said Aristippus, "your freedom shall be your reward. I shall, perhaps, take some comfort in life, when I have got rid of this wicked woman. I have for some time been uneasy within myself: I have suspected her; but, having no proofs, I was silent. But what must we do now?"—"You know," said she, "the garden where is the monument of the Epicureans: come there in the evening, and wait for me." And having so said, away she goes; and coming to Demæneta, "Dress yourself," she cries, "immediately; neglect nothing that can set off your person; everything that I have promised you is ready."— Demæneta did as she was desired, and adorned herself with all her skill; and in the evening Thisbe attended her to the place of assignation. When they came near she desired her to stop a little; and going forwards she begged Arsinoë to step into the next house, and leave her at liberty in her own; for she wished to spare the young man's blushes, who was but lately initiated into love affairs; and, having persuaded her, she returned, introduced Demæneta, put her to bed, took away the light (lest, forsooth, you, who were then safe at Ægina, should discover her), and entreated her to enjoy the good fortune which awaited her in silence. "I will now go," said she, "and bring the youth to you; he is drinking at a house in the neighborhood."—Away she flies where Aristippus was waiting, and exhorts him to go immediately and bind the adulterer fast. He follows her, rushes into the house, and, by help of a little moonlight which shone, with difficulty finding the bed, exclaims, "I have caught you now, you abandoned creature!" Thisbe immediately upon this exclamation bangs to the door on the other side, and cries out, "What untoward fortune! the adulterer has escaped; but take care at least that you secure the adulteress."—"Make yourself easy," he replied; "I have secured this wicked woman, whom I was the most desirous of taking:" and seizing her, he began to drag her towards the city. But she feeling deeply the situation she was in, the disappointment of her hopes, the ignominy which must attend her offences, and the punishment which awaited them, vexed and enraged at being deceived and detected, when she came near the pit which is in the Academy (you know the place where our generals sacrifice to the Manes of our heroes), suddenly disengaging herself from the hands of the old man, flung herself headlong in: and thus she died a wretched death, suited for a wretch like herself.

"'Upon this Aristippus cried out, "You have yourself anticipated the justice of the laws," and the next day he laid the whole matter before the people; and having with difficulty obtained his pardon, consulted his friends and acquaintance how best he could obtain your recall. What success he has met with I cannot inform you of; for I have been obliged, as you see, to sail here on my own private business. But I think you have the greatest reason to expect that the people will consent to your return, and that your father will himself come to seek you, and conduct you home.'—Here Charias ended his recital. How I came to this place, and what have been my fortunes since, would take up more time and words than there is at present opportunity for."

Having said this, he wept; the strangers wept with him, seemingly for his calamities, really, perhaps, in remembrance of their own: nor would they have ceased from lamentation, had not sleep coming over them through the luxury of grief, at length dried their tears. They then lay in repose, but Thyamis (for that was the name of the pirate captain) having slept quietly the first part of the night, was afterwards disturbed by wandering dreams; and starting from his sleep, and pondering what they should mean, was kept awake by his perplexities the remainder of the night. For about the time when the cocks crow (whether a natural instinct induces them to salute the returning sun, or a feeling of warmth and a desire of food and motion excites them to rouse those who are about them with their song) the following vision appeared to him.

He seemed to be in Memphis, his native city; and entering into the temple of Isis, he saw it shining with the splendour of a thousand lighted lamps; the altars were filled with bleeding victims of all sorts; all the avenues of the temple were crowded with people, and resounded with the noise of the passing throngs. When he had penetrated to the inmost sanctuary of the edifice, the goddess seemed to meet him, to give Chariclea into his hands, and to say, "O Thyamis, I deliver this maiden to you; but though having you shall not have her, but shall be unjust, and kill your guest; yet she shall not be killed."—This dream troubled him, and he turned it every way in his mind; at length, wearied with conjectures, he wrested its signification to his own wishes. You shall have her, and not have her; that is, you shall have her as a wife, not as a virgin: and as for the killing, he understood it to mean, thou shalt wound her virginity, but the wound shall not be mortal. And thus, led by his desires, he interpreted his vision.—When the morning dawned, he called his principal followers about him, and ordered their booty, which he called by the specious name of spoils, to be brought out into the midst; and sending for Cnemon, directed him to bring with him the captives whom he had the care of. When they were being brought, "What fortune," they exclaimed, "awaits us now?" and besought the protection and assistance of Cnemon. He promised to do all that was in his power for them, and comforted and encouraged them. He told them that the pirate captain had nothing barbarous in his disposition; that his manners were rather gentle; that he belonged to an illustrious family, and from necessity alone had embraced this kind of life. When all were met together, and they too made their appearance, Thyamis, seating himself on an eminence, and ordering Cnemon, who understood the Egyptian tongue, (whereas he himself could not speak Greek) to interpret what he said to the captives, thus addressed the assembly:—

"You know, comrades, what my sentiments have always been towards you. You are not ignorant, how being the son of the high-priest of Memphis, and being frustrated of succeeding to the office after the departure of my father, my younger brother against all law depriving me of it, I fled to you, that I might revenge the injury, and recover my dignity. I have been thought worthy to command you, and yet I have never arrogated any particular privileges to myself: if money was to be distributed, I desired only an equal share of it; if captives were to be sold, I brought their price into the common stock; for I have always deemed it to be the part of a valiant leader, to take the larger share of toil, and only an equal share of spoils. As to the captives, those men whose strength of body promised to be serviceable to us, I kept for ourselves; the weaker I sold. I never abused the women. Those of any rank I suffered to redeem themselves with money; and sometimes, out of compassion, dismissed them without ransom: those of inferior condition, who, if they had not been taken, would have passed their lives in servile offices, I employed in such services as they had been accustomed to. But now I *do* ask of one part of these spoils for myself, this foreign maiden. I might take her by my own authority, but I would rather receive her by your common consent; for it were foolish in me to do anything with a prisoner against the will of my friends. Neither do I ask this favour of you gratis; I am willing, in recompense for it, to resign my share in all the other booty. For since the priestly caste despises common amours, I am determined to take this maiden to myself, not out of mere lust, but for the sake of offspring. And I will explain to you the reasons which induce me to do so.

"In the first place she appears to me to be well born: I form this conjecture both from the riches which were found about her, and from her not being depressed by her calamities, but, seeming to rise superior to them; I am convinced that her disposition is good and virtuous; for, if in beauty she surpasses all, and by her looks awes all beholders into respect, can we do otherwise than think highly of her? But what recommends her above every thing to me is, that she appears to be a priestess of some god; for, in all her misfortunes, she has with a pious regard refused to lay aside her sacred robe and chaplet. Where then can I a priest find a partner more fitting for me, than one who is herself a priestess?"

The applause of the whole company testified their approbation. They exhorted him to marry, and wished him all possible happiness. He then pursued his discourse:—"I thank you, comrades; but it will now be proper to inquire how far my proposal is agreeable to this maiden. Were I disposed to use the power which fate has put into my hands, my will would be sufficient; they who can compel have no need to entreat. But in lawful marriage, the inclination of both parties ought to coincide." And turning to Chariclea, he said, "How, maiden, do you like my offer? What is your country, and who were your parents?" She, keeping her eye a considerable time on the ground, and moving slowly her head, seemed to meditate what she should answer. At length, raising herself gently towards Thyamis, and dazzling him with more than her usual charms (for her eyes shone with uncommon lustre, and the circumstances she was in gave an additional glow to her cheeks), Cnemon serving as interpreter, she thus addressed him:

"It might perhaps have been more proper for my brother Theagenes to speak on this occasion; for silence, I think, best becomes women, especially in a company of men. Since, however, you address yourself to me, and shew this first mark of humanity, in that you seek to obtain what you desire, by persuasion rather than force; since the main subject of your discourse relates to me alone; I am compelled to lay aside the common reserve of my sex, and to explain myself in regard to the proposal of marriage which you have made, even before such an audience. Hear then what is our state and condition.

"Our country is Ionia; our family one of the most illustrious in Ephesus. In early youth, as the laws appointed, we entered into the priesthood. I was consecrated to Diana, my brother to Apollo. But as the office is an annual one, and the time was elapsed, we were going to Delos to exhibit games according to the custom of our country, and to lay down the priesthood. We loaded a ship therefore with gold, silver, costly garments, and other things necessary for the show and the entertainment which we were to give to the people. We set sail; our parents being advanced in years, and afraid of the sea, remained at home: but a great number of our fellow citizens attended us, some on board our ships, others in vessels of their own. When we had completed the greatest part of our voyage, a tempest suddenly arose; winds and hurricanes, raising the waves, drove the ship out of its course. The pilot yielded at length to the fury of the storm; and deserting the government of the ship, let her drive at the mercy of the winds. We scudded before them for seven days and nights; and at length were cast upon the shore where you found us, and where you saw the slaughter which had happened there. Rejoicing at our preservation, we gave an entertainment to the ship's company. In the midst of it, a party of the sailors, who had conspired to make themselves masters of our riches, by taking away our lives, attacked us; our friends defended us; a dreadful combat ensued, which was continued with such rage and animosity, on both sides, that of the whole number engaged we alone survived (would to God we had not!), miserable remains of that unhappy day; in one thing alone fortunate, in that some pitying deity has brought us into your hands; and, instead of death which we feared, we are now to deliberate upon a marriage. I do not by any means decline the offer. Prisoner as I am, I ought to esteem it an honour and a happiness to be permitted to aspire to the bed of my conqueror. It seems too, to be by a particular providence of the gods, that I, a priestess, should be united to the son of a high priest. One thing alone I beg of you, O Thyamis. Permit me, at the first city I arrive at in which there is a temple or altar of Apollo, to resign my priesthood, and lay aside these badges of my office: this perhaps would with most propriety be done in Memphis, when you shall have recovered the dignity you are entitled to. Thus would our wedlock be celebrated with better auspices, joined with victory and prosperous success: but, if you would have it sooner, be it as you please; let me only first perform those rites which the custom of my country demands. This I know you will not refuse me, as you have yourself been, as you say, dedicated to holy things from childhood, and have just and reverend notions of what relates to the gods."

Here she ceased, and her tears began to flow. Her speech was followed by the approbation and applause of the company, who bid her do thus, and promised her their aid. Thyamis could not help joining with them, though he was not entirely satisfied, for his eager desire to possess Chariclea made him think even the present hour an unreasonable delay. Her words, however, like the siren's song, soothed him, and compelled his assent; he thought, too, he saw in this some relation to his dream, and brought himself to agree that the wedding should be celebrated at Memphis. He then dismissed the company, having first divided the spoils, a great part of the choicest of which were forced upon him by his people.

He gave orders that, in ten days, they should all be ready to march to Memphis; and sent the Greeks to the habitation in which he had before placed them. Cnemon, too, by his command, attended them no longer now as a guard, but as a companion: their entertainment was the best which Thyamis could afford; and Theagenes, for his sister's sake, partook of the same handsome treament. He determined within himself to see Chariclea as seldom as possible, lest the sight of her should inflame the desire which tormented him, and urge him on to do anything inconsistent with what he had agreed to and promised. He deprived himself, therefore, of that company in which he most delighted, fearing that to converse with her, and to restrain himself within proper bounds, would be more than he could answer for. When the crew had dispersed, each to his habitation in the lake, Cnemon went to some distance from it, in search of the herb which he had promised to procure for Theagenes;

and Theagenes, taking the opportunity of his absence, began to weep and lament, not addressing himself to Chariclea, but calling earnestly upon the gods: and she with tender solicitude inquiring whether he was only lamenting their common misfortunes, or suffering any new addition to them?—"What can be newer or more unworthy," he replied, "than the breaking of vows and promises? than that Chariclea, entirely forgetting me, should give her consent to another marriage?"—"God forbid!" replied the maiden; "let not your reproaches increase the load of my calamities; nor, after so long an experience of my fidelity, lightly suspect a measure which the immediate necessity of the moment compelled me to adopt: sooner will you change than find me changed in regard to you. I can bear ill fortune; nor shall any force compel me to do anything unworthy of the modesty and virtue of my sex. In one thing alone, I own, I am immoderate, my love for you; but then it is a lawful one; and, however great, it did not throw me inconsiderately into your power; I resigned myself to you on the most honourable conditions; I have hither to lived with you in the most inviolate purity, resisting all your solicitations, and looking forward to a lawful opportunity of completing that marriage to which we are solemnly pledged. Can you then be so unreasonable as to think it possible that I should prefer a barbarian to a Greek? a pirate, to one to whom I am bound by so many ties?"—"What, then," said Theagenes, "was the meaning of that fine speech of yours? To call me your brother, indeed, was prudent enough, to keep Thyamis from suspecting the real nature of our love, and to induce him to let us continue together. I understood, too, the meaning of your veiling the true circumstances of our voyage under the fictions of Ionia and Delos. But so readily to accept his proposals, to promise to marry him, nay, to fix a time for the ceremony—this, I own, disturbs me, and passes my comprehension; but I had rather sink into the earth than see such an end of all my hopes and labours on your account."

Chariclea flung her arms round Theagenes, gave him a thousand kisses, and bedewing him with tears, cried out, "How delightful to me are these apprehensions of yours! They prove that all the troubles you have undergone have in no degree weakened your love; but know, O my dear Theagenes, that unless I had promised as I did, we should not now be talking together. You must be sensible that contradiction only adds force to violent passion; seeming compliance allays the impulse in its birth, and the allurement of promises lulls the violence of desire. Your rough lovers think they have got something when they have obtained a promise: and, relying upon the faith of it, become quieter, feeding themselves with hope. I, being aware of this, in words resigned myself up to him, committing what shall follow to the gods, and to that genius who presides over our loves.

"A short interval of time has frequently afforded means of safety, which the wisest counsels of men could not have foreseen. I saw nothing better to be done than to endeavour to ward off a certain and imminent danger, by a present, though uncertain, remedy. We must, therefore, my dearest Theagenes, use this fiction as our best ally, and carefully conceal the truth even from Cnemon; for though he seems friendly to us, and is a Greek, yet he is a captive, and likely, perhaps, to do anything which may ingratiate him with his master. Our friendship with him is as yet too new, neither is there any relation between us sufficiently strong to give us a certain assurance of his fidelity. If he suspects, therefore, and inquires into our real situation, we must deny it: for even a falsehood is commendable when it is of service to those who use it, and does no injury to the hearers of it."

While Chariclea was thus suggesting this course, Cnemon comes running in, with an altered countenance, and seemingly in much agitation. "O Theagenes," he cried, "I have brought you the herb I mentioned; apply it, and it will heal your wounds; but you must now, I fear, prepare yourself for others, and a slaughter equal to that which you have lately been an actor in." Theagenes desiring him to explain himself, "There is no time at present;" he replied, "for explanation; action will probably anticipate words; but do you and Chariclea follow me as fast as you can;" and taking them with him, he brought them to Thyamis. They found him employed in burnishing his helmet and sharpening his spear. "Very seasonably," he exclaimed, "are you employed about your arms; put them on as fast as you can, and command all your men to do the same, for a hostile force is approaching greater than ever threatened us before, and they must now be very near. I saw them advancing over the top of the neighbouring hill, and have made all possible haste to bring you information, giving the alarm to every one I met with in my passage."

Thyamis, at these tidings, started up and cried out, "Where is Chariclea?" as if he were more apprehensive for her than for himself. When Cnemon showed her standing near the door. "Lead this maiden privately," says he, "into the cave where I keep my treasures, and forget not to replace as usual the covering of it; having done this, return to me as fast as you can: meanwhile, I will prepare for the storm of battle which awaits us." Having said this, he ordered his lieutenant to bring forth a victim, that he might begin the engagement after a due sacrifice to his country's gods. Cnemon proceeded to execute his commission, and leading off Chariclea, who turned earnestly towards Theagenes, and lamented her hard fate, he let her down into the cave. This was not, as many are, the work of nature, an accidental excavation, but the contrivance of the pirates, who, imitating her operations, had hollowed out an artificial cavern for the reception of their treasures. It was formed in this manner: its entrance, narrow and dark, was under the doors of a hidden chamber, the threshold became, in case of need, a second door, for farther descent; it fitted exactly, and could be lifted up with great facility; the rest of the cave was cut into various winding passages, which, now diverging, now returning, with a multitude of ramifications, converged at last into an open space at the bottom, which received an uncertain light from an aperture at the extremity of the lake. Here Cnemon introduced Chariclea, and led her to the farthest recess, encouraging and promising her that he and Theagenes would come to her in the evening; and that he would not suffer him to engage in the battle which impended. Chariclea was unable to answer him; and he went out of the cave, leaving her half dead, silent, and stupified, as if her soul had been separated from her with Theagenes. He shut down the door, dropping a tear for her as he did it, and for the necessity he was under of burying her in a manner alive, and consigning the brightest of human forms to darkness and obscurity. He made what haste he could to Thyamis. He found him burning with ardour for the fight, and Theagenes by his side splendidly armed; he was even to frenzy rousing the spirits of his followers who surrounded him, and thus began to address them:

"There is no need, comrades, to address you in a long exhortation; you want no encouragement, to whom war is the breath of life; and the sudden approach of the enemy cuts off all space for words; it becomes us to prepare to resist force by force; not to do so would betray an absence of all energy. I do not put you in mind of your wives and children as is usual on these occasions, though nothing but victory can preserve them from destruction and violation. This contest is for our very being and existence; no quarter, no truce, ever takes place in piratic warfare; we must either conquer or die. Let us exert, then, our force to the utmost, and with determined minds fall upon the enemy."

Having said this, he looked round for his lieutenant, Thermuthis, and called him several times by his name. When he nowhere appeared, throwing out hasty threats against him, he rushed on towards the ferry. The battle was already begun, and he could see at a distance those who inhabited the extremities and approaches of the lake in the fact of being routed by the enemy, who set on fire the boats and huts of those who fell or fled. The flames spread to the neighbouring morass, caught hold of the reeds which grew there in great abundance, dazzled every eye with an almost intolerable blaze, and, crackling and roaring, stunned their ears.

War now appeared in all its horrid forms: the inhabitants for some time, with readiness and energy, supported and repelled the attack; but being astonished by the sudden incursion, and pressed by the superior numbers of the enemy, those on the land gave way, and many of those on the lake, together with their boats and habitations, were overwhelmed in the waters! every dreadful sound now struck the air, as the conflict raged both by land and water; groans and shouts were mingled, the lake was discoloured with blood, all were involved in fire or water. Thyamis, at this sight, called to mind his dream, and the temple of Isis shining with lamps, and flowing with the blood of victims; he saw a resemblance in it to the scene before him, and began to fear that he must give up his former favourable interpretation; that Chariclea was destined to fall in this tumult, and that so having had her in his possession, he should now have her no longer; that she would be slain, not merely be wounded in her virginity; exclaiming, therefore against the goddess, for having deceived him, and unable to bear the thought that any one else should possess Chariclea, he ordered the men who were about him to halt, and if they were obliged to engage, to defend themselves as well as they could, by retiring behind, and making sallies from, the numerous little islands: as by so doing they might, for some time, be able to resist the attack of the enemy. He then, under pretence of going to seek Thermuthis, and sacrificing to his household gods, returned in great agitation to his tent, suffering no one to follow him.

The disposition of the barbarians is obstinate and determined; when they despair of their own safety, they are accustomed to destroy those who are most dear to them; either wildly imagining that they shall enjoy their company after death; or thinking that by so doing they shall deliver them from the injuries and insults of the enemy. Stimulated by some of these motives, Thyamis, forgetting the urgent danger which pressed upon him, and the enemies by whom he was surrounded as by a net; burning with anger, love, and jealousy, rushed headlong to the cave: he

HELIODORUS OF EMESA

poured out his Egyptian exclamations with a loud voice, and soon after his entrance, being addressed by some one in the Greek tongue, the voice guided him to the person; he seized her hair with his left hand, and with his right plunged his sword into her bosom: the unfortunate creature sank down, uttering a last and piteous groan. Issuing forth and closing the trap-door, he threw a little dust over her, and dropping a tear he exclaimed, "Are these then the nuptial presents you were to expect from me!" When he arrived at the boats, he saw his people ready to fly as the enemy approached near, and Thermuthis having now made his appearance, preparing to begin the sacrifice: having abused him for his unseasonable absence, and told him that he had already offered up the most beauteous of victims, he, Thermuthis and the rower got into a boat: their small vessels would not hold more, being made out of the trunk of a tree rudely hollowed. Theagenes and Cnemon got into another, and in the same manner all the rest embarked.

When they had proceeded a little from the shore, rowing round the side rather than launching out into the deep, they lay upon their oars, and drew up in a line, to receive the enemy; but at their approach, a sudden panic seized the pirates, and not sustaining the first hostile shout of their opponents, they fled in disorder: Cnemon and Theagenes gradually retired, but not from fear: Thyamis alone disdained to fly; and perhaps not wishing to survive Chariclea, rushed into the midst of his foes. A cry was instantly heard among them, "This is Thyamis, let all have an eye to him:" immediately they turned their boats and surrounded him; he, vigorously fighting, wounded some and killed others, and yet strange was that which ensued: out of so great a multitude no one lifted up a sword, or cast a dart at him, but every one did their utmost to capture him alive. He continued manfully to resist, till at length his spear was wrested from him, and he had lost his lieutenant, who had nobly seconded him; and who, having received, as he thought, a mortal wound, leaped into the lake, and with great difficulty reached the shore, no one offering to pursue him; for now they had laid hold on Thyamis, and esteemed the capture of one man a victory; and though he had destroyed so many of their men, their joy at having taken him alive far exceeded their grief for the loss of their comrades; for gain is dearer to robbers than their lives; and friendship and relationship are only so far considered among them as they conduce to this main end.

The leaders of this attack were the men who had fled from Thyamis and his followers at the Heracleotic mouth of the Nile: they, enraged at the loss of a booty, which through plunder, they considered as their own, gathered their friends together, and many others from the neighbouring towns, by proposing to them an equal division of the spoils; and became their guides in the expedition.

The reason why they were so desirous of taking Thyamis alive was this: Petosiris, who resided at Memphis, was his younger brother; by his artifices he had unlawfully deprived Thyamis of the priesthood, and hearing that he was now at the head of the pirates, he feared that he might take some opportunity to attack him, or that in time his treachery might be discovered; he was besides suspected of having made away with his brother, who nowhere appeared. For these reasons he proclaimed great rewards among all the nests of pirates in his neighbourhood, to any one who should capture him alive: they, stimulated by these offers, and in the heat of battle, not losing sight of gain, took him prisoner at the price of many of their lives. They sent him, under a strong guard, to the main land, he reproaching them all the while for their seeming lenity, and bearing bonds much more indignantly than he would have borne death. The rest proceeded towards the island in quest of treasures and spoil; but when, after a long and strict search, they found nothing of any consequence, some few things excepted, which out of hurry or forgetfulness were left out of the cavern, they set fire to the tents; and the evening coming on, fearing to remain there any longer, lest they should be surprised by the enemy whom they had driven thence, they returned to their companions upon the continent.

Book II

In this manner, as we have related, were the flames spread over the lake; the conflagration escaped the notice of Theagenes and Cnemon while the sun was above the horizon, the superior lustre of that planet overcoming the blaze; but when it set, when night came on, and the fire had no longer any rival to contend with, it appeared at a distance to their great consternation, as they began to raise themselves out of the morass. Theagenes tearing his hair, thus broke out into passionate exclamations; "May this day be the last of my life; may my fears, cares, and dangers now have an end, and my hopes and love conclude together. Chariclea is no more, and I am undone; in vain, wretch, that I am, have I become a coward, and submitted to an unmanly flight, that I might preserve myself for you, the delight of my life. For you, alas! I live no longer; you have fallen by an untimely death, nor was he on whom you doated present to receive your latest breath; but you are become the prey of flames, and these are the nuptial torches which cruel fate has lighted up for you. All is consumed, and there now remains no trace of the most perfect of human forms: O! most cruel and envious deities! a last embrace is denied me:" and thus lamenting, he felt about for his sword— Cnemon arrested his hand, and cried out, "Why, Theagenes, do you lament her who is safe? Chariclea is alive; be comforted." "Away!" he replied, "this is a tale for children; why do you keep me from the death I long for?" Cnemon swore to the truth of what he had said, told him the orders of Thyamis, described the cave where he had placed Chariclea; and assured him there was not the smallest danger of the flames (cut off as they would be) penetrating through the deep and winding avenues by which she was protected.

Theagenes at these assurances began to recover his spirits, and hastened towards the island, having Chariclea, and a joyful meeting in the cave before his eyes, ignorant, alas! of the woes which awaited him there. They proceeded forwards with great ardour, plying the oars themselves, for their rower had fallen overboard in the confusion of the first flight; they went on with an unsteady course from inexperience in rowing, not able to keep stroke, and the wind being against them; but their ardour overcame their unskilfulness, and with great difficulty at last, and bathed in sweat, they reached the shore, and ran eagerly towards the tents. Of these they saw only the ashes, they having been totally consumed; the stone, however, which formed the threshold and entrance of the cavern, was conspicuous enough; for the huts being built of reeds and such slender materials, were soon consumed and turned into a light ash, which the wind scattering away, left the earth bare in many places for a passage, cooling it at the same time with the blast.

Finding some torches half burnt, and lighting some reeds which remained, they opened the cave's mouth, and under the guidance of Cnemon, descended into it. When they had gone a little way, Cnemon suddenly exclaimed, "O God! what is this? we are undone, Chariclea is slain;" and flinging his torch on the ground, extinguished it, and falling on his knees, and covering his face with his hands, began to weep. Theagenes threw himself upon the body, and held it a long time in his arms, closely embraced; Cnemon seeing him overwhelmed with this stroke, and fearing when he recovered his senses he would make some attempt upon himself, took away unobserved the sword which hung by his side, and leaving him for a moment, ran out to light his torch. While he was gone, the unhappy lover broke out into mournful and tragic exclamations, "O intolerable calamity, and never-to-be-appeased wrath of the gods! what insatiable demon thus rages to my destruction? who, after having driven me from my country through a thousand dangers of seas and pirates, having delivered me up to marauders, and stript me of all I had, when one only comfort was left me, has now deprived me of that! Chariclea is no more, she lies slain by a violent death; doubtless, she has fallen in defence of her chastity, determined to preserve herself unspotted for my sake. In vain has her beauty bloomed both for herself and me; but, O my love! have not you one last word left to speak to me? Are life and breath for ever gone? Alas! you are silent; that mouth, formerly the interpreter of the will of heaven, is dumb, and darkness and destruction have overwhelmed the priestess of the gods. Those eyes glance no more whose lustre dazzled all beholders, whose brightness, if your murderer had met, he could not have executed his purpose; what shall I call you, my wife? but we were not married; my contracted spouse? but the contract has been a fruitless one; let me call you by the sweetest of all appellations, Chariclea. O Chariclea! if, where you are, you are capable of receiving comfort, be comforted; you have a faithful lover; we shall soon meet again; behold, I sacrifice myself to your Manes, to you I pour out my own blood in libations; this cavern, a rude sepulchre, shall retain both our bodies; we shall be united in our deaths, though fate forbade it in our lives." Saying this, he felt for his sword, and not finding it, "O Cnemon," he exclaimed, "you have undone me, and Chariclea too, for the second time depriving her shade of the company it desires." While he was thus speaking, a voice from the windings of the cave was heard, calling Theagenes; he, not in the least alarmed, replied, "I come, my dearest life; your soul, I see, still hovers above the earth, partly, perhaps, because unwilling to leave that body, from which it has by violence been expelled; and partly, because wanting the rites of sepulture, you may be refused admittance in the shades below." Cnemon now approached with the torch; again the voice was heard, calling Theagenes; Cnemon instantly exclaimed, "Ye gods! is not this the voice of Chariclea? Theagenes, I think she is safe, for the sound seems to me to proceed from that very part of the cavern where I know I left her."—"Will you never cease attempting to deceive me," replied Theagenes?—"I am much deceived myself," replied the other, "if we find this corpse which lies before us to be that of Chariclea;" and stooping down to examine the countenance, "O heavens!" he cried out, "what do I see? the face of Thisbe!" and starting back, he stood petrified with astonishment. Theagenes, on the contrary, now began to recover his spirits, and in his turn supported and encouraged Cnemon, who was ready to faint; and besought him that he would lead him instantly to Chariclea; Cnemon, by degrees coming to himself, again examined the body, which really was that of Thisbe; he knew, too, by its hilt, the sword which Thyamis from rage and haste had left sticking in the wound. He perceived also a tablet appearing out of her bosom; he took it, and was beginning to read what was written upon it; but Theagenes would not suffer him, and earnestly entreated him, if all he saw was not the illusion of some demon, that he would take him to Chariclea; you may afterwards, said he, read this tablet. Cnemon obeyed; and, taking up the tablet and the sword, hastened towards Chariclea. She, creeping on hands and knees towards the sound of their voices as well as she could, at length saw the light, flew to Theagenes, and hung upon his neck. And mutually exclaiming, "And are you restored to me, my dear Theagenes?"—"Do you live, sweetest Chariclea?" they fell in each others' arms upon the ground; their voices murmuring and themselves dying away. So much does a sudden rush of joy overpower the human faculties, and excess of pleasure passes into pain. Thus these lovers, unexpectedly preserved, seemed again in danger, till Cnemon, observing a little water in a cleft of the rock, took it up in the hollow of his hand, and sprinkling it over their faces and nostrils, they came by degrees to themselves. But when they discovered their situation, lying on the ground in each other's arms, they rose immediately, and blushing a little, especially Chariclea, began to make excuses to Cnemon. He, smiling, turned the matter into pleasantry.

"You will not find a severe censor in me," said he; "whoever is but moderately acquainted with the passion of love, will easily forgive its excesses. But there is one part of your conduct, Theagenes, which I cannot approve of—indeed I was ashamed to see it—when you fell down, and bewailed in so lamentable a manner a foreign woman, and one of no good character, while I was all the time assuring you, that she, whom you professed to love best, was alive and near you."—"Have done, Cnemon," he replied; "do not traduce me to Chariclea. You know I lamented her, under the person of another; but since the kind gods have shewn me that I was in an error, pray call to mind a little your own fortitude. You joined your tears, at first, with mine; but when you recognized the body which lay before you, you started as from a demon on the stage, you in armour, and with a sword, from a woman; you, a Grecian warrior, from a corpse!"

This raillery drew a short and forced smile from them, mingled with tears; for such was their calamitous situation, that grief and thought soon overpowered this gleam of cheerfulness. A short silence ensued; when Chariclea gently moving her finger upon her cheek under the ear, exclaimed, "I shall always esteem her blest, whoever she be, for whom Theagenes is concerned; but, if you do not think that love makes me too inquisitive, I should be glad to know who is this happy damsel who has been thought worthy of his tears; and by what error he could take a stranger for me."—"You will wonder when you hear," replied Theagenes. "Cnemon affirms, that these are the remains of Thisbe, the Athenian singer, the plotter against him and Demæneta."—"How," said the astonished Chariclea, "could she be brought here, from the middle of Greece to the extremity of Egypt, like a deity in a tragedy? and how could she be concealed from us at our entrance?"—"As to that, I am as much at a loss about it as you can be," said Cnemon; "all I know of her adventures is this: After the tragical end of Demæneta, my father laid before the people what had happened. They pitied and pardoned him; and he was earnestly employed in soliciting my recall. Thisbe made use of the leisure she had upon her hands; and at different entertainments set her musical skill and her person to sale.

"She now received more favour from the public than Arsinoë, who grew careless in practising her talents; while Thisbe shewed greater perfection, both in voice and execution. But she was not aware that by this she had excited the inextinguishable envy of a courtezan. This was increased by her having seduced Nausicles, a rich merchant of Naucratium, formerly a lover of Arsinoë; but who had left her on pretence of being disgusted with the distortions of her eyes and countenance, while she was playing on the flute. Anger and jealousy raging in her bosom, she went to the relations of Demæneta, and discovered to them the snare which Thisbe had laid for their kinswoman; partly from her own conjectures, and partly from what Thisbe had told her. Their anger, however, fell first upon my father; and they engaged the most skilful counsel to accuse him to the people, as if he had put Demæneta to death without trial or conviction; and had made use of the adultery only as a pretext for her murder; and loudly called upon him to produce the adulterer, or at least to name him; they concluded by insisting that Thisbe should be put to the torture. My father readily agreed to this, but she was not to be found; for, upon the first stirring of the matter, she had taken flight with her merchant. The people, angry at her escape, were in an ill humour to hear the defence of the accused. They did not indeed convict him of the murder, but found him guilty of being concerned in the contrivance against Demæneta, and of my unjust banishment. They exiled him from the city, and fined him to the amount of the greatest part of his fortune. Such were the fruits of his second marriage.

"The wretched Thisbe, whose punishment I now see before me, sailed safe from Athens: this is all I know about her, and this I had from Anticles at Ægina. I sailed with him to Egypt in hopes of finding Thisbe at Naucratium, that I might bring her back to Athens, and clear my father from the suspicions and accusations he laboured under, and procure her to be justly punished for her crimes against us. What I have since undergone you shall hear at a more convenient season; let us now examine into the cause of the tragedy which is here presented to us. But how Thisbe came into this cavern, and how she has been murdered in it, must be explained to us, I believe, by some deity, for it passes human comprehension; let us examine, however, the tablet that was found in her bosom; perhaps that will give us some information." With this he took it, and began to read as follows:

"Thisbe, formerly his enemy, but now his avenger, to her master, Cnemon:

"In the first place I inform you of the death of Demæneta, brought about on your account by my means; how it happened, if you will admit me to your presence, I will relate to you in person. I have been ten days on this island, having been made captive by one of the robbers, who boasts that he is lieutenant to the chief, and keeps me closely confined—as he says, out of love; as I suppose, lest I should be taken from him. By the kindness of the gods, I have seen and recognized you, and send this tablet to you privately by an old woman who waits upon me, commanding her to deliver it to a handsome Greek, a favourite of the chief. Deliver me from the power of these pirates, and receive to yourself your handmaid; and, if you can prevail upon yourself, preserve her; knowing that in what I acted against you I was compelled, but the revenging you of your enemy was my own voluntary act. But, if you still feel an inextinguishable resentment against me, satiate it as you please; only let me be in your hands, even if I am to die by them; I prefer death from you, and to have the rites of my country performed over my remains, to a life that is more dreadful than death; and to the love of a barbarian, more odious to me than the hatred of a Greek."—This was the contents of the tablet.

"O Thisbe," said Cnemon, "the gods have wisely ordained your death; and that you should become, even after your slaughter, the relater of your calamities; the Fury who has driven you through the world, has not ceased her avenging pursuit, till she has made me, whom you have injured, even in Egypt, a spectator of your punishment. But what accident is it which has stopped your career, while perhaps this letter of yours was only the forerunner of some new practice against me? for I cannot help suspecting you even now that you are dead. I fear lest the account of Demæneta's death should be a fiction; lest those who have informed me of it should have deceived me; lest you should have crossed the seas with a design to renew in Egypt the tragedies you have acted against me in Attica."—"O you courageous fellow!" cries out Theagenes, "will you never cease to terrify yourself with shades and fancies? You cannot pretend that she has bewitched me, at any rate, for I have had no part in the drama; assure yourself that no harm can arise to you from this dead corpse, and pluck up your spirits: but who has been so far your benefactor as to slay your enemy, and how and when she descended here, I am utterly at a loss to imagine."—"As to the matter in general I am so too," replied Cnemon; "but he who slew her was certainly Thyamis, as I conjecture from the sword which was found near the body; I know it to be his, by the ivory hilt carved into the form of an eagle."—"But can you conjecture," said the other, "how, and when, and for what cause, he committed this murder?"—"How should I know that?" he answered. "This cavern has not had the virtue of inspiring me, like that of Delphi or Trophonius."

The mention of Delphi seemed to agitate Theagenes, and drew tears from Chariclea; they repeated the name with great emotion. Cnemon was surprised, and could not conceive why they were so affected by it. In this manner they were engaged in the cave. Meanwhile Thermuthis, the lieutenant of Thyamis, after he had been wounded and had got to land in the manner we have related, when night came on, hastened towards the cavern in search of Thisbe; for he it was who had placed her there. He had some days before taken her by force from the merchant Nausicles in a narrow mountain pass. On the tumult and attack which soon after ensued, when he was sent by Thyamis in search of a victim, he let her down into this cavern, that she might be out of the reach of danger, and in his hurry and confusion left her near the entrance of it. Here she remained out of fear, and ignorance of the winding passages which led to the bottom; and here Thyamis found and killed her by mistake for Chariclea. Thermuthis proceeded on his way to Thisbe. Upon reaching the island he hastened to the tents; these he found in ashes: and having with some difficulty discovered the entrance of the cavern, by means of the stone covering, he lighted a handful of reeds which yet remained there, and hastened to descend into it.

He called Thisbe by her name, in Greek; but when he saw her lying dead at his feet, he stood motionless with horror and surprise. At length he heard a murmur and distant sound of voices issuing from the hollow recesses of the cave; for Theagenes and Cnemon were still conversing together.

These he concluded to be the murderers of Thisbe, and was in doubt what he should do; for as was natural in a ferocious pirate, his rage, raised to the highest pitch by this disappointment of his desires, urged him to rush at once upon the supposed authors of it; but his want of arms made him unwillingly more cautious. He concluded therefore that it was best at first not to present himself as an enemy, but if by any means he could possess himself of arms, then to attack them on a sudden. With this design he advanced towards Theagenes, throwing wild and fierce glances around him, and discovering in his looks the purpose of his heart.

They were surprised at the sudden appearance of a stranger, almost naked, wounded, and with his face bloody. Chariclea, startled and ashamed, retired into the inmost part of the cave. Cnemon too drew a little back, knowing Thermuthis, seeing him unexpectedly, and fearing that he came there on no good account. But Theagenes was more irritated than terrified, and presenting the point of his sword, called out, "Stand where you are, or you shall receive another wound; thus far I spare you, because I know your face, and am not sure of your designs."—Thermuthis stretched out his unarmed hands, and besought his compassion; forced, notwithstanding his rugged temper, from the circumstance he was in, to become a supplicant. He called on Cnemon for assistance, and said he deserved help from him, having never injured him; having lived with him as a comrade, and coming now as a friend. Cnemon was moved by his entreaties; raised him from the knees of Theagenes which he had embraced, and eagerly inquired where was Thyamis. The latter related all he knew—how his leader had attacked the enemy; how he had rushed into the midst of the battle, sparing neither his foes nor himself; the slaughter he made of them; and the protection which the proclamation to take him alive afforded him. He mentioned his own wound and escape, but knew nothing of his captain's fate; and was come here in search of Thisbe. They inquired how he became so interested about Thisbe; and how she came into his possession. He told them everything: how he had taken her from a merchant; how he fell violently in love with her, and had concealed her some time in his tent, and at the approach of the attacking party had placed her in the cave where he now saw her slain; that he was perfectly ignorant of the authors of her death, but would most gladly find them out if he could, and ascertain their motive.

Cnemon, eager to free himself from suspicion, told him it was certainly Thyamis who slew her; and shewed him the sword which was found beside her; which, when Thermuthis saw, still reeking with blood, and warm from the wound, and knew it to have belonged to Thyamis, he uttered a deep groan, still more perplexed how to account for the accident, and in dumb gloomy astonishment moved towards the mouth of the cave. Here throwing himself upon the bosom of the deceased, he embraced the body, and repeating nothing but the name of Thisbe, fainter by degrees and fainter, oppressed with grief and fatigue, sunk at last into a sleep.

The remainder of the company in the cave began now to consult what steps it was proper for them to pursue. But the multitude of their past calamities, the pressure of the present misfortunes, and the uncertainty of what might happen to them, obscured the light, and weakened the force, of their reason. Each looked at the other, expecting him to say something; and being disappointed, turned his eyes to the ground; and raising them again, sighed, lightening a little his grief by this expression of it. At length Cnemon sat down on the ground; Theagenes threw himself on a rock, and Chariclea reclined upon him. In this posture they a long time resisted the attacks of sleep, desirous, if they could, to devise some scheme of action; but, overcome at last with grief and fatigue, they unwillingly yielded to the law of nature, and fell into a sweet slumber from the very excess of sorrow. Thus is the intelligent soul obliged sometimes to sympathise with the affections of the body.

When sleep had for a little while just weighed their eye-lids down, the following vision appeared to Chariclea. A man with his hair in disorder, a downcast look, and bloody hands, seemed to come and thrust out her right eye with a sword. She instantly cried out, and called upon Theagenes. He was soon awakened, and felt for her uneasiness, though it was only in a dream. She lifted her hand to her face, as if in search of the part she had lost, and then exclaimed, "It was a dream; my eye is safe!"—"I am glad," replied Theagenes, "that those bright sunbeams are uninjured. But what has ailed you? how came you so terrified?"—"A savage and violent man," says she, "not fearing even your valour, attacked me with a sword as I lay at your feet; and, as I thought, deprived me of my right eye; and would that it had been a reality and not a vision!"—"Now Heaven forefend! why do you make so shocking a wish?"—"Because I would much rather lose one of my eyes than be under apprehensions for you; for I greatly fear that the dream regards you, whom I esteem as my eyes, my soul, my all."—"Cease," called out Cnemon (who had heard all that had passed, having been awakened by the first exclamation of Chariclea), "for I think the vision has another interpretation. Had you any parents living when you left Greece?"—"I had," she replied.—"Believe then now that your father is dead. I form my conjecture from hence: Our parents are the authors of our being; therefore they may properly enough in a dream be shadowed out under the similitude of eyes, the organs of light, which convey to us things visible."

"The loss of my father," replied Chariclea, "would be a heavy blow; but let even your interpretation be the true one, rather mine. I consent to pass for a false prophet!"—"Be it so," replied Cnemon; "but we are indeed dreaming, while we are examining fancies and visions, and forget to apply ourselves to our real business, especially while the absence of the Egyptian (meaning Thermuthis), who is employed in lamenting his deceased love, gives us an opportunity."—"O Cnemon," said Theagenes, "since some god has joined you to us, and made you a partaker in our calamities, do you advise us what to do, for you are acquainted with the country and language; and we, oppressed with a greater weight of misfortunes, are less fit for counsel."

"Which of us has the greater load of misfortunes to struggle with, is by no means clear," said Cnemon. "I have my full share of them; but, however, as I am the elder, and you command me to speak, I will obey you. The island where we are, you see, is desolate, and contains none but ourselves. Of gold, silver, and precious garments, plundered from you and others, and heaped together by the pirates, there is plenty; but of food and other necessaries, it is totally destitute. If we stay here, we are in danger of perishing by famine, or of being destroyed by some of the invaders, or by the buccaneers, if, knowing of the treasures which are left here, they return again in search of them. There will then be no escape; either we shall perish, or be exposed to their violence and insults. They are always a faithless race, and will now be more disorderly and dreadful, having lost their chief. We must fly, therefore, from this place, as from a snare and a prison, sending Thermuthis away first, if we can, under pretext of inquiring after Thyamis, for we shall be more at liberty to consult and act by ourselves. It is prudent, too, to remove from us a man of an unconstant temper, of savage manners, and who, besides, suspects us on account of the death of Thisbe, and probably only waits for an opportunity to commit some violence against us."

The advice of Cnemon was approved of; and they determined to follow it; and moving towards the mouth of the cave, the day now beginning to dawn, they roused Thermuthis, who was still sunk in sleep; and telling him as much as they thought proper of their design, easily persuaded a fickle-minded man. They then took the body of Thisbe, drew it into a hollow of the rock, covered it as well as they could with ashes from the tents, and performed what funeral rites the time and place would admit of, supplying what was deficient by tears and lamentations.

They next proceeded to send out Thermuthis on the expedition they had projected for him. He set out, but soon returned, declaring he would not go alone, nor expose himself to the danger of so perilous a search, unless Cnemon would bear him company. Theagenes, observing that this proposal was by no means agreeable to Cnemon, who betrayed evident marks of fear and apprehension when informed of it, said to him, "You are valiant in council, Cnemon, but a laggard in action;

you have shown this more than once; pluck up your spirits, and prove yourself a man. It is necessary that this fellow should have no suspicion, at present, of our design to leave him. Seem to agree, therefore, to what he proposes, and go with him at first; for there is no danger to be apprehended from an unarmed man, especially by you who are armed. You may take your opportunity, and leave him privately, and come to us at some place which we shall fix upon; and we will, if you please, mention some neighbouring town, if you know any, where the inhabitants are a little civilized."

Cnemon agreed to this, and named Chemmis, a rich and populous place, situated on a rising ground on the banks of the Nile, by way of defence against the incursions of the pirates, about one hundred furlongs distant from the lake directly south. "I fear," said Theagenes, "that Chariclea will find some difficulty in getting thither, as she is unused to walking; however, we will attempt it, and pretend that we are beggars who seek our living by showing juggling tricks."

"Truly," said Cnemon, "your faces are sufficiently disfigured for such a business, particularly Chariclea's, who has just lost an eye; after all, though, I fear you will rather appear guests for the table than petitioners for scraps at the door."—This sally was received with a forced and languid smile, which played only on the lips. They then prepared to depart, swearing never to desert each other, and calling the gods to witness it.

Cnemon and Thermuthis set out early in the morning; and, crossing the lake, took their way through a thick and difficult wood. Thermuthis went first, at the persuasion of Cnemon, on the pretext that, as he was acquainted with the country, he was better qualified to lead; in reality, that the other might more easily find an opportunity of deserting him. They met with some flocks in their way; and the shepherds fled, at their approach, into the thickest of the wood. They seized a ram, roasted him at a fire the shepherds had lighted, and hardly staying till it was sufficiently dressed, devoured the flesh with eagerness. Hunger pressed them; they fell upon it like wolves; swallowed whole pieces, just warmed through, and still dropping with blood. When they had satisfied their hunger, and allayed their thirst with milk, they pursued their way. Evening now approached, and they were ascending a hill under which was situated a town, where Thermuthis said it was very probable that Thyamis was either detained a captive or had been slain. Here Cnemon pretended that he felt great pain; that his stomach was exceedingly disordered by his inordinate repast of meat and drink, and that he must retire to ease it. This he did two or three times, that his companion might suspect nothing, and complained that it was with great difficulty he could follow him. When he had accustomed the Egyptian to his staying behind, he took an opportunity at last to let him go on forwards farther than usual; and then, turning suddenly back, he ran down the hill as fast as he could into the thickest part of the bushes. Thermuthis, when he had arrived at the summit, sat himself down on a rock, expecting the approach of night, which they had agreed to wait for before they entered into the town to inquire after Thyamis. He looked about for his companion, having no good designs against him, for he was still persuaded that he had slain Thisbe, and was considering how he might serve him in the same manner; proposing afterwards to attack Theagenes. But when Cnemon appeared nowhere, and night advanced, he fell asleep—a deadly and last sleep it proved to him, for an asp, which had lain concealed in a thicket, bit him, and put a fitting end to his life.

But Cnemon, after he had left Thermuthis, stopped not in his flight till the darkness of the night obliged him to make a halt. He then endeavoured to conceal himself by lying down and covering himself as well as he could with leaves. Here he passed a restless and almost sleepless night, taking every noise, every gust of wind, and motion of a leaf, for Thermuthis. If at any time he dropped into a slumber, he thought he was fleeing; and looking behind, imagined he saw him pursuing, who was now unable to follow him; till at last he resisted all approaches of sleep, his dreams becoming more dreadful to him than even his waking apprehensions.

He was uneasy at the duration of the night, which appeared to him the longest he had ever spent. At length, to his great joy, day appeared. He then proceeded to cut his hair short, which he had suffered to grow, in imitation of, and to recommend himself to, his piratical companions, for the pirates, willing to render themselves as formidable as they can, among other things, cherish long hair, which they suffer to grow down their foreheads, and play over their shoulders, well knowing that flowing locks, as they make the lover more amiable, so they render the warrior more terrible. When Cnemon, therefore, had shaped his hair into the common form, he proceeded to Chemmis, where he had appointed to meet Theagenes. As he drew near the Nile, and was preparing to pass over it to Chemmis, he perceived an old man wandering upon its banks, walking several times up and down the stream, as if he were communicating his cares to the river. His locks were as white as snow, and shaped like those of a priest; his beard flowing and venerable; his habit Grecian. Cnemon stopped a little; but when the old man passed by many times, seemingly unconscious that any one was near (so entirely was he immersed in care and meditation), he placed himself before him, and, in the Grecian manner of salutation, bid him be of good cheer. The other replied, his fortunes were such that good cheer was out of the question. Cnemon, surprised, asked: "Are you a stranger from Greece, or from whence?"—"I am neither a Grecian nor a stranger," said he, "but an Egyptian of this country."—"Why, then, have you a Grecian dress?"—"My misfortunes," says he, "have put me into this splendid habit." The other, wondering how misfortunes could improve a man's appearance, and seeming desirous to be informed—"You carry me into a 'tale of Troy divine,'" replied the old man; "and a swarm of evils, the recital of which would oppress you. But whence do you come, O young man, and whither are you going? and how come I to hear the Greek tongue in Egypt?"—"It is a little unreasonable in you," replied Cnemon, "to ask these questions of me, you who will tell nothing about yourself, though I made the first inquiries."—"I admit it," said the other; "but do not be offended. You seem to be a Greek, and to have yourself undergone some transformation from the hand of fortune. You are desirous to hear my adventures; I am no less so to relate them. Probably I had told them to these reeds, as the fable goes, if I had not met with you. But let us leave the Nile and its banks; for a situation exposed to the meridian sun is not a proper place for a long narration. If you have no urgent business which hinders you, let us go to the town which you see opposite to us. I will entertain you, not in my own house, but in that of a good man who received me when I implored his protection. There you may listen to my story, and in your turn relate your own."—"With all my heart," said Cnemon, "for I myself was going to this town to wait for some friends of mine, whom I had appointed to meet there." Getting, therefore, into a boat, many of which were lying by the river's side, to transport passengers, they crossed over into the town, and arrived at the house where the stranger was lodged. The master of the house was not at home; but his daughter, a marriageable maiden, received them with great cheerfulness, and the servants waited upon the old man as if he had been their father, most probably by their master's orders. One washed his feet, and wiped off the dust from under his knees; another got ready his bed, and strewed it with soft coverings; a third brought an urn, and filled it with fire; a fourth prepared the table, and spread it with bread and various kinds of fruit.

Cnemon, wondering at their alacrity, exclaimed, "We have certainly got into the house of Jove the Hospitable, such is the attention and singular benevolence with which we are received."—"You have not got into the habitation of Jove," replied the other, "but into that of a man who exactly imitates his hospitable and charitable qualities: for his life has been a mercantile and wandering one; he has seen many cities, and observed the manners of many nations; he is naturally therefore inclined to compassionate the stranger, and receive the wanderer, as he did me not many days ago."—"And how came you to be a wanderer, father?"— "Being deprived," said he, "of my children by robbers; knowing those who had injured me, but unable to contend with them; I roam about this spot, mourning and sorrowing; not unlike a bird whose nest a serpent has made desolate, and is devouring her young before her eyes. She is afraid to approach, yet cannot bear to desert them; terror and affection struggle within her; she flies mournfully round the scene of her calamities, pouring in vain her maternal complaints into ears deaf to her waitings and strangers to mercy."—"Will you then relate," said Cnemon, "when and how you encountered this grievous war of woe?"—"By-and-bye," he replied; "but let us now attend to our craving stomach; which, because it considers itself of more consequence than any other organ, is called by Homer *destructive*. And first, as is the custom of the Egyptian sages, let us make a libation to the gods. Nothing shall make me omit this; nor shall grief ever so entirely possess my mind, as to render me forgetful of what I owe to heaven." With this he poured pure water out of the vase, and said, "I make this libation to the gods of this country, and those of Greece; to the Pythian Apollo, and also to Theagenes and Chariclea, the good and beautiful, since I reckon them also among the gods:" and then he wept, as if he were making another libation to them with his tears. Cnemon, greatly struck at what he heard, viewed the old man from head to foot, and exclaimed, "What do you say? Are Theagenes and Chariclea really your children?"—"They are my children," replied the stranger, "but born to me without a mother. Fortune, by the permission of the gods, gave them to me; I brought them forth with the travail of my soul. My great inclination towards them supplied the place of nature; and I have been esteemed by them, and called their father. But tell me, how came you acquainted with them?"—"I am not only acquainted with them," said Cnemon, "but can assure you that they are alive and well."—"O Apollo, and all the gods!" he exclaimed, "where are they? Tell me, I beseech you; and you will be my preserver and equal to the gods!"—"But what shall be my reward?" replied the other.—"At present that of obliging me; no mean reward to a wise man: I know many who have laid up this as a treasure in their hearts. But if we arrive in my country, which, if I may believe the tokens of the gods, will ere long be, your utmost desires shall be satisfied with wealth."

"You promise me," said Cnemon, "things uncertain and future, when you have it in your power to reward me immediately."—"Show me anything I can now do for you," said the old man, "for I would willingly part even with a limb to satisfy you."—"Your limbs need be in no danger," replied the Grecian; "I shall be satisfied if you will relate to me from whence these strangers come, who were their parents, how they were brought here, and what have been their adventures."—"You shall have a treat," replied the old man; "so great as to be second to none other, not even if you should obtain all earthly treasures. But let us now take a little food; for my narration and your listening will take up a considerable time."

When they had eaten, therefore, some nuts and figs, and fresh-gathered dates, and such other things as the old man was used to feed upon (for he never deprived any animal of life for his own nourishment), he drank a little water, and Cnemon some wine; and, after a short pause, the latter said: "You know, O father, that Bacchus delights in convivial conversations and stories; and as I am now under his influence, I am very desirous of hearing some, and I claim from you my promised reward: it is time to bring your piece upon the stage, as the saying goes."—"You shall be satisfied," replied the stranger: "but I wish the good Nausicles were here, who has often earnestly desired to hear this detail from me, and as often, on some pretext or other, has been put off."—At the name of Nausicles, Cnemon asked where he was. "He is gone a hunting," replied the other.—"And after what kind of game?"—"Why, not indeed of wild beasts, but of men as savage as they, who are called buccaneers, who live by robbery, who are very difficult to be taken, and lurk in marshes, caverns, and lakes."—"What offence have they given him?"—"They have taken his mistress from him, an Athenian girl, whom he called Thisbe."—"Ah!" said Cnemon, in a tone of surprise, and immediately stopped, as if checking himself.—"What ails you?" said the old man.—The other, evading the question, proceeded, "I wonder with what forces he means to attack them?"—

"Oroondates, viceroy of Egypt, under the Great King, has appointed Mithranes commandant of this town; Nausicles, by means of a large sum of money, has prevailed upon him to march with a body of horse and foot against them; for he is exceedingly annoyed at the loss of this Grecian girl; not only because he liked her himself, and because she was well skilled in music; but because he was going to take her with him to the king of Ethiopia, by way of attendant upon the queen, as he said, and to amuse her after the Grecian fashion. Being deprived, therefore, as he supposes, by her loss, of a great reward which he expected for her, he is using his utmost efforts to recover her. I encouraged him too to this expedition, thinking it possible he might find and recover my children also." "Enough of buccaneers, and viceroys, and kings," cried out Cnemon, impatiently; "your discourse is wandering from the point I aim at. This episode has nothing to do with the main plot; come back to the performance of your promise; you are like the Pharian Proteus; not turning indeed into false and fleeting shapes, but trying to slip away from me."—"Be satisfied," said the old man, "you shall know all. I will explain to you first what relates to myself, shortly, and without reserve; which will be a proper introduction to that which is to follow.

"I am a citizen of Memphis. The name of my father was Calasiris, as is likewise mine. Though now a wanderer, I was not long ago a high priest. I had a wife, but have now lost her; after her death I lived for some time quietly, delighting myself with two sons whom she had left me. But in a few years, the fated revolution of the heavenly bodies altered every thing; the eye of Saturn scowled upon my family, and portended a change in my fortunes for the worse. I had skill enough to foresee the ills which threatened me, but not to avoid them; for no foresight can enable us to escape the immutable decrees of fate: it is, however, an advantage, to have some foreknowledge of them, as it blunts the violence of the stroke. Unexpected misfortunes, my son, are intolerable; those which are foreseen are more easily borne: the mind is confused and disarmed by sudden fear; custom and reason strengthen it. My calamities began in this manner:

"A Thracian woman, in the bloom of youth and in beauty second only to Chariclea, whose name was Rhodope, unfortunately for those who became acquainted with her, travelled through Egypt. In her progress she came in 'revel-rout' to Memphis, with great luxury and pomp of attendance, and adorned with every grace, and exercising all the arts of love. It was almost impossible to see her, and not fall into her snares; such irresistible witchery accompanied the eyes of this fair harlot. She frequently came into the temple of Isis, where I officiated as high priest. She worshipped the goddess with sacrifices and costly offerings. I am ashamed to proceed; yet I will not conceal the truth. The frequent sight of her overcame me at last, in spite of the command I had long been accustomed to maintain over my passions. I struggled long against my bodily eyes and the eyes of my fancy, but in vain; I yielded at last, and sank under the dominion of love. I perceived that the arrival of this woman was to be the beginning of those misfortunes which the heavens foretold to me; and that my evil genius was to make her one of the principal instruments of them. I determined, however, to do nothing to disgrace that office of priesthood which had descended to me from my ancestors, nor to profane the altars and temples of the gods: and as to the transgression which my evil stars had determined I should fall into, not in act, indeed (heaven forbid!) but in desire; I constituted reason my judge, and made her impose the penalty of exile from my native land, yielding to the necessity of fate, submitting to its decrees, and flying from the ill-omened Rhodope. For I will own to you, O stranger! that I was afraid, lest, under the present baleful influence of the constellations, I might be tempted to do something unbecoming my character. Another, and a principal reason for my absenting myself, was, on account of my children; for my skill in divination shewed me that they were in a short time to contend with each other in arms.

"Snatching myself away, therefore, from a spectacle so dreadful to a father's eyes (sufficient to turn aside the aspect of the sun, and make him hide his beams), I departed from my country, from my house, and family, making no one acquainted with the course I intended to take, but pretending that I was going to Egyptian Thebes, to see my eldest son Thyamis, who was there on a visit to his grandfather."—Cnemon started again at the name of Thyamis; but restrained himself, and was silent, desirous to hear the sequel. The old man, after observing—

"I pass over the intermediate part of my journey, for it has no relation to what you desire to know," thus proceeded: "But having heard that there was a famous city in Greece, called Delphi, sacred to Apollo, abounding in temples, the resort of wise men, retired, and free from popular tumults; thither I bent my steps, thinking that a city destined for sacred rites was a proper retreat for one of my profession. I sailed through the Crissæan gulf, and landing at Cirrha, proceeded to the city: when I entered it, a voice, no doubt divine, sounded in my ears;

and as in other respects this place seemed a fit habitation for a superior race, so particularly on account of its situation. The mountain Parnassus hangs over it, as a kind of natural fortification and citadel, stretching out its sides, and receiving the city into its bosom." "Your description is most graphic, cried out Cnemon, "and seems really made under the influence of the Pythic inspiration; for in this manner I remember well my father described Delphi, when he returned from the council of the Amphictyons, to which the city of Athens had deputed him as sacred secretary."—"You are an Athenian then, my son?"—"Yes."—"Your name?"—Cnemon."—"What have been your fortunes?"—"You shall hear by-and-bye. Now however continue your own narration."—"I will," replied the old man.

"I ascended into the place, I admired the city of race-courses, of market-places, and of fountains, especially the famed one of Castalia, with the water of which I sprinkled myself, and hastened to the temple; for the thronging of the multitude, which pressed towards it, seemed to announce the time when the priestess was about to be under the sacred impulse; and having worshipped and uttered a petition for myself, I received the following oracle:

> *Thou from the fertile Nile, thy course dost bend,*
> *Pause here awhile, and sojourn as my friend:*
> *Stern fate thou fly'st, her strokes with courage bear;*
> *Ere long of Egypt thou shalt have a share.*

"As soon as the priestess had pronounced this, I fell upon my face, and besought the deity to be propitious to me in everything. The crowd who surrounded the shrine, joined in praising the deity for having deigned to answer me on my first entreaty; they congratulated me, and paid me great respect, saying, that I seemed to be the greatest favourite with the deity who had appeared there since Lycurgus, a Spartan. They permitted me at my request to inhabit the precincts of the temple, and passed a decree that I should be maintained at the public expense. My situation, in short, was a very agreeable one; I either assisted at the ceremonies and sacrifices which were every day performed and offered by strangers as well as natives, or conversed with the philosophers, for many of this description flocked to Delphi. The city is in truth a university, inspired by the deity who presides over inspiration and the muses. Various subjects were discussed; sometimes the manner of our religious rites in Egypt, and why certain animals were counted sacred more than others; and the different histories which belonged to each. Another inquired about the construction of the Pyramids and the Catacombs. In short, there was nothing relative to Egypt which they did not scrutinize into; for it is wonderful how the Greeks listen to, and are delighted with, accounts of that country. At length one among the more accomplished of them touched upon the Nile, its fountains, and inundations, wondering why it alone, of all rivers, should in the summer time swell and overflow. I told them what I knew on that subject, which I had gathered from the sacred books which the priests alone are permitted to consult. I related how it had its rise on the south-east confines of Libya and Ethiopia; that it increased in the summer, not because its waters, as some supposed, were driven back by the Etesian winds, but because these winds, about the time of the summer solstice, drive the clouds before them from the northern into the southern parts, which are by this means collected in the torrid zone, where their farther motion is stopped by the extreme vehemence of the heat. They are then condensed, and pressed by degrees, till they dissolve, and fall in copious showers. These swell the river till it disdains its banks, and, bursting over Egypt like a sea, fertilizes the plains it overflows. Its waters are very sweet to drink, as they are furnished by the rains from heaven; they are not hot to the touch as they are higher up, but nevertheless are tepid; they exhale no vapours like other rivers, which they certainly would do, if (as some learned Grecians suppose) their rise was owing to the melting of the snows.

"While I was discoursing in this manner, one of the priests of Apollo, whose name was Charicles, with whom I had contracted some intimacy, said, 'I am pleased with what you say, and agree with you entirely, for I have heard the same account of this matter from the priests at the cataracts of the Nile.'—'And have you been as far as there,' said I?—'I have,' he replied.—'On what account?'—'On occasion of some family misfortunes, which, however, at last became the course of my happiness.' When I expressed some surprize at this, 'You would not wonder,' said he, 'if you were to hear the whole matter as it happened; and you may hear it whenever you please.'—'I should be very glad to hear it at once,' said I.—'Attend then,' said Charicles; 'for I have long, and from an interested motive, wished for an opportunity of relating my story to you:'—and, dismissing the general company, he began as follows:

"'I had been married a considerable time without having children; I wearied the gods with supplications; and at last, in an advanced stage of life, I became the father of a little daughter, but who was born, as the gods foretold, not under auspicious destiny. She became marriageable, and had many suitors. I married her to him whom I thought most worthy of her; and on the very wedding night she was burnt in her bed, her apartment having been set on fire either by accident or lightning. The hymeneal song, which was still resounding, was turned into a dirge: she was carried from the marriage apartment to her grave; and the torches, which had illuminated the nuptial procession, now lighted the funeral pile.

"'My evil genius added yet another calamity to this tragedy, and took from me the mother of my child, who sank under her sorrows.

"'Such a series of misfortunes was almost too much for me. It was with difficulty I abstained from laying violent hands upon myself; I had however strength of mind sufficient to refrain from an action which the teachers of religion pronounce unlawful. But being unable to bear the solitude and silence of my house, I left my country, for to deaden memory by turning the eyes upon new objects is a great palliative to grief. I wandered into various parts, and came at last into your Egypt, and to Caladupa, in order to visit the cataracts of the Nile: this, my friend, was the occasion of my coming into your country, which you inquired after. I must now proceed to a digression, though it more properly forms the principal reason of my entering at all into this narration.

"'While I was wandering at leisure through the city, and buying some things of the Greeks (for time having now considerably alleviated my grief, I thought of returning into my country), I was accosted by a middle-aged man, with the complexion of an Ethiopian, but of a grave deportment, and bearing marks of prudence in his aspect: he saluted me, and in broken Greek said he wished to speak to me. I readily consenting, he took me into a neighbouring temple, and said: "I saw you cheapening some Indian, Ethiopian, and Egyptian roots and herbs; if you really have a desire to buy some, I can furnish you."—"I shall be very glad to see them," I replied.—"You must not beat me down too much," said he.—"Do not then be too exorbitant on your part," was my answer.—With that he pulled a small pouch from a pocket under his arm, and showed me some jewels of inestimable value: there were pearls as big as nuts, perfectly round, and of the purest white; emeralds and amethysts—the former as green as the vernal corn, and shining with a kind of oily lustre; the latter resembling the colour of the sea-beach, when played upon by the shadows of an overhanging rock, which impart to it a purple tinge. The mingled brilliancy of the whole collection astonished and delighted my eyes.

"'After having contemplated them for some time, I said, "You must seek some other purchaser; my whole fortune would scarcely be sufficient to procure one of these gems."—"But if you cannot buy them," he replied, "you may receive them as a present."—"Certainly! but why are you jesting with me?"—"I am not jesting with you, I am serious in what I say; and I swear to you by the deity whose shrine we are before, that I will give you everything which I have shown you, if, in addition to these, you will receive from my hands a present far more precious than all which you behold."—I could not help smiling: he asked the cause of it.—"Because it seems to me ridiculous," said I, "that when you promise me gifts of such price, you should besides make me expect a present still more valuable."—"Nevertheless, believe me," he replied, "and swear to me that you will use my gift well, and in the manner which I shall exact from you."—I wondered and doubted, but at last swore to him, allured by the hopes of such treasures. When I had taken such an oath as he required, he conducted me to his house, and showed me a girl of wonderful and more than mortal beauty: He affirmed she was but seven years old; but she appeared to me to be almost of a marriageable age, so much did her uncommon beauty seem to add even to her stature. I stood for some time motionless, ignorant of what was to follow, and ravished with the sight before me; when my conductor thus addressed me:

""'The child whom you behold, O stranger, was exposed, when an infant, by her mother, and left at the mercy of fortune, for a reason which you shall hear by-and-bye. It happened luckily that I found, and took her up; for I could not allow myself to desert in its danger a soul which had once entered a human body: in so doing I should have transgressed the precepts of our Gymnosophists, of whom I had been privileged to be a disciple. Something, too, uncommon and divine, seemed to beam from the eyes of the infant, which were cast upon me with sparkling yet engaging lustre. There was exposed with her this profusion of jewels which I have shown you. There was a silken fillet, on which was written some account of the child, in letters of her native country; her mother, I suppose, taking care to place these explanations with her. When I had read it, and knew from whence and whose the infant was, I took her to a farm at a distance from the city, and placed her in the hands of shepherds to be nourished, enjoining them to keep her as private as possible. I myself kept the jewels which were exposed with her, lest they might tempt any one to destroy the child. The whole transaction remained for a while a secret; but, in process of time, as she grew up and increased more than commonly in stature and in beauty (so much so, indeed, that her charms would not have been concealed even in the bowels of the earth), fearing some discovery to her prejudice, and that I, too, might come into some trouble about her: I procured myself to be sent ambassador into Egypt. I came here: I brought the girl with me, being very desirous of placing her in some secure situation. The viceroy of this country has appointed to give me audience to-day: meanwhile I deliver up to you, and to the gods, the disposers of all events, this child; trusting that you will observe the conditions you have sworn to; that you will preserve her free, as you have received her, and marry her to a free man. I confide in your performing all you have promised; not depending alone on your oaths, but on your disposition and general conduct, which I have observed for the many days which you have spent in this city, and which I see to be truly worthy of Greece, that renowned country to which you owe your birth. This is all I can say to you at present, as the business of my embassy calls me; but, if you will meet me at the temple of Isis to-morrow, you shall have a more particular and exact account of your charge."

"'I did as I was desired. I took the girl home with me to my house: I treated her with respect and tenderness, giving thanks to the gods for the event; and from that time calling and esteeming her as my daughter. The next morning I hastened to the temple of Isis, where the stranger had appointed me; and after I had walked about and waited a considerable time, and saw nothing of him, I went to the palace of the viceroy, and inquired if any one had seen the Ethiopian ambassador. I was there told that he had left the city, or rather had been driven out of it, the evening before,—the viceroy threatening him with death if he did not immediately quit the province. When I inquired into the cause of so sudden a proceeding, I learned that he had, with some haughtiness, forbidden the governor to meddle with the emerald mines, which he claimed as belonging exclusively to Ethiopia. I returned home vexed and disappointed, as I was by this accident prevented from knowing the condition, the country, and parents of the child.'"

"I am vexed, too, as much as he was," said Cnemon, "for my curiosity on these subjects is nearly as great; but, perhaps, it may be satisfied in the progress of your narration." "Possibly it may," replied Calasiris; "but now, if you please, let Charicles proceed with his own story," which he thus continued:—

"When I arrived at my house, the child came out to meet me. She could not speak to me, knowing nothing of Greek; but she saluted me with her hand, and the sight of her began to console me for my disappointment. I saw, with admiration, that, as a generous race of hounds fawn upon those who notice them; so she seemed to have a strong sense of my kindness for her, and to consider me in the light of a father. I determined to stay no longer at Caladupa, lest some envious deity should deprive me of my second daughter. Embarking, therefore, on the Nile, I reached the sea, got on board a ship, and arrived in Greece. This child is now with me: I have given her my name, and all my cares are centred in her. Her improvements exceed my warmest wishes. She has learned my language with surprising quickness: she has grown up to perfection like a nourishing plant. Her beauty is so transcendent as to attract every eye upon her, both Grecian and foreign. Wherever she appears—in the temple, in the course, or in the market-place—she draws to her the looks and thoughts of all, like the model statue of some goddess. Yet, with all this, she is the cause of great uneasiness to me: she obstinately refuses to marry, determines to lead a life of celibacy, consecrates herself to Diana, and spends most of her leisure hours in the chase, and with her bow. This is a severe disappointment to me, for I wished to give her to my sister's son, an accomplished and graceful young man; but my wishes are frustrated by this preposterous fancy of hers. Neither entreaties, nor promises, nor reasoning, can work upon her; and, what is most vexatious, she wounds me, as they say, with a shaft drawn from my own bow, and employs the eloquence which I have taught her in magnifying the way of life she has chosen. She is inexhaustible in the praises of virginity; places it next the life of the gods—pure, unmixed, uncorrupt. She is equally skilful in depreciating love, and Venus, and marriage. I implore your assistance in this matter; for which reason I was glad to seize the opportunity you gave me, and have troubled you with a long story. Do not desert me on this occasion, my good Calasiris, but employ the wisdom you are master of, or even any charm you may know; persuade her by words, or work upon her by incantations, to leave this unnatural course, and to feel that she is born a woman: you can, I know, do this if you will. She is not averse to the conversation of men; she has been used to their company from her childhood. She lives, too, very near you, here within the precincts of the temple. Condescend, I beseech, to hear me, and grant what I desire. Suffer me not to spend a melancholy and lonely old age, without hopes of having my family continued; I entreat you by Apollo, and your country's gods.'"

"I was moved by his supplications, Cnemon. I could scarcely refrain from tears: his own flowed in great abundance. I promised, in short, to use my utmost skill in attempting what he desired. We were still talking, when a messenger arrived in haste, and told us that the head of the Ænianian embassy was at the door, and extremely impatient for the priest to appear, and begin the sacred rites. When I inquired who the Ænianians were, what was the nature of the embassy which they had sent, and what sacrifice he was going to perform; he told me that the Ænianians were a principal nation of Thessaly, entirely Grecian, being descended from Deucalion—that their country extended along the Malian bay—that they called their metropolis Hypata; as they would insinuate, because it was fit to rule over all the cities of the province; as others pretended, because it was situated under Mount Œta—that the embassy was sent by the Ænianians every fourth year, at the time of the Pythian games—and the sacrifice offered to Neoptolemus, the son of Achilles, who was here surprised and slain, at the very altar of Apollo, by Orestes the son of Agamemnon. But the embassy of the present year will be yet more magnificent than any of the former ones; for the head of it prides himself in being descended from Achilles.

"I met the young man the other day, and indeed he seems worthy of the family of Peleus: such is the nobleness of his stature and deportment, that you will easily believe him sprung from a goddess.

"When I wondered how it came to pass, that he, being an Ænianian, should pretend that he was of the race of Achilles (for Homer, our great Egyptian poet makes Achilles a Phthiotian), 'the young man,' said Charicles, 'claims him entirely as their own: for Thetis, he says, certainly married Peleus out of the Malian bay; and the country which extended along that bay was anciently called Phthia: but the glory of the hero has induced others to claim him falsely as their countryman. He is, besides, in another way, related to the Æacidæ: Mnestheus is his ancestor, the son of Sperchius and Polydora, the daughter of Peleus, who went with Achilles to the siege of Troy; and, being so nearly connected with him, was among the chief leaders of the Myrmidons.

"'The ambassador abounds in arguments to support the claim of his country to Achilles. He insists much upon this present embassy and sacrifice to Neoptolemus; the honour of performing which, all the

Thessalians have, by common consent, yielded up to the Ænianians, whereby they admit that they are most nearly related to him.'

"'Whether this be truth or vain assumption,' said I, 'be so good now, if you please, as to call in the ambassador, for I am extremely desirous to see him.'

"Charicles immediately sent to him, and the young man entered with an air and aspect truly worthy of Achilles. His neck straight and erect, his hair thrown back off his forehead; his nose and open nostrils giving signs of an impetuous temper; his eyes of a deep blue, inclining to black, imparting an animated but amiable look to his countenance, like the sea smoothing itself from a storm into a calm.

"After he had received and returned our salutations, he said it was time to proceed to the sacrifice, that there might be sufficient space for the ceremonies which were to be performed to the Manes of the hero, and for the procession which was to follow them.—'I am ready,' replied Charicles, and rising, said to me, 'If you have not yet seen Chariclea, you will see her to-day; for, as a priestess of Diana, she will be present at these rites and the procession.'

"But I, Cnemon, had often seen the young woman before; I had sacrificed and conversed with her upon sacred subjects. However, I said nothing of it; and, waiting for what might happen, we went together to the temple. The Thessalians had prepared everything ready for the sacrifice. We approached the altar; the youth began the sacred rites; the priest having uttered a prayer, and from her shrine the Pythoness pronounced this oracle:

> *Delphians, regard with reverential care,*
> *Both him the goddess-born, and her the fair;*
> "Grace" *is the sound which ushers in her name,*
> *The syllable wherewith it ends, is* "Fame."
> *They both my fane shall leave, and oceans past,*
> *In regions torrid shall arrive at last;*
> *There shall the gods reward their pious vows,*
> *And snowy chaplets bind their dusky brows.*

"When they who surrounded the shrine heard this oracle, they were perplexed, and doubted what it should signify. Each interpreted it differently, as his inclinations and understanding led him: none, however, laid hold of its true meaning. Oracles indeed, and dreams, are generally to be explained only by the event. And beside, the Delphians, struck with the preparations which were making for the procession, hastened to behold it, neglecting or deferring any farther scrutiny into the oracular response."

Book III

When the ceremony was over, and the procession had passed by," continued Calasiris—"But," said Cnemon, interrupting him, "the ceremony is not over, Father; you have not made me a spectator of the procession, whereas I am very desirous both of hearing and seeing; you treat me like a guest who, as they say, is come a day after the feast: why should you just open the theatre, only to close it again?"—"I was unwilling," said Calasiris, "to detain you from what you are most desirous to know, by a detail which has little or nothing to do with the principal end of my narration; but since you must be a passing spectator, and by your fondness for shows declare yourself to be an Athenian, I will endeavour briefly to describe the exhibition to you; and I shall do so the more willingly, on account of the consequences which followed it.

"The procession began with an hecatomb of victims, led by some of the inferior ministers of the temple, rough-looking men, in white and girt-up garments. Their right hands and breasts were naked, and they bore a two-edged axe. The oxen were black, with moderately arched and brawny necks—their horns equal, and very little bent; some were gilt, others adorned with flowers—their legs bent inwards—and their deep dewlaps flowing down to their knees—their number, in accordance with the name, exactly a hundred. A variety of other different victims came afterwards, each species separate and in order, attended with pipes and flutes, sending forth a strain prelusive of the sacrifice: these were followed by a troop of fair and long-waisted Thessalian maidens, with dishevelled locks—they were distributed into two companies; the first division bore baskets full of fruits and flowers; the second, vases of conserves and spices, which filled the air with fragrance: they carried these on their heads; thus, their hands being at liberty, they joined them together, so that they could move along and lead the dance. The keynote to the melody was sounded by the next division, who were to sing the whole of the hymn appointed for this festival, which contained the praises of Thetis, of Peleus, and their son, and of Neoptolemus. After this, O Cnemon——" "But *Cnemon* me no *Cnemons*," said the latter; "why not recite the hymn to me instead of depriving me of so much pleasure? Make me, I beseech you, an auditor at this festival as well as a spectator."—"You shall be so if you desire it," said Calasiris; "the hymn, as nearly as I can recollect, ran as follows:

"'Thetis, the golden-haired, we sing.
She who from Nereus erst did spring,
The Venus of our fatherland.
To Peleus wed, at Jove's command,
Her—of the thunderbolt of war, }
Famed for his beamy spear afar, }
Achilles—Greece the mother saw }
Wedded to whom did Pyrrha bear,
Great Neoptolemus his heir,
Of Grecian land the boast and joy,
The destined scourge of lofty Troy.
Thou who in Delphic land dost rest,
Hero, by thee may we be blest;
Accept our strains, and oh, by thee,
May every ill averted be!
Thetis the golden-haired we sing,
She who from Peleus erst did spring.

"The dance which accompanied this song was so well adapted to it, and the cadence of their steps agreed so exactly with the melody of the strain, that for a while, in spite of the magnificence of the spectacle, the sense of seeing was overpowered and suspended by that of hearing; and all who were present, attracted by the sounds, followed the advancing dancers. At length a band of youths on horseback, with their splendidly dressed commander, opening upon them, afforded a spectacle far preferable to any sounds. Their number was exactly fifty; they divided themselves into five-and-twenty on each side guarding their leader, chief of the sacred embassy, who rode in the midst: their buskins, laced with a purple thong, were tied above their ancles; their white garments, bordered with blue, were fastened by a golden clasp over their breasts. Their horses were Thessalian, and by their spirit gave token of the open plains they came from; they seemed to champ with disdain the foaming bit, yet obeyed the regulating hand of their riders, who appeared to vie with each other in the splendour of their frontlets and other trappings, which glittered with gold and silver. But all these, Cnemon, splendid as they were, were utterly overlooked, and seemed to vanish, like other objects before a flash of lightning, at the appearance of their leader, my dear Theagenes, so gallant a show did he make. He too was on horseback, and in armour, with an ashen spear in his hand;

his head was uncovered; he wore a purple robe, on which was worked in gold the story of the Centaurs and the Lapithæ; the clasp of it was of electrum, and represented Pallas with the Gorgon's head on her shield. A light breath of wind added to the grace of his appearance; it played upon his hair, dispersed it on his neck, and divided it from his forehead, throwing back the extremities of his cloak in easy folds on the back and sides of his horse. You would say, too, that the horse himself was conscious both of his own beauty and of the beauty of his rider; so stately did he arch his neck and carry his head, with ears erect and fiery eyes, proudly bearing a master who was proud to be thus borne. He moved along under a loose rein, balancing himself equally on each side, and, touching the ground with the extremity of his hoofs, tempered his pace into almost an insensible motion.

"Every one, astonished at the appearance of this young man, joined in confessing, that beauty and strength were never before so gracefully mingled. The women in the streets, unable to disguise their feelings, flung handfuls of fruit and flowers over him, in token of their admiration and affection: in short, there was but one opinion concerning him— that it was impossible for mortal form to excel that of Theagenes. But now, when

Rosy-finger'd morn appeared,

as Homer says, and the beautiful and accomplished Chariclea proceeded from the temple of Diana, we then perceived that even Theagenes might be outshone; but only so far as female beauty is naturally more engaging and alluring than that of men. She was borne in a chariot drawn by two white oxen—she was dressed in a purple robe embroidered with gold, which flowed down to her feet—she had a girdle round her waist, on which the artist had exerted all his skill: it represented two serpents, whose tails were interlaced behind her shoulders; their necks knotted beneath her bosom; and their heads, disentangled from the knot, hung down on either side as an appendage: so well were they imitated, that you would say they really glided onward. Their aspect was not at all terrible; their eyes swam in a kind of languid lustre, as if being lulled to sleep by the charms of the maiden's breast. They were wrought in darkened gold, tinged with blue, the better to represent, by this mixture of dark and yellow, the roughness and glancing colour of the scales. Such was the maiden's girdle. Her hair was not entirely tied up, nor quite dishevelled, but the greater part of it flowed down her neck, and wantoned on her shoulders—a crown of laurel confined the bright and ruddy locks which adorned her forehead, and prevented the wind from disturbing them too roughly—she bore a gilded bow in her left hand; her quiver hung at her right shoulder—in her other hand she had a lighted torch; yet the lustre of her eyes paled the brightness of the torch."

"Here are, indeed, Theagenes and Chariclea," cried out Cnemon. "Where, where are they?" exclaimed Calasiris; who thought that Cnemon saw them.—"I think I see them now," he replied, "but it is in your lively description."—"I do not know," said Calasiris, "whether you ever saw them such as all Greece and the sun beheld them on that day—so conspicuous, so illustrious; she the object of wish to all the men, and he to all the women; all thought them equal to the immortals in beauty. But the Delphians more admired the youth, and the Thessalians the maid; each most struck with that form which they then saw for the first time. Such is the charm of novelty.

"But, Cnemon! what a sweet expectation did you raise in me when you promised to show me these whom I so fondly loved! and how have you deceived me! You winged me with hope to expect that they would presently be here, and exacted a reward for these good tidings; but, lo! evening and night have overtaken us, and they nowhere appear."—"Raise up your spirits," said Cnemon, "and have a good heart; I assure you they will soon arrive. Perhaps they have met with some impediment by the way, for they intended to arrive much earlier. But I would not shew them to you, if they were here, till you had paid me the whole of my reward; if, therefore, you are in haste to see them, perform your promise, and finish your story."—"It is now," replied Calasiris, "become a little irksome to me, as it will call up disagreeable remembrances; and I thought, besides, that you must by this time be tired with listening to so tedious a tale; but, since you seem a good listener, and fond of hearing stories worth the telling, I will resume my narration where I left it off. But let us first light a torch, and make our libations to the gods who preside over the night; so that, having performed our devotions, we may spend, without interruption, as much as we please of it in such discourses as we like." A maid, at the old man's command, brought in a lighted taper; and he poured out a libation, calling upon all the gods, and particularly upon Mercury; beseeching them to grant him pleasant dreams, and that those whom he most loved might appear to him in his sleep. Calasiris then proceeded in this manner:

"After, Cnemon, that the procession had thrice compassed the sepulchre of Neoptolemus, and that both men and women had raised over it their appropriate shout and cry; on a signal being given, the oxen, the sheep, the goats, were slaughtered at once, as if the sacrifice had been performed by a single hand. Heaps of wood were piled on an immense altar; and the victims being placed thereon, the priest of Apollo was desired to light the pile, and begin the libation.

"'It belongs, indeed, to me,' said Charicles, 'to make the libation; but let the chief of the sacred embassy receive the torch from the hands of Diana's priestess, and light the pile; for such has always been our custom.' Having said this, he performed his part of the ceremony, and Theagenes received the torch from Chariclea. From what now happened, my dear Cnemon, we may infer that there is something divine in the soul, and allied to a superior nature; for their first glance at each other was such, as if each of their souls acknowledged its partner, and hastened to mingle with one which was worthy of it.

"They stood awhile, as if astonished; she slowly offering and he slowly receiving the torch; and fixing their eyes on one another, for some space, they seemed rather to have been formerly acquainted, than to have now met for the first time, and to be returning gradually into each other's memory. Then softly, and almost imperceptibly smiling, which the eyes, rather than the lips, betrayed, they both blushed, as if ashamed of what they had done; and again turned pale, the passion reaching their hearts. In short, a thousand shades of feeling wandered in a few moments over their countenances; their complexion and looks betraying in various ways the movements of their souls.

"These emotions escaped the observation of the crowd, whose attention was engaged on other things. They escaped Charicles too, who was employed in reciting the solemn prayers and invocations, but they did not escape me, for I had particularly observed these young people, from the time that the oracle was given to Theagenes in the temple; I had formed conjectures as to the future from the allusion to their names, though I could not entirely comprehend the latter part of the prediction.

"At length Theagenes slowly and unwillingly turning from the maiden, lighted the pile, and the solemn ceremony ended. The Thessalians betook themselves to an entertainment, and the rest of the people dispersed to their own habitations. Chariclea putting on a white robe, retired with a few of her companions to her apartment, which was within the precincts of the temple; for she did not live with her supposed father, but dwelt apart for the better performance of the temple services.

"Rendered curious by what I had heard and seen, I sought an opportunity of meeting Charicles. As soon as he saw me, he cried out, 'Well, have you seen Chariclea, the light of my eyes, and of Delphi?'—'I have,' I replied, 'but not now for the first time; I have frequently before seen her in the temple, and that not in a cursory manner. I have often sacrificed with her, and conversed with and instructed her, on various subjects, divine and human.'—'But what did you think of her to-day, my good friend? Did she not add some ornament to the procession?'—'Some ornament, do you say? you might as well ask me whether the moon outshines the stars.'—'But some praise the Thracian youth, and give him at least the second place to her.'—'The second, if you will, and the third; but all allow that your daughter was the crown and sun of the ceremonial.' Charicles was delighted with this, and smiling said, 'I am just going to see her.' I, too, was pleased, for my view was to inspire him with content and confidence. 'If you will,' he added, 'we will go together, and see whether she is the worse for the fatigues she has undergone.' I gladly consented, but pretended I went to oblige him; and that I gave up other business of my own.

"When we arrived at her apartment, we found her lying uneasily upon her couch, her eyes melting with languor and passion. Having as usual saluted her father, he asked what was the matter with her? She complained that her head ached; and said that she wished to take a little rest. Charicles, alarmed, went out of the chamber, ordering her maids to keep every thing quiet about her; and, turning to me, 'What languor,' said he, 'my good Calasiris, can this be, which seems to oppress my daughter?'—'Wonder not,' I replied, 'if, in such an assembly of people, some envious eye has looked upon her.' 'And do you, too,' he returned, smiling ironically, 'think, with the vulgar, that there is any thing in fascination?'—'Indeed I do,' said I; 'and thus I account for its effects: this air which surrounds us, which we take in with our breath, receive at our eyes and nostrils, and which penetrates into all our pores, brings with it those qualities with which it is impregnated; and, according to their different natures, we are differently affected. When any one looks at what is excellent, with an envious eye, he fills the surrounding atmosphere with a pernicious quality, and transmits his own envenomed exhalations into whatever is nearest to him. They, as they are thin and subtle, penetrate even into the bones and marrow; and thus envy has become the cause of a disorder to many, which has obtained the name of fascination.

"'Consider besides, O Charicles, how many have been infected with inflammation of the eyes, and with other contagious distempers, without ever touching, either at bed or board, those who laboured under them, but solely by breathing the same air with them. The birth of love affords another proof of what I am explaining, which, by the eyes alone, finds a passage to the soul; and it is not difficult to assign the reason; for as, of all the inlets to our senses, the sight is the most quick and fiery, and most various in its motions; this animated faculty most easily receives the influences which surround it, and attracts to itself the emanations of love.

"'If you wish for an example from natural history, here is one taken out of our sacred books. The bird Charadrius cures those who are afflicted with the jaundice. If it perceives, at a distance, any one coming towards it, who labours under this distemper, it immediately runs away, and shuts its eyes; not out of an envious refusal of its assistance, as some suppose, but because it knows, by instinct, that, on the view of the afflicted person, the disorder will pass from him to itself, and therefore it is solicitous to avoid encountering his eyes. You have heard, perhaps, of the basilisk, which, with its breath and aspect alone, parches up and infects everything around it. Nor is it to be wondered at, if some fascinate those whom they love and wish well to; for they who are naturally envious do not always act as they would wish, but as their nature compels them to do.' Here Charicles, after a pause, said, 'You seem to have given a very reasonable account of this matter; and as you appear to admit that there are various kinds of fascination, I wish hers may be that of love; I should then think that she was restored to health, rather than that she was disordered. You know I have often besought your assistance in this matter. I should rejoice rather than grieve, if this were the affection she labours under, she who has so long set at nought Venus and all her charms. But, I doubt, it is the more common sort of fascination, that of an evil eye, which afflicts her. This your wisdom will certainly enable you to cure, and your friendship to us will incline you to attempt it.' I promised to do all in my power to relieve her, should this be the case; and we were still talking, when a man arrives in haste, and calls out—'One would imagine, my good friends, that you were invited to a fray instead of a feast, you are so tardy in coming up; and yet it is the excellent Theagenes who prepares it for you; and Neoptolemus, the first of heroes, who presides at it. Come away, for shame, and do not make us wait for you until evening. Nobody is absent but yourselves.'

"'This,' whispers Charicles, 'is but a rough inviter; the gifts of Bacchus have not mended his manners. But let us go, lest he come from words to blows.' I smiled at his pleasantry, and said I was ready to attend him. When we entered, Theagenes placed Charicles next to himself; and paid some attention to me, out of respect to him. But why should I fatigue you with a detail of the entertainments; the dancing and singing girls, the youths in armour, who moved in Pyrrhic measures; the variety of dishes with which Theagenes had decked his table, in order to make the feast more jovial? But what follows is necessary for you to hear, and pleasant for me to relate. Our entertainer endeavoured to preserve a cheerful countenance, and forced himself to behave with ease and politeness to his company, but I perceived plainly what he suffered within; his eyes wandered, and he sighed involuntarily. Now he would be melancholy and thoughtful; then on a sudden, recollecting himself, his looks brightened, and he put on a forced cheerfulness. In short, it is not easy to describe the changes he underwent; for the mind of a lover, like that of one overcome with wine, cannot long remain in the same situation, both their souls fluctuating with weak and unsteady passion. For which reason a lover is disposed to drink; and he who has drunk is inclined to love.

"At length, from his yawning, his sighs, and his anxiety, the rest of the company begun to perceive that he was indisposed; so that even Charicles, who had not hitherto observed his uneasiness, whispered me, 'I fancy an envious eye has looked upon him also; he seems to be affected much in the same manner as Chariclea.' 'Indeed, I think so, too,' I replied; 'and it is probable enough, for next after her in the procession, as being most conspicuous, he was most exposed to envy.'

"But now the cups were carried round; and Theagenes, out of complaisance rather than inclination, drank to every body. When it came to me, I said I was obliged to him for the compliment, but must beg to be excused tasting of the cup. He looked displeased and angry, as if he thought himself affronted; when Charicles explained the matter, and told him I was an Egyptian, an inhabitant of Memphis, and a priest of Isis, and consequently abstained from wine and all animal food. Theagenes seemed filled with a sudden pleasure when he heard that I was an Egyptian and a priest; and raising himself up, as if he had suddenly found a treasure, he called for water, and drinking to me, said, 'O sage, receive from me this mark of good-will, in the beverage which is most agreeable to you; and let this table conclude a solemn treaty of friendship between us.'—'With all my heart," I replied,' most excellent Theagenes; I have already conceived a friendship for you;' and taking the cup, I drank—and with this the company broke up, and dispersed to their several habitations; Theagenes embracing me at parting with the warmth and affection of an old friend.

"When I retired to my chamber, I could not sleep the first part of the night. My thoughts continually ran upon these young people, and upon the conclusion of the oracle, and I endeavoured to penetrate into its meaning. But, towards the middle of the night, methought I saw Apollo and Diana advancing towards me (if it were indeed only imagination, and not a reality): one led Theagenes, the other Chariclea. They seemed to deliver them into my hands; and the goddess calling me by my name, thus addressed me:

"'It is time for you now to return to your country, for such is the decree of fate. Depart therefore yourself, and take these under your protection; make them the companions of your journey; treat them as your children; and carry them from Egypt, where and howsoever it shall please the gods to ordain.'—Having said this, they disappeared, signifying first that this was a vision, and not a common dream.

"I understood plainly the commands they gave me; except that I doubted what land it was, to which I was at last to conduct these persons."—"If you found this out afterwards, Father," said Cnemon, "you will inform me at a proper season; in the mean time tell me in what manner they signified, as you said, that this was not a common dream, but a real appearance."—"In the same manner, my son, as the wise Homer intimates; though many do not perceive the hidden sense that is contained in these lines:

Ἴνια γὰρ μετόπισθε ποδῶν ἠδέ κνημάων
Ῥεῖ᾽, ἔγνων ἀπιοντός, ἀρίγνωτοί τε θεοί περ.

"As they departed, I their legs and feet
To glide did see; the gods are known with ease."

"I must confess," said Cnemon, "that I am one of the many, and perhaps you imagined so when you quoted these verses. I have understood the common sense of the words, ever since I first read them, but cannot penetrate any hidden theological meaning that may be couched under them."—Calasiris considering a little, and applying his mind to the explanation of this mystery, replied:

"The gods, O Cnemon, when they appear to, or disappear from us, generally do it under a human shape—seldom under that of any other animal; perhaps, in order that their appearance may have more the semblance of reality. They may not be manifest to the profane, but cannot be concealed from the sage. You may know them by their eyes; they look on you with a fixed gaze, never winking with their eye-lids— still more by their motion, which is a kind of gliding, an aerial impulse, without movement of the feet, cleaving rather than traversing the air: for which reason the images of the Egyptian gods have their feet joined together, and in a manner united. Wherefore Homer, being an Egyptian, and instructed in their sacred doctrines, covertly insinuated this matter in his verses, leaving it to be understood by the intelligent. He mentions Pallas in this manner:

... δεινὼ δὲ οἱ ὄσσε φάανθεν.

'Fierce glared her eyes.'

and Neptune in the lines quoted before—'ῥεῖν ἔγνων,'—as if gliding in his gait; for so is the verse to be construed—'ῥεῖν ἀπιόντος,' gliding away; not, as some erroneously think, 'ῥεῖ' εγνων,' I easily knew him."

"You have initiated me into this mystery," replied Cnemon; "but how come you to call Homer an Egyptian? It is the first time I ever heard him called so. I will not insist that he is not your countryman; but I should be exceedingly glad to hear your reasons for claiming him as such."—"This is not exactly the time," said Calasiris, "for such a discussion; however, as you desire it, I will shortly mention the grounds upon which I go.

"Different authors have ascribed to Homer different countries— indeed the country of a wise man is in every land; but he was, in fact, an Egyptian, of the city of Thebes, as you may learn from himself. His supposed father was a priest there; his real one, Mercury. For the wife of the priest whose son he was taken to be, while she was celebrating some sacred mysteries, slept in the temple. Mercury enjoyed her company; and impregnated her with Homer; and he bore to his dying day a mark of his spurious origin. From Thebes he wandered into various countries, and particularly into Greece; singing his verses, and obtaining the name he bore. He never told his real one, nor his country, nor family; but those who knew of this mark upon his body, took occasion from it to give him the name of Homer; for, immediately from his birth, a profusion of hair appeared upon both his thighs."

"On what account, my father, did he conceal the place of his birth?"— "Possibly he was unwilling to appear a fugitive; for he was driven out by his father, and not admitted among the sacred youths, on account of the peculiar mark he bore on his body, indicating his spurious origin. Or, perhaps, he had a wise design in keeping the real spot of his nativity a secret, as by so doing he might claim every land he passed through as his fatherland."—"I cannot help," said Cnemon, "being half persuaded of the truth of this account you give of Homer. His poems breathe all the softness and luxuriance of Egypt; and from their excellency, bespeak something of a divine original in their author.

"But after that, by Homer's assistance, you had discovered the true nature of these deities, what happened?"—"Much the same as before: watchings, thoughts, and cares, which night and darkness nourish. I was glad that I had discovered something, which I had in vain attempted to explain before; and rejoiced at the near prospect of my return to my country. But I was grieved to think that Charicles was to be deprived of his daughter. I was in great doubt in what manner the young people were to be taken away together; how to prepare for their flight; how to do it privately, whither to direct it; and whether by land or by sea. In short, I was overwhelmed with a sea of troubles and spent the remainder of the night restless, and without sleep. But the day scarce began to dawn, when I heard a knocking at the gate of my court, and somebody calling my servant.

"The boy asked who it was that knocked, and what he wanted. The person replied, that he was Theagenes the Thessalian.—I was very glad to hear this, and ordered him to be introduced; thinking this an excellent opportunity to lay some foundation for the design I meditated. I supposed that, having discovered at the entertainment that I was an Egyptian, and a priest, he came to ask my advice and assistance in the attachment which now influenced him. He thought, perhaps, as many wrongly do, that the science of the Egyptians was only of one sort. But there is one branch in the hands of the common mass, as I may say, crawling on the ground; busied in the service of idols, and the care of dead bodies; poring over herbs, and murmuring incantations; neither itself aiming, nor leading those who apply to it to aim, at any good end; and most frequently failing in what it professes to effect. Sometimes succeeding in matters of a gloomy and despicable nature; showing imaginary visions as though real; encouraging wickedness; and ministering to lawless pleasures. But the other branch of Egyptian science, my son, is the true wisdom; of which that which I have just mentioned is the base-born offspring. This is that in which our priests and seers are from their youth initiated. This is of a far more excellent nature; looks to heavenly things, and converses with the gods; inquires into the motions of the stars, and gains an insight into futurity; far removed from evil and earthly matters, and turning all its views to what is honourable and beneficial to mankind. It was this which prompted me to retire a while from my country—to avoid, if possible, the ills which it enabled me to foresee, and the discord which was to arise between my children. But these events must be left to the gods, and the fates, who have power either to accomplish or to hinder them; and who, perhaps, ordained my flight, in order that I might meet with Chariclea. I will now proceed with my narration.

"Theagenes entered my apartment; and, after I had received and returned his salute, I placed him near me on the bed, and asked what was the occasion of so early a visit.—He stroked his face, and, after a long pause, said: 'I am in the greatest perplexity, and yet blush to disclose the cause of it:'—and here he stopped. I saw that this was the time for dissimulation, and for pretending to discover what I already knew. Looking therefore archly upon him, I said, 'Though you seem unwilling to speak out, yet nothing escapes my knowledge, with the assistance of the gods.'—With this I raised myself a little, counting over certain numbers upon my fingers, (which in reality meant nothing); shaking my locks, like one moreover under a sudden influence of the divinity, I cried out, 'My son, you are in love.'—He started at this; but, when I added—'and with Chariclea,' he thought I was really divinely inspired; and was ready to fall at my feet, and worship me. When I prevented this, he kissed my head, and gave thanks to the gods that he had really found my knowledge as great as he expected. He besought me to be his preserver; for, unless preserved by my assistance, and that quickly, he was undone, so violent a passion had seized upon him; desire so consumed him—him, who now first knew what it was to love.

"He swore to me, with many protestations, that he never had enjoyed the company of women—that he had always rejected them—and professed himself an enemy to marriage, and a rebel to Venus, until subdued by the charms of Chariclea—that this did not arise from any forced temperance, or natural coldness of constitution; but he had never before seen a woman whom he thought worthy of his love—and having said this, he wept, as if indignant at being subdued by a weak girl. I raised him, comforted, and bade him be of good cheer; for, since he had applied to me, he should find that her coyness would yield to my art. I knew that she was haughty, protesting against love, so as not to bear even the name of Venus or wedlock; but I would leave no stone unturned to serve him. 'Art,' said I, 'can not outdo even nature: only be not cast down, but act as I shall direct you.'

"He promised that he would obey me in every thing; even if I should order him to go through fire and sword. While he was thus eager in protestations, and profuse in his promises of laying at my feet all he was worth, a messenger came from Charicles, saying that his master desired me to come to him—that he was near, in the temple of Apollo, where he was chanting a hymn to appease the deity; having been much disturbed in the night by a dream.

"I arose immediately, and dismissing Theagenes, hastened to the temple; where I found Charicles reclining sorrowfully upon a seat, and sighing deeply. I approached him, and inquired why he was so melancholy and cast down.—'How can I be otherwise,' he replied, 'when I have been terrified by dreams? and hear too, this morning, that my daughter still continues indisposed, and has passed a sleepless night. I am the more concerned at this, not only on her own account, but also because to-morrow is the day appointed for the display of those who run in armour; at which ceremony the priestess of Diana is to preside, and hold up a torch. Either, therefore, the festival will lose much of its accustomed splendour by her absence; or if she comes against her will, she may increase her illness. Wherefore let me now beseech you, by our friendship, and by the god at whose altar we are, to come to her assistance, and think of some remedy. I know you can easily, if you please, cure this fascination, if such it be—the priests of Egypt can do far greater things than these.'

"I confessed that I had been negligent (the better to carry on the deception); and requested a day's time to prepare some medicines, which I thought necessary for her cure. 'Let us now, however,' I continued, 'make her a visit; consider more accurately the nature of her complaint; and, if possible, administer to her some consolation. At the same time, Charicles, I beg you will say a few words to her concerning me; inspire her with regard for my person, and confidence in my skill, that so the cure may proceed the better.' He promised that he would do so; and we went together. But why say much of the situation in which we found the luckless Chariclea? She was entirely prostrated by her passion; the bloom was flown from her cheeks; and tears flowing like water had extinguished the lustre of her eyes. She endeavoured, however to compose herself, when she saw us; and to resume her usual voice and countenance. Charicles embraced, kissed and soothed her. 'My dear daughter,' he cried, 'why will you hide your sufferings from your father? and while you labour under a fascination, you are silent as if you were the injurer, instead of being the injured party: an evil eye has certainly looked upon you. But be of good cheer; here is the wise Calasiris, who has promised to attempt your cure; and he, if any one is able, can effect it; for he has been bred up from his youth in the study of things divine, and is himself a priest; and what is more than all, he is my dearest friend. Resign yourself up, therefore, entirely to his management; suffer him to treat you as he pleases, either by incantations or any other method—you have, I know, no aversion to the company and conversation of the wise.'

"Chariclea motioned her consent, as though not displeased at the proposal—and we then took our leave; Charicles putting me in mind of what he had first recommended to my anxious care; beseeching me, if possible, to inspire his daughter with an inclination for love and marriage. I sent him away in good spirits: assuring him that I would shortly bring about what he seemed to have so much at heart."

Book IV

T he ensuing day ended the Pythian games; but not the conflict of the youthful pair; Love was the arbiter, and in the persons of these his combatants, determined to exhibit his mightiest contest. Towards the end of the ceremony, when all Greece was looking on, and the Amphictyons sat as judges; when the races, the wrestlings, and the boxing matches were over; a herald came forward, and made proclamation for the men in armour to appear. At that instant the priestess Chariclea shone out like some fair star at the end of the course; for she had prevailed with herself, however unfit, to come forth, that she might comply with the custom of her country: and perhaps not without a secret hope of seeing Theagenes. She bore a torch in her left hand, and a branch of palm in her right. At her appearance every eye in the assembly was turned upon her, but none sooner than that of Theagenes; for what is so quick as the glance of a lover? He, who perhaps had heard that it was probable she might come, had his whole mind intent upon that expectation; and, when she appeared, was not able to contain himself; but said softly to me, who sat next to him, ''Tis she herself; 'tis Chariclea!' I bid him be silent, and compose himself. And now, at the summons of the herald, a warrior stood forth; splendidly armed, of noble air, and distinguished appearance; who had formerly been victor in many contests, but at this meeting had not engaged in any, probably because he could not find a competitor; and none now appearing to oppose him, the Amphyctyons ordered him to retire, the law not permitting any one to be crowned who had not contended. He begged the herald might be suffered again to make proclamation, which he did, calling upon some one to enter the lists.

"Theagenes said to me, 'This man calls upon me.'—'How so?' said I,—'He does indeed,' he replied; 'for no other, while I am present and behold it, shall receive a crown from the hands of Chariclea.'—'But do you not consider the disgrace, if you should fail of success?'—'Will any one outrun me in speed and in desire to see and be near Chariclea? To whom will the sight of her add swifter wings and more impetuous speed? You know that the painters make Love winged, signifying thereby how rapid are the motions of his captives; and, were I inclined to boast, I could say that no one hitherto has been able to excel me in swiftness.'—And immediately he sprang up, came forward, gave in his name and family, and took his allotted place.

"He stood there in complete armour, expecting with trembling eagerness the signal of the trumpet, and scarce able to wait for it. It was a noble and all-engrossing spectacle, as when Homer describes Achilles contending on the banks of Scamander. The whole assembly was moved at his unexpected appearance, and felt as much interested in his success as they would have done for their own; such power has beauty to conciliate the minds of men. But Chariclea was affected more than all: I watched her countenance, and saw the changes of it. And when the herald proclaimed the names of the racers—Ormenus the Arcadian, and Theagenes the Thessalian—when they sprang forward from the goal, and ran together with a swiftness almost too rapid for the eye to follow—then the maiden was unable to contain herself; her limbs trembled, and her feet quivered, as if they could assist the course of her lover, on whom her whole soul was intent. The spectators were on the very tiptoe of expectation, and full of solicitude for the issue; and I more than all, who had now determined to regard Theagenes as my own son."

"No wonder," said Cnemon, "that those present were in an agony of expectation; when I, even now, am trembling for Theagenes. Deliver me, therefore, I beseech you, as soon as you can, out of my suspense."

"When they had not finished more than half their course," continued Calasiris, "Theagenes turning a little, and casting a stern glance at Ormenus, lifted up his shield on high, and stretching out his neck, and fixing his eyes intently on Chariclea, flew like an arrow to the goal, leaving the Arcadian far behind him. When he reached the maiden, he fell upon her bosom; not, I imagine, without design, but in appearance as if unable to check on a sudden the rapidity of his pace. When he took the palm from her hand, I observed he kissed it."

"You have relieved my mind," said Cnemon; "I rejoice that he has both obtained the victory, and kissed his mistress. But what happened afterwards?"—"You are not only insatiable of hearing, Cnemon, but invincible by sleep; a great part of the night is now spent, and you are still wakeful, still attentive to my tedious story."—"I am at feud with Homer, father, for saying that love, as well as everything else, brings satiety in the end; for my part I am never tired either of feeling it myself, or hearing of its influence on others; and lives there the man of so iron and adamantine an heart, as not to be enchanted with listening to the loves of Theagenes and Chariclea, though the story were to last a year? Go on, therefore, I beseech you."

"Theagenes," continued Calasiris, "was crowned, proclaimed victor, and conducted home with universal applause. But Chariclea was utterly vanquished; the second sight of Theagenes fixed deep that love which the first had inspired; for the mutual looks of lovers revive and redouble their passion; sight inflames the imagination, as fuel increases fire. She went home, and spent a night as bad or worse than the former one. I, too, was sleepless as before, ruminating how I should conceal our flight, and into what country it was the intention of the gods that I should conduct my young companions. I conjectured, from the words of the oracle, that it was to be by sea:

——'and oceans past,
In regions torrid shall arrive at last;'

but I could think only of one method to obtain some information whither I ought to take them; and that was, if I could gain a sight of the fillet which was exposed with Chariclea; on which, as Charicles said, some particulars relating to her were written. It was probable that I might learn from thence the names of her parents, and of her country, which I already guessed at; and it was thither, most likely, that the fates would direct her course. I went, therefore, in the morning, to the apartment of Chariclea; I found all her servants in tears, and Charicles in the deepest distress. I inquired into the cause of this agitation.

"'My daughter's malady,' he replied, 'increases visibly; she has passed a wretched night, worse than the preceding one.'—Upon this I desired that he, and all who were present, would leave the room; and that some one would procure for me a tripod, laurel, fire, and frankincense; and that no one would disturb me till I should call for them. Charicles ordered everything to be disposed as I desired. When I was left at liberty, I began a kind of scenical representation; I burnt my incense, I muttered a few prayers, and with the branch of laurel stroked Chariclea several times from head to foot. At last, after having played a hundred fooleries with myself and the maiden, I began yawning, grew tired of the mummery, and ceased. She smiled, shook her head, and signified that I was in an error, and had entirely mistaken the nature of her disorder. I approached nearer to her, and bid her be of good cheer, for her malady was by no means, uncommon or difficult of cure—that she was undoubtedly fascinated, perhaps when she was present at the procession, but most probably when she presided at the race—that

I suspected who had fascinated her—that my suspicions fell upon Theagenes, who ran the armour race; for I had observed with what an intent and ardent eye he gazed upon her.

"'Whether he looked at me or not,' she replied, 'say no more of him; yet tell me who is he, and whence does he come? I saw many admiring him.'—I told her that she had already heard from the herald that he was a Thessalian—that he himself claimed to be of the family of Achilles; and, I thought, not without great appearance of truth: for his beauty and stature bespoke him a descendant from that hero. Yet he was not, like him, insolent or arrogant, but possessed an elevated mind, tempered with sweetness; 'and though he has an evil eye, and has fascinated you, he suffers worse torments than he has inflicted.'

"'Father,' said she, 'I am obliged to you for the compassion you express for me; but do not wish ill to one who perhaps has not committed any wrong. My malady is not fascination, but, I think, of another kind.'—'Why do you conceal it then, my daughter, and not tell it freely, that you may meet with some relief? Consider me as a father to you, in age at least, and more in good-will. Am not I well known to, and the intimate friend of, Charicles? Tell me the cause of your disorder: put confidence in me; I swear I will not betray it. Speak freely, and do not increase your sufferings by concealing them: there is no disease, which when easily known, is not easily cured; but that which is become inveterate by time is almost incurable—silence nourishes anguish; what is disclosed admits of consolation and relief.'—After a pause, in which her countenance betrayed the various agitations of her mind, she said, 'Suffer me to continue silent to-day, I will be more explicit hereafter; if the art of divination, in which you are skilled, has not already discovered to you all I have to tell you.'

"Upon this I arose and took my leave, hinting to the maiden the necessity of overcoming her modesty and reserve. Charicles met me. 'What have you to tell me?' said he. 'All good news,' I replied. 'To-morrow your daughter shall be cured of her complaint, and something else shall happen which you greatly desire; in the meantime, however, it may not be amiss to send for a physician:' and having said this, I retired, that he might ask me no more questions.

"I had not gone far, when I saw Theagenes wandering about the precincts of the temple, talking to himself, and seeming satisfied if he could only see the place where Chariclea dwelt. Turning aside, I passed by as if I had not observed him; but he cried out, 'Calasiris, I rejoice to see you! listen to me; I have been long waiting for you.' I turned suddenly. 'My handsome Theagenes,' said I, 'I did not observe you.' 'How can he be handsome,' he replied, 'who cannot please Chariclea?' I pretended to be angry. 'Will you not cease,' I said, 'to dishonour me and my art, which has already worked upon her, and compelled her to love you? and she now desires, above all things, to see you.' 'To see me!' he exclaimed; 'what is it you tell me? why do not you instantly lead me to her:' and immediately he began advancing. I caught hold of his robe: 'Hold,' I cried, 'however famous you are for speed, this is not a business to be ventured upon in haste; it requires consideration and management, and many preparations, in order to ensure success and safety. You must not think to bear off by force so rich a prize. Do not you know that her father is one of the principal men of Delphi; and that such an attempt would here incur a capital punishment?' 'I regard not death,' he replied, 'if I can possess Chariclea; however, if you think it better, let us ask her in marriage of her father. I am not unworthy of his alliance.' 'We should not obtain her,' I answered; 'not that there can be any objection to you, but Charicles has long ago promised her to his sister's son.' 'He shall have no reason to rejoice in his good fortune,' said Theagenes. 'No one, while I am alive, shall make Chariclea his bride; my hand and sword have not yet so far forgot their office.' 'Moderate your passion,' I replied; 'there is no occasion for your sword; only be guided by me, and do as I shall direct you. At present retire, and avoid being seen often in public with me; but visit me sometimes, quietly and in private.' He went away quite cast down.

"On the morrow Charicles met me: as soon as he saw me he ran up to me, and repeatedly kissed my head, crying out, 'How great is the force of wisdom and friendship! You have accomplished the great work. The impregnable is taken. The invincible is vanquished. Chariclea is in love!'

"At this I began to arch my eyebrows: I put on a consequential air, and proudly paced the room. 'No marvel,' said I, 'that she has not been able to resist even the first application of my spells, and yet I have hitherto employed only some of the weakest of them. But how came you acquainted with what you are rejoicing at?' 'According to your advice,' said he, 'I sent for some physicians of whom I had a high opinion. I took them to visit my daughter, promising them large fees if they could afford her any relief. As soon as they entered her apartment they inquired into the cause of her complaint. She turned from them, made no reply to their inquiries, and kept repeating a verse from Homer, the sense of which is,—

"Achilles, Peleus' son, thou flower of Greeks."

At length the sagacious Acestinus (perhaps you know him) seized her unwilling hand, hoping to discover by her pulse the movements of her heart. He felt it, and, after some consideration, said, "O Charicles, it is in vain you call upon us for assistance; the leech's art can here be of no use." "My God," cried I, "what is it you say? My daughter is dying, and you give me no hope." "Compose yourself," he replied, "and attend to me;" and taking me aside he thus addressed me:—

"'Our art professes to heal only the disorders of the body, not those of the mind, except only when the mind suffers with the afflicted body; when one is cured the other is relieved. Your daughter certainly labours under a malady, but it is not a corporeal one. She has no redundant humours, no head-ache, no fever, no distemper which has its origin in the body—this I can venture to pronounce." I besought him, if he knew what really ailed her, that he would tell me. At last he said, "Does she not know herself that the malady is a mental one—that it is, in one word, love? Do you not see how her swelled eyes, her unsettled look, her pale countenance, betray the wounded heart? Her thoughts wander, her discourse is unconnected, she gets no sleep, and visibly falls away; some relief must be sought for, but he alone for whom she pines can, I think, afford it." Having so said, he took his leave. I hastened to you, as to a god and preserver, who alone have it in your power, as both I and my daughter acknowledge, to do us good. For when I was pressing her, in the most affectionate manner, to discover to me the cause of her complaint, she answered that she knew not what was the matter with her; this only she knew, that Calasiris alone could heal her, and besought me to call you to her; from which I perceive that she has the greatest opinion of, and confidence in, your wisdom.'

"'Since you have found out that she is in love,' I replied, 'can you conjecture with whom?' 'No, by Apollo,' said he; 'how should I discover that? I wish with all my heart it may be with Alcamenes, my sister's son. I have long destined him for her spouse, if my wishes can have weight with her.' I told him it was easy to make the experiment, by bringing the young man into her presence. He seemed to approve of this and went away.

"Soon after I met him in the market-place. 'I have very disagreeable news,' said he, 'my daughter is certainly possessed, she behaves in so strange a manner. I introduced Alcamenes to her, as you desired; and he had taken care about his personal appearance, but she, as if she had seen the Gorgon's head, or anything more frightful, gave a piercing shriek, turned her face aside, and, grasping her neck with both her hands, protested that she would strangle herself, if we did not instantly leave the room. This, you may imagine, we hastened to do upon seeing such monstrously strange conduct. And we again entreat you to save her life, and to fulfil, if possible, our wishes.'

"'O Charicles,' I replied, 'you were not mistaken in saying your daughter was possessed. She is, indeed, beset by those powers which I was obliged to employ against her. They are very potent, and are compelling her to that from which her nature and constitution is averse. But it seems to me that some opposing deity counteracts my measures, and is fighting against my ministers; wherefore it is necessary that I should see the fillet which you told me was exposed with your daughter, and which you had preserved with the other tokens: I fear it may contain some witcheries and magic which work upon her mind, the contrivance of an enemy, who wishes her to continue all her life single, childless, and averse to love.' Charicles assented to what I said, and presently brought me the fillet. I begged and obtained time to consider it. I took it eagerly with me to my apartment, and began immediately to read what was written on it. The characters were Ethiopian; not the common ones, but such as those of royal birth make use of, which are the same as the sacred writings of the Egyptians; and this was the tenor of the inscription:—

"'Persina, Queen of Ethiopia, inscribes this, her lament, as a last gift to an unfortunate daughter, who has not yet obtained a name, and is known to her only by the pangs she cost.'

"I shuddered, Cnemon, when I read the name of Persina; however, I read on as follows:—

"'I call the Sun to witness, the author of my race, that I do not expose you, my child, and withdraw you from the sight of your father Hydaspes, on account of any crime of mine. Yet I would willingly excuse myself to you, if you should happen to survive, and to him who shall take you up, if propitious providence vouchsafes to send you a preserver, and relate to the world the cause of my exposing you.

"'Of the gods we count the Sun and Bacchus among our ancestors; of the heroes, Perseus, Andromeda, and Memnon. Our kings, at various times, have adorned the royal apartments with pictures of them and their exploits; some ornamented the porticoes and men's apartments:

our bed-chamber was painted with the story of Perseus and Andromeda. There, in the tenth year after our marriage, when as yet we had no child, I retired to repose myself during the scorching heat of noon; and here your father, Hydaspes, visited me, being warned to do so by a dream. In consequence of this visit I became pregnant. The whole time of my pregnancy was a continual feast, a course of sacrifices and thanksgivings to the gods, for the near prospect, long wished for, of a successor to the kingdom. But when at last I brought you forth, a white infant, so different from the Ethiopian hue, I was at no loss to explain the cause, since, in the embraces of your father, I had kept my eyes fixed on the picture of Andromeda, whom the painter had represented just unchained from the rock, and my imagination had communicated her complexion to my unhappy offspring. But this, though satisfactory to me, might not have been so to any one else. I dreaded the being accused of adultery, and the punishment which awaits that crime: I committed you, therefore, to the wide world and to fortune. I thought this better even for you than death, or the disgrace of being called a bastard, one of which fates must have awaited you had I preserved you at home. I told my husband that my child was dead, and exposed you privately, placing as many valuables with you as I could collect, by way of reward for whoever should find and bring you up. Among other ornaments I put this fillet upon you, stained with my own blood and containing this melancholy account, which I have traced out in the midst of tears and sorrows, when I first brought you into the world, and was overwhelmed with grief and consternation. And, oh my sweet, yet soon lost daughter, if you should survive, remember the noble race from which you spring; honour and cultivate virtue and modesty, the chief recommendations of a woman, and ornaments of a queen. But, among the jewels which are exposed with you, remember to inquire after, and claim for yourself a ring which your father gave me when he sought me in marriage. The circle of it is inscribed with royal characters, and in its bezil the stone Pantarbè, which possesses occult and powerful virtue. I have given you this account in writing, since cruel fortune denies me the happiness of doing it in person; my pains may have been taken to no purpose, but they may be of use to you; the designs of fate are inscrutable by mortals. These words (oh vainly beautiful, and bringing, by your beauty, an imputation on her who bore you), if you should be preserved, may serve as a token to discover your race; if otherwise (which may I never hear!) they will be the funeral lament of an afflicted mother.'

"When I read this, Cnemon, I acknowledged and wondered at the dispensations of the deities. I felt both pleasure and pain by a new kind of sensation; I rejoiced and wept at the same time. I was glad to have discovered what I was before ignorant of, together with the meaning of the oracle: but I was apprehensive for the event of the design I was engaged in; and lamented the instability and uncertainty, the changes and the chances of human life, of which the fortunes of Chariclea afforded so remarkable an instance. I recollected that, with her high birth, heiress of the royal family of Ethiopia, she was now banished to a vast distance from her native country, and reputed as a bastard. I continued a considerable time in these contemplations, deploring her present situation, and hardly daring to flatter myself with better hopes for the future. At length I collected my scattered spirits, and determined that something must be done, and that quickly. I went, therefore, to Chariclea; I found her alone, almost overcome by what she suffered: her mind willing to bear up against her malady; but her body labouring, yielding, and unable to resist its attacks. When I had sent out her attendants, and given orders that no one should disturb us, on pretence that I had some prayers and invocations to make use of over her, I thus addressed her:

"'It is now time, my dear Chariclea, to disclose to me (as you promised yesterday) the cause of your sufferings. Hide nothing, I beseech you, from a man who has the greatest regard for you; and whose art is besides able to discover whatever you may obstinately endeavour to conceal.'—She took my hand, kissed it and wept. 'Sage Calasiris,' said she, 'permit me, I beg of you, to suffer in silence; and do you, as you have it in your power, discover of yourself the cause of my disease. Spare me the ignominy of confessing that which it is shameful to feel, and still more shameful to avow. Whatever I undergo from my disorder, I suffer more from the thought of my own weakness, in permitting myself to be overcome by it, and not resisting it at the beginning. It was always odious to me; the very mention of it contaminates the chaste ears of a virgin.'

"'I acquiesce, my daughter,' I replied, 'in your silence. I do not blame your reserve, and that for two reasons. In the first place, I have no need to be told that which I have before discovered by my art; and then an unwillingness to speak of a matter of this nature, becomes well the modesty of your sex. But since you have at last felt love, and are manifestly smitten by Theagenes (for this the gods have disclosed to me), know that you are not the first, or the only one, who has succumbed under this passion. It is common to you with many celebrated women, and many maidens in other respects most irreproachable; for love is a very powerful deity, and is said to subdue even the gods themselves. Consider then what is best to be done in your present circumstances. If it be the greatest happiness to be free from love, the next is, when one is taken captive, to regulate it properly: this you have in your power to do; you can repel the imputation of mere sensual love, and sanctify it with the honourable and sacred name of wedlock.'

"When I said this, Cnemon, she showed much agitation, and great drops of sweat stood on her forehead. It was plain that she rejoiced at what she heard, but was anxious about the success of her hopes; and ashamed and blushing at the discovery of her weakness. After a considerable pause she said,

"'You talk of wedlock, and recommend that, as if it were evident that my father would agree to it, or the author of my sufferings desire it.'—'As to the young man, I have not the least doubt; he is more deeply smitten than yourself, and suffers full as much on your account as you can do on his. For, as it seems, your souls at their first encountering knew that they were worthy of each other, and felt a mutual passion; this passion, out of regard to you, I have heightened by my art in Theagenes. But he whom you suppose your father, proposes to give you another husband, Alcamenes, whom you well know.'—'He shall sooner find Alcamenes a grave, than find him a wife in me,' said she; 'either Theagenes shall be my husband, or I will yield to the fate which presses upon me. But why do you hint that Charicles is not really my father?'

"'It is from this that I have my information,' I replied, shewing her the fillet.—'Where did you get this?' said she, 'or how? for since I was brought, I hardly know how, from Egypt, Charicles has kept it safely locked up in a chest lest any accident should happen to it.'—'How I got it,' I returned, 'you shall hear another time; at present tell me if you know what is written on it.'—She owned that she was entirely ignorant of its contents.—'It discovers,' said I, 'your family, your country, and your fortunes.'—She besought me to disclose the purport of it; and I interpreted the whole writing to her, word for word. When she came to know who she was, her spirit seemed to rise, in conformity to her noble race. She asked me what was to be done at this conjuncture. I then became more unreserved and explicit in my advice to her.

"'I have been, my daughter,' said I, 'in Ethiopia; led by the desire of making myself acquainted with their wisdom. I was known to your mother Persina, for the royal palace was always open to the learned. I acquired some reputation there, as I increased my own stock of Egyptian knowledge by joining it to that of Ethiopia: and when I was preparing to return home, the queen unbosomed herself to me, and disclosed everything she knew relative to you, and your birth, exacting from me first an oath of secrecy. She said she was afraid to confide in any of the Ethiopian sages; and she earnestly besought me to consult the gods as to whether you had been fortunately preserved; and if so, into what part of the world you were: for she could hear no tidings of you in Ethiopia, after a most diligent inquiry. The goodness of the gods discovered by their oracles everything to me: and when I told her you were still alive, and where you were, she was very earnest with me to seek you out, and induce you to return to your native land; for she had continued sorrowful and childless ever since you were exposed; and was ready, if you should appear, to confess to her husband everything which had happened. And she was inclined to hope that he would now acknowledge you; having had so long experience of her virtue and good conduct, and seeing an unexpected prospect arise of a successor to his family. This she said, and besought me earnestly by the Sun, an adjuration which no sage dare violate, to do what she desired of me. I am now here, desirous to execute what I have been so strongly conjured to do: and though another cause brought me into this country, I esteem the pains of my wandering well repaid; and give thanks to the gods that I have found you here, whom I have long been desirous of meeting with. You know with what care I have cultivated your friendship—that I concealed whatever I knew concerning you, till I could obtain possession of this fillet, as a pledge of the truth of my relation. You may now, if you will be persuaded, leave this country with me, before you are obliged, by force, to do anything against your inclinations; for I know that Charicles is taking every measure to bring about your marriage with Alcamenes. You may return to your country, revisit your family, and be restored to your parents accompanied by Theagenes, your intended husband; and you may change your life of exile and uncertainty for that of a princess, who shall hereafter reign with him whom she most loves, if we may place confidence in the predictions of the gods.' I then put her in mind of the oracle of Apollo, and gave her my explanation of it. She had heard of it before, for it was much talked of, and its meaning inquired into. She paused at this: at last she said, 'Since such, you think, is the will of the gods, and I am inclined to believe your interpretation, what,

Father, will be best for me to do?'—'You must pretend,' said I, 'that you are willing to marry Alcamenes.'—'But this is odious to me,' she replied; 'it is disgraceful to give even a feigned promise to any but Theagenes: but since I have given myself up to your direction, and that of the gods, how far will this dissimulation lead me, so that I be not entangled in any disagreeable circumstances by it?'—'The event will show you,' said I; 'to tell you beforehand might cause some hesitation upon your part, whereas suddenness in action will bring with it confidence and boldness. Only follow my advice: seem, for the present, to agree to the marriage which Charicles has so much at heart; he will not proceed in it without my knowledge and direction.' She wept, yet promised to be guided by me, and I took my leave of her.

"I had scarcely got out of the chamber when I met Charicles, with a very downcast and sorrowful air.—'You are a strange man,' said I: 'when you ought to rejoice, sacrifice, and give thanks to the gods, for having obtained what you so long have wished for; when Chariclea at last, with great difficulty, and the utmost exertions of my art and wisdom, has been brought to yield to love, and to desire marriage; you go about sad and drooping, and are ready to shed tears. What can be the matter with you?'—'I have but too much reason for sorrow,' he replied, 'when the delight of my eyes, before she can be married, as you say she is inclined to be, is threatened to be hurried away from me, if any faith is to be given to dreams, which on several nights, and particularly on the last, have tormented me. Methought I saw an eagle take his flight from the hand of Apollo, and stooping down suddenly upon me, snatch my daughter, alas! out of my very bosom, and bear her away to some extreme corner of the earth, full of dusky and shadowy forms. I could not discover what became of them; for soon the vast intermediate interval hid them from my sight.' I instantly conjectured what this dream portended; but I endeavoured to comfort him, and to prevent his having the smallest suspicion of the real truth. 'Considering that you are a priest,' I said, 'and are dedicated to that deity who is most famous for oracles, you seem to me not to have much skill in the interpretation of dreams. This darkly signifies the approaching marriage of your child, and the eagle represents her intended spouse: and when Apollo intimates this to you, and that it is from his hands that your daughter is to receive a husband, you seem displeased, and wrest the dream to an ominous interpretation. Wherefore, my dear Charicles, let us be cautious what we say; let us accommodate ourselves to the will of the gods, and use our utmost endeavours to persuade the maiden.'

"'But how shall we manage,' he replied, 'to render her more compliant?'—'Have you,' said I, 'any valuables laid up in store, garments, or gold, or necklace? if you have, produce them, give them to her as a marriage present, and propitiate her by gifts. Precious stones and ornaments have a magic influence upon a female mind. You must proceed too, as fast as you can, in all your preparations for the nuptials; there must be no delay in hastening them forward, while that inclination, forced upon her mind by art, remains yet undiminished.'— 'Nothing shall be wanting which depends upon me,' replied Charicles; and immediately he ran out, with alacrity and joy, to put his words in execution. I soon found that he lost no time in doing what I had suggested; and that he had offered to Chariclea dresses of great price, and the Ethiopian necklace which had been exposed with her as tokens by Persina, as if they were marriage presents from Alcamenes.—Soon after I met Theagenes, and asked him what was become of all those who had composed his train in the procession.—He said the maidens had already set forward on their journey, as they travelled slowly; and that the youths, impatient of delay, were becoming clamorous, and pressing him to return home. When I heard this, I instructed him what to say to them, and what he should do himself; and bidding him observe the signals that I should give him, both of time and opportunity, I left him.

"I bent my course towards the temple of Apollo, intending to implore him to instruct me, by some oracle, in what manner I was to direct my flight with my young friends. But the divinity was quicker than any thought of mine—he assists those who act in conformity to his will, and with unasked benevolence anticipates their prayers; as he here anticipated my question by a voluntary oracle, and in a very evident manner manifested his superintendence over us. For as I was hastening, full of anxiety, to his shrine, a sudden voice stopped me—'Make what speed you can,' it said; 'the strangers call upon you.'—A company of people were at that time celebrating, to the sound of flutes, a festival in honour of Hercules. I obeyed, and turned towards them, as soon as I heard this warning, careful not to neglect the divine call. I joined the assembly, I threw incense on the altar, and made my libations of water. They ironically expressed their admiration at the cost and profusion of my offerings, and invited me to partake of the feast with them. I accepted the invitation, and having reclined on a couch adorned with myrtle and laurel, and tasted something of what was set before me, I said to them, 'My friends, I have partaken of a very pleasant entertainment with you, but I am ignorant whom I am among; wherefore it is time now for you to tell me who you are, and from whence: for it is rude and unbecoming for those who have begun a kind of friendship, by being partakers of the same table and sacrifice, and of the same sacred salt, to separate without knowing at least something of each other.'—They readily replied that they were Phœnician merchants from Tyre—that they were sailing to Carthage with a cargo of Ethiopian, Indian, and Phœnician merchandize—that they were at that instant celebrating a sacrifice to the Tyrian Hercules, on account of a victory which that young man (showing one of their company) had gained at the Pythian games; esteeming it a great honour that a Phœnecian should be declared a conqueror in Greece. 'This youth,' said they, 'after we had passed the Malian promontory, and were driven by contrary winds to Cephallene, affirmed to us, swearing by this our country's god, that it was revealed to him in a dream that he should obtain a prize at the Pythian games; and persuaded us to turn out of our course, and touch here. In effect, his presages have been fulfilled; and the head of a merchant is now encircled with a victor's crown. He offers therefore this sacrifice to the god who foretold his success, both as a thanksgiving for the victory, and to implore his protection in the voyage which we are about to undertake; for we propose to set sail early to-morrow morning, if the winds favour our wishes.'

"'Is that really your intention?' I said.—'It is indeed,' they answered.— 'You may then,' I replied, 'have me as a companion in your voyage, if you will permit it; for I have occasion to go into Sicily, and in your course to Africa you must necessarily sail by that island.'—'You shall be heartily welcome,' they replied; 'for nothing but good can happen to us from the society of a sage, a Grecian, and, as we conjecture, a favourite of the gods.'—'I shall be very happy to accept your offer,' I said, 'if you will allow me one day for preparation.'—'Well,' said they, 'we will give you to-morrow; but do not fail in the evening to be by the water-side; for the night is favourable to our navigation; gentle breezes at that season blow from the land, and propel the ship quietly on her way.'

"I promised them to be there without fail at the time appointed, and exacted an oath from them that they would not sail before. And with this I left them, still employed in their pipes and dances, which they performed to the brisk notes of their music, something after the Assyrian fashion; now bounding lightly on high, and now sinking to the ground on bended knees, and again whirling themselves round with rapidity, as if hurried on by the influence of the divinity. I found Chariclea admiring as they lay in her lap the presents which Charicles had made her; from her I went to Theagenes: I gave each of them instructions what they were to do, and returned to my apartment, solicitous and intent upon the prosecution of my design; which I did not long delay to put in execution. When it was midnight, and all the city was buried in sleep, a band of armed youths surrounded the habitation of Chariclea. Theagenes led on this amatory assault: his troop consisted of those who composed his train. With shouts, and clamour, and clashing their shields, to terrify any who might be within hearing, they broke into the house with lighted torches; the door, which had on purpose been left slightly fastened, easily giving way to them. They seized and hurried away Chariclea, who was apprized of their design, and easily submitted to the seeming violence. They took with her a quantity of valuable stuff, which she indicated to them; and the moment they had left the house, they raised again their warlike shouts, clashed their shields, and with an awful noise marched through the city, to the unspeakable terror of the affrighted inhabitants; whose alarm was the greater, as they had chosen a still night for their purpose, and Parnassus resounded to the clang of their brazen bucklers. In this manner they passed through Delphi, frequently repeating to each other the name of Chariclea. As soon as they were out of the city, they galloped as fast as they could towards Mount Œta. Here the lovers, as had been agreed upon, withdrew themselves privately from the Thessalians, and fled to me. They fell at my feet, embraced my knees in great agitation, and called upon me to save them; Chariclea blushing, with downcast eyes, at the bold step she had taken. 'Preserve and protect,' said Theagenes, 'strangers, fugitives, and suppliants, who have given up everything that they may gain each other; slaves of chaste love; playthings of fortune; voluntary exiles, yet not despairing, but placing all their hopes of safety in you.' I was confused and affected with this address: tears would have been a relief to me; but I restrained myself, that I might not increase their apprehensions. I raised and comforted them; and bidding them hope everything which was fortunate, from a design undertaken under the direction of the gods, I told them I must go and look after what yet remained to be done for the execution of our project; and desiring them to stay where they were, and to take great care that they were not seen by any body, I prepared to leave them; but Chariclea caught hold of my garment, and detained me.

"'Father,' she cried, 'it will be treacherous and unjust in you to leave me already, and alone, under the care of Theagenes only. You do not consider how faithless a guardian a lover is, when his mistress is in his power, and no one present to impose respect upon him. He will with difficulty restrain himself, when he sees the object of his ardent desires defenceless before him; wherefore I insist upon your not leaving me, till I have exacted an oath from Theagenes, that he will not attempt to obtain any favours which I am not disposed to grant, till I arrive in my country, and am restored to my family; or, at least, if the gods should envy me that happiness, till I am by my own consent become his wife.'

"I was surprised yet pleased with what she said, and agreed entirely with her in her sentiments. I raised a flame upon the hearth in place of an altar, threw on a few grains of frankincense, and Theagenes took the oath, indignant at its being required of him, and that such an obligation should deprive him of showing voluntarily that respect to Chariclea, which he was already determined to show without any such compulsion. He should now, he said, have no merit in it; all the restraint he put upon himself would be imputed to the fear of perjury. He swore, however, by the Pythian Apollo, by Diana, by Venus herself, and the Loves, that he would conform himself in every instance to the will of Chariclea. These and other solemn vows having been mutually taken under the auspices of the gods, I made what haste I could to Charicles.

"I found his house full of tumult and grief, his servants having already informed him of the rape of his daughter; his friends flocking round him with useless consolation, and equally useless advice; himself in tears, and totally at a loss what to do. I called out with a loud voice, 'Knaves that you are, how long will you stand here stupid and undetermined, as if your misfortunes had taken away your senses? Why do you not arm instantly, pursue and take the ravishers, and revenge the injuries you have received?' 'It will be to no purpose,' replied Charicles, in a languid tone; 'I see that all this is come upon me by the wrath of heaven; the gods foretold to me that I should be deprived of what I held most dear, since the time that I entered unseasonably into the temple, and saw what it was not lawful for me to behold. Yet there is no reason why we should not contend, in this instance, even against a calamity, though sent by the deities, if we knew whom we have to pursue, and who have brought this misfortune upon us.' 'We do know them,' said I; 'it is Theagenes, whom you made so much of and introduced to me, and his companions. Perhaps you may find some of them still about the city, who may have loitered here this evening. Arise, therefore, and call the people to council.'

"What I desired was done: the magistrates sent the herald about, to convoke an assembly by the sound of trumpet. The people presently came together, and a night meeting was held in the theatre. Chariclis drew tears of compassion from all, when he appeared in the midst in mourning garments, with dust upon his face and head, and thus began:

"'Delphians, you may perhaps imagine that I have called together this meeting, and am now addressing it solely on account of my own great calamities; but that is not entirely the case. I suffer indeed what is worse than death. I am left deserted, afflicted by the gods, my house desolate, and deprived of that sweet conversation which I preferred to all the pleasures in the world; yet hope, and the self-conceit common to us, still sustains me, and promises me that I shall again recover my daughter. But I am moved with indignation at the affront which has been offered to the city, which I hope to see punished even before my own wrongs are redressed, unless the Thessalian striplings have taken away from us our free spirit, and just regard for our country and its gods; for what can be more shameful than that a few youths, dancers forsooth, and followers of an embassy, should trample under their feet the laws and authority of the first city in Greece, and should ravish from: the temple of Apollo its chiefest ornament, Chariclea, alas! the delight of my eyes; How obstinate and implacable towards me has been the anger of the gods! The life of my own daughter, as you know, was extinguished with the light of her nuptial torches. Grief for her death brought her mother soon to the grave, and drove me from my country; but, when I found Chariclea, I felt myself consoled; she became my life, the hope of succession in my family, my sweet anchor, I may say, my only comfort. Of all these this sudden storm has bereft me, and that at the most unlucky time possible, as if I were to be the scorn and sport of fate, just when preparations were making for her marriage, and you were all informed of it.'

"While he was speaking, and indulging himself in lamentations, the chief magistrate Hegesias interrupted and stopped him. 'Let Chariclis, fellow-citizens,' said he, 'lament hereafter at his leisure; but let not us be so hurried away, and affected by concern for his misfortunes, as to neglect opportunity, which in all things is of great moment, and particularly in military affairs. There is some hope that we may overtake the ravishers if we follow them instantly, for the delay which must take place on our part will naturally make them less speedy in their march: but if we spend our time in womanish bewailings, and by our delays give them an opportunity to escape, what remains but that we shall become a common laughing-stock, the laughing-stock of youths, whom the moment we have taken we should nail to so many crosses, and render their names, and even their families, infamous? This we may easily effect, if we endeavour to rouse the indignation of their countrymen against them, and interdict their descendants, and as many of themselves as may happen to escape, from ever being present at this annual ceremonial and sacrifice to the Manes of their hero; the expense of which we defray out of our public treasury.' The people approved what he advised, and ratified it by their decree. 'Enact, also,' said he, 'if you please, that the priestess shall never in future appear to the armed runners; for, as I conjecture, it was the sight of her at that time which inflamed Theagenes, and excited in him the impious design of carrying her off; it is desirable, therefore, to guard against anything which may give occasion to such an attempt for the time to come.'

"When this also was unanimously agreed to, Hegesias gave the signal to march, the trumpet sounded, the theatre was abandoned for war, and there was a general rush from the assembly for the fight. Not only the robust and mature followed him, but children and youths likewise, supplying with their zeal the place of age; women, also, with a spirit superior to their strength, snatching what arms they could meet with, tried in vain to keep up with them, and, by the fruitless attempt, were obliged to confess the weakness of their sex. You might see old men struggling with their age, their mind dragging on their body, and indignant at their physical weakness, because of the vigour of their minds. The whole city, in short, felt so deeply the loss of Chariclea, that, without waiting for day, and moved by a common impulse, it poured forth in pursuit of her ravishers."

Book V

How the city of Delphos succeeded in their pursuit, I had no opportunity of learning; their being thus engaged, however, gave me an excellent opportunity for the flight which I meditated. Taking, therefore, my young companions, I led them down to the sea, and put them aboard the Phœnician vessel, which was just ready to set sail, for day now beginning to break, the merchants thought they had kept the promise they had made, of waiting for me a day and a night. Seeing us however appear, they received us with great joy, and immediately proceeded out of the harbour, at first using their oars, then a moderate breeze rising from the land, and a gentle swell of the sea caressing as it were the stern of our ship, they hoisted sail, and committed the vessel to the wind.

"We passed with rapidity the Cirrhæan gulf, the promontory of Parnassus, the Ætolian and Calydonian rocks, and the Oxian isles, *sharp* both in name and figure, and the sea of Zacynthus began to appear as the sun sank towards the west. But why am I thus tedious? Why do I forget you and myself, and, by extending my narration, embark you upon a boundless ocean? Let us stop here a while, and both of us take a little rest; for though I know you are a very patient hearer, and strive excellently against sleep, yet I have prosecuted the account of my troubles to so unseasonable an hour, that I think you at last begin to give in. My age, too, and the remembrance of my sufferings, weigh down my spirits, and require repose."

"Stop then, Father," replied Cnemon, "not on my account, for I could attend untired to your story many days and nights; it is to me as the siren's strains; but I have for some time heard a tumult and noise in the house; I was rather alarmed at it, but my great desire to hear the remainder of your discourse prevented me from interrupting you."

"I was not sensible of it," said Calasiris, "owing, I suppose, partly to the dulness of my hearing, the common malady of age, and partly to my being intent on what I was saying. But I fancy the stir you hear is occasioned by the return of Nausicles, the master of the house; I am impatient to know how he has succeeded."—"In every thing as I could wish, my dear Calasiris," said Nausicles, who entered at that moment. "I know how solicitous you were for my success, and how your best wishes accompanied me. I have many proofs of your good will towards me, and among others the words which I have just heard you uttering. But who is this stranger?"—"A Greek," said Calasiris; "what farther regards him you shall hear another time; but pray relate to us your success, that we may be partakers in your joy." "You shall hear all in the morning," replied Nausicles: "at present let it suffice you to know, that I have obtained a fairer Thisbe than ever; for myself, wearied with cares and fatigues, I must now take a little repose." Having said this, he retired to rest.

Cnemon was struct at hearing the name of Thisbe; racking his mind with anxiety, he passed a sleepless night, nor could he at intervals restrain his sighs and groans, which at last awakened Calasiris, who lay near, from a sound sleep. The old man, raising himself upon his elbow, asked him what was the matter with him, and why he vented his complaints in that almost frantic manner. "Is it not enough to drive me mad," replied Cnemon, "when I hear that Thisbe is alive?"—"And who is this Thisbe?" said Calasiris, "and how came you acquainted with her? and why are you disturbed at supposing her to be alive?"—"You shall hear at large," returned the other, "when I relate to you my story; at present I will only tell you that I saw her dead with these eyes, and buried her with my own hands among the buccaneers." "Take some rest now," said the old man; "this mystery will soon be cleared up."—"I cannot sleep," he said; "do you repose yourself if you will; I shall die if I do not find out, and that immediately, under what mistake Nausicles is labouring; or whether among the Egyptians alone the dead come to life again." Calasiris smiled at his impatience, and betook himself again to sleep.

But Cnemon arose, and, going out of his chamber, encountered all those difficulties which it was probable a stranger would meet with, who wanders at night, and in the dark, in an unknown house; but he struggled with them all, such was his horror of Thisbe, and his anxiety to clear away the apprehensions which were raised in his mind by what fell from Nausicles. After passing and repassing many times, without knowing it, the same passages, at last he heard the soft voice of a woman lamenting, like a vernal nightingale pouring out her melancholy notes at eventide. Led by the sound, he advanced towards the apartment; and putting his ear to the division of the folding doors, he listened, and heard her thus lamenting:—

"What an unhappy fate is mine! I thought I had escaped from the hands of the robbers, and avoided a cruel death. I flattered myself that I should pass the remainder of my life with my beloved; wandering indeed, and in foreign lands, but with him it would have been sweet; and every difficulty would have been supportable. But my evil genius is not yet satisfied; he gave me a glance of hope, and has plunged me afresh in despair. I hoped I had escaped servitude, and am again a slave; a prison, and am still confined. I was kept in an island, and surrounded with darkness; my situation is not now very different, indeed, perhaps rather worse, for he who was able and willing to console me is separated from me. The Pirates' cave which I yesterday inhabited, seemed indeed an avenue to the shades below; more like a charnel house than a dwelling; but his presence in whom I delighted made it pleasant; for he lamented my fate living, and shed tears over me when he thought me dead. Now I am deprived of every comfort; he who partook of and lessened the burden of my misfortunes is ravished from me; and I, deserted and a captive, am exposed alone to the assaults of cruel fortune; and endure to live only because I have a glimmering of hope that my beloved still survives. But where, O delight of my soul, are you? What fate has awaited you? Are you also forced to be a slave—you, whose spirit is so free, and impatient of all slavery except that of love? Oh, may your life be safe, at least; and may you, though late, see again your Thisbe! for so, however unwilling, you must call me."

When Cnemon heard this, he could no longer restrain himself, or have patience to listen to what was to follow; but guessing from what he had already heard, and particularly from what was last uttered, that the complainer could be no other than Thisbe, he was ready to fall into a swoon at the very doors; he composed himself, however, as well as he was able, and fearing lest he should be discovered by any one (for morning now approached, and the cock had twice crowed), he hurried back with a tottering pace.

Now his foot stumbled; now he fell against the wall, and now against the lintels of the door; sometimes he struck his head against utensils hanging from the ceiling; at last, with much difficulty, and after many wanderings, he reached his own apartment, and threw himself upon the bed. His body trembled, and his teeth chattered, and it might have become a very serious matter had not Calasiris, alarmed at the disorder in which he returned, come to his assistance, and soothed and comforted him. When he came a little to himself, he inquired into the cause of it.

"I am undone," exclaimed Cnemon; "that wretch Thisbe is really alive;" and having said this, he sank down again and fainted away.

Calasiris having with much ado recovered him, attempted to cheer his mind. Some envious demon, who makes human affairs his sport, was no doubt practising his illusions upon Cnemon, not suffering him to enjoy his good fortune unalloyed with trouble; but making that which was afterwards to be the cause of his greatest pleasure wear at first the appearance of calamity: either because such is the perverse disposition of those beings, or because human nature cannot admit pure and unmixed joy. Cnemon, at this very time, was flying from her whom he above all things desired to meet, and frightened at that which would have been to him the most pleasing of sights; for the lady who was thus lamenting was not Thisbe but Chariclea. The train of accidents which brought her into the house of Nausicles was as follows:—

After Thyamis was taken prisoner, the island set on fire, and its pirate inhabitants expelled, Thermuthis, his lieutenant, and Cnemon crossed over the lake in the morning to make inquiries after Thyamis. What happened on their expedition, has been before related. Theagenes and Chariclea were left alone in the cave, and esteemed what was to prove only an excess of calamity, a great present blessing; since now for the first time, being left alone, and freed from every intruding eye, they indulged themselves in unrestrained embraces and endearments; and forgetting all the world, and clinging together as though forming but one body, they enjoyed the first fruits of pure and virgin love; warm tears were mingled with their chaste kisses; chaste I say, for if at any time human nature was about to prevail on Theagenes he was checked by Chariclea, and put in mind of his oath; nor was it difficult to bring him back within due bounds, for though not proof against pure love, he was superior to mere sensual desire. But when at length they called to mind that this was a time for consultation they ceased their dalliance, and Theagenes began as follows:—

"That we may spend our lives together, my dearest Chariclea, and obtain at last that union which we prefer to every earthly blessing, and for the sake of which we have undergone so much, is my fervent prayer, and may the gods of Greece grant it! But since every thing human is fluctuating, and subject to change, since we have suffered much, and have yet much to hope, as we have appointed to meet Cnemon at Chemmis, and are uncertain what fortunes may await us there, and, in fine, as the country to which all our wishes tend is at a great distance, let us agree upon some token by which we may secretly hold communication when present; and, if at any time separated, may trace out each other in absence; for a token between friends is an excellent companion in a wanderer's journey, and may often be the means of again bringing them together."

Chariclea was pleased with the proposal; and they agreed, if they were divided, to write upon any temple, noted statue, bust of Mercury, or boundary-stone, Theagenes the word Pythicus, and Chariclea Pythias; whether they were gone to the right or the left; to what city, town, or people; and the day and hour of their writing. If they met in any circumstances, or under any disguise, they depended upon their mutual affection to discover one another, which they were certain no time could efface, or even lessen. Chariclea, however, showed him the ring which had been exposed with her, and Theagenes exhibited a scar made upon his knee by a wild boar. They agreed on a watch-word: she, *lampas* (a lamp), he, *phoinix* (a palm-tree). Having made these arrangements, they again embraced each other, and again wept, pouring out their tears as libations, and using kisses as oaths.

At last they went out of the cave, touching none of the treasures it contained, thinking riches obtained by plunder an abomination. They selected, however, some of the richest jewels which they themselves had brought from Delphi, and which the pirates had taken from them, and prepared for their journey. Chariclea changed her dress, packing up in a bundle her necklace, her crown, and sacred garments; and, the better to conceal them, put over them things of less value. She gave the bow and quiver (the emblems of the god under whom he served) to Theagenes to bear: to him a pleasant burden.

They now approached the lake, and were preparing to get into a boat, when they saw a company of armed men passing over toward the island. Rendered dizzy by the sight, they stood for some time astounded, as if deprived of all feeling by the continued assaults of unwearied evil fortune. At last, however, and just as the men were landing, Chariclea proposed to retire again into the cave, and endeavour to conceal themselves there; and was running towards it, when Theagenes stopped her, and exclaimed, "Why should we vainly endeavour to fly from that fate which pursues us every where? Let us yield to our fortune, and meet it with fortitude: what besides should we gain but unending troubles, a wandering life, and still renewed assaults of the evil genius who mocks and persecutes us? Have you not experienced how he has added, with savage eagerness, the assaults of pirates to exile, and worse perils by land to those we suffered by sea; how he terrified us first with fightings, afterwards threw us into the hands of buccaneers, detained us some time in captivity, then left us solitary and deserted, just gave us a prospect of flight and freedom, and now sends ruffians to destroy us; plays off his warfare against us and our fortunes, and gives them the appearance of a continually shifting scene, and sadly varied drama? Let us put an end then to the tragedy, and give ourselves up to those who are prepared for our destruction, lest the continued pressure and increase of our misfortunes oblige us, at last, to lay violent hands upon ourselves."

Chariclea did not entirely agree with all which her lover in his passion said. She admitted the justice of his expostulations with fortune, but could not see the propriety of giving themselves up into the hands of the armed men. It was not certain that they meant to destroy them; the evil genius who pursued them would not, perhaps, be kind enough to put so quick an end to their miseries; he probably reserved them to experience the hardships of servitude; and was it not worse than death to be exposed to the insults and indignities of the barbarians? "Let us endeavour, therefore," said she, "by all means in our power to avoid this fate. We may, from past experience, have some hopes of success: we have frequently, already, escaped from dangers which appeared inevitable."

"Let us do as you please," said Theagenes; and followed her, unwillingly, as she led the way. They could not, however, escape in safety to the cave; for while they were looking only at the enemy in front, they were not aware of another troop which had landed on a different part of the island, and which was taking them from behind, as in a net. They were now utterly confounded, and stood still, Chariclea keeping close by Theagenes, so that if they were to die they might die together. Some of the men who approached were just preparing to strike; but when the youthful pair, looking up, flashed upon them the full splendour of their beauty, their hearts failed them, and their hands grew slack; for the arm even of a barbarian reverences the beautiful, and the fiercest eye grows milder before a lovely countenance. They took them prisoners, therefore, and conducted them to their leader, anxious to lay before him the first and fairest of the spoils. It was the only booty, however, which they were likely to obtain, for they could find nothing else, after the strictest search throughout the island. Everything on the surface of it had been destroyed by the late conflagration. They were ignorant of the cave and its contents. They proceeded then towards their commander: he was Mithranes, commandant to Oroondates, viceroy of Egypt, under the Great King, whom Nausicles (as has been said) had induced, by a great sum of money, to make this expedition into the island in search of Thisbe. Upon the approach of Theagenes and Chariclea, Nausicles, with the quick-sighted craft of a merchant, started forward, and running up, exclaimed, "This is indeed Thisbe, the very Thisbe ravished from me by those villain pirates, but restored by your kindness, Mithranes, and by the gods." He then caught hold of Chariclea, and seemed in an ecstacy of joy; at the same time he spoke to her privately in Greek, in a low voice, and bid her, if she valued her life, pretend that her name was Thisbe.

This scheme succeeded. Chariclea, pleased at hearing her native language, and flattering herself with the hopes of comfort and assistance from the man who spoke it, did as he bid her; and when Mithranes asked her her name, said it was Thisbe. Nausicles then ran up to Mithranes, kissed his head, flattered the barbarian's vanity, extolled his good fortune, and congratulated him that, besides his many other exploits, this expedition had had such good success. He, cajoled by these praises, and really believing the truth of what was said (being deceived by the name), though smitten with the beauty of the maiden, which shone out under a sorry garb, like the moon from beneath a cloud; yet, confounded by the quickness of Nausicles's manœuvres, and having no time given to his fickle mind for change of purpose, said, "Take, then, this maiden, whom my arms have recovered for you;" and so saying, he delivered her into his hands, unwillingly and frequently looking back upon her, as if he would not have parted with her had he not thought himself pledged, by the reward he had received, to give her up. "But as for her companion," he added, pointing to Theagenes, "he shall be my prize. Let him follow me under a guard; he shall be sent to Babylon: with such a figure as his, he will become the service of the great king." And having thus signified his pleasure, they passed over the lake, and were separated from each other. Nausicles took the road to Chemmis, with Chariclea; Mithranes visited some other towns which were under his command, and very soon sent Theagenes to Oroondates, who was then at Memphis, accompanied with the following letter:—

"Mithranes, Commandant, to the Viceroy Oroondates.

"I have taken prisoner a Grecian youth of too noble an appearance to continue in my service, and worthy to appear before, and serve only, the Great King. I send him to you, that you may offer him to our common master, as a great and inestimable present, such a one as the royal court has never yet beheld, and probably never will again."

Scarcely had the day dawned when eager curiosity carried Calasiris and Cnemon to the apartment of Nausicles, to inquire farther into his adventures. He told them all that I have related: how he arrived at the island; how he found it deserted; the deceit he had put upon Mithranes, in passing off another maiden upon him for Thisbe; he was better pleased, he said, with his present prize than if he had really found Thisbe; there was no more comparison between their several beauties than between a mortal and a goddess; hers was unrivalled, it was impossible for him to express how beautiful she was; but, as she was under his roof, they might satisfy themselves with their own eyes. When they heard this, they began to suspect a little of the truth, and besought him to send for her immediately, as knowing that words could not do justice to her personal appearance.

When she was introduced (with downcast eyes, and her face veiled to her forehead), and Nausicles had besought her to be of good cheer, she looked up a little, and saw (beyond her hopes), and was seen by, her unexpected friends. Immediately a sudden cry was heard from all. These exclamations burst out at once, "My father!"—"My daughter! Chariclea herself! and not Cnemon's Thisbe." Nausicles stood mute with astonishment when he saw Calasiris embracing Chariclea, and weeping for joy. He wondered what this could be which had the air of a recognition on the stage, when Calasiris ran to him, and embracing him, cried out, "O best of men, may the gods shower on you every blessing you desire, as you have been the preserver of my daughter, and have restored to my longing eyes the delight of my life. But, my child, my Chariclea! where have you left Theagenes?" She wept at the question, and, pausing a little, said, "He who delivered me to this gentleman, whoever he may be, has led him away captive." Calasiris besought Nausicles to discover to him all he knew about Theagenes; under whose power he now was; and whither they had taken him.

The merchant gave him all the information he was able, conceiving this to be the pair about whom he had frequently heard the old man speak, and whom he knew he was seeking in sorrow. He added, that he feared his intelligence would not be of much service to persons in their humble circumstances; he doubted, indeed, whether any sum of money would induce Mithranes to part with the youth. "We are rich enough," said Chariclea softly to Calasiris; "promise him as much as you please; I have preserved the necklace which you know of, and have it with me." Calasiris recovered his spirits at hearing this; but not choosing to let Nausicles into the secret of their wealth, replied, "My good Nausicles, the wise man is never poor; he measures his desires by his possessions, and receives from those who abound what it is honourable for him to ask. Tell us then where the person is who has Theagenes in his power; the divine goodness will not be wanting to us, but will supply us with as much as is sufficient to satisfy the avarice of this Persian."

Nausicles smiled incredulously. "I shall," said he, "be persuaded that you can suddenly grow rich, as by a miracle, when you have first paid down to me a ransom for this maiden; you know that riches have as many charms for a merchant as for a Persian."—"I know it," replied the old man, "and you shall have a ransom. But why do you not anticipate my wishes, and, with your customary benevolence, offer, of your own accord, to restore my daughter? Must I be forced to entreat it of you?"—"You shall have her on proper terms," said the merchant. "I do not grudge you her; but now (as I am going to sacrifice) let us join in supplication to the gods, and pray that they would increase my wealth, and bestow some on you."—"Spare your ridicule," replied Calasiris, "and be not incredulous; make preparations for the sacrifice, and we will attend you when everything is ready."

Nausicles agreed to this, and soon after sent a message to his guests to desire their presence. They obeyed cheerfully, having before concerted what they were to do. The men accompanied Nausicles to the altar, with many others who were invited, for it was a public sacrifice. Chariclea went with the merchant's daughter and some other females, whose encouragements and entreaties had prevailed upon her to be present at the ceremony; and they would hardly have persuaded her had she not secretly pleased herself with the thought of taking this opportunity to pour out her vows and prayers for Theagenes.

They came to the temple of Mercury (for him, as the god of gain and merchants, Nausicles particularly worshipped); and when the sacred rites were performed, Calasiris inspected the entrails of a victim, and changing his countenance according as they portended joyful or adverse events, at last stretched out his hand, (murmuring certain words) and pretending to take something from among the ashes, presented a ring of great value to Nausicles, which he had brought with him for that purpose: "And here," said he, "the gods, by my hands, offer you this as a ransom for Chariclea."

The ring was a perfect marvel, both for material and workmanship. The circle was of electrum, within the bezil was an Ethiopian amethyst, of the size of a maiden's eye, finer much than those of Spain or Britain;

for these latter have a dullish tinge of purple, like a rose just bursting from its bud, and beginning to redden under the sun's beams; whereas the Ethiopian amethyst shines with a deeper and more sparkling lustre; if you turn it about it scatters its rays on all sides, not dulling but lighting up the sight.

They are besides of much greater virtue than the western ones; they do not belie their name, but will really keep those who wear them sober amid great excesses. This property is common to all the Indian and Ethiopian stones: but that which Calasiris now gave Nausicles far surpassed them. It was carved with wonderful art, and represented a shepherd tending his sheep. He sat upon a rock, gently elevated from the ground, surveying his flock, and distributing them into different pastures by the various notes of his pipe; they seemed to obey, and to feed as the sound directed them. You would say that they had golden fleeces, the natural blush of the amethyst, without the aid of art, casting a glow upon their backs. Here you might observe the frolics of the little lambs; some climbing up the ascent, others gambolling around the shepherd, converted the rock into a pastoral theatre. Some wantoning in the flame of the gem as in the sun, just touched in bounding the rocky surface; others, older and more bold, seemed as if they would overleap the circle; but here art had hindered them, and surrounded the jewel in the rock with the golden bezil. The rock was not counterfeit, but real; the artist, to represent it, had inclosed the edges of the stone, and was not put to the trouble of feigning what in reality existed. Such then was the ring.

Nausicles was struck at the seeming miracle, and delighted with the beauty of the gem, which he esteemed to be of more value than all he was worth.—"I was but jesting," said he, "my dear Calasiris, when I talked of a ransom for your daughter; my design was to restore her to you freely; and without price; but since, as they say, the gifts of the gods are not to be refused, I accept this jewel which is sent from heaven; persuaded that it is a present from Mercury, the best of deities, who has furnished you with it through the fire, and indeed you see how it sparkles itself with flames: besides, I think that the pleasantest and most lawful gain is that which, without impoverishing the giver, enriches the receiver."

Having said this, he took the ring, and proceeded with the rest of the company to an entertainment; the women by themselves, in the interior of the temple; the men in the vestibule. When they had satisfied their appetite, and the board was crowned with cups, they sang a suitable hymn to Bacchus, and poured out libations to him; the women sang a hymn of thanksgiving to Ceres. Chariclea, retiring from the rest, occupied with her own thoughts, prayed for the health and safe return of Theagenes.

And now, the company being warmed with wine, and rife with mirth, Nausicles, holding out a goblet of pure water, said, "Good Calasiris, let us offer this to the nymphs, the sober nymphs your deities, who have no sympathy with Bacchus, and are nymphs in very deed; but if you will entertain us with such a relation as we wish to hear, it will be more pleasant to us than even our flowing bowls. You see the women have already risen from the table, and are amusing themselves with dancing; but neither dancing nor music will be so pleasant to us as the narrative of your wanderings, if you will favour us with it. You have often excused yourself from the task on account of the troubles with which you were overwhelmed, and the lowness of your spirits; but there cannot be a more proper time for it than the present, when everything contributes to remove the one and to raise the other. You have recovered your daughter, and have hopes of recovering your son; especially if you do not affront me, by deferring your story any longer."

"Now may all good attend you, Nausicles," said Cnemon, putting in his word; "who, although you have provided all manner of music for our recreation, are willing to forego such delights (leaving them to ordinary minds), and to listen to higher and mysterious matters, seasoned with a divine interest. You show judgment in coupling together the deities, Mercury and Bacchus, thus mingling the pleasures of discourse with those of wine. Though I admire the whole order of this splendid sacrifice, yet I know nothing which will render the god of eloquence more propitious, than if this good old man will contribute his narrative to the rest of the entertainment."

Calasiris obeyed, as well to oblige Cnemon, as to conciliate the favour of Nausicles, whose services he foresaw he should have occasion for, and entered upon his story. He began with what he had already related to Cnemon; he was now, however, less minute, and entirely passed over some matters which he did not choose Nausicles to know; and when he had proceeded to the point where he had before left off, he went on as follows:

"As the wind was at first very favourable to us, the fugitives from Delphi began to flatter themselves with the hopes of a prosperous voyage; but when we got into the straits of Calydon, the swell and rolling of the waves alarmed them not a little;" here Cnemon, interrupting, begged him to explain, if he could, the cause of that agitation. "The Ionian sea," continued Calasiris, "from being wide beyond, is there contracted, and pours itself, by a narrow channel, into the Crissæan gulf; whence, hastening to mingle its waters with the Ægean, it is stopped and thrown back again by the Isthmus of Peloponnesus; which is opposed, probably, as a rampart by divine providence, lest it should overflow the opposite land: and a greater reflux being occasioned in the strait than in the rest of the gulf, from the encounter of the advancing and retreating tides the waves, owing to this repercussion, boil, swell, and break in tumult one over the other." This explanation was received with the applause and approbation of all; and the old man continued his narration.

"Having passed the strait, and lost sight of the Oxian Isles, we thought we discovered the promontory of Zacynthus, which rose on our sight like an obscure cloud, and the pilot gave orders to furl the sails. We inquired why he slackened the vessel's speed, when we had a prosperous wind: 'Because,' said he, 'if we continue to sail at the rate we do at present, we shall arrive off the island about the first watch of the night; and I fear lest, in the darkness, we may strike upon some of the rocks which abound under the sea on that coast: it is better therefore for us to keep out at sea all night, carrying only so much sail as may suffice to bring us under the island in the morning.' This was the opinion of the pilot: however we made land sooner than he expected, and cast anchor at Zacynthus just as the sun rose.

"The inhabitants of the port, which was not far distant from the city, flocked together at our arrival, as to an unusual spectacle. They admired the construction of our vessel, framed with regard both to size and beauty; and from thence formed an idea of the skill and industry of the Phœnicians. Still more did they wonder at our uncommon good fortune in having had so prosperous a passage, in the midst of winter, and at the setting of the Pleiades.

"Almost all the ship's company, while the vessel was being moored, hurried off to the city to buy what things they wanted. I strolled about in search of a lodging, somewhere on the shore, for the pilot had told me that we should probably winter at Zacynthus: to remain on board the ship would have been very inconvenient, because of the noisy crew, and our fugitives could not be so well concealed in the city as their situation required.

"When I had walked a little way, I saw an old fisherman sitting before his door, and mending his nets. I approached and addressed him—'Can you inform me, my good friend,' said I, 'where I can hire a lodging?'—'It was broken,' said he, 'near yonder promontory, having caught upon a rock.'—'This was not what I inquired,' said I; 'but you would do me a kind office if you will either receive me into your own house, or show me another where I may be taken in.'—'It was not I who did it, I warrant you,' said he; 'I was not in the boat; old age has not yet so dulled the faculties of Tyrrhenus. It was the fault of the lubberly boys which occasioned this mishap, who, from ignorance of the reefs, spread their nets in the wrong place.'

"Perceiving now that he was hard of hearing, I bawled out at the top of my voice, 'Good day to you! Can you show us, who are strangers, a place where we may find lodging?'—'The same to you,' answered he. 'You may, if you please, lodge with me; unless, perhaps, you are one of those who require a great many beds and chambers, and have a large number of servants with you.' Upon my saying: 'I have only two children with myself,'—'A very good number,' he replied, 'for you will find my family consist of only one more. I have two sons who live with me; their elder brothers are married and settled by themselves; I have, besides, the nurse of my children, for their mother has been some time dead; wherefore, good sir, do not hesitate, nor doubt that we shall receive gladly one whose first aspect is venerable and prepossessing.' I accepted his offer: and when I returned afterwards with Theagenes and Chariclea, the old fisherman received us with great cordiality, and assigned us the warmest and most convenient part of his habitation.

"The beginning of the winter passed here not unpleasantly. We lived together in the day time: at night we separated. Chariclea slept in one apartment, with the nurse, I in another, with Theagenes, and Tyrrhenus in a third, with his children. Our table was in common, and well supplied; the old man furnished it abundantly with provision from the sea. We frequently amused our leisure by assisting him in fishing, in which art he was very skilful, and had tackle for it in abundance, and suited for every season. The coast was convenient for placing his nets, and abounded with fish, so that most people attributed his success in his occupation to his good fortune alone, which was in part, however, owing to his skill. Thus, for some time, we lived in peace; but it is not permitted to the unhappy to be long at ease; nor could the charms of Chariclea, even in this solitude, be exempt from disturbance.

"The Tyrian merchant, that victor in the Pythian games, with whom we sailed, was very annoying to me; he took every opportunity of pressing me with earnestness, as a father, to grant him Chariclea in marriage. He vaunted his family and his fortune. He said that the vessel in which we sailed was entirely his property; and the greatest part of her cargo, which consisted of gold, precious stones, and silk. He crowned all these, and many other recommendations of himself, with his victory in Greece, which he thought reflected no small lustre upon him. I objected my present poverty, and that I could never bring myself to dispose of my daughter in a foreign country, and at such a distance from Egypt. 'Talk not of poverty,' he would reply; 'I shall esteem the gift of Chariclea's hand more than a portion of a thousand talents. Wherever she is, I shall look upon that place as my country; I am ready to change my destined course to Carthage, and sail with you wherever you please.'

"When, after some time, I saw the Phœnician relax nothing of his importunity, but that he grew more urgent every day in his solicitations, I determined to flatter him with fallacious hopes, lest he should offer some violence to us in the island, and promised I would do everything which he wished when we arrived in Egypt. But I had no sooner thus quieted him a little, than a new wave of trouble came rolling in upon me.

"Old Tyrrhenus accosted me one day as I was wandering in a retired part of the coast. 'My good Calasiris,' said he, 'Neptune is my witness, and all the gods, that I regard you as my brother, and your children as my own. I am come to discover to you a gathering danger which will occasion you great uneasiness, but which I cannot, with any regard to the laws of hospitality, conceal from one who lodges under my roof, and which it concerns you much to be acquainted with. A nest of pirates, concealed under the side of yonder promontory, are lying in wait for your Phœnician vessel. They are continually on the watch for your sailing out of port. I caution you, therefore, to beware, and to consider what you have to do; for it is on your account, or rather, as I suspect, on account of your daughter, that they have conceived this audacious design, which they are but too well prepared for.'

"'May the gods reward you,' said I, 'for your kind information; but, my dear Tyrrhenus, how did you obtain, your intelligence?'—'My trade,' he answered, 'makes me acquainted with these men; I take fish to them, for which they pay me a better price than others; and yesterday, as I was taking up my nets on the shore, Trachinus, the captain of the pirates, came and asked me if I knew when the Phœnicians intended to set sail. I, suspecting his intent, replied, that indeed I did not exactly know, but I supposed that it would be early in the spring. "Does the fair maiden, who lodges at your house, sail with them?"—"I really don't know," said I. "But why are you so curious?"—"Because I love her to distraction," he returned. "I did so at first sight. I never saw a form comparable to hers; and yet my eyes have been used to beauty, and I have had in my power some of the most charming captives of all nations."

"'I wished to draw him on a little, that I might get acquainted with his design. "Why," said I, "should you attack the Phœnicians; cannot you take her away from my house without bloodshed, and before they embark?"—"The regard I have for you," he returned, "prevents me from doing this. There is a sense of honour even among pirates towards friends and acquaintances. If I were to carry off the strangers from your house, it might bring you into some trouble; they would probably be required at your hands. Besides, by waiting for them at sea, I obtain two ends: I may make myself master of a rich vessel, as well as of the maid I love. One of these I must necessarily give up, if I make the attempt by land; neither would it be without danger so near the city: the inhabitants would soon become acquainted with my enterprize, and pursuit would be immediate." I praised his prudence, and left him. I now discover to you the design of these villains, and beseech you to adopt means for the preservation of yourself and your children.'

"Having heard this, I went away in great trouble, and revolving various thoughts in my mind, when I met, by accident, with my Tyrian merchant. He talked to me on the old subject, and gave me occasion to try him on a scheme which just then struck me. I related to him just as much of the fisherman's discovery as I thought proper. I told him that one of the inhabitants of Zacynthus, who was too powerful for him to resist, had a design to carry off Chariclea. 'For my part,' I added, 'I had much rather give her to you, as well on account of our acquaintance as of your opulent condition; and, above all, because you have promised to settle in our country after your marriage; if, therefore, you have this alliance much at heart, we must sail from hence in all haste, before we are prevented, and violence is offered.' He was much pleased at hearing me talk in this manner. 'You are much in the right, my father,' he said; and, approaching, kissed my head, and asked me when I would have him to set sail, for though the sea was at this season hardly navigable, yet we might make some other port, and so, escaping from the snares laid for us here, might wait with patience the approach of spring.—'If,' I replied, 'my wishes have weight with you, I would sail this very night.'— 'Be it so,' said he, and went away.

"I returned home. I said nothing to Tyrrhenus; but I told my children that, at the close of the day, they must embark again on board the vessel. They wondered at this sudden order, and asked the reason of it. I excused myself from explaining it then; but said, it was absolutely necessary that it should be obeyed.

"After a moderate supper I retired to rest; but I had no sooner fallen asleep, than an old man seemed to appear to me, in a dream: withered and lean, in other respects, but showing, from the muscular appearance of his knees, the marks of former strength. He had a helmet on his head; his countenance was intelligent and shrewd, and he seemed to drag one thigh after him, as if it had been wounded. He approached me, and said with a sarcastic smile,—'Do you alone treat me with contempt? All those who have sailed by Cephalene, have been desirous to visit my habitation, and to contemplate my glory; you only seem to despise me, and have not given me so much as a common salutation, though you dwell in my neighbourhood. But you shall soon suffer for this negligence; and shall experience the same calamities, and encounter the same enemies, both by sea and land, which I have done. But address the maiden you have with you in the name of my consort; she salutes her, as she is a great patroness of chastity, and foretells her, at last, a fortunate issue to all her troubles.'

"I started up, trembling, at the vision. Theagenes asked what ailed me. 'We shall be too late,' said I, 'for the ship is sailing out of port; it is this thought which has disturbed and awakened me; but do you get up and collect our baggage, and I will go and see for Chariclea.' She appeared at my first summons: Tyrrhenus, too, got up, and inquired what we were about. 'What we are doing,' said I, 'is by your advice; we are endeavouring to escape from those who are lying in wait for us; and may the gods preserve and reward you for all your goodness to us: but do you add this to all the favours you have already bestowed upon us; pass, I pray you, into Ithaca, and sacrifice for us to Ulysses, and beseech him to moderate the anger which he has conceived against us, and signified to me this night in a dream.' He promised he would do so, and accompanied us to the ship, shedding tears abundantly, and wishing us a prosperous voyage, and all sorts of happiness. In short, as soon as the morning star appeared, we set sail, much against the will of the crew, who were with difficulty persuaded by the Tyrian merchant, when they were told, that it was in order to escape from a pirate, who lay in wait for them. He knew that what they thought a fiction, was the sober truth.

"We encountered adverse winds, a swelling sea, and almost continual tempests; we lost one of our rudders; had our yard-arms much injured, and were in imminent danger of perishing, when we reached a promontory of Crete: here we determined to stay a few days, to repair our vessel and refresh ourselves. We did so, and fixed for putting again to sea the first day of the new moon, after her conjunction with the sun.

"We set sail, with a gentle south-west wind, directing our course towards Africa, which our pilot used all his endeavours to reach as soon as he could; for he said he had for some time observed a vessel hovering at a distance, which he took for a pirate. 'Ever since we left Crete,' says he, 'she has followed us; she steers the same course, and without doubt it is by design, not accident; for I have often changed my track, on purpose to see if she would do the same, and she has always invariably done so.' A great part of the crew were alarmed at this intelligence, and began to exhort each other to prepare for defence; others neglected it, and said it was a very common thing for small ships to follow in the wake of larger ones, for the sake of being directed in their way.

"While they were thus disputing, evening approached; the wind slackened gradually, breathed gently on the sails and now made them flutter a little, but hardly swelled them at all. At length it subsided into a dead calm, setting with the sun, or retiring, as I may say, to give advantage to our pursuers; for while there was a fresh gale our ship, spreading more canvas, far out-sailed them; but when the wind dropped, when the sea was smooth, and we were driven to make use of our oars, this light and small vessel soon came up with our large and heavy one. When they came near, one of the crew, an inhabitant of Zacynthus, cried out: 'We are undone, this is a pirate crew: I am well acquainted with the ship of Trachinus.'

"We were thunderstruck at this intelligence, and, in the midst of a sea calm, our vessel shook with a tempest of confusion; it was full of tumult, lamentation, and hurrying up and down. Some ran into the hold; others encouraged one another to resist and fight; a third party were for getting into the boat, and so attempting an escape. While they were thus in confusion, and mutually hindering each other, the approach of danger put an end to their disputes, and every one seized upon the weapon which was nearest to him.

"Chariclea and myself, embracing Theagenes, were hardly able to restrain his ardent spirit which was boiling for the fight; she assuring him that death should not separate them; but that the same sword which wounded him, should put an end to her life. I, as soon as I knew that it was Trachinus who pursued us, began to consider how best to promote our future safety. The pirates coming close up with us, crossed our course, and being very desirous of taking us, did not use their arms; but rowing round us, prevented our farther progress, like besiegers wishing to make us surrender upon terms. 'Fools,' they cried out, 'why are you so mad as to make a show of defence against so superior a force? drawing upon yourselves certain destruction! We are as yet disposed to treat you kindly; you may even now, if you please, get into your boats, and save your lives.'

"So long as a bloodless war was waged, the Phœnicians were bold enough and refused to quit the vessel. But when one of the pirates, more daring than his fellows, leapt into the ship, and began to cut at them right and left with his sword, and they became sensible that the matter was now serious, and that wounds and blood must settle it, they repented of their boldness, fell at their enemies' feet, begged for quarter, and promised to do whatever they were ordered.

"The pirates, although they had already begun the fight, and though the sight of blood commonly whets the angry passions, yet, at the command of Trachinus, unexpectedly spared the suppliants. A truce ensued, but a truce more dreadful, perhaps, than battle: it had the name of peace, but war would have been scarcely less grievous. The conditions of it were, that every man should quit the ship, with a single garment, and death was denounced against any one who should violate these terms. But life, it seems, is preferred by mankind before all other things; and the Tyrians (robbed as they were of their ship and wealth), as if they had gained rather than lost, contended with each other who should be the first to leap into the boat and so preserve their lives.

"When we came into his presence, according to command, Trachinus, taking Chariclea by the hand said; 'We wage not war against you, my charmer; although the hostilities are undertaken on your account. I have all along been following you, ever since you left Zacynthus, despising for your sake the sea and danger; be of good cheer, then, I will make you mistress, with myself, of all these riches.' It is the part of prudence to seize upon the opportunity. So she, remembering some of my instructions, smoothed her brow, which this sudden storm had ruffled, and composed her countenance to winning smiles.—'I give the gods thanks,' says she, 'for inspiring you with merciful sentiments towards us; but if you would win, and keep my confidence, give me this first mark of your goodwill—preserve to me my brother and my father, and do not order them to quit the ship, for I cannot live without them;' and with this she fell at his feet, and embraced his knees.

"Trachinus, thrilling with pleasure at her touch, that he might enjoy it the longer, purposely delayed granting her request. At last, melted by her tears, and subdued by her looks, he raised her up, and said—'I grant your prayer, as to your brother with pleasure, he seems a youth of spirit and may help us in our trade; but as for the old man, who is but useless lumber, if I preserve him, it is only out of great regard to your entreaties.'

"While this was passing the sun set, and the dusk of twilight surrounded us; the sea began to swell on a sudden, whether on account of the change of season, or the will of fortune, I know not; the sound of rising wind was heard. In a moment it swept down upon the sea, in stormy gusts, and filled the hearts of the pirates with tumult and apprehension; for they were overtaken with it after they had left their own bark, and had got on board our ship for the sake of plunder; this, from its size, they were unused to, and unable to manage: their seamanship was all extemporised and self-taught, each for himself, boldly exercised some department of his art. Some furled the sails, others clumsily pulled the ropes; one bungler ran to the prow, another attempted to manage the tiller at the stern; so that we were in imminent danger, not so much from the fury of the storm, which was not yet very violent, as from the ignorance and unskilfulness of the sailors and pilot, who as long as there was any glimmering of light, made a show of resisting the tempest; but, when darkness overshadowed us, totally gave the matter up. The waves now burst over us, and we were in peril of going to the bottom, when some of the pirates made an attempt to get again on board of their own bark, but were hindered and stopped by the rage of the increasing tempest, and by the exhortations of Trachinus; who told them, that if they would preserve the ship on board of which they were, together with its wealth, they might buy a thousand such boats as their own. At length they cut the cable by which it was kept in tow, maintaining that it might be the cause of a fresh storm to them, and that by so doing he provided for their future security; for if they should touch at any port, bringing an empty bark with them, an inquiry would naturally be made as to its crew. His comrades approved of what he had done, and found him to have shown his sense in two respects; for they felt the ship a good deal eased after the bark was turned adrift, but the tempest was by no means appeased; they were still tossed by wave following upon wave, the vessel suffered much injury, and was in great danger. Having with difficulty weathered the night, we drove all the next day, and towards the end of it made land, near the Heracleotic mouth of the Nile, and, against our wills, disembarked on the coast of Egypt. Our companions were full of joy; we were overcome with grief, and we felt ill-will to Neptune for our preservation—we should have preferred a death free from insult at sea, to a more dreadful expectation on land, and a continual exposure to the lawless wills of the pirates. They began to act in accordance with their nature on landing; for, proposing to offer a sacrifice of thanksgiving to Neptune, they brought Tyrian wine, and other requisites for the ceremony, out of the ship; and sent some of their comrades with store of money into the country, to buy up cattle, bidding them pay whatever price was asked. As soon as these returned with a whole herd of sheep and swine, the pirates who had stayed behind immediately set fire to a pile, sacrificed the victims, and prepared the feast.

"Trachinus took an opportunity of leading me aside, and thus addressed me;—'Father, I have betrothed your daughter to myself; and am preparing to celebrate the marriage this very day, combining the most delightsome festival with this sacrifice to the gods. That you may partake cheerfully of the approaching entertainment, and that you may inform your daughter, who, I hope, will receive the intimation with joy, I give you this previous notice of my intentions; not that I want your consent to put them in execution; my power is a pledge for the performance of my will: but I have thought it fitting and auspicious to receive a willing bride from the hands of a parent, who shall have before apprised and persuaded her.'

"I pretended approval of what he said, and gave thanks to the gods who had destined my daughter to the honour of being his spouse; and then retiring, I began to consider what I could do in this conjuncture. I soon returned, and besought him that the nuptials might be celebrated with greater pomp and circumstance than he seemed to hint at—that he would assign the vessel as a bridal chamber for Chariclea; that he would give orders that none might enter or disturb her there, that she might have time to get ready her wedding dress, and make other needful preparations for the ceremony; for it would be most unseemly, that she, whose family was illustrious, and wealth considerable; and above all, she who was about to be the bride of Trachinus, should not have what preparation and ornament the present occasion would permit; although the shortness of the notice, and inconvenience of the place, would not allow the celebration of the nuptials with that splendour which was befitting their station.

"Trachinus was overjoyed at hearing me talk in this manner; and said he would, with the greatest pleasure, order everything as I desired. In consequence of this, he gave strict directions that no one should approach the ship after they had taken everything out of it they wanted. They conveyed out tables, cups, carpets, canopies—the works of Tyrian and Sidonian hands, and every requisite for ministering to and adorning a feast. They carried in disorder upon their shoulders, heaps of rich furniture and utensils, collected with great care and parsimony, but now destined to be defiled by the licentiousness of a tumultuous entertainment. I took Theagenes, and went to Chariclea; we found her weeping. 'You are accustomed, my daughter,' said I, 'to these reverses, and yet you lament as if they were new to you. Has any fresh misfortune happened?'

"'Everything is unfortunate,' she replied; 'above all, the fatal passion of Trachinus, which there is now but too much reason to fear, both from his circumstances and opportunities, that he will soon attempt to gratify. Unexpected success inflames the desires of a licentious mind; but he shall have reason to rue his detested love. Death, certain death, shall withdraw me from his pursuit: yet the thought of being divided from you, and from Theagenes, if such a separation should become necessary, dissolves me into tears.'—'Your conjectures are but too true,' I replied: 'Trachinus is resolved to turn the entertainment, which usually follows a sacrifice, into a nuptial ceremony, and there you are to be the victim. He discovered his design to me, as to your father; but I was long ago acquainted with his violent passion for you, even ever since the conversation which I had with Tyrrhenus, at Zacynthus. But I concealed what I knew, that I might not prematurely afflict you with the dread of impending calamity, especially as I had hopes of escaping it. But since, my children, fate has ordered otherwise, and we are now in such hazardous circumstances; let us dare some noble and sudden deed; let us meet this extremity of danger courageously, and either preserve our lives with bravery and freedom, or resign them with fortitude and honour.' When they had promised to act as I should order, and I had directed them what they were to do, I left them to prepare themselves, and sought the pirate next in command to Trachinus. His name, I think, was Pelorus: I accosted him and told him that I had something agreeable to disclose to him. He followed me readily to a retired place, and I went on:

"'Son,' said I, 'hear in few words, what I have to say to you; the opportunity admits not of delay, or long discourse—to be brief, my daughter is in love with you. No wonder; you have fascinated her with your appearance, but she suspects that your captain will seize this opportunity of the sacrifice to marry her himself: for he has ordered her to be dressed and adorned as elegantly as her present time admits of. Consider then how you may best frustrate his intention, and obtain the damsel for yourself, who says she will rather die than become the spouse of Trachinus.' Pelorus listened eagerly to me: and then replied, 'Be of good cheer, father; I have long felt an equal affection for your daughter, and was seeking an opportunity of getting into her good graces. Trachinus therefore shall either voluntarily resign this maiden to me (to whom besides, I have a just claim, as having been the first to board your vessel), or he shall feel the weight of my hand, and his nuptials shall bear bitter fruits.' After this conversation I retired, that I might raise no suspicion. I went to my children—I comforted them—I told them that our scheme was in a very good train. I supped afterwards with our captors. When I observed them warm with wine, and ready to be quarrelsome, I said softly to Pelorus (for I had designedly placed myself near him), 'Have you seen how the maiden is adorned?'—'No,' said he.—'You may then, if you please,' I returned, 'if you will go aboard the vessel; privately though, for Trachinus has forbidden all access to it. You may there see her sitting, like the goddess Diana; but moderate your transports; take no freedoms, lest you draw down death both on yourself and her.'

"After this he took the first opportunity of withdrawing secretly, and entered with all speed into the ship. He there beheld Chariclea, with a crown of laurel on her head, and refulgent in a gold-embroidered robe, (for she had dressed herself in her sacred Delphic garments, which might, as the event should turn out, be either funereal or triumphant); everything about her was splendid, and bore the semblance of a bridal chamber. Pelorus was all on fire at the sight. Desire and jealousy raged in his bosom. He returned to the company, with a look which indicated some furious design. Scarcely had he sat down, when he broke out—'Why have I not received the reward which is justly due to me for having first boarded our prize?'—'Because you have not demanded it,' replied Trachinus. 'Besides, there has yet been no division of the booty.'—'I demand then,' said Pelorus, 'the maiden whom we have taken,'—'Ask any thing but her,' said the captain, 'and you shall have it.'—'Then,' returned the other, 'you break cutter's law, which assigns to the first who boards an enemy's ship, and meets the danger, the free and unrestricted choice of taking what he will.'—'I do not mean to break our private law,' said Trachinus; 'but I rest upon another law, which commands you all to be obedient to your captain. I have a violent affection for this maiden—I propose to marry her; and think I have a right, in this instance, to a preference: if you oppose my will, this cup which I hold in my hand, shall make you rue your opposition.' Pelorus, glancing his eyes on his companions—'See,' says he, 'the guerdon of our toils; just so may each of you be deprived of your rewards!' How, Nausicles, shall I describe the scene which followed? You might compare the company to the sea agitated by a sudden squall of wind: rage and wine hurried them headlong into the wildest excesses of tumult. Some took part with their captain, others with his opponent; some called out to obey their captain, others to vindicate the violated law. At length Trachinus raised his arm in act to hurl a goblet at Pelorus; but at that instant the other plunged a dagger into his side, and he fell dead on the spot. The fray now became general: dreadful blows were dealt on all sides; some in revenge of their captain, others in support of Pelorus; wounds were inflicted and received by sticks and stones, by cups and tables—shouts of victory and groans of defeat resounded everywhere. I retired as far as I could from the tumult, and gaining a rising ground, became, from a secure spot, a spectator of the dreadful scene. Theagenes and Chariclea did not escape a share in it; for he, as had been before agreed upon, joined himself sword in hand, to one of the parties, and fought with the utmost fury; she, when she saw the fight began, shot her arrows from the ship, sparing only Theagenes. She herself did not join either side, but aimed at the first fair mark she saw, herself being all the while concealed, but sufficiently discovering her enemies by the light of their fires and torches: they, ignorant of the hand which smote them, thought it a prodigy, and a stroke from heaven.

"All the crew besides being now stretched on the ground, Theagenes was left closely engaged in fight with Pelorus, an antagonist of tried courage, exercised in many a scene of bloodshed. Chariclea could now no longer assist him with her shafts, she dreaded lest in this hand-to-hand engagement, she might wound her lover instead of his antagonist. The event of the fight was for some time doubtful; at length Pelorus began to give way. Chariclea, deprived of all other means of assisting him, encouraged him with her voice. 'Be strong,' she cried out, 'be of good cheer, take courage, my life!'

"Her words inspired her lover with fresh spirit and resolution: they reminded him, that she, the prize of victory, still lived. Regardless of several wounds which he had received, he now made a desperate effort, rushed upon Pelorus, and aimed a fearful sword-cut at his head; a sudden swerve occasioned him to miss his blow, but his blade descended on his enemy's shoulder, and lopped off his arm above the elbow. The barbarian now had recourse to flight; Theagenes pursued him. What followed I am not able to relate—he came back without my perceiving it. I still remained on the eminence to which I had retired, not daring, in the night time, to proceed any farther in a hostile country. But he had not escaped the eye of Chariclea. I saw him at break of day lying, in a manner, dead; she sitting by, lamenting, and ready to kill herself upon him, but restrained by a glimmering of hope that he might still survive. I, thunderstruck at the suddenness with which our misfortunes by land had succeeded those by sea, was not able to speak. I could neither inquire into the particulars of the situation in which he had returned, nor attempt to comfort her, nor relieve him.

"At break of day, after I had descended from my eminence, I saw a band of Egyptian pirates coming down from a mountain which overlooked the sea. In a twinkling they had seized, and were carrying off, the youthful pair, together with what plunder they could take with them from the ship. I followed them at a distance, lamenting my own, and my children's misfortunes, unable to succour them, and thinking it best not to join them; cherishing some faint hope of future assistance. But I soon felt my own unfitness for the task, being left far behind by the Egyptians, and unable to follow them through steep and rugged roads. Since that time, until the recovery of my daughter, by the favour of the gods, and your goodness, O Nausicles, my days have passed in sorrow and tears."

Having said this, he wept. All who heard him wept with him; and a lamentation, not wholly unmixed with pleasure, pervaded the whole company. Tears readily flow when the head is warm with wine. At length Nausicles applied himself to comfort Calasiris.

"Father," said he, "be of good cheer, you have already recovered your daughter, and this night alone divides you from the presence of your son. To-morrow we will wait upon Mithranes, and do all in our power to ransom and free Theagenes."—"No wish is nearer to my heart," replied Calasiris, "but it is now time to break up our entertainment: let us remember the gods, and join with our libations, thanksgiving for my child's deliverance." Upon this the vases for libation were carried round, and the company dispersed.

Calasiris looked about for Chariclea; and having long watched the crowd as they came out, and not seeing her, at length he inquired for her of one of the women, and by her information went into the temple, where he found her fallen into a deep sleep, embracing the feet of the image of the deity, wearied by long prayer, and exhausted by grief. He dropped a tear over her, breathed out a petition for her happiness, and, gently waking her, conducted her to his lodging, blushing at her imprudence, in having suffered herself to be surprised by sleep in such a place. Here, in her chamber, with the daughter of Nausicles, she laid herself down to rest, but wakefulness compelled her to ruminate upon her sorrows.

Book VI

Calasiris and Cnemon betook themselves to their apartments on the men's side of the house, and composed themselves to rest. The night was quickly past, great part of it having been consumed in the preceding feast, and subsequent narration; but it passed too slowly for their impatience; and almost before day they were up, and presented themselves to Nausicles, urging him to inform them where he thought Theagenes was, and to lead them to him as soon as possible. He was not slow in complying with their request, and they set out under his direction. Chariclea was very earnest to accompany them, but they pressed, and at last obliged, her to remain where she was; Nausicles assuring her that they were not going far, and that they would soon return, and bring Theagenes with them. Here then they left her, struggling between sorrow for their departure, and joy for the promised hope of seeing her lover.

They had scarcely got out of the village, and were proceeding along the banks of the Nile, when they saw a crocodile creeping from the right side of the river to the left, and making his way swiftly down the stream. The rest of the party being used to the sight, regarded it with indifference, although Calasiris secretly thought that it portended some impediment in their expedition. But Cnemon was very much frightened at its appearance, though he could hardly be said to have seen the animal itself, but had rather had a glimpse of the shadow: he was so terrified as almost to run away. Nausicles burst into a laugh. "Cnemon," said Calasiris, "I thought you were apt to be terrified only in the darkness and obscurity of the night; but I see your courage shows itself even in the day-time. It is not only names that affright you, but the commonest and most every-day appearance puts you quite into a trepidation."—"Prithee tell me what god, or what demon is it," said Nausicles, "whose name this valiant Grecian cannot bear?"

"If it were the name of a deity," replied the old man, "there might be something in it; but it is the appellation of a mortal, and that not of a celebrated hero, nor even of a man; but of a weak woman, and, as he says, of a dead one too, at the mention of which he is disordered and trembles. That night in which you returned from the buccaneers, bringing with you my dearest Chariclea, this said name was, somehow or other, mentioned in his hearing: it put him into such an agitation, that he had no sleep all night, nor suffered me to enjoy any; he was half dead with fear, and I had the greatest difficulty in the world to bring him to himself; and were I not afraid of terrifying, or giving him pain, I would now mention the name, that you might laugh the more:"—and immediately he uttered the word *Thisbe*. But Nausicles did not laugh, as he expected; he became grave and pensive, doubting and pondering why and by reason of what intimacy Cnemon felt so much at the mention of Thisbe.

Cnemon upon this burst out into an immoderate fit of laughter in his turn. "See," said he, "my dear Calasiris, the mighty magic of this name; it is not only a bugbear which disturbs, as you say, all my faculties, but it has the same effect upon Nausicles; with this difference, however, that the certainty of her death inclines me to laughter, when the same news seems to make him sorrowful, who was before so disposed to be merry at the expense of others."—"Spare me," said Nausicles; "you have sufficiently revenged yourself: but I conjure you by the gods of hospitality and friendship—by the kind and sincere reception which you have met with at my house and table—that you will tell me how you became so well acquainted with the name of Thisbe—whether you really have known her, or only pretend to have done so, out of sport, and to vex me?"—"It is now your turn, Cnemon," said Calasiris, "to turn narrator. You have frequently promised to make me acquainted with your condition and adventures, and as often, on some pretext or other, have put it off: you cannot have a better opportunity of doing so than the present: you will oblige both Nausicles and me; and lighten, by your story, the fatigues of our journey."

Cnemon suffered himself to be persuaded, and entered upon his history, relating briefly, what he had before told more at length to Theagenes and Chariclea—That he was an Athenian—that his father was Aristippus, and his stepmother Demæneta—her execrable love, and the snares she laid for him on its disappointment, by the ministry of Thisbe—the particulars of these—his flight from his country, and condemnation as a patricide—his exile at Ægina—his hearing from Charias of the death of Demæneta, betrayed by her own wicked assistant Thisbe—what Anticles related to him of the distress his father fell into; the family of Demæneta combining against him, and persuading the people that he had murdered her—the flight of Thisbe from Athens, with a Naucratian merchant, who was in love with her—his sailing with Anticles to Egypt, in search of Thisbe; in order, if he could find her, to bring her back to Athens, to clear his father, and punish her—

the various difficulties and dangers he went through, both by sea and pirates—how, having escaped these, and arrived in Egypt, he was again taken by the pirates—his meeting and connection with Theagenes and Chariclea—the death of Thisbe—and every thing in order, till he came to his meeting with Calasiris and Nausicles, and to those facts and events with which they were acquainted.

Nausicles meanwhile revolved a thousand thoughts in his mind—now he was about to disclose all his transactions with Thisbe, and now inclined to defer it to another opportunity; but his eagerness for speaking had almost got the better of him, when some remains of reserve, and an accident which happened by the way, prevented his unbosoming himself for the present. They had travelled about eight miles, and were near to the village where Mithranes dwelt, when Nausicles meeting an acquaintance, inquired whither he was going in so much haste.

"Do you not know," he replied, "that all my exertions have now but one aim, that of executing the behests of Isias of Chemmis? I labour for her, I supply her with every thing she wants. I wake day and night in her service. I refuse no commission, small or great, which the dear Isias imposes on me, though toil and loss are all I have hitherto gotten for my pains. I am now making what haste I can with this bird which you see, a flamingo of the Nile, carrying it to my mistress, according to her commands."—"What an amiable mistress you have got," said Nausicles, "how light are her commands! how fortunate you are that she has not ordered you to bring her a phœnix, instead of a phœnicopter!"—"She does all these things," said the other, "out of wanton sport to make a jest of me—but may I ask where you are bending your course?"

When he had learned that they were going to Mithranes—"You are on a sleeveless errand," said he, "for Mithranes is not now here; he has this evening led out his troops on an expedition against the buccaneers of Bessus; for Thyamis, their leader, has made an incursion into his territories, and taken from him one of his captives, a Grecian youth, whom he was preparing to send to Oroondates, at Memphis; and from thence, as I suppose, as a present to the Great King. But I must be gone to Isias, (who is now, perhaps, looking for me with eager eyes), lest my delay offend my charmer; she is but too ready to seize a pretence, however slight, to flout and quarrel with me." While these words were yet in his mouth, he hurried off, leaving his hearers confused and stupified at his tidings.

Nausicles was the first who broke silence. He tried to encourage his companions; and told them, that they ought not to lose heart, and entirely lay aside their undertaking, on account of this short and temporary disappointment. That now, indeed, it was necessary to return to Chemmis, as well to consult upon what they had farther to do, as to make preparations for a longer expedition, which must be undertaken in search of Theagenes, whether he was with the buccaneers or anywhere else; but that he had good hopes of finding and recovering him: for he conceived that it was not without some kind interposition of Providence, that they had so fortunately met with an acquaintance whose intelligence put them into the right track, and plainly pointed out to them the pirate-settlement, as the first place where they were to seek their friend.

They assented, without difficulty, to his proposal; what they had heard giving them a glimmering hope, and Cnemon privately assuring Calasiris that he was sure that Thyamis would watch over the safety of Theagenes. They determined therefore to return to Chemmis, where, being arrived, they found Chariclea at the house door, with outstretched neck and eager eyes, looking on every side for their appearance. As soon as she saw them, and no Theagenes with them, fetching a deep and melancholy sigh—"Are you alone!" she cried, "Father? Do you return even as you set out?—Theagenes then is no more! Tell me, by the gods I beseech you, if you have any tidings for me! and whatever they may be, do not increase my misery by delaying them. There is a degree of humanity in discovering quickly unfortunate intelligence: the soul collects at once all its powers of resistance, and the shock is sooner over."

Cnemon hastening to repress her rising anguish—"How ready are you," said he, "to foretell calamities! You generally, however, prove a false prophetess, and so far you do well—Theagenes is not only living, but, I trust in the gods, safe;"—and he told her, briefly, in what condition, and where he was. "Ah, Cnemon!" said Calasiris, "one would think, from what you say, that you had never been in love! Do not you know that they who really love are apprehensive of the slightest trifles, and believe only their own eyes, when the situation of their lovers is concerned? Absence always fills their languishing souls with fear and torment; they imagine that nothing but the most invincible necessity can ever make them separate from each other. Forgive Chariclea, therefore, who labours under the extremity of this passion, and let us enter the house, and consider what we have to do;"—and taking Chariclea's hand, and soothing her with paternal tenderness, he led her in.

Nausicles, willing to solace his friends after their fatigues, and having, besides, a farther private end of his own, prepared a more than usually choice entertainment for them alone and his daughter, whom he commanded to dress and adorn herself with uncommon bravery and splendour. Towards the end of the feast he thus addressed them:

"I call the gods to witness, my friends, that your company is so agreeable to me, that I should be happy if you would spend the remainder of your lives here, and enjoy, in common with me, my wealth and pleasures. I wish to consider you so much more in the light of friends than guests, that I shall think nothing too much which I can bestow upon, or partake with you. I am ready also to give you every advice and assistance in my power, towards the recovery of your lost relation, as long as I can stay with you; but you know that I am a merchant, and that it is by this profession that I procure and increase my substance. And now, as the west winds have set in favourably, have opened the sea for navigation, and promise a prosperous season, my affairs call loudly upon me to sail into Greece. I am very desirous, therefore, of hearing what you propose to do, that I may endeavour, as much as possible, to accommodate my schemes to yours." Here he paused; and Calasiris, after a short pause, answered him:—"O Nausicles! may your voyage be fortunate!—may Hermes, the patron of gain, and Neptune the preserver, protect and accompany your expedition—may they lead you through smooth seas, may they make every haven safe—every city easy of access to you, and every inhabitant favourable to your undertakings—these are the sincere and grateful wishes of those whom you have received, and now, at their own request, dismiss after observing the exact law of friendship and hospitality. Though it is grievous and painful to us to leave you, and to depart from your house, which with so much generosity you have taught us in a manner to consider as our own; yet it is incumbent upon, and unavoidable for us, to apply ourselves immediately to the search and recovery of our lost friend. This is the fixed purpose of myself and Chariclea: let Cnemon speak for himself—whether he had rather gratify us, by accompanying us in our wanderings, or has any other project in his mind." Cnemon seemed now desirous of answering in his turn; and, preparing to speak, fetched, on a sudden, a deep sigh, and tears for some time stopped his utterance: at length collecting and composing himself as well as he could, he said—

"O fortune, fickle and uncertain goddess! how dost thou shower down misfortunes upon us miserable mortals! but upon none have thy persecutions been exerted with more unremitting severity than upon me. You deprived me of my family and father's house; banished me from my country and friends—after a long interval of calamities which I pass over, shipwrecked me upon the coast of Egypt; delivered me over to pirates; shewed me, at last, a glimmering of comfort, by making me acquainted with men, unfortunate, indeed, like myself, but at the same time Greeks, and such as I hoped to spend the remainder of my life with; but now you deprive me of this consolation, where shall I turn myself? What ought I to do? Shall I desert Chariclea, who has not yet recovered Theagenes? That would be infamous and abominable? Or shall I follow and attend her in her search? If there were a probable prospect of finding him, the hope of success would sweeten, and authorize my toils; but if that expectation is distant and uncertain, and the undertaking discouraging and difficult, who can tell where my wanderings will end? May I not, then, hope that you, and the deities of friendship, will forgive me, if I venture to mention a return to my family and country? especially since the gods offer me so unlooked-for an opportunity, in the voyage which Nausicles proposes making into Greece. Ought I to let slip so favourable an occasion? since, should any thing have happened to my father, his house will be left desolate, and his name and estate without a successor: and though I may be destined to spend the remainder of my days in poverty, yet it will be desirable and right in me, to preserve in my own person the remnant of my race. But, O Chariclea! I am most anxious to excuse myself to you, and to beg your forgiveness, which I beseech you to grant me. I will follow you as far as the quarters of the buccaneers; and will beg the favour of Nausicles, however pressed he may be in time, to wait for me so long. If perchance I should be so fortunate as to deliver you there into the hands of Theagenes, I shall then appear to have been a faithful guardian of the precious deposit which has fallen under my care, and shall set out on my own expedition with lucky omens, and a quiet conscience. But if (which the gods forbid!) I should be deceived in this hope, I shall still, I trust, appear excusable, in that I have gone so far, and have not left you alone, but in the hands of the excellent Calasiris, your father, and best preserver."

Chariclea meanwhile conjecturing, from many circumstances, that Cnemon was in love with the daughter of Nausicles (for one who is herself enamoured most easily detects the like affections in another), and seeing, from the behaviour and expressions of Nausicles, that he was very desirous for the alliance, that he had long been working at it, and endeavouring to allure Cnemon into it; and thinking it, besides, not perfectly proper, or free from suspicion, that he should any longer be the companion of her journey—"My friend," said she, "let us entreat you to act as is most agreeable to yourself: receive our best and most grateful thanks for all the favours you have bestowed upon us, and the good offices you have performed. For the future we have not so much need of your cares and attention, nor is there now any necessity that you should endanger your own fortunes, by waiting any longer upon ours. Go, then, under happy auspices, to Athens; may you there again find your family, and recover your estate. It would be blameable on you to neglect the opportunity which Nausicles offers you: I and Calasiris will struggle with the cross accidents which pursue us, till we may perhaps, at last, find some end to our wanderings. If we meet with no assistance from men, the gods, we trust, will not forsake us."

"May the immortals," said Nausicles, "accompany Chariclea, according to her prayers, and assist her in every thing! and may she soon recover her friend and parents: her generous spirit and excellent understanding well deserve success. Do you, Cnemon, regret no longer that you do not bring Thisbe back again with you to Athens, especially when you may accuse me of having carried her off clandestinely from thence; for the merchant of Naucratium, the lover of Thisbe, was no other than myself; nor have you any reason to apprehend distress or poverty. If your inclinations coincide with mine, you may not only recover your country and family, under my guidance, but enrich yourself to the extent of any reasonable desires. If you are willing to marry, I offer you my daughter, Nausiclea, with an ample portion, judging that I have received enough in that I have learned your family and nation."

Cnemon, seeing what had long been the object of his wishes and prayers, now unexpectedly offered him beyond his hopes, eagerly replied, "I take your offer with great joy, and gratitude;" and Nausicles immediately delivered his daughter into his outstretched hand, and betrothed her to him; and ordering those who were present to raise the nuptial song, he himself opened the dance, making the entertainment furnish forth a sudden wedding.

All the company were engaged in this joyous ceremony, the more pleasant, because unlooked for: the song resounded through the apartments, and during the whole night, the house shone with the marriage torches. But Chariclea, retiring from the rest, betook herself to her solitary chamber; where, having secured the door, and risking as she thought no intrusion, she surrendered herself to all the stings of frenzy. She let her dishevelled tresses fall upon her shoulders, tore and discomposed her garments, and thus broke out:—"Aye! let me too, in the manner he likes best, lead the dance before the overruling evil genius; let lamentations be my songs, and tears my libations: let darkness surround me, and obscure night preside over what I am about;" and with this she extinguished her torch against the ground. "What a dainty nuptial chamber has he provided me! He claims me for himself, and keeps me solitary. Cnemon marries and joins in the dance; Theagenes wanders a captive, perhaps, and in bonds; and provided he lives even that were well. Nausiclea is betrothed and separated from me, who, till this night, partook of my bed; and I am left alone and destitute. Heaven knows that I grudge them not their good fortune; I wish them all felicity; but I repine that I have no share of it myself. The tragedy of my misfortunes has been prolonged beyond example. But what avails it to spend my time in womanish lamentations! let the measure of my calamities be filled up, since such is the will of heaven. But, O Theagenes, my sweet and only care, if you are dead, and the dreadful tidings (which may the gods forbid!) should ever wound my ear, I swear instantly to join you in the shades below. Meanwhile let me offer to your spirit (if it has left the lovely body) these funeral rites" (and immediately she plucked off handfuls of her hair and laid them on the bed): "Let me pour a libation to you out of those eyes which you hold so dear;" and with this she bedewed her couch with her tears. "But, if you are alive and safe, appear to me, my life, in a dream; and repose with me, but preserve, even then, the respect you have sworn to your betrothed." So saying, she flung herself on the bed, embraced and kissed it; till sobs and groans, fatigue and grief, gradually overwhelmed with a cloud all her reasoning faculties; and she sunk, at last, into a deep sleep, which continued till late the following morning.

Calasiris, wondering that she did not appear as usual, went up to her chamber to inquire after her; where, knocking loudly at the door, and calling her repeatedly by her name, he at length awakened her. She, alarmed at this sudden call, and confused at the disorder both of her person and apartment; yet, went to the door, unbolted it, and let him in. He, when he saw her hair dishevelled, her garments torn, her eyes restless, and breathing still too much of that passion with which they had been inflamed before she dropped asleep, began to suspect something of the cause of this agitation. Leading her, therefore, again to the bed, placing her upon it, and helping her to compose her dress a little— "Why, Chariclea," says he, "do you indulge these transports? Why do you grieve thus beyond measure, and abjectly sink under the calamities which oppress you? I am now at a loss to discover that nobleness of mind, and chastened spirit, with which you have hitherto borne your ills. Have done with these unbecoming extravagancies—consider that you are a mortal creature; a thing unstable, subject to the blasts of good and evil fortune. Why abandon yourself to despair, perhaps, on the eve of a change of fortune? Preserve yourself, my child; if not for your own sake, at least for Theagenes, who lives only in and for you."

Chariclea blushed at his chiding, and at the circumstances in which he had surprised her. She was for some time silent. At last she said— "You have reason, I own, to blame me, Father: but, perhaps, you will not think me without excuse. My love for Theagenes is no new or vulgar passion, but pure and chaste; it is directed towards one who, though not my wedded husband, is my betrothed: I am grieved and disappointed at not seeing him return with you; and am in a thousand doubts and fears about his life and safety."

"Be comforted then," replied Calasiris, "trust in the oracles of the gods, and believe, that under their guidance and protection, he is both safe and well. You should remember what we heard yesterday—that he was taken by Thyamis, as he was being carried to Memphis; and, if he is in his power, you may be satisfied that he is safe; for there was a friendship between them even before. It is our business now to make what haste we can to the town of Bessa, in order to seek, you for your lover, and I for my son; for you have already heard that Thyamis stands in that relation to me."

Chariclea appeared very pensive at this.—"If indeed," said she, "this is your son, and not some other Thyamis, our affairs are in great jeopardy." Calasiris wondering at, and inquiring the cause of, her apprehensions,— "You know," she continued, "that I was for some time in the power of the pirates: there these unhappy features of mine inspired Thyamis with love. I fear lest, if in our inquiry we should meet with him, he should immediately recognize me, and compel me to a marriage which, on various pretences, I before with difficulty eluded."—"I trust," said the old man, "that the sight of me will inspire him with reverence and respect, and that a father's eye will repress and restrain his intemperate desires: however, there is no reason why we should not endeavour, by some artifice, to guard against what you fear; and you seem expert at finding out excuses and delays, against those who show themselves too pressing."

Chariclea, recovering her spirits a little at this pleasantry—"I do not know whether you are in jest or earnest:" said she, "but I can relate to you the contrivance of Theagenes and myself, when we attempted to make our escape from the pirates' island; and, if you approve of it, we may make use now of the same stratagem; and may it be more fortunate than it was then! We determined to change our garments, to metamorphose ourselves into beggars, and in this squalid garb to pass through the towns and villages. Let us now then, if you please, put on the appearance of wretchedness: we shall be less subject to inquiry and observation. The greatest security is found in the lowest estate. Poverty is an object of pity, not of envy; and we shall more easily procure our daily bread: for, in a foreign land, every thing is sold dear to strangers; but is cheaply given to the wretched."

Calasiris approved of the project, and besought her to be ready as soon as possible to set out. They acquainted Nausicles and Cnemon with their intentions, and in three days were prepared to enter on their expedition. They took no beast of burden with them, though they might have had one, nor suffered any one to attend them. Nausicles and Cnemon, and all their family, accompanied them as far as they would permit it. Nausiclea, too, having by earnest entreaties obtained her father's permission, set out with her friend; her love for Chariclea making her break through that reserve and retirement which young women are expected to preserve during the first days of their nuptials. They accompanied them about half a mile; and then, saluting each other, and mingling tears and every good wish with their embraces, they took their leave. Cnemon repeatedly besought them to pardon those nuptial engagements which prevented his going with them; and promised that, whenever he had an opportunity, he would endeavour to find them out.

At length they separated. Nausicles, and his train, took the road to Chemmis. Chariclea and Calasiris began the transformation which they had meditated, and clothed themselves in tattered garments, which they had got ready. She stained her cheeks with a compound of soot and dust, and threw an old torn veil negligently over her face. She carried a bag under her arm, which had the appearance of being a receptacle for scraps and broken victuals, but contained, in reality, the sacred vestments she had brought from Delphi—her garlands, and the precious tokens which her mother had exposed with her.

Calasiris carried her quiver, wrapt up in a piece of old leather, as a burden, across his shoulders; and, loosening the string of her bow, made use of it as a walking-stick. If any one approached, he leant heavily upon it, stooping more than his years actually obliged him to do; and, limping with one leg, suffered himself frequently to be led by Chariclea.

When the metamorphosis was completed they could not help smiling at each other's appearance, and, in the midst of their grief, a few jokes upon it escaped them; and beseeching the deities who persecuted them to cease at length from their anger, they made what haste they could to the town of Bessa, where they hoped to find Theagenes and Thyamis. But in this they were disappointed; for arriving near Bessa at sun-setting, they saw the ground strewed with a considerable number of dead bodies, newly slain; most of them were Persians, whom they knew by their habits, but some were the natives of the place. They conjectured this to have been the work of war, but were at a loss to know who had been the combatants. At length, while they were searching and examining the corpses, dreading lest they might find a friend among them (for strong affection is unreasonably apprehensive on the slightest grounds), they saw an old woman, hanging over the body of one of the natives, and loud in her lamentations. They resolved therefore to endeavour to get what intelligence they could from her; and, accosting her, they first tried to soothe her vehement affliction; and then, when she became a little calmer, Calasiris, in the Egyptian tongue, ventured to ask her what was the cause of the slaughter they saw before them, and who it was whom she so lamented. She answered, briefly, that she was mourning for her son; that she came on purpose to the field of battle that some one of the combatants, if any should return, might deprive her of life, now become a burden to her; that meanwhile, amid tears and lamentations, she was endeavouring, as well as she could, to perform funeral rites for her child. The cause of the engagement, says she, was as follows:—"A foreign youth, of remarkable beauty and stature, was proceeding under the direction of Mithranes, the Persian Commandant, in his way to Memphis, where he was to be presented to Oroondates, the Viceroy of the Great King. Mithranes had taken him captive, and thought he could not offer a more agreeable gift. The inhabitants of our town pretending, whether truly or not I cannot say, that they had some knowledge of this young man, came suddenly upon the soldiers of Mithranes, and rescued him. Mithranes, when he heard of it, was violently enraged, and two days ago led his troops against the town. My countrymen are used to war; they lead a piratical life, and despise death when gain or revenge are in view. Many are the widows and orphans they have made, and many mothers have they deprived of their children, as I, unhappy woman, am at this day. As soon, therefore, as they had certain intelligence of the Persians' expedition, they left the city, chose a proper place for an ambuscade, and posting, in concealment, a select body of troops where they knew the enemy must pass, as soon as they appeared, attacked them resolutely in front, while the rest of their companions rushed suddenly, with a great shout, from their ambush, fell upon their flank, and soon put them to the rout. Mithranes fell among the first, and most of his troops with him; for they were so surrounded, that there was little opportunity for flight. A few of our people were slain, and among those few my son, transfixed, as you see, with a Persian dart; and now I, unhappy that I am, am bewailing his loss; and, perhaps, am still reserved to lament that of the only son I have now left, who marched yesterday with the army against the city of Memphis."

Calasiris inquired into the cause of this expedition. The old woman told him what she had heard from her son: That the inhabitants of Bessa, after they had slaughtered the officer and soldiers of the Great King, saw plainly that there was no room for excuse or pardon; that Oroondates, as soon as the intelligence reached Memphis, would immediately set out with his army, surround, besiege, and utterly destroy their town; that therefore they had resolved to follow up one bold deed by a bolder; to anticipate the preparations of the Viceroy; to march, in short, without delay to Memphis, where, if they could arrive unexpectedly, they might possibly surprise and seize his person, if he were in the city; or if he were gone, as was reported, upon an expedition into Ethiopia, they might more easily make themselves masters of a place which was drained of its troops, and so might for some time ward off their danger; and could also reinstate their captain, Thyamis, in the priesthood, of which he had been unjustly deprived by his younger brother. But if they should fail in the bold attempt, they would have the advantage of dying in the field, like men, and escape falling into the hands of the Persians, and being exposed to their insults and tortures. "But, as for you," continued the old woman, "where are you going?"—"Into the town," said Calasiris.—"It is not safe for you," returned she, "at this late hour, and unknown as you are, to go among strangers."—"But if you will receive us into your house," replied the other, "we shall think ourselves safe."—"I cannot receive you just at this time," said she, "for I must now perform some nocturnal sacrifices. But if you can endure it—and indeed you must do so, retire to some distance from the slain, and endeavour to pass the night as well as you can in the plain; in the morning I will gladly receive and entertain you as my guests." When she had said this, Calasiris took Chariclea, and shortly explained to her what had passed between them; and going to a rising ground, not very far from the field of battle, he there reclined himself, putting the quiver under his head.

Chariclea sat down on her wallet—the moon just rising, and beginning to illuminate all around with her silver light; for it was the third day from the full. Calasiris, old, and fatigued with his journey, dropped asleep; but Chariclea's cares kept her waking, and made her spectatress of an impious and accursed scene, but not an unusual one, among the Egyptians. For now the old woman, supposing herself at liberty, and unobserved, dug a sort of pit, and lighted a fire of sticks which she had collected together, on each side of it. Between the two fires she placed the dead body of her son, and taking an earthen cup from a neighbouring tripod, she poured first honey into the trench, then milk, and then wine. She next worked up a kind of paste of dough into something of the similitude of a man, and crowning it with laurel and fennel, cast that too into the ditch. Then snatching up a sword, with many frantic gestures and barbarous invocations to the moon, in an unknown tongue, she wounded herself in the arm, and dipping a branch of laurel in her blood, sprinkled it over the fire. And after many other wild and mystic ceremonies, she stooped down at length to the corpse of her son, whispered something in its ear, and, by the power of her spells, raised and forced it to stand upright.

Chariclea, who had observed the former part of this ceremony, not without apprehension, was now seized with affright and horror, and awakened Calasiris, that he too might be a spectator of what was being done. They, being themselves shrouded in darkness, observed in security what passed by the light of the fires, and were near enough too to hear what was said; the old woman now questioning the dead body in a loud voice,—"Whether its brother, her son, would return in safety?"—it answered nothing; but nodding its head by a doubtful signal, gave its mother room to hope, and then, on a sudden, fell down again upon its face. She turned the body on its back, repeated her question, and whispered, as it should seem, still stronger charms in its ear; and brandishing her sword now over the fire, and now over the trench, raised the corpse again, and putting the same interrogation to it, urged it to answer her, not by nods and signs only, but in actual and distinct words.

Here Chariclea addressed Calasiris, and besought him to approach, and ask something about Theagenes; but he refused altogether; declaring, that it was much against his inclination that he became a compulsory spectator of so impious a scene; for it did not become a priest to be present at, much less to take a part in, such a deed.—"Our divinations," said he, "are made by means of lawful sacrifices, and pure prayers; not by profane ceremonies, and unhallowed conjurations of dead carcases, such as our wayward fate has now obliged us to be witnesses of." But while he was proceeding, the body, with a deep and hollow voice, began to speak, as if its words were uttered from the inmost recesses of a winding cave. "I spared you at first, O mother, although you were transgressing the laws of nature, disregarding the decrees of the fates, and disturbing by your enchantments, what ought to remain at rest. There is, even among the departed, a reverence for parents; but since, as far as in you lies, you destroy that reverence, and persist in pushing your wicked incantations to the utmost—since you are not content with raising up a dead body, and forcing it to make signs, but will proceed to compel it to speak; regardless of the care you owe to your son's remains, preventing his shade from mixing with those who are gone before him, and mindful only of your own private convenience and curiosity—hear what I piously avoided disclosing to you before:

"Your son shall return no more; and you yourself shall perish by the sword, and shortly conclude your course by a violent death, worthy of the execrable practices in which you have spent your life; you who are not now alone, as you suppose yourself; but are performing your horrid rites, worthy of being buried in the deepest silence and darkness, in the sight of others, and betraying the secrets of the dead in the hearing of witnesses. One of them is a priest; and his wisdom indeed is such, that he may perhaps see the propriety of concealing what he has seen. He is dear to the gods; and if he hastens his journey, he may prevent his sons from engaging singly with each other in a bloody and deadly fight, and compose their differences. But what is infinitely worse, a maiden has heard and seen everything which has taken place. She is deeply in love, and is wandering through the world in search of her lover, whom, after many toils and dangers, she shall at last obtain, and, in a remote corner of the earth, pass with him a splendid and royal life."

Having said this, the body fell again prone on the ground. The old woman concluding that the strangers were the spectators meant, ran furiously, in all the disorder of her dress, and sword in hand, to seek for them among the dead, where she imagined they had concealed themselves; determined to destroy, if she could find them, the witnesses of her abominable incantations. But while searching incautiously among the carcases, and blinded by her fury, she stumbled, and fell headlong upon a fragment of a spear stuck upright in the earth, which, piercing through her body, soon put an end to her wicked life, and quickly fulfilled the fatal prophecy of her son.

Book VII

O n the other hand, Calasiris and his fair companion, having been in such danger, in order to be free from their present terrors, and hastening, on account of the prophecy they had heard, continued, with diligence, their journey to Memphis. They arrived at the city at the very time when those events were being fulfilled which had been foretold in the incantation scene. The citizens of Memphis had just time to shut their gates, before the arrival of Thyamis and his robber band; a soldier from the army of Mithranes, who had escaped from the battle of Bessa having foreseen, and foretold, the attempt.

Thyamis having ordered his men to encamp under the walls, rested them after the fatigues of their march; and determined forthwith to besiege the city. They in the town who, surprised at first, expected the attack of a numerous army, when they saw from their walls the small number of their assailants, put themselves in motion, and collecting the few troops, archers and cavalry, left for the defence of the place, and arming the citizens as best they could, were preparing to issue out of the gates, and attack their enemy in the field. But they were restrained by a man of some years and authority among them, who said, that although the Viceroy Oroondates was absent in the Ethiopian war, it would be improper for them to take any step without the knowledge and direction of his wife, Arsace; and that the soldiers who were left, would engage much more heartily in the cause, if fighting under her orders.

The multitude joined with him in opinion, and followed him to the palace which the viceroy inhabited in the absence of the sovereign. Arsace was beautiful, and tall; expert in business; haughty because of her birth, as being the sister of the Great King; extremely blameable, however, in her conduct, and given up to dissolute pleasure. She had, in a great measure, been the cause of the exile of Thyamis: for when Calasiris, on account of the oracle which he had received relative to his children, had withdrawn himself privately from Memphis, and on his disappearing, was thought to have perished; Thyamis, as his eldest son, was called to the dignity of the priesthood, and performed his initiatory sacrifice in public. Arsace, as she entered the temple of Isis, encountered this blooming and graceful youth, dressed on the occasion with more than usual splendour. She cast wanton glances at him, and by her gestures gave plain intimation of her passion. He, naturally modest, and virtuously brought up, did not notice this, and had no suspicion of her meaning, nay, intent on the duties of his office, probably attributed her conduct to some quite different cause. But his brother Petosiris, who had viewed with jealous eyes his exaltation to the priesthood, and had observed the behaviour of Arsace towards him, considered how he might make use of her irregular desires, as a means of laying a snare for him whom he envied.

He went privately to Oroondates, discovered to him his wife's inclinations, and basely and falsely affirmed that Thyamis complied with them. Oroondates was easily persuaded of the truth of this intelligence, from his previous suspicions; but took no notice of it to her, being unable clearly to convict her; and dreading and respecting the royal race she sprang from, thought it best to conceal his real opinion. He did not, however, cease uttering threats of death against Thyamis, until he drove him into banishment; when Petosiris was appointed to the priesthood in his room.

These events happened some years before the time of which I am at present speaking. But now the multitude surrounded the palace of Arsace, informed her of the approach of a hostile army (of which however she was aware) and besought her to give orders to the soldiers to march out with them to attack the enemy.

She told them that she thought she ought not to comply with their request, till she had made herself a little acquainted with the number of the enemy—who they were—from whence they came—and what was the cause of their expedition. That for that purpose she thought it would be proper for her first to ascend the walls, to take a survey from thence; and then having collected more troops, to determine, upon consideration, what was possible and expedient to be done.

The people acquiesced in what she said, and advanced at once towards the wall; where, by her command, they erected upon the ramparts a tent, adorned with purple and gold-embroidered tapestry; and she, royally attired, placed herself under it, on a lofty throne, having around her, her guards in arms, glittering with gold; and holding up a herald's wand, the symbol of peace, invited the chiefs of the enemy to a conference under the walls.

Thyamis and Theagenes advanced before the rest, and presented themselves under the ramparts, in complete armour, their heads only uncovered: and the herald made proclamation:—

"Arsace, wife of the chief viceroy, and sister of the Great King, desires to know who you are—what are your demands—and why you presume to make incursions into the territory of Memphis?"—They replied, that their followers were men of Bessa.—Thyamis, moreover, explained who he was: how being unjustly deprived of the priesthood of Memphis by the suspicions of Oroondates, and the arts of his brother Petosiris, he was come to claim it again at the head of these bands—that if they would restore him to his office, he asked no more; and his followers would withdraw in peace, without injuring any one; but if they refused this just demand, he must endeavour to do himself justice by force and arms— that it became Arsace to revenge herself upon Petosiris for his wicked calumnies against her; by which he had infused into the mind of her husband suspicions against her honour; and had driven him, his brother, into exile.

These words made a great impression upon the citizens: they well recollected Thyamis again; and now knowing the cause of his unexpected flight, of which they were ignorant before, they were very much disposed to believe that what he now alleged was truth. But Arsace was more disturbed than any one, and distracted by a tempest of different cares and thoughts. She was inflamed with anger against Petosiris, and calling to mind the past, resolved how she might best revenge herself upon him. She looked sometimes at Thyamis, and then again at Theagenes: and was alternately drawn by her desires towards both. Her old inclination to the former revived; towards the latter a new and stronger flame, hurried her away: so that her emotion was very visible to all the by-standers. After some struggle, however, recovering herself, as if from convulsive seizure, she said, "What madness has engaged the inhabitants of Bessa in this expedition? and you, beautiful and graceful youths of noble birth, why should you expose yourselves to manifest destruction for a band of marauders, who, if they were to come to a battle, would not be able to sustain the first shock? for the troops of the Great King are not so reduced as not to have left a sufficient force in the city to surround and overwhelm all of you, although the viceroy be absent in a foreign war. But since the pretext of this expedition is of a private nature, why should the people at large be sufferers in a quarrel in which they have no concern? Rather let the parties determine their dispute between themselves, and commit their cause to the justice and judgment of the gods. Let, then, the inhabitants both of Memphis and the men of Bessa remain at peace; nor causelessly wage war against each other. Let those who contend for the priesthood engage in single combat, and be the holy dignity the prize of the conqueror."

Arsace was heard by the inhabitants of Memphis with pleasure, and her proposal was received with their unanimous applause. They suspected the wickedness and treachery of Petosiris, and were pleased with the prospect of transferring to his single person the sudden danger which threatened the whole community. But the bands of Bessa did not so readily agree; they were at first very averse to expose their leader to peril on their behalf, until Thyamis at length persuaded them to consent; representing to them the weakness and unskilfulness of Petosoris, whereas he should engage in the combat with every possible advantage on his side. This reflection probably influenced Arsace in proposing the single combat. She hoped to obtain by it her real aim, revenge upon Petosiris, exposing him to fight with one so much his superior in skill and courage.

The preparations for the encounter were now made with all celerity; Thyamis, with the utmost alacrity, hastening to put on what still he wanted to complete his armour. Theagenes encouraging him, securely buckled on his arms, and placed, lastly, a helmet on his head, flashing with gold, and with a lofty crest.

On the other hand, Petosiris protested against the combat. He was obliged by violence to put on his arms; and, by the command of Arsace, was thrust out of the gates. Thyamis seeing him—"Do you observe, Theagenes," said he, "how Petosiris shakes with fear?"—"Yes," replied the other; "but how (resumed he) will you use the victory which seems ready to your hands; for it is no common foe whom you are going to encounter, but a brother?"—"You say well;" he returned, "and have touched the very subject of my thoughts. I intend to conquer him with the assistance of the gods, but not to kill him. Far be it from me to suffer myself to be so far transported by anger, resentment, or ambition, as to pursue revenge for past injuries, or purchase future honours at the expense of a brother's blood!"

"You speak nobly," said Theagenes; "and as one who feels the force of natural ties; but have you any commands for me?"—"The combat I am going to engage in," said Thyamis, "is a mere trifle, fit to be despised; but since Fortune sometimes sports with mortals, and strange accidents happen, I will just say, that if I prove victor, you shall accompany me into the city, live with me, and partake equally with myself, of everything which my fortune and station can afford. But if, contrary to my expectation, I should be vanquished, you shall command the bands of Bessa, with whom you are in great favour, and shall lead for a time the life of a freebooter, till the Deity shall place you in more prosperous circumstances." Having said this, they embraced each other with great affection; and Theagenes sat down to observe the issue of the fight.

In this situation he unconsciously afforded Arsace an opportunity of feeding herself upon his presence, as she surveyed his person, and gratified at least her eyes. And now Thyamis advanced towards Petosiris; but Petosiris could not sustain his approach, and on his first movement turned about towards the gate, and attempted to re-enter the city, but in vain; for those who were stationed at the entrance drove him back; and those who were upon the walls gave notice throughout the whole circuit of the place, that he should nowhere be admitted. He fled then as fast as he could around the city, and at length threw away his arms. Thyamis pursued him; and Theagenes followed, solicitous for his friend, and desirous of seeing what would happen. He took no arms with him, lest it might appear that he came to assist Thyamis; but, placing his spear and shield where he had before sat, and leaving them for Arsace to contemplate in his stead, he attended closely on the steps of the brothers.

Petosiris was not yet taken, nor was he far in advance; he was every minute in danger of being reached, and had only so much the advantage of the course, as it was reasonable to suppose an unarmed man would have over one who was in armour. In this manner they twice circled the walls; but the third time Thyamis approached near enough to threaten the back of his brother with his spear. He called on him to stop and turn, if he would avoid receiving a wound; the multitude meanwhile upon the walls, as in a theatre, being spectators and judges of the contest.

Just at this instant, either the interposition of the Deity, or the caprice of Fortune, who rules the affairs of men, introduced an episode upon the stage, and supplied, as if out of rivalry, a beginning for another drama. Calasiris, who had submitted to a voluntary exile, and had supported innumerable perils, both by sea and land, in order to avoid the dreadful sight, was brought to the spot at that very hour, and compelled by inevitable fate to become a witness of the encounter of his sons, as the oracle had long ago foretold he should be. As soon as he arrived near enough to see what was passing under the walls of Memphis—when he recognised his children, recollected the prophecy, and saw the arms of one of them raised against the other, he hastened with greater speed than his age seemed to admit of, (doing violence to his weight of years), to prevent the dreaded issue of the combat.

Having nearly reached them, he exclaimed with all his might—"My children! what mean you? what madness is this!" They, intent on what they were themselves engaged in, did not recognise their father, covered as he was with beggar's weeds, but took him for some wandering vagrant, who was probably beside himself. Those who were on the walls, wondered at his so rashly exposing himself between the combatants. Others laughed at what they thought his mad and fruitless efforts. When the good old man perceived that he was not known under these mean garments, he cast aside the tatters under which he was disguised; let his sacred locks flow down upon his shoulders, threw away his scrip and staff, and stood before them with a reverend and priest-like aspect; gently inclining his body, and stretching out his hands as a suppliant: his tears flowed apace, while he exclaimed—"O my sons, I am Calasiris—I am your father— stay your hands—repress your fatal rage—receive, acknowledge, and reverence your parent."

Almost ready to swoon, the young men slackened in their course, and cast themselves before his feet, hardly believing what they saw; but when they were convinced that it was really Calasiris, and no phantom, they embraced his knees, and clung to him, their minds labouring with various and conflicting feelings. They were rejoiced at seeing their father unexpectedly safe—they were ashamed and hurt at the circumstances in which he had found them—they were confused and solicitous at the uncertainty of what was to follow.

The spectators from the city gazed with wonder at what was passing, and observed it in silence, without interfering. They were, in a manner, astounded with ignorance and surprise, and stood like figures on a painter's canvas, rivetted upon the scene before them, when lo! a new actress made her appearance on the stage. Chariclea followed close after Calasiris. The eye of a lover is quick as lightning in recognising the object of its passion—a single gesture, the fold of a garment, seen behind, or at a distance, is sufficient to confirm its conjectures. When she knew Theagenes afar off, transported at the long-wished-for sight, she ran franticly towards him, and, falling on his neck, embraced him closely, breathing out her passion in inarticulate murmurs.

He, when he saw a squalid face, disguised, and industriously discoloured, her tattered garments, and vile appearance, repulsed and threw her from him with disgust, as some common beggar; and when she still persisted, and hindered his seeing Calasiris and his children, he smote her on the face. She softly said to him—"O Pythias, have you then forgotten the torch?" He, startled as at the sudden stroke of an arrow, recognized the token which had been agreed upon between them; and, looking at the countenance of Chariclea, which broke on him like the sun from behind a cloud, rushed into her embrace. All those upon the walls, including Arsace herself, who swelled with displeasure and already viewed Chariclea with jealous eyes, were overcome with wonder, as at some scenic exhibition.

The unnatural warfare between the brothers was now ended; the tragedy which threatened blood, had passed into a comedy. The father, who had seen them armed against each other, and had nearly been a spectator of the wounds of one of them, became the instrument of peace. He who was unable to avoid the fated spectacle of his sons' hostilities, was fortunate enough to rule the issue of what fate had ordered.

They recovered their father after a ten years' exile; and they hastened to crown and invest him again with the ensigns of that dignity, which had nearly been the cause of a bloody contest between them. But amid all these successes the love scene of the drama triumphed—Theagenes and Chariclea, blooming in youth and beauty, and sparkling with pleasure at having recovered one another, attracted the eyes of every beholder. Nearly the whole city poured out through the gates, and a multitude of every age and sex hurried into the plain. The young men surrounded Theagenes; those in the prime of life, and who had formerly known him, crowded round Thyamis; the maidens who already indulged in dreams of wedlock followed Chariclea; the old men and priests attended upon and congratuled Calasiris:—thus a kind of sacred procession was formed upon the instant.

Thyamis dismissed the men of Bessa with much gratitude, and many thanks for their ready assistance. He promised by the next full moon to send them a hundred oxen, a thousand sheep, and ten drachmas each; and then, placing his neck within the embrace of the old man, he supported on one side the tottering steps of his weary father, whom fatigue, surprise, and joy had well nigh exhausted. Petosiris on his side did the same: and thus they led him, with lighted torches, and the applause and congratulations of the surrounding multitude, to the temple of Isis; pipes and sacred flutes attending the procession, and stimulating the spirits of the young to activity in the holy dance. Neither was Arsace herself absent from the ceremony, for with guards, attendants, and much pomp, she proceeded to the temple of Isis, where she offered gold and precious stones, under pretence of setting an example to the city, but having eyes for Theagenes alone, and gazing upon him with more eagerness than did all the others; yet the pleasure she received was not unmixed. Theagenes held Chariclea by the hand, and for her he removed the surrounding crowd, and the keen stings of jealousy sunk deep into the breast of Arsace.

But Calasiris, when he arrived at the innermost part of the temple, threw himself on his face, and continued so long prostrate and motionless at the feet of the sacred image, that he was near expiring under emotion. The bystanders gently raised and set him on his feet; and when with difficulty, and by degrees, he came to himself, he poured out a libation to the goddess, and, in the midst of vows and prayers, took the sacred diadem of the priesthood from his own head, and placed it on that of his son Thyamis; saying to the spectators—"That he felt himself old, and saw his end approaching—that his eldest son was his lawful successor in the office—and that he possessed the needful vigour, both of mind and body, for exercising the functions of it."

The multitude testified, by their acclamations, their approbation of what he said; and he retired with his sons, and Theagenes, to those apartments of the temple which are set apart for the high-priest. The crowd separated to their several habitations; and Arsace at length departed, unwillingly, and often turning back, under pretence of greater respect to the goddess; at last, however she did depart, casting back her eyes as long as possible upon Theagenes.

As soon as she arrived at her palace, she hurried to her chamber, and, throwing herself upon the bed, in the habit she had on, lay there a long time speechless. She was a woman ever inclined to sensual passion; and was now inflamed above measure by the beauties and grace of Theagenes, which excelled any she had ever beheld. She continued restless and agitated all night, turning from one side to the other, fetching deep and frequent sighs; now rising up, and again falling back on her couch; now tearing off her clothes, and then again throwing herself upon her bed; calling in her maids without cause, and dismissing them without orders. In short, her unrestrained love would certainly have driven her into frenzy, had not an old crone, Cybele by name, her bedchamber woman, well acquainted with her secrets, and who had ministered to her amours, hurried into the chamber.

Nothing had escaped her notice, and she now came to add fuel to the flame; thus addressing her:—"What ails you, my dear mistress?

What new passion tortures you? Whose countenance has raised such a flame in my nursling's soul? Is there any one foolish or insolent enough to overlook or contemn advances from you? Can any mortal see your charms unmoved, and not esteem your favours as a most supreme felicity? Conceal nothing from me, my sweet child. He must be made of adamant, indeed, whom my arts cannot soften. Only tell me your wishes, and I will answer for the success of them. You have more than once made trial of my skill and fidelity." With these and such like insinuating persuasions, and falling at the feet of Arsace, she entreated her to disclose the cause of her sufferings and agitations. The princess at last, composing herself a little, said—

"Good nurse! I have received a deeper wound than I have ever yet felt; and though I have frequently, on similar occasions, successfully experienced your abilities, I doubt whether they can avail me now. The war which threatened our walls yesterday, has ended without bloodshed, and has settled into peace; but it has been the cause of raising a more cruel war within my bosom, and of inflicting a deep wound, not on any part of my body, but on my very soul, by offering to my view, in a luckless hour, that foreign youth who ran near Thyamis during the single combat. You must know whom I mean, for his beauty shone so transcendently among them all, as to be conspicuous to the rudest and most insensible to love, much more to one of your matured experience. Wherefore my dearest nurse, now that you know my wound, employ all your skill to heal it; call up every art, work with every spell and will which years have taught you, if you would have your mistress survive; for it is in vain for me to think of living, if I do not enjoy this young man."

"I believe I know the youth of whom you speak," replied the old woman; "his chest and shoulders were broad; his neck, straight and noble; his stature, raised above his fellows; and he outshone, in short, every one around him:—his eyes sparkling with animation, yet their fire tempered with sweetness; his beautiful locks clustered on his shoulders; and the first down of youth appeared upon his cheek. An outlandish wench, not without beauty, but of uncommon impudence, ran suddenly up to him, embraced him, and hung upon his neck.—Is not this the man you mean?"

"It is indeed," replied Arsace; "I well remember the last circumstance you mention; and that strolling hussy, whose home-spun made-up charms have nothing more in them than common, but are, alas! much more fortunate than mine, since they have obtained for her such a lover."

The old woman smiled at this, and said,—"Be of good cheer, my child; the stranger just now, perhaps, thinks his present mistress handsome; but if I can make him possessor of your beauties he will find himself to have exchanged brass for gold, and will look with disdain upon that conceited and saucy strumpet."—"Only do this, my dearest Cybele, and you will cure, at once, two dreadful distempers—love and jealousy; you will free me from one, and satisfy the other."—"Be it my care," replied the nurse, "to bring this about; do you, in the meantime, compose yourself; take a little rest; do not despair before the trial, but cherish soothing hope." Having said this, she took up the lamp, and, shutting the door of the chamber, went away.

Soon after sunrise, taking one of the eunuchs of the palace with her, and ordering a maid to follow her with cakes and other requisites for sacrifice, she hastened to the temple of Isis. Upon arriving at the entrance, she said—she came to offer a sacrifice for her mistress Arsace, who had been disturbed by portentous dreams, and wished to propitiate the goddess. One of the vergers opposed, and sent her away, telling her—that the temple was overwhelmed with sorrow—that Calasiris, returned from his long exile, had feasted with his friend the evening before, unbending his mind with unusual cheerfulness and mirth:—after the entertainment he made a libation, and poured out many prayers to the goddess—he told his sons that they would not see him much longer—and earnestly recommended to their protection the young Greeks who came with him; begging them to have the tenderest care of, and assist them in everything:—he then retired to rest; and whether excess of joy had relaxed his nerves and exhausted his spirits more than his old and worn-out frame could bear, or whether he had asked, and obtained, this favour of the gods, towards cock-crowing he was found to have expired, by his sons, who, alarmed at his presages, had watched over him all night. "And now," continued he, "we have sent into the city, to assemble together the rest of the priestly caste, that we may celebrate his funeral rites according to the custom of our country. You must therefore retire; for it is not lawful for any one, except the priests, to enter the temple, much less to sacrifice, for at least seven days."

"What then will become of the Grecian strangers during this interval?" said Cybele.—"Thyamis," he replied, "our new high-priest, has ordered apartments to be fitted up for them, beyond its precincts; and they are even now complying with our custom, by quitting the temple, and during this melancholy space of time, will lodge without."

The old woman, thinking this an admirable occasion to spread her nets and prepare her snares, said, "Good verger, now is the time to be of service to the strangers, and to oblige Arsace, sister of the Great King. You know how fond she is of Greeks, and how ready to show hospitality to foreigners; let these young people know, that with the knowledge, and by the consent of Thyamis, apartments are prepared for them in our palace."

The verger, suspecting nothing of Cybele's designs, imagined that he was doing a very good office for the strangers if he could get them received into the Viceroy's palace; that he should also oblige those who asked this of him, and hurt nobody. He sought therefore Theagenes and Chariclea. He found them drowned in tears, and overwhelmed with sorrow. "You do not act," said he, "conformably to the principles of your country or religion in lamenting so deeply the departure of a holy man, who, besides, foretold it to you, and forbade you to grieve at it. Reason and the divine word should rather encourage you to attend him, mentally, with rejoicing and congratulation as resting from his labours, and having exchanged this troublesome state for a better. On your own account, however, I can excuse your giving way, at first, to grief, having lost your father, your protector, and chief support; but you must not despair; Thyamis succeeds not only to his father's dignity, but to his affections towards you. He has manifested the greatest regard for you. His first thoughts have been for your accommodation. He has been able to procure a retreat for you, so splendid, as not only foreigners in low estate like you, but the greatest of the inhabitants, would envy. Follow then this woman," pointing to Cybele—"consider her as your mother, and accept the hospitality to which she will introduce you."

Theagenes and Chariclea did as they were directed. Grief had so overwhelmed their faculties, that they hardly knew what they were about; and in their present forlorn state were willing to fly to any refuge. But could they have foreseen the calamities which awaited them in the house they were about to enter, they would have shrunk back. Fortune, whose sport they were, seemed now to promise them a short space for rest, and a prospect of joy, only to plunge them deeper in misfortunes. They went voluntary prisoners; and young, strangers, and unsuspecting, deceived by the fair show of hospitality, they delivered themselves up to their enemy. Thus subject is a wandering life to the cloud of error, and thus easily is the unhappy traveller deluded and imposed upon.

The lovers, when they arrived at the viceregal palace, and saw its magnificent vestibules (far more splendid than any private house), the guards, and array of attendants and courtiers, were surprised and disturbed, observing the habitation to be very much beyond what was suitable to the present condition of their fortunes. However, they followed Cybele, who exhorted and encouraged them—called them her friends and children, and bid them form the most pleasing expectations for their future. At length, when she had brought them to her own apartment, which was remote and private, she caused them to sit down, and thus addressed them:

"My children, I am acquainted with the cause of your present sorrow; and that you lament, with great reason, the death of the high priest, Calasiris, who was in the place of a father to you; but it is proper for you now to tell me who you are, and from whence you come. So far I know, that you are Greeks; and, as I judge from your appearance, of a good family; for a countenance so ingenuous, so graceful and engaging an air, bespeak a noble race. But from what country and city of Greece you come, and by what chance you have wandered hither, I wish to know; and it will be for your interest to acquaint me, that I may inform my mistress Arsace, the sister of the Great King, and wife of the most powerful of the viceroys, Oroondates. She is hospitable, refined, and a lover of the Greeks. When she has had some previous information about you, you will appear before her with less embarrassment, and more honour. And whatever you disclose, will not be to an entire stranger, for I also am a Greek by nation. I am a native of Lesbos. I was brought here a captive; but I find my life in captivity pleasanter than any I could have hoped to pass at home, for I enjoy the entire confidence of my mistress; she sees only with my eyes, and hears with my ears; but I make use of the credit I have with her to introduce only worthy and honourable persons to her acquaintance."

Theagenes, comparing in her mind what Cybele now said, with the behaviour of Arsace the day before; recollecting how intently she had fixed her eyes upon him, and calling to memory her wanton signs and glances, foreboded no good to himself from what was to follow: he prepared, however, to say something in answer to Cybele, when Chariclea whispered in his ear—"Remember that I am your *sister* in what you are going to say." He, taking the hint, began—

"You know already, Mother! that we are Greeks—this young woman is my sister—our parents were carried off by pirates—we set out in search of them, and ourselves met with worse fortunes, falling into the hands of cruel men, who robbed us of our all, which was considerable, and were, with difficulty, persuaded to spare our lives. Some pitying deity brought us acquainted with the hero Calasiris (now beatified): under his guidance we arrived here, flattering ourselves that we should spend the remainder of our lives under his protection; but now we are as you see, left alone, and desolate; bereft of our own parents, and of him who promised to supply the place of them. This is our present situation. To you we return our best thanks for your good offices and hospitality; and you would greatly enhance the favour by suffering us to live retired, and by ourselves; deferring, for some time at least, the favour you hinted at, that of introducing us to Arsace. Strangers, wanderers, and unfortunate as we are, we are very unfit to appear in her splendid court. Acquaintance and intercourse are best suited for those who are of equal rank." Cybele could hardly restrain herself at this intelligence. She betrayed, by her countenance, evident marks of the joy she felt at hearing that Chariclea was the sister of Theagenes, concluding that she would now be no obstacle to the amorous designs of her mistress.

"Fair youth," said she, "you will have different sentiments of Arsace when you are acquainted with her. She condescends, and accommodates herself to every kind of fortune. She has a particular pleasure in comforting and assisting those who have met with unworthy treatment. Though she is by birth a Persian, in disposition she is a Greek. She delights in the company and conversation of those who, like yourselves, are lately come from Greece. She greatly affects both the Grecian ways and manners: be of good cheer then; you will not fail to receive every attention and honour which a man can wish for, and your sister will be her companion and favourite. But now tell me your names?" Having heard them, she ran to Arsace, ordering them to wait her return, and giving directions to her portress (an old woman like herself,) not to suffer any one to enter the apartment, nor to permit those who were inside to leave it.

"But," said the other, "what if your son Achæmenes should return; he went out just before your departure to the temple, in order to get some application to his eyes, which are still very troublesome to him?"—"Neither must he enter," replied she; "make fast the doors, and tell him that I am gone away, and have taken the key with me."

The portress did as she was directed; and Cybele was no sooner departed than the unhappy lovers could no longer restrain their bitter thoughts and lamentations. Almost in the same instant he cried out "O Chariclea!"—She, "O Theagenes!" They proceeded to deplore their misfortunes in the same frame of mind and nearly in the same words.

They mingled embraces with their complaints, and kisses with their tears. The remembrance of Calasiris drove them at last into audible grief; into cries and sobs; Chariclea particularly, who had known him longer—who had experienced more of his attention, benevolence, and affection. "O Calasiris!" she cried out, as well as her sobs would let her, "for I can no longer call you by the sweet name of father; the evil genius who persecutes me, has on all sides deprived me of that endearing appellation. My real father I have never known. I betrayed, alas! and deserted him who adopted me; and have lost him who received, preserved, comforted, and instructed me; and the custom of the priests does not permit me to pay the last tribute of tears over his dear remains. Yet, O my preserver (and I will once more call you father), here at least, while I may, I will pour out a libation to you with my tears, and give you offerings from my hair." So saying, she plucked handfuls from her beauteous tresses. Theagenes caught her hands, and besought her to forbear.

She, however proceeded in tragic strain—"Why do I continue to live, deprived of such a hope? Calasiris is gone!—the support of my wanderings—my leader in a foreign country, and only guide to my native one—he who could lead me to the knowledge of my parents—our comfort in adversity, our defender from misfortune, our strength, and stay, is lost; and has left us, a miserable pair, ignorant and forlorn, in a foreign land. For want of guidance, it is impossible for us to continue our journey. That grave, bland, wise, and of a truth, *hoary*, soul is fled, and will not see the event of its labours on our behalf."

While she was going on thus dolefully, and Theagenes, though he felt deeply for himself, was attempting to compose her, and to repress the violent expressions of her grief, Achæmenes returned; and finding the doors fast, inquired of the old portress the reason. She told him, that it was by his mother's order. While he was wondering what could be her motive, he heard Chariclea lamenting within; and stooping down, and looking through the crevices of the door, he could easily see what passed in the chamber. Again he asked the old woman who those were whom he saw within. She told him—"She knew no more of them, than that they were a youth and maiden, foreigners, as she guessed, whom Cybele had not long before brought with her."

Again he stooped down, and took a more careful survey of them. Chariclea was entirely unknown to him. He admired her beauty, and figured to himself what it must be when not obscured by dejection, and overwhelmed with grief; and his admiration began to lead him insensibly into love. As for Theagenes, he had some distant and obscure recollection of having seen him before. While he was gazing on one, and then trying to recall the other to his mind, Cybele returned. She had told Arsace everything she had done, relative to the young pair. She congratulated her on her good fortune, which had effected without trouble what she could else hardly have hoped to obtain by a thousand schemes and contrivances; which had lodged her lover under her own roof, and afforded her the unrestrained and unsuspected liberty of seeing, and being seen by him.

With this discourse she stimulated her passion to such a degree, that she could scarcely prevent her hastening to an immediate interview with Theagenes, by suggesting that it should not take place while as yet her face was pale, and her eyes swelled, from the distraction in which she had passed the preceding night. She advised her to compose herself for that day, and stay till she had recovered her former beauty. She arranged with her how she was to treat and manage her guests; and left her full of hopes and flattering expectations. Then returning to her apartment, and coming upon her son employed as he was about the door, she asked him what he was so curiously prying into.

"I am examining the strangers within," said he; "who are they? from whence do they come?"—"It is not permitted you to know," she replied; "nay, I advise you to conceal what you have already discovered of them; and to avoid their company as much as possible, for such is my mistress's pleasure." The young man, easily persuaded by his mother, retired; comprehending that Theagenes was reserved for the private gratification of Arsace, and saying to himself as he went away—"Is not this the man whom I received from the Commandant Mithranes, to carry to Oroondates, that he might be sent to the Great King?—Was he not taken away from me by Thyamis, and the men of Bessa, when I narrowly hazarded my life, and was almost the only one of the party who escaped?—It surely is so, if I can believe my eyes, which are now better, and serve me nearly as well as ever. Besides, I heard that Thyamis returned here yesterday, and, after a single combat with his brother, recovered the priesthood. This is undoubtedly the man I mean: for the present, however, I will conceal my knowledge of him, and observe in silence my mistress's intentions with regard to these young people."— Thus he muttered to himself.

Cybele hastened to her guests, and detected some traces of the sorrows which had them employed in her absence; for though, at the noise she made in opening the doors, they endeavoured to compose their dress and looks and manner as well as they were able, yet they could not conceal from the penetrating old woman that they had been agitated and in tears.

"My dear children," she cried out, "why do I see this ill-timed grief, when you ought to rejoice, and congratulate yourselves upon your good fortune? Arsace manifests the kindest disposition towards you; she will permit you to come into her presence to-morrow, and, in the mean time, has ordered you to be received and treated with every attention and regard. Dry then these unseasonable and childish tears, clear your countenances, and compose and conform yourselves in everything, according to the pleasure of your great benefactress."—"The remembrance of Calasiris," replied Theagenes, "and the loss we have sustained in being so soon deprived of his friendly attentions, called forth our tears."—"This is foolish," said the old woman; "why are you so affected at so common and trifling an event? Calasiris was but an adopted father, and, by the course of nature, could not last long; whereas you are now in favour with one who will shower upon you rank, riches, pleasures, everything which your age (now that you are in the bloom of youth) can enjoy, or your warmest wishes hope for. Look on Arsace as your good genius—as your goddess Fortune—and fall down before her! Only be ruled by me in what manner you are are to approach her, and comport yourselves when she admits you to an interview; conform yourselves to her pleasure, and obey her orders; for she is young, a princess, proud also of her beauty, and will not bear to have her will disputed, or her commands disregarded."

Theagenes made no answer, his mind misgiving him that matters of an unworthy and unwelcome nature were being hinted at. In the meantime some eunuchs arrived, bringing with them, in golden dishes, delicacies which remained from the royal table, which were in the highest degree sumptuous and choice. After saying that their mistress sends them out of honour to the strangers, and having placed them upon the board, they departed. The young people, at the suggestion of Cybele, and that they might not seem to despise the favour of the princess, just tasted what was set before them: and the like honour was repeated to them in the evening as well as on other days. Early the next morning the same eunuchs again appeared, and thus addressed Theagenes:

"Most enviable among men! you are sent for by my mistress: she has ordered us to introduce you to her presence—an honour and happiness which falls to the lot of very few." He paused a little: at length he arose, with a very unwilling air: and asked,—"If he alone were sent for, and not his sister also?"—"He only, at present," they replied: "his sister should have a private interview another time; now several of the Persian nobles were with Arsace: and besides, it was the custom that men and women should be separately received and admitted to an audience." Theagenes, stooping, whispered to Chariclea:—"All is not right; this is most suspicious."—She softly advised him, not at first to contradict Arsace, but to feign a willingness to comply with everything which was desired of him.

He then followed his conductors who officiously instructed him in what manner he should address and converse with the princess; and what ceremonies and obeisances were usual and necessary in appearing before her: but he answered nothing. At length they arrived in her presence: they found her sitting on a lofty throne—her dress gorgeous with gold and purple—her tiara and necklace sparkling with the most costly gems—and her whole person set off with all the appliances of art—her guards standing around her, and some of the principal nobles and magistrates sitting on each side. Theagenes was neither dazzled nor confounded by all this splendour: he forgot, in a moment, the simulated complaisance which had been recommended to him by Chariclea: rather did he feel his pride rebel at sight of the Persian pomp: neither bending the knee, nor prostrating himself, but with an erect countenance—"Hail," he said, "O royal Arsace!" They in the presence were indignant, and a murmur of disapprobation ran through the circle: every one blamed the daring rudeness of Theagenes, who presumed to address the princess without the usual prostration. But she, smiling, said—

"Forgive a foreigner, unaccustomed to forms; and, above all, a Greek, infected with the national contempt towards Persians." And then she raised the tiara from her head, to the astonishment, and manifest dislike, of those about her; for this is what the viceroys do when they return the salute of those who pay them homage. "Be of good cheer, stranger," said she, by an interpreter (for though she understood Greek she did not speak it); "if you desire anything, scruple not to acquaint me, nor doubt to obtain your wish:" and then making a signal to her eunuchs, she dismissed him, and he was ceremoniously re-conducted, with a train of guards, to his apartments.

Achæmenes having now had a nearer view of him, recollected him well—wondered at, yet suspected the cause of the honours which were paid him, but kept the silence which was recommended to him by his mother. Arsace proceeded to receive her nobles at an entertainment, apparently out of respect to them, but really to celebrate her own joy at having had an interview with Theagenes. To him she sent not only portions of the viands set before her, as usual, but carpets and embroidered tapestry, the work of Tyrian and Lydian skill. She sent likewise two beautiful slaves to wait upon them—a maid to Chariclea, and a boy to Theagenes, both from Ionia, and in the bloom of youth.

She was urgent with Cybele to lose no time, but to bring about, as soon as possible, what she had so much at heart: for her passion was now too strong for her endurance. Cybele, accordingly, was to relax none of her endeavours, but was to circumvent Theagenes with all her arts. She did not openly explain the wishes of her mistress, but gave him to guess at them by hints and circumlocutions. She magnified her good-will towards him—took every occasion to extol the beauties of her person, as well those which appeared to every beholder as those which her attire kept concealed: she commended her graceful manners and amiable disposition, and assured him that a brave and handsome youth was certain of finding favour with her. All this while she endeavoured in what she said to sound his temper, whether it were amorous and easily inflamed.

Theagenes thanked her for her good inclinations towards the Greeks, and professed himself obliged by the peculiar kindness and benevolence with which she had treated him. But all her innuendoes, relating to other matters, he passed over, and appeared as though he did not understand them. This was a vast annoyance to the old beldame, and her heart began almost to fail her; for she had penetration enough to see that Theagenes understood very well the end she aimed at, but was averse to, and determined to repel, all her overtures. She knew that Arsace could not brook a much longer delay. She had already experienced the violence of her temper, which was now inflamed by the ardour of her present passion. She was daily demanding the fulfilment of her promise, which Cybele put off on various pretences; sometimes saying, that the youth's inclinations towards her were chilled by his timidity—at others, feigning that some indisposition had attacked him. At length, when nearly a week had ineffectually elapsed, and the princess had admitted Chariclea to more than one interview; when out of regard to her pretended brother, she had treated her with the greatest kindness and respect; Cybele was at length obliged to speak out more plainly to Theagenes, and make an unvarnished declaration of her mistress's love to him.

She blamed his backwardness, and promised that his compliance should be followed by the most splendid rewards. "Why," said she, "are you so averse to love? Is it not strange that one of your age should overlook the advances of a woman like Arsace—young, and beautiful as yourself—and should not esteem her favours as so much treasure-trove, especially when you may indulge your inclinations without the smallest apprehension of danger—her husband being at a distance, and her nurse the confidante of her secrets, and entirely devoted to her service, being here, ready to manage and conceal your interviews? There are no obstacles in your way. You have neither a wife nor a betrothed; although in such circumstances, even these relations have been overlooked by many men of sense, who have considered that they should not really hurt their families, but should gain wealth and pleasure to themselves." She began to hint, at last, that there might be danger in his refusal. "Women," says she, "tender-hearted and ardent in their desires, are enraged at a repulse, and seldom fail to revenge themselves upon those who overlook their advances.—Reflect, moreover, that my mistress is a Persian, of the royal family, and has ample means in her hands of rewarding those whom she favours, and punishing those who she thinks have injured her. You are a stranger, destitute, and with no one to defend you. Spare yourself danger, and spare Arsace a disappointment: she is worthy of some regard from you, who has shown and feels such intensity of passion for you: beware of a loving woman's anger, and dread that revenge which follows neglected love. I have known more than one repent of his coldness.—These grey hairs have had longer experience in love affairs than you, yet have I never seen any one so unimpressible and harsh as you are."

Addressing herself then to Chariclea (for, urged by necessity, she ventured to hold this discourse before her), "Do you, my child," says she, "join your exhortations to mine; endeavour to bend this brother of yours, to whom I know not what name to give. If you succeed, you shall find the advantage great to yourself; you will not lose his love and you will gain more honour; riches will shower down upon you, and a splendid match will await you. These are enviable circumstances to any the chiefest of the natives; how much more to foreigners who are in poverty!" Chariclea, with a bitter smile, replied—

"It were to be wished that the breast of the most excellent lady, Arsace, had felt no such passion; or that, having felt it, she had had fortitude sufficient to bear and to repress it. But if the weakness of her nature has sunk under the force of love, I would counsel my brother no longer to refuse responding to it, if it may be done with any degree of security—if it may be possible to avoid the dangers which I see impending from the Viceroy's wrath, should he become acquainted with the dishonourable affair which is going on."

At these words Cybele sprang forwards, and, embracing and kissing Chariclea, "How I love you, my dear child;" she exclaimed, "for the compassion you shew for the sufferings of one of your own sex, and your solicitude for the safety of your brother. But here you may be perfectly at ease—the very sun shall know nothing of what passes." "Cease for the present," replied Theagenes seriously, "and give me time for consideration."

Cybele upon this went out, and—"O Theagenes!" said Chariclea, "the evil genius who persecutes us has given us a specious appearance of good fortune, with which there is really intermixed more of evil; but since things have so turned out, it is a great part of wisdom to draw some good, if possible, from each untoward accident. Whether you are determined to comply with the proposal which has been made to you, it is not for me to say. Perhaps, if our preservation depended upon your compliance, I might reconcile myself to it; but if your spirit revolts at the complaisance which is expected from you, feign at least that you consent, and feed with promises the barbaric woman's passion. By these means you will prevent her from immediately determining any thing harshly against us: lead her on by hope, which will soften her mind, and hinder her anger from breaking out: thus we shall gain time, and in the interval some happy accident, or some propitious deity, may deliver us from the perplexities with which we are surrounded. But beware, my dear Theagenes, that by dwelling in thought upon the matter you do not fall into the sin in deed."

Theagenes, smiling, replied,—"No misfortunes, I see—no embarrassments can cure a woman of the innate disease of jealousy: but be comforted, I am incapable of even feigning what you advise. In my mind, it is alike unbecoming to do or to say an unworthy thing; and there will be one advantage in driving Arsace to despair—that she will give us no farther trouble on this subject; and whatever else I am destined to suffer, my bent of mind and my bitter experience have but too well prepared me to bear."—Chariclea having said, "I fear you are bringing ruin upon our heads,"—held her peace.

While this conversation employed the lovers, Cybele went to Arsace, and encouraged her to hope for a favourable issue to her desires, for that Theagenes had intimated as much, she returned to her own apartments. She said no more that evening; but having in the night earnestly besought Chariclea, who shared her bed, to co-operate with her, in the morning she again attacked Theagenes, and inquired what he had resolved upon; when he uttered a plain downright refusal, and absolutely forbad her expecting any complaisance from him of the sort she wished. She returned disappointed and sorrowful to her mistress; who, as soon as she was made acquainted with the stern refusal of Theagenes, ordering the old woman to be ejected headlong out of the palace, entered into her chamber, and, throwing herself upon the bed, began to tear her hair, and beat her breast.—Cybele was returning home in disgrace, when her son Achæmenes met her, and, seeing her in tears, asked—"if any misfortune had happened to her?—Or has our mistress," said he, "received any bad news?—Has any calamity befallen the army?—Has Oroondates been defeated by the Ethiopians?"

He was running on in this manner with his questions, when his mother stopped him.—"Have done trifling," said she, "and let me alone." She was going away: he followed her, and taking her by the hand, besought her earnestly to explain to him, her son, the cause of her sorrow. She suffered herself to be led by him into a retired part of the garden, and then said—

"I would not to any one else disclose my own and my mistress's distresses; but since she is in the extremest agitation, and I am in danger of my life (for I fear the worst from her rage and disappointment), I will venture to speak, in case you should be able to think of any thing that may comfort and assist your poor mother. Arsace is in love with the young man who is now at my apartments: she burns with no common affection, but with inflamed and ungovernable passion; and when both of us thought it an easy matter for her to satisfy her inclinations, we have been miserably disappointed. To this cause you are to attribute the attentions which have been paid to, and the favours which have been showered upon, the strangers; but since this stupid, rash, and unbending youth has rejected all our advances, she, I think, will not survive it; and I anticipate destruction for myself. This, my child, is the cause of my present affliction:—if you have it in your power to assist me, do it quickly, or else prepare shortly to pay the last rites over my tomb."

"What shall be my reward?" replied Achæmenes, "for it is necessary to come directly to the point: it is not a time, in your present confusion and distress, to delay you with long discourse."

"Ask whatever you please," replied Cybele: "I have already, by my interest, made you head-cupbearer: if you are desirous of any greater dignity, tell me so: there is no degree of wealth, or honour, to which you may not aspire, if you can procure Arsace the means of satisfying her inclinations."

"I have long suspected this passion of the princess," replied the young man, "but kept silence, waiting the event. I am not covetous of riches, or ambitious of place; if she can procure me in marriage the maiden who is called the sister of Theagenes, I think I may promise that every thing else shall happen according to her wishes. I am desperately in love with this young woman. Your mistress, who knows by experience the force of this passion, may very reasonably be brought to assist a fellow sufferer in it, especially when, by so doing, she may probably meet with success in her own pursuits."

"Doubt not," said Cybele, "of her gratitude. She will do anything for you, if you can be of real service to her in this affair; nay, we may perhaps, ourselves persuade the maiden; but explain, I beg of you, in what manner you propose to assist us."

"I will not say a word," he replied, "till Arsace has promised, and sworn, to grant me what I desire: and do not you by any means at present enter upon the subject with the young woman. She too, I can see, is of a high and lofty spirit; you may spoil all by undue rashness."—"I will act just as you shall direct," replied Cybele; and running into her mistress's apartment, she fell at her feet, and bid her be of good cheer, for every thing now should happen as she would have it—"Only," said she, "admit my son Achæmenes to an audience."

"Let him come in," replied the princess; "but take care that you do not again deceive me." Achæmenes was upon this introduced—his mother explained his wishes, and made known his promises—and Arsace swore to procure for him the hand of Chariclea. He then said—

"Let Theagenes give over all his airs; he who is a slave, yet dares to behave with insolence to his mistress."—Being desired to explain himself, he related all he knew—How Theagenes was taken captive in war by Mithranes, who was about to send him to Oroondates, in order that he might convey him to the Great King—that he was rescued in the way by Thyamis and the men of Bessa—that he, Achæmenes, with difficulty escaped from them—that he was fortunate enough to have with him the letters of Mithranes. And upon this he produced and shewed them to Arsace; and appealed to Thyamis for the truth of all he had said.

Arsace began to conceive hope from these tidings, and, immediately issuing from her chamber, repaired to the hall of audience, where, seating herself upon her throne, she commanded Theagenes to be brought before her.

When he appeared, she asked him if he knew Achæmenes, whom she pointed out to him, standing near her. He replied that he did.—"Was he not," said she, "bringing you hither a captive, some short time ago?" He admitted that also.—"You are my slave then," said she, "and as such, shall do as I direct you, and, whether you will or not, be obedient to my commands. This sister of yours I give in marriage to Achæmenes, who fills a principal station in my court, as well for his own good deserts, as out of the regard I have for his mother; and I will defer the nuptials only till a day is fixed, and preparation made for due splendour in their celebration."

Theagenes was pierced as with a sword at this address, but determined not to thwart her, but rather to elude her attack as that of a wild beast.—"O princess," he replied, "in the midst of my calamities I give the gods thanks, that since I, whose life was originally fortunate, and family illustrious, am destined to be a slave, I have fallen into your power, rather than into that of any other; into yours, who, while you considered us as strangers and foreigners, have treated us with so much compassion and humanity. As for my sister, although, not being a captive, she is not a slave; yet her own inclination will lead her to serve and obey you in every thing: dispose of her, therefore, as shall seem good in your eyes."—"Let him," Arsace then said, "be placed among the waiters at the royal table; let Achæmenes instruct him in the art of cup-bearing, that he may, without delay, become expert in the services which will be required of him."

Theagenes was now permitted to retire, which he did; sorrowing, and meditating deeply on what he had farther to do.

Achæmenes, elated with the success of his project, had the cruelty to insult him.—"You," said he, "who were just now so haughty, who seemed alone a freeman among slaves; who held your head so high, and refused to bow it even before the princess must now learn to bend it, or else my knuckles shall teach you better manners."

Arsace was left alone with Cybele.—"Now," said she, "nurse, every excuse is taken from this proud Grecian; go to him and tell him, that if he will comply with what I require of him, he shall obtain his liberty, and spend his life in affluence and pleasure; but if he still continues sullen and reluctant, assure him that he shall feel the wrath of an angry mistress, and a disappointed woman: that punishments of every kind await him, and that he shall be condemned to the lowest and most disgraceful slavery." Cybele performed her embassy without delay; and added, from herself, whatever she thought most likely to work upon his hopes or fears.

Theagenes demanded a short time for consideration; and going alone to Chariclea, he exclaimed—"We are undone, my dearest Chariclea! every cable of safety is broken, every anchor of hope is lost; nor have we now the name of liberty to console us in our misfortunes, but are again fallen into servitude."—He explained his meaning, and related what had happened.—"We are now," he added, "exposed to the insults of barbarians; we must obey all their commands or suffer the extremest punishments; and as if this were not sufficient, what is above all the rest intolerable, know that Arsace has promised to give you in wedlock to Achæmenes, the son of Cybele; but this, while I have life, an arm, and a sword, I will either prevent or never see. But what ought we now to do? What contrivance can we imagine to avoid this detestable union, of you with Achæmenes, of me with Arsace?"

"If you will condescend to the one yourself," replied Chariclea, "you will easily find means to hinder the other."

"Have a care what you say!" replied Theagenes, eagerly, "God forbid that any persecution of fate should drive the faithful, though yet unrewarded lover of Chariclea, to stoop to another, and that an unlawful union; but a thought comes into my head, for necessity is the mother of invention;" and so saying, he immediately sought Cybele, and bade tell her mistress that he wished to have an interview with her alone.

The old woman, concluding that he was now about to give way, joyfully delivered the message, and Arsace ordered her to bring him to the palace after supper. Cybele bade those in waiting withdraw, so that her mistress might be in private and undisturbed, and introduced Theagenes when the shades of night began to envelope every thing in obscurity. A single lamp burnt in the chamber; and as soon as they were entered, she was preparing to retire, but Theagenes stopped her.—"Let Cybele, O princess!" said he, "if you please, remain for the present; I know she is a very faithful keeper of secrets;" and taking Arsace's hand, he went on: "O my mistress! I did not presume at first to dispute your will, or defer my submission to your commands, for any other reason than that I might obey them with greater security; but now, since the will of fortune has in its kindness made me your slave, I am much more ready to obey your pleasure. One thing only I desire of you—of you who have promised me so many—break off the marriage of Chariclea with Achæmenes; for, to waive other objections, a maiden of her noble birth is no fit wife for the son of a slave. If this be not granted me, I swear by all that is sacred that I will never comply with your wishes; and if the least violence is offered to Chariclea, you shall soon see me dead at your feet."

"You may be sure," replied Arsace, "that I, who am willing to surrender even myself, desire in everything to oblige you; but I have sworn to give your sister to Achæmenes."—"Let not that trouble you," said he, "you may give him any sister of mine; but my mistress, my intended, my betrothed in short, you neither would wish to bestow, nor shall you bestow, upon him."

"What mean you?" said she.—"Nothing but the truth," replied he, "for Chariclea is really not my sister, but my intended wife; you are, therefore, absolved from your oath; and if you wish for a farther confirmation of my words, you may, as soon as it please you, give order for the celebration of our nuptials."

Arsace was much annoyed; and heard, not without jealousy, the true relation in which Chariclea stood to Theagenes; but, at present, only said,—"If you will have it so, this marriage shall be broken off, and I will seek out another wife for Achæmenes."—"When this matter is settled," replied Theagenes, "dispose of me as you please, I will perform all I have promised." He then approached in order to kiss her hands. She, however, instead of presenting her hand, saluted him with her lips; and he left the presence kissed, but not kissing in return.

On his return to Chariclea, he disclosed to her all that had passed, (at which she, too, was not free from jealousy,) setting before her the secret intention of his promise, the good results which he anticipated from it. In the first place, the project of Achæmenes' marriage would be marred, a fair pretext would be afforded for deferring at present the completion of Arsace's wishes; and what was worth more than all, there was the certainty that Achæmenes would make "confusion worse confounded," upon finding his expectations blighted, and himself supplanted in the princess's good graces by another favourite. I took care (he said) to have his mother present at the interview, and a witness that our intercourse was but in *words*; she will keep nothing secret from her son. It may suffice perhaps (he added) to avoid all occasion for an evil conscience, and to trust only in the protection of the gods; but it is good also to avoid all occasion for an evil conscience in the sight of men, so as to pass through this transitory life with virtuous boldness. "There is every reason to believe," added he, "that a slave like Achæmenes, will conspire against his mistress; for the subject commonly hates the cause of his subjection, and this man has no occasion to invent a pretext for rebellion (as has been the case with many), he is really wronged, has been deceived, and sees another preferred before him; he is conscious to the profligacy of his mistress, and has a motive ready to his hand."

He held this discourse to Chariclea, endeavouring to revive in her a hope of better things. On the morrow he was sent for by Achæmenes to serve at the table, for such were Arsace's commands. He was arrayed in a Persian robe of great value, which was sent by her at the same time, and adorned partly against his will, with bracelets and jewelled necklaces.

Upon arriving at the palace, Achæmenes offered to instruct him in the functions of his office; but, hastening to the sideboard, and taking up a precious goblet, he said,—"I need no instructor, self-taught, I will wait upon my mistress, making no bustle about such trifles. Your fortune has forced you perhaps to learn your trade; nature and the spur of the moment will teach me what I am to do." So saying, he lightly, and with a grace, poured out the wine, and handed the cup upon his finger ends.

The draught inflamed the mind of Arsace more than ever. Slowly sipping, she fixed her eyes intently upon Theagenes, taking in at the same time large draughts of love; neither did she drain the goblet, but left a portion of its contents, in which Theagenes might pledge her. A wound of a very different nature rankled in the bosom of Achæmenes: anger, envy, and resentment manifested themselves on his countenance, so that Arsace could not help observing it, and whispered something to those who were nearest her.

When the entertainment broke up—"Grant me," said Theagenes, "my mistress! this first boon which I shall ask—permit me alone to wear this dress when serving at your table." Arsace agreed to his request, and putting on his ordinary raiment, he departed. Achæmenes followed him, sharply upbraided him with his want of manners; telling him, too, that there was a forwardness and familiarity in him, which, though they might at first be overlooked, in consideration of his youth and inexperience, would in the end, if not corrected, infallibly give offence.

He gave him these cautions, he said, out of a friendly feeling, and particularly as he was shortly to become related to him by marrying his sister, according to his mistress's promise.

He was proceeding with his good advice; but Theagenes, his eyes fixed in deep thought on the ground, seemed not to hear, and was preparing to leave him, when Cybele joined them, on her way to conduct her mistress to take her usual siesta. Seeing her son sorrowful, and apparently out of humour, she inquired into the cause of it.—"This foreign youth," said he, "thanks to his specious person, is preferred to all of us, the ancient chamberlains and cupbearers; to-day he has already wormed himself into our mistress's good graces, and has waited nearest her royal person, presenting the cup to her, and thrusting us out of our former dignity, which has become no more than an empty name. We ought, perhaps, to bear without murmuring, if we cannot feel without envy, the honours he receives, and the confidence to which he is admitted, since we have had the weakness, by our negligence and silence, to assist in his success; our mistress, however, might have done all this without affronting and disgracing her old servants, who moreover are in all her secrets. But some other time will serve for speaking farther on this subject: at present, let me go and see my charming Chariclea, my promised bride; that, by her sweet aspect, I may soothe the annoyance of my mind."

"What bride do you talk of?" replied Cybele, "you seem to me to take fire at small and imaginary offences, and to be ignorant of the real and deep ones which you have received. Chariclea is no longer destined for your wife."

"What say you?" he exclaimed, "am not I a very fitting match for my fellow-slave? What can have wrought this sudden change?"—"Our own too great fidelity and zeal in serving Arsace;" replied Cybele, "for after that we have preferred her caprices to our own safety; when, in compliance with her desires, we have endangered ourselves, and have put the accomplishment of her wishes into her power, this noble youth, this dainty favourite, enters her chamber, and at first sight persuades her to break through all her oaths, and to promise Chariclea to himself; who now, as he affirms, is no longer his sister, but his mistress."

"And is Chariclea indeed promised to Theagenes?" said Achæmenes.—"It is but too true," replied Cybele, "I was present myself and heard it; they even talked of the nuptial feast, and of celebrating it shortly; proposing to satisfy you with the hand of some one else."

At this mortifying intelligence Achæmenes, smiting his hands together, and uttering a deep groan—"I will make this wedding a fatal one to them all," said he; "only do you assist me in endeavouring to put it off for a few days. If any one inquires after me, say that I am indisposed and gone into the country. This precious stranger's calling her his betrothed is a mere pretext to break through the engagements that have been made to me; his kissing, his embracing her, nay, his sleeping with her, would not clearly convince me that she is not his sister. I will sift this business, and will vindicate the violated oaths and the insulted gods." So saying, raging with love, jealousy, and disappointment (feelings all the more violent in a barbarian's breast), he rushed out of the room; and without giving himself time for consideration, in the first moments of his passion, he secretly mounted, in the evening, an Armenian horse, reserved for state occasions, and fled full speed to Oroondates.

The Viceroy was then in the neighbourhood of the celebrated Thebes, marshalling all his forces, and preparing to lead them on an expedition against the Ethiopians.

Book VIII

The king of Ethiopia had deceived Oroondates by a stratagem, and made himself master of one of the objects of the war—the city of Philœ, always ready to fall a prey to the first invader—and, by so doing, had reduced him to great straits, and to a necessity of using sudden and hurried efforts for its recovery.

Philœ is situated a little above the smaller cataracts of the Nile, about twelve miles distant from Syene and Elephantis. The city was formerly seized upon and inhabited by a band of Egyptian fugitives, which made it debateable land between the governments of Egypt and Ethiopia. The latter were for extending their dominions as far as the cataracts, while the former claimed even the city of Philœ, pretending that they had conquered it in war, because it had been occupied by their exiles. It had been taken and retaken several times by both nations; and was, just before the time I am speaking of, held by an Egyptian and Persian garrison.

The king of Ethiopia dispatched an embassy to Oroondates, to demand the restoration of the city and the emerald mines; and meeting, as has been before observed, with a refusal, he sent ambassadors a second time towards Egypt; (they going in advance) he following a few days later, with a numerous army, set on foot beforehand, but keeping all the while their destination a profound secret.

When he concluded that his envoys had passed Philœ, and had lulled the inhabitants and garrison there into negligence and security, by persuading them, as they were instructed, that they were preparing to proceed farther on a peaceful embassy; he on a sudden appeared before Philœ, in a few days overwhelmed its surprised and unprepared defenders (unable to resist his superior force and his artillery), and took possession of the city, which he kept, without injuring any who dwelt in it.

In the midst of these troubles Achæmenes found Oroondates, and by his sudden and unexpected appearance, helped to increase them.—"Has any misfortune," hastily he inquired, "happened to Arsace, or to any other of my family?" "A misfortune has happened," replied Achæmenes, "but I would speak to you in private."

When every one had retired he entered upon his story. He related the capture of Theagenes by Mithranes; how he was sent to him (Oroondates), in order to be conveyed, if he thought proper, as a present to the Great King, to whose court and table the youth would be a worthy ornament. He proceeded to narrate his rescue from them in their journey by the men of Bessa, the death of Mithranes in his defence, and his own subsequent arrival at Memphis, introducing into his narrative the affairs also of Thyamis.

At length he came to the ungoverned passion of Arsace—the transfer of Theagenes into the palace—his too kind reception there—his attendance and his cup-bearing—"Hitherto," he added, "I believe nothing has actually taken place, for the youth is coy and unwilling; but if this temptation be not taken away from before her eyes—if Theagenes be not speedily removed from Memphis—there is the greatest reason to apprehend that time, fear, and artifices of various kinds, will at length conquer his disinclination. On these accounts I have taken an opportunity to leave the city privately, and to come in all haste to make this discovery to you, thinking it my duty no longer to conceal a matter in which your honour and interest are so intimately concerned."

When he had raised the resentment of Oroondates by these tidings, and filled him with indignation and a desire of revenge, he inflamed his desires when he came to dwell upon the charms of Chariclea. He extolled her to the skies, spoke of her beauty as divine; saying that her equal never had, and never would be seen. "None of your concubines," said he, "not those alone who are left at Memphis, but those even who follow your person, are in any degree to be compared with her." In this manner Achæmenes went on, raising the curiosity and wishes of Oroondates, reckoning, that although the viceroy might indulge his fancy for Chariclea for a time, yet he might afterwards easily be induced to give her up to him in marriage, as a reward for his discoveries.

Urged on by anger and desire, the viceroy instantly summoned the eunuch Bagoas, who was in great favour and authority, and commanded him to proceed directly to Memphis with a troop of fifty horse, and without fail or delay to bring Theagenes and Chariclea to his camp, wherever he should find them.

He wrote at the same time a letter to Arsace to this effect:

"Oroondates to Arsace.

"Send to me Theagenes and Chariclea, the captive pair, who are slaves to the Great King, and under orders to be transmitted to him. Send them willingly, since, even if you be unwilling, they will be taken from you; and then the report of Achæmenes will be believed."

To the chief eunuch at Memphis he wrote as follows:

"You shall hereafter give an account of your negligence as to my household; at present deliver the Grecian captives to Bagoas, that they may be brought to me, whether Arsace consent to it or not. Deliver them, I say, or the bearer of these presents has orders to bring you hither in chains, when you shall be flayed alive."

Bagoas took the letters, signed with the viceroy's signet, that they might obtain full credit, and set out for Memphis to execute his master's orders.

Oroondates now put himself in motion against the Ethiopians, commanding Achæmenes to follow him, who was watched and guarded without his knowing it, till it should appear whether the information he had given were true. Meanwhile at Memphis, soon after the departure of Achæmenes, Thyamis had been completely invested with the office of high priest, and, as such, was become one of the chiefs of the city.

After he had celebrated, with proper piety, the funeral of Calasiris, and observed, in mourning and retirement, the appointed number of days—as soon as the sacred laws permitted him to hold communication with those who were without the temple, his first care was to inquire after Theagenes and Chariclea.

He learned, with some difficulty, that they had been removed to the viceroy's palace; and immediately on receiving this intelligence he hastened to Arsace, to make inquiries after them. He was solicitous about them on various accounts; and particularly as his father had, with his last breath, recommended them, in the strongest manner, to his care and protection.

He returned thanks to the princess for her goodness in receiving and entertaining the young Grecian strangers, during that space of time in which it was not lawful for them to continue within the precincts of the temple; and he now begged permission to resume the pledge entrusted to his care.

"I wonder," replied Arsace, "that while you are praising my kindness and humanity, you should at the same time intimate a doubt of their continuance; and conceive any apprehension that I shall not still be able and willing to entertain these foreigners, and assign to them such honour as is due."

"You mistake me," replied Thyamis; "I know that they would live here in much more splendour and affluence than they can with me, even did they wish to remain under my roof: but having met with many misfortunes, born of an illustrious family, and now wandering here, far from their native home; the first wish of their hearts is, to recover their friends, and to return to their country: my pledge to aid them was the inheritance left me by my father; and I have, too, myself many motives for friendship towards them."

"You act discreetly," replied Arsace, "in asking as a favour, rather than demanding as a right: for a favour it would be in me to give up to your friendship, those over whom I have a right as slaves."—"Slaves!" cried Thyamis, in amazement, "what mean you?"—"I mean captives," said she, "by the right of war."

Perceiving that she meant to insist upon their having been taken by Mithranes, he thus resumed:—"O Arsace! it is not now war, but peace; if that brings servitude, this restores liberty again; the one is the result of a tyrant's will, the other is a truly royal gift. Besides, it is not the mere name but the disposition of those using them, which really constitute either peace or war. By attending to these considerations you will define better wherein equity consists: there can be no doubt as to what honour and expediency demand in the present case. How can it be honourable, or expedient, in you to persist obstinately in the detention of these strangers, and to avow your determination of so doing?"

Arsace could no longer contain herself; but acted, like most who are in love, while they imagine their passion concealed they feel timidity; when discovered they lose all shame; concealment makes them timid, discovery audacious: she stood self-accused; and she could not help perceiving, or thinking she perceived, that Thyamis suspected her. Throwing aside therefore all reserve, and all regard to the dignity of the high priest, she broke out on a sudden—"Be assured that you too shall answer for the share you have had in the attack upon Mithranes; Oroondates will make a strict inquiry after, and punish with severity, all those who were concerned in the slaughter of him and of his troops. As to these foreigners, I will not give them up; they are now my slaves; shortly they will be sent, according to our custom, to my brother, the Great King: declaim as you please on what is decent, proper, and expedient; those in power need not such things; they find them all in the indulgence of their own sovereign will. Retire, then, from the palace at once and willingly, lest you be restrained against your will."

Thyamis retired, invoking the gods and predicting to her no good event from such behaviour, and considering whether he should disclose these proceedings to the citizens, and call upon them for assistance.

"I value not your priesthood or your prophecy," said Arsace, "the only prophecy which love regards, is the prospect of success." So saying, she withdrew to her chamber, and sending for Cybele, consulted with her upon the measures which she had next to pursue. She suspected the flight of Achæmenes, and the motive of it; for Cybele, whenever she was questioned on the subject, made various excuses for his absence, and studiously endeavoured to persuade her that he was anywhere else, rather than in the camp of Oroondates. These excuses, never wholly credited, became each day less credible.

When Cybele therefore approached her, she thus began: "What shall I do, nurse? How can I ease the torments which oppress me? My love is as intense as ever; nay, I think it burns more violently: but this youth, so far from being softened by kindness and favours, becomes more stubborn, and intractable. Some time ago he could bring himself to soothe me by fallacious promises, but now he seems openly and manifestly averse to my desires: I fear he suspects, as I do, the cause of Achæmenes' absence, and that this has made him more timorous. It is *his* disappearance, indeed, which gives me most uneasiness: I cannot help thinking that he is gone to Oroondates, and perhaps will wholly or in part succeed in persuading him of the truth of what he says. Could I but see Oroondates, he would not withstand one tear or caress of mine; a woman's well-known features exert a mighty magic over men. It will be a grievous thing, before I have enjoyed Theagenes, to be informed against, nay, perhaps put to death, should his mind be poisoned before I have the means of seeing and conversing with him: wherefore, my dear Cybele, leave no stone unturned, strain every engine; you see how pressing and critical the business now becomes; and you may well believe that, if I myself am driven to despair, I shall not easily spare others. You will be the first to rue the machinations of your son: and how you can be ignorant of them I cannot conceive."

"The event," replied Cybele, "will prove the injustice of your suspicions, both with regard to my son and me: but when you are yourself so supine in the prosecution of your love, why do you lay the fault on others? You are flattering this youth like a slave, when you should command him as a mistress. This indulgent mildness might be proper at first, for fear of alarming his tender and inexperienced mind; but when kindness is ineffectual, assume a tone of more severity; let punishments, and even stripes, force from him that compliance which favours have failed in doing. It is inborn in youth to despise those who court; to yield to those who curb them: try this method and you will find him give to force that which he refused to mildness."

"Perhaps you may be right," replied Arsace, "but how can I bear to see that delicate body, which I doat on to distraction, torn with whips, and suffering under tortures?"

"Again you are relapsing into your unseasonable tenderness," said Cybele; "a few turns of the rack will bring about all you desire, and for a little uneasiness which you may feel, you will soon obtain the full accomplishment of your wishes. You may spare your eyes the pain of seeing his sufferings—deliver him to the chief eunuch, Euphrates; order him to correct him, for some fault which you may feign he has committed—our ears are duller, you know, in admitting pity, than are our eyes. On the first symptoms of compliance, you may free him from his restraint."

Arsace suffered herself to be persuaded; for love, rejected and despairing, pities not even its object, and disappointment seeks revenge. She sent for the chief eunuch, and gave him directions for the purpose which had been suggested to her. He received them with a savage joy, rankling with the envy natural to his race, and from what he saw and suspected, particularly angry with Theagenes. He put him immediately in chains, cast him into a deep dungeon, and punished him with hunger and stripes: keeping all the while a sullen silence; answering none of the miserable youth's inquiries, who pretended, (though he well knew the cause), to be ignorant of the reason why he was thus harshly treated. He increased his sufferings every day, far beyond what Arsace knew of or commanded, permitting no one but Cybele to see him; for such, indeed, were his orders.

She visited him every day, under pretence of comforting, of bringing him nourishment; and of pitying him, because of their former acquaintance: in reality, to observe and report what effect his punishment had upon him, and whether it had mollified his stubborn heart; but his spirit was still unconquered, and seemed to acquire fresh force from the duration of his trials. His body, indeed, was torn with tortures, but his soul was exalted by the consciousness of having preserved its purity and honour. He gloried that while fortune was thus persecuting him, she was conferring a boon upon his nobler part—the soul. Rejoicing in this opportunity of showing his fidelity to Chariclea, and hoping only she would one day become acquainted with his sufferings, for her sake he was perpetually calling upon her name and styling her his light! his life! his soul!

Cybele (who had urged Euphrates to increase the severity of his treatment, contrary to the intentions of Arsace, whose object was by moderate chastisement, to bend but not to kill him), saw it was all to no purpose, and began to perceive the peril in which she stood. She feared punishment from Oroondates, if Achæmenes should incautiously discover too much of the share she had in the business; she feared lest her mistress should lay violent hands upon herself, either stung by the disappointment, or dreading the discovery of her amour. She determined, therefore, to make a bold attempt, to avoid the danger which awaited her, either by bringing about what Arsace desired, or to remove all concerned in, and privy to the matter, by involving them in one common destruction.

Going therefore to the princess—"We are losing our labour," she said: "this stubborn youth, instead of being softened, grows every day more self-willed; he has Chariclea continually in his mouth, and, by calling upon her alone, consoles himself in his misfortunes. Let us then, as a last experiment, cut the cable, as the proverb says, and rid ourselves of this impediment to our wishes: perhaps, when he shall hear that she is no more, he may despair of obtaining her, and surrender himself to your desires."

Arsace eagerly seized upon this idea: her rage and jealousy had but too well prepared her for embracing the cruel expedient.—"You advise well," she replied, "I will take care to have this wretch removed out of our way."—"But who will you get to put your design into execution?" said Cybele, "for though your power here is great, the laws forbid you to put any one to death without the sentence of the judges. You must undergo, therefore, some trouble and delay in framing a fictitious charge against this maiden; and there will, besides, be some difficulty in proving it. To save you the pain and hazard of this proceeding, I am ready to dare and suffer anything. I will, if you think fit, do the deed with poison, and by means of a medicated cup remove our adversary."

Arsace approved, and bid her execute her purpose. She lost no time, but went to the unhappy Chariclea, whom she found in tears, and revolving how she could escape from life of which she was now weary; suspecting as she did the sufferings and imprisonment of Theagenes, though Cybele had endeavoured to conceal them from her, and had invented various excuses for his unusual absence.

The beldame thus addressed her:—"Why will you consume yourself in continual, and now causeless, lamentations? Theagenes is free, and will be with you here this evening. His mistress, angry at some fault which he had committed in her service, ordered him into a slight confinement, but has this day given directions for his release, in honour of a feast which she is preparing to celebrate, and in compliance with my entreaties. Arise, therefore, compose yourself, and refresh your spirits with a slight refection."

"How shall I believe you?" replied the afflicted maiden, "you have deceived me so often, that I know not how to credit what you say."

"I swear to you, by all the gods," said Cybele, "all your troubles shall have an end this day; all your anxiety shall be removed, only do not first kill yourself by abstaining obstinately, as you do, from food. Taste, then, the repast which I have provided."

Chariclea was, with difficulty, persuaded, though she very naturally entertained suspicions; the protestations, however, of the old woman, and the pleasing hopes suggested prevailed at length; (for what the mind desires it believes), and they sat down to the repast.

Cybele motioned to Abra, the slave, who waited upon them, to give the cup, after she had mixed the wine, first to Chariclea; she then took another herself and drank. She had not swallowed all that was presented to her, when she appeared seized with dizziness; and throwing what remained in the cup upon the ground, and casting a fierce look upon the attendant, her body was attacked with violent spasms and convulsions. Chariclea, and all who were in the room, were struck with horror, and attempted to raise and assist her; but the poison, potent enough to destroy a young and vigorous person, wrought more quickly than can be expressed upon her old and worn-out body. It seized the vitals; she was consumed by inward fire; her limbs, which were at first convulsed, became at length stiff and motionless, and a black colour spread itself over her skin. But the malice of her soul was more malignant even than the poison, and Cybele, even in death did not give over her wicked arts; but by signs and broken accents, gave the assistants to understand that she was poisoned by the contrivance of Chariclea. No sooner did she expire than the innocent maiden was bound, and carried before Arsace.

When the princess asked her if she had prepared the fatal draught, and threatened her, if she would not confess the whole truth, that torments should force it from her, her behaviour astonished all the beholders. She did not cast down her eyes; she betrayed no fear; she even smiled, and treated the affair with scorn, disregarding, in conscious innocence, the incredible accusation, and rejoicing in the imputation of the guilt, if through the agency of others, it should bring her to a death, which Theagenes had already undergone. "If Theagenes be alive," said she, "I am totally guiltless of this crime; but if he has fallen a victim to your most virtuous practices, it needs no tortures to extract a confession from me: then am I the poisoner of your incomparable nurse, treat me as if I were guilty, and by taking my life, gratify him who loathed your unhallowed wishes."

Arsace was stung into fury by this: she ordered her to be smitten on the face, and then said—"Take this wretch, bound as she is, and show her her precious lover suffering, as he has well deserved; then load every limb with fetters and deliver her to Euphrates; bid him confine her in a dungeon till to-morrow, when she will receive from the Persian magistrates the sentence of death."

While they were leading her away, the girl who had poured out the wine at the fatal repast, who was an Ionian by nation, and the same who was sent at first by Arsace to wait upon her Grecian guests—(whether out of compassion for Chariclea, whom nobody could attend and not love, or moved by a sudden impulse from heaven,) burst into tears, and cried out—"O most unhappy and guiltless maiden!" The bystanders wondering at this exclamation and pressing her to explain its meaning, she confessed that it was she who had given the poison to Cybele, from whom she had received it, in order that it might be administered to Chariclea. She declared, that either overcome by trepidation at the enormity of the action, or confused at the signs made by Cybele, to present the goblet first to the young stranger, she had, in her hurry, changed the cups, and given that containing the poison to the old woman.

She was immediately taken before Arsace, every one heartily wishing that Chariclea might be found innocent; for beauty, and nobleness of demeanour, can move compassion even in the minds of barbarians.

The slave repeated before her mistress all she had said before, but it was of no avail towards clearing the innocent maiden, and served only to involve herself in the same punishment; for Arsace, saying she was an accomplice, commanded her to be bound, thrown into prison, and reserved with the other for trial; and she sent directly to the magistrates, who formed the Supreme Council; and to whom it belonged to try criminals and to pronounce their sentence, ordering them to assemble on the morrow.

At the appointed time, when the court was met, Arsace stated the case, and accused Chariclea of the poisoning; lamenting, with many tears, the loss she had sustained in a faithful and affectionate old servant, whom no treasures could replace; calling the judges themselves to witness the ingratitude with which she had been treated, in that, after she had received and entertained the strangers with the greatest kindness and humanity, she had met with such a base return: in short, her tone was throughout bitter and malignant.

Chariclea made no defence, but confessed the crime, admitting that she had administered the poison, and declaring, that had she not been prevented, she would have given another potion to Arsace; whom she attacked in good set terms; provoking, in short, by every means in her power, the sentence of the judges.

This behaviour was the consequence of a plan concerted between her and Theagenes the night before, in the prison, where they had agreed that she should voluntarily meet the doom with which she was threatened, and quit a wandering and wretched life, now become intolerable by the implacable pursuits of adverse fortune. After which they took a last melancholy embrace; and she bound about her body the jewels which had been exposed with her, which she always carried about her, concealing them under her garments to serve as attendants upon her obsequies; and she now undauntedly avowed every crime which was laid to her charge, and added others which her accusers had not thought of; so that the judges, without any hesitation, were very near awarding her the most cruel punishment, usual in such cases, among the Persians. At last, however, moved perhaps by her youth, her beauty, and noble air, they condemned her to be burnt alive.

She was dragged directly out of the court, and led by the executioners without the walls, the crier proclaiming that a prisoner was going to suffer for the crime of poisoning; and a vast multitude flocking together, and following her, poured out of the city.

Among the spectators upon the walls Arsace had the cruelty to present herself, that she might satiate her revenge, and obtain a savage consolation for her disappointment, in viewing the sufferings of her to whom she imputed it. The ministers of justice now made ready and lighted an immense pile; and were preparing to place the innocent victim upon it, when she begged a delay of a few moments, promising that she would herself voluntarily ascend it—and now turning towards the rising sun, and lifting up her eyes and hands to heaven, she exclaimed—"O sun! O earth! O celestial and infernal deities who view and punish the actions of the wicked! I call upon you to witness how innocent I am of the crime of which I am accused. Receive me propitiously, who am now preparing to undergo a voluntary death, unable to support any longer the cruel and unrelenting attacks of adverse fortune;—but may your speedy vengeance overtake that worker of evil, the accursed and adulterous Arsace; the disappointment of whose profligate designs upon Theagenes has urged her thus to wreak her fury upon me." This appeal, and these protestations, caused a murmur in the assembly. Some said the matter ought to undergo a further examination—some wished to hinder, others advanced to prevent her mounting the pile: but she put them all aside, and ascended it intrepidly.

She placed herself in the midst of it, and remained for a considerable time unhurt, the flames playing harmlessly around her, rather than approaching her; not injuring her in the least—but receding whithersoever she turned herself; so that their only effect seemed to be to give light and splendour to her charms; as she lay like a bride upon a fiery nuptial couch.

She shifted herself from one side of the pile to another, marvelling as much as any one else, at what happened, and seeking for destruction, but still without effect; for the fire ever retreated, and seemed to shun her approach. The executioners on their part were not idle, but threw on more fuel (Arsace by signs inciting them), dry wood, and reeds, and every thing that was likely to raise and feed the flame; yet all was to no purpose; and now a murmur growing into a tumult, began to run through the assembly: they cried out—"This is a divine interposition!—the maiden is unjustly accused!—she is surely innocent!"—and advancing towards the pile, they drove away the ministers of justice, Thyamis, whom the uproar had roused from his retirement, now appearing at their head, and calling on the people for assistance. They were eager to deliver Chariclea, but durst not approach too near. They earnestly desired her, therefore, to come down herself from the pile; for there could be no danger in passing through the flames, to one who appeared even to be untouched by them. Chariclea seeing and hearing this, and believing too that some divinity was really interposing to preserve her, deemed that she ought not to appear ungrateful, or reject the mercy, and leapt lightly from the pile: at which sight the whole city raised a sudden shout of wonder, joy, and thanksgiving to the gods.

Arsace, too, beheld this prodigy with astonishment, but with very different sensations. She could not contain her rage. She left the ramparts, hurried through a postern gate, attended by her guards and the Persian nobles, and herself laid violent hands on Chariclea. Casting a furious glance at the people—"Are ye not ashamed," she cried, "to assist in withdrawing from punishment a wretched creature detected in the very fact of poisoning, and confessing it? Do ye not consider, that while shewing a blameable compassion to this wicked woman, ye are putting yourselves in opposition to the laws of the Persians—to the judges, the peers, the viceroys, and to the Great King himself. The fact of her not burning has perhaps moved you, and ye attribute it to the interposition of the gods, not considering that this yet more fully proves her guilt. Such is her knowledge of charms, and witchcraft, that she is enabled to resist even the force of fire. Come all of you to-morrow to the examination which shall be held in public, and you shall not only hear her confess her crimes herself, but shall find her convicted also by her accomplices whom I have in custody."

She then commanded Chariclea to be led away, still keeping her hold upon her neck, and ordering her guards to disperse the crowd, who were with difficulty prevented from interfering for her rescue; but who at length gave way, partly suspecting her to be a sorceress, and partly through awe of the person, and dreading the power, of Arsace.

Chariclea then was again committed to the custody of Euphrates; again thrown into prison, and reserved for a second trial, and a second sentence; rejoicing however amidst her troubles, that she should once more have an opportunity of seeing, and conversing with, Theagenes; for Arsace, out of a refinement of cruelty, had ordered them to be confined in one dungeon, that each might be a spectator of the other's sufferings; for she well knew that a tender heart is much more hurt by the pains of those it loves than by its own. In this instance, however, her savage mind was disappointed; and what she meant as a punishment turned out a consolation. They took a melancholy pleasure in suffering for each other, and in suffering equally. Had a greater share of torments been inflicted upon either, the other would have been jealous, and thought his love defrauded—moreover they were now together—they could converse with, comfort, and encourage one another to bear their calamities with fortitude, and to resist courageously every trial that might endanger their purity or fidelity. They passed the greatest part of the night in speaking on such topics, as might indeed be expected from a pair, whose whole delight was in their mutual conversation, and who despaired of ever passing another night together again.

At length they came to the miraculous event which happened at the pyre. Theagenes attributed it to the benevolence of the gods, who were angry at the injustice of Arsace, and who pitied Chariclea's innocence and piety. She herself was in doubt whether to thank or complain of heaven. The manifest interposition of the gods at the place of execution, was a mark of their kindness and protection; but to be preserved from death, only to be plunged afresh in new and unceasing troubles, was rather a sign of their having incurred, and still continuing under, the divine displeasure: unless indeed, it were some wonder-working method of the deity delighting to plunge them into the deepest misery, in order to show its power of saving them when their condition appeared desperate.

She was going on in a complaining style, when Theagenes stopped her, bidding her speak more reverently, nor to scrutinize the conduct of the Deity. Suddenly she exclaimed,—"May the gods be propitious to us, for I just now call to mind a dream, (or rather waking vision), which I had last night, and which the unexpected sight of you again, and the various matters which we have since talked of, had driven from my memory. The vision was this:—The beatified Calasiris appeared to me (whether in reality or in idea, I am not certain) and repeated these lines, for the words fell into verse;

> *'Wearing Pantarbè, fear not flames, fair maid,*
> *Fate, to whom nought is hard, shall bring thee aid.'"*

Theagenes on his part appeared suddenly like one under supernatural impulse, for springing forwards, as far as his fetters would permit him, he exclaimed—"The gods be gracious to us! recollection makes me also a poet; I had, myself, a like vision. Calasiris, or some deity in his shape, appeared to me, and addressed me in these lines:

> *'From Arsace, the morrow sees thee free—*
> *To Ethiopia with the virgin flee.'*

"Now, I readily comprehend the meaning of the oracle which is given to me. By Ethiopia, is signified the dark abode of those who dwell under the earth—by the virgin, Proserpine—by freedom, my release from this wretched body: but I do not so readily understand that which relates to you—there appears to be a contradiction in it. The name of Pantarbè means 'all fear,' and yet from it you are promised assistance."

"My dearest Theagenes," replied Chariclea, "you have been so accustomed to misfortunes that you use yourself to interpret every thing in its worst sense—the mind of man so readily takes a colour from its circumstances. The oracles appear to me to admit of much more favourable meaning. The virgin, instead of Proserpine, means perhaps me, with whom you are to escape to Ethiopia, my country, after you shall have been delivered from the prisons of Arsace. How all this is to be brought about is not very apparent, but it is not incredible. Every thing is possible to the gods; and they who have favoured us with this prediction, will watch over its accomplishment. The prophecy which relates to me, so far from being obscure, is, as you see, fulfilled; and I am, contrary to all expectation, alive, and unhurt, at least by the flames: I was hitherto ignorant that I carried the cause of my preservation about me, but now I fancy that I understand the words. I took particular care at the time of my trial, as indeed I had been wont to do before, to have the jewels which were exposed with me, bound closely about my body, concealing them under my garments—in case I should escape, they would help to support my life—if I were doomed to suffer, they would adorn my funeral. Among these, which consist of costly necklaces, and Indian and Ethiopian jewels, there is a ring, given by my father to my mother when they were betrothed: within the bezil is a stone called Pantarbè; it is inscribed with sacred letters, and endowed with mystic virtues, from whence, as I conjecture, it obtains the power to preserve those who wear it from the force of fire. This, therefore, most probably, and the good pleasure of the gods, is what has preserved me. I remember too, that our friend, Calasiris, (now in happiness,) told me that something of this virtue was hinted at in the writing inscribed on the fillet which was exposed with me, and which I always wear round my waist."

"What you say," replied Theagenes, "may perhaps be true—what has happened seems to confirm your conjecture: but what Pantarbè will deliver us from the dangers which threaten us to-morrow? This stone, though it preserves from fire, does not confer immortality, and the wicked Arsace will find out some other, and new kind of punishment. How do I wish that she would involve us both in the same sentence, that one and the same hour might end our troubles! I should not esteem such a departure death, but repose and ease to our manifold miseries."

"Be not so cast down," said Chariclea, "the oracle promises us another Pantarbè. Let us trust in the gods, so will our deliverance be more grateful; or, if we be doomed to die, piety will soften and sanctify our sufferings."

In such conversations were the unfortunate lovers employed; each more solicitous for the fate which awaited the other, than for his own. They vowed to be faithful, and love one another till death; and beguiled the melancholy moments in these, which they thought would be their last, protestations. Meanwhile Bagoas and his troop of horse arrived at Memphis, in the middle of the night, while every one was buried in sleep. And when they had, without tumult, roused the guards, and made known who they were, they were admitted and entered into the court of the Viceroy's palace. Bagoas caused his men to surround the building, that he might be prepared, in case of meeting with any resistance; and he himself gaining admission by a crazy postern gate, and commanding silence to the person there, hastened, with ease, from his knowledge of the place, to the apartments of Euphrates, the moon affording a little light. Euphrates was in bed; but being roused by the noise made at his door, started up, and called out "Who is there?" "It is I," said Bagoas; "make no noise, but order a light to be brought."—The other ordered a boy, who slept in his chamber, to bring a light, but to take care not to awaken any one else.

When the light came, and the boy had retired, Euphrates began— "What new calamity does this sudden and unexpected appearance of yours announce?"—"There is no need," returned the other, "of many words; take and read this letter. Recognise the seal of Oroondates, and obey his commands, this very night, with secrecy and expedition: Make use of the soldiers whom I have brought with me, that you may give the less alarm. I leave you to judge for yourself whether you will or will not first disclose the business to Arsace."

Euphrates took the letters, and perused them both. "This," says he, "will be a fresh blow to my mistress, and she needs no additional affliction; for she was yesterday seized with a sudden disorder, as if by a stroke from heaven, and she now lies in a burning fever, and is in the utmost danger of her life. As for these letters, I would not show them to her at present, even were she in good health, for I know that she would sooner die herself, and involve us in the same destruction, than part with these young people. You are arrived just in time to save them. Come then forthwith—receive those whom you seek—take them away—use them kindly yourself, and endeavour to procure for them the same treatment from others. Their situation may well excite your compassion; for I have been obliged, much against my will, but at the inexorable command of Arsace, to inflict upon them a variety of punishments and tortures. They seem, besides, to be well born, and, to judge from their habitual conduct, possessed of discretion and good sense." And so saying, he rose and conducted Bagoas to the prison, who, as soon as he saw the young captives, pale and exhausted as they were with their sufferings, he could not help being wonderfully struck with their form and beauty. They, concluding that this unseasonable visit announced their fate, and that Bagoas was come to lead one of them, at least, to trial and execution, were at first rather agitated; but soon recovering an air of cheerfulness, they appeared pleased rather than grieved.

Euphrates advanced; and as he was preparing to loose their fetters from the wooden block, Theagenes exclaimed, "Accursed Arsace! She hopes to conceal her abominable actions in darkness and obscurity. But let her know that the eye of justice is most piercing; that it will bring to light her most secret crimes and display her wickedness in the face of the sun. But do you, ministers of her cruelty, execute her commands. Grant us, however, one last and only favour: whether we be doomed to die by fire, by water, or by the sword, let us suffer together, and end our wretched being by one and the same kind of death." Chariclea joined in this supplication. The eunuchs, who understood what they said, shed tears, and brought them out in chains as they were.

When they had left the palace, Euphrates remained where he was; and Bagoas, ordering his followers to take off all their fetters, except such as were just necessary to prevent an escape, placed them on horseback, surrounded with his troop, and took, with all expedition, the road to Thebes.

They rode all that night, and the next day till nine o'clock, when, being spent with want of sleep, and exposed to the summer rays of an Egyptian sun, Chariclea particularly, unused to this kind of travelling, being nearly exhausted with fatigue, they resolved, at last, to make a halt, to breathe their horses, and to refresh themselves. They chose for this purpose an elevated and projecting place on the banks of the Nile, where the river, turning from its direct course, and winding into a semicircle, forms a spot something resembling the gulf of Epirus, which, being kept continually moist, abounded in grass and herbage proper for their beasts. Here, too, were peach trees, sycamores, and others which love to grow in the neighbourhood of the Nile, these over-arched and afforded them a pleasant shade. Bagoas availed himself of their shelter instead of tents, and here he took some refreshment, inviting Theagenes and Chariclea to partake of his repast. They refused at first; he pressed them; and when they replied that it was needless for those who were going to execution to trouble themselves about nourishment, he told them they were much mistaken if they thought their lives in any danger; for he was not leading them to death, but to the viceroy Oroondates.

The meridian heat of the sun had now passed; it was no longer vertical, but its beams struck upon them laterally. Bagoas thereupon prepared to pursue his march, when a courier arrived with great precipitation, himself out of breath, and his horse dropping with sweat, and ready to sink under him with fatigue. As soon as he had spoken a word to Bagoas in private, he remained in silence. The eunuch fixing for some time his eyes on the ground, with a serious and reflecting air, at last said, "Rejoice, strangers! You are revenged of your enemy. Arsace is no more. As soon as she heard that you were gone away with me, she strangled herself, and has prevented an inflicted, by a voluntary, death; for her crimes have been such, that she had no hope of escaping the just resentment of Oroondates and the sentence of the Great King, and must either have lost her life, or have spent the remainder of it in infamy and confinement. Be of good cheer, then; fear nothing; I know your innocence, and your persecutor is removed."

Bagoas said this as he stood near them, with difficulty expressing himself in the Greek tongue, and using many uncouth words; but he spoke with sincerity of heart, for he rejoiced at the death of Arsace, whose dissolute manners and tyrannical disposition he abominated; and he wished to comfort and encourage the young people; he thought moreover that he should recommend himself to Oroondates by a very acceptable service, by preserving for him this young man, who would throw into the shade all the rest of his attendants; and by presenting him with a maiden worthy in every respect to supply the place of Arsace.

Theagenes and Chariclea, too, rejoiced at this intelligence. They adored the justice of the gods; and felt that, after this sudden and deserved end of their enemy, they should not feel their misfortunes, however severe—so welcome is death to some if only it be shared in by their foes. Evening now approached. A refreshing breeze sprang up, and invited them to continue their journey. They travelled all that night, and part of the next morning, making all possible expedition to Thebes, in hopes of finding Oroondates there. In this hope, however, Bagoas was disappointed. Before he arrived at that city, a courier met him, and informed him that Oroondates had set out for Syene, leaving the strictest orders to his officers to collect every man, even from the garrisons, and march them after him to that place; for the greatest apprehensions were entertained that the town would be taken before the satrap could arrive to its succour, the Ethiopian army having appeared at its gates before any intelligence was received that it was in motion. Bagoas, therefore, turned out of the road to Thebes, and took that of Syene.

When he came near the place, he fell in with a troop of Ethiopians, who had been sent out to scour the country, and to ascertain the safety of the roads for the march of their own army. Overtaken by night, and ignorant of the ground, they had concealed themselves behind some bushes (in obedience to the orders given them), watching for the passing by of any prey which they might seize, and also providing for their own security. At break of day they perceived the approach of Bagoas and his company. They despised the smallness of their number, but let them all pass by, in order to assure themselves that there was no greater force behind; and then suddenly rushing from their concealment in the marsh, they pursued and attacked them with a great shout.

Bagoas and his men, astonished at the sudden noise and assault, seeing from their colour that they were Ethiopians, and from their number (which amounted to near a thousand light-armed men), that resistance was vain, did not await their approach, but took to flight. They retreated at first with some degree of order, to avoid the appearance of a complete rout. The enemy detached after them a band of two hundred Troglodites. The Troglodites are a pastoral nation, on the borders of Arabia, of great natural agility, which they increase by exercise. They are unused to heavy armour, but, with slings and missile weapons, endeavour to make an impression upon the enemy at a distance, from whom, if they find them superior, they immediately retreat. The enemy do not take the trouble to pursue them, knowing them to be swift as the wind, and given to hide themselves in caverns, which they make their habitations. They, though on foot, soon overtook Bagoas and his flying squadron, and making use of their slings, wounded some of them from afar, yet, on their facing about, did not await their assault, but retreated headlong to their own comrades.

The Persians seeing this, and perceiving the smallness of their number, ventured to attack them; and having easily repulsed them for a space, turned again, and putting spurs to their horses, continued their flight with slackened rein and with the utmost speed. Some, deserting the main body, and hurrying to a bend in the Nile, hid themselves under its banks. The horse of Bagoas fell with him; one of his legs was fractured with the fall, and being unable to move, he was taken prisoner.

Theagenes and Chariclea, too, were made captives. They thought it dishonourable to desert Bagoas, who had shown them much kindness, and from whom they hoped more in future. They kept, therefore, by his side, dismounting from their horses, and voluntarily offered themselves to the enemy; Theagenes saying to Chariclea, "This explains my dream: these are the Ethiopians into whose lands we are fated to go: let us give ourselves up into their hands, and await an uncertain fortune with them, rather than expose ourselves to manifest danger with Oroondates."

Chariclea thought she could now perceive herself to be led on by the hand of destiny: a secret hope of better fortune began to insinuate itself into her bosom, and she could not help considering those who attacked them as friends rather than enemies; but not venturing to disclose her presages to Theagenes, she contented herself with expressing her consent to his advice.

When the Ethiopians approached, and observed Bagoas, from his features, to be a eunuch, and incapable of resistance, and the others unarmed and in chains, but of extraordinary grace and beauty, they inquired who they were. They made use of an Egyptian interpreter, whom they carried with them, who understood besides a little Persian, concluding that the prisoners spoke one or other of these tongues; for experience had taught them that a body detached as spies and scouts ought always to have some one with them who naturally speaks or understands the language of the country which they are sent to reconnoitre.

Theagenes, who, from his long residence in the land, had acquired something of the Egyptian tongue, replied, that the eunuch was one of the chief officers of the Persian viceroy; that he himself and Chariclea were Grecians by birth, taken prisoners, first by the Persians, and now voluntary captives to the Ethiopians, as they hoped, under better auspices.

The enemy determined to spare their lives, and to deliver them, as the first fruits of victory, to their sovereign, looking upon them as amongst the most valuable possessions of the satrap; eunuchs are reckoned as the eyes and ears of a Persian court, having neither children nor connexions to turn aside their fidelity, they are wholly attached to the person and service of their master; their young prisoners, too, appeared to them to be the most beautiful persons they had ever seen, and promised to be conspicuous ornaments to the royal household. They mounted them, therefore, upon horses, and carried them along with them, though the accident of Bagoas, and the fetters of the others, prevented their travelling very fast.

Here, then, was a kind of prologue to another drama:—just before they were prisoners in a foreign land, and on the verge of being brought out to a public and ignominious execution; now they were being carried, or rather escorted, though in captive guise, by those destined, ere long, to be their subjects. Such was their present situation.

Book IX

S yene was now closely blockaded, and on every side, as with a net, invested by the Ethiopian army.

Oroondates, as soon as he was informed of the design and sudden approach of the enemy (who, having passed the cataracts, were pressing towards the place), using the utmost diligence and expedition, had contrived to throw himself into the city before their arrival; and after planting his engines and artillery upon the walls, awaited the attack, and made every preparation for a vigorous defence.

Hydaspes, the king of Ethiopia, though he was deceived in the hope of surprising the town before they had any notice of his approach, invested it, however, on all sides, and surrounding it with a line of circumvallation, made for the present no attack, but sat down quietly before it, filling and exhausting the plains of Syene with myriads of men, beasts, and cattle. Here the party which has been mentioned brought their captives into his presence.

He was delighted at the sight of the young people; his soul, by a secret prescient movement, of which he knew not the cause, inclining towards his children. He thought this too an omen of victory, and joyfully exclaimed—"See! the gods, as our first spoils, deliver up to us our enemies in bonds. Let these then, as our first captives, be carefully preserved for our triumphant sacrifices to be offered, as the customs of Ethiopia require, to the gods of our country, when we shall have subdued our foes." And having praised and rewarded the captors, he sent them, together with their prisoners, to the rear of the army, ordering the latter to be kept under a guard (many of whom understood their language), to be treated, attended, and provided for in the most careful and splendid manner, and especially to be preserved from all contamination, as destined to be sacred victims. He directed their iron chains to be taken off, and fetters of gold to be put on in their room— for this metal is used by the Ethiopians in the way in which other nations use iron. His commands were obeyed; and the lovers, when they saw their first chains taken off, began to entertain hopes of liberty, which were soon crushed by the appearance and application of the golden ones.

Theagenes could not forbear smiling, and exclaimed—"Here is, indeed, a splendid mutation of fortune; the goddess is very kind to us, and changes our iron for gold: enriched by our fetters, we are become prisoners of high price."

Chariclea smiled at this sally, and tried to keep up his spirits, insisting that the more favourable predictions of the gods were beginning to be fulfilled, and endeavouring to soothe his mind with better hopes.

Hydaspes, who had flattered himself that he should take Syene at his first appearance, without opposition, being very nearly repulsed by the garrison, defending themselves bravely, irritated besides by insulting speeches, determined no longer to continue the blockade, by which, the city might at last be taken, to the destruction of some and the escape of others: but, by a new and unusual way of assault, to involve the town, and its defenders, in one common and universal ruin.

His plan of attack was this: he described a circle round the walls, which he divided into portions of ten cubits each, assigning ten men to every division, and ordering them to dig a wide and deep ditch. They dug it accordingly, while others, with the earth they threw out, raised a mound or wall parallel with, and nearly equal in height, to that of the place which they were besieging. The garrison made no attempt to hinder these operations—the besieging army was so numerous, that they durst not venture on a sally—and the works were carried on at such a distance from the walls, as to be out of the reach of their missile weapons.

When he had completed this part of his plan, with wonderful dispatch, owing to the multitude of men employed in it, and the diligence with which he urged on their labours, he proceeded to execute another work. He left a part of the circle, to the space of about fifty feet, plain and unfilled up. From each extremity of the ditch above described, he extended a long mound down to the Nile, raising it higher and higher as it approached the river. It had the appearance of two long walls, preserving all the way the breadth of fifty feet.

When he had carried on his lines so that they joined the river, he cut a passage for it, and poured its waters into the channel, which he had provided for them. They, rushing from higher into lower ground, and from the vast width of the Nile into the narrow channel, and confined by the mounds on each side, thundered through the passage and channel with a noise and impetuosity that might be heard at a great distance.

The fearful sight and sound struck the ears and met the eyes of the astonished inhabitants of Syene. They saw the alarming circumstances in which they were, and that the view of the besiegers was, to overwhelm them with the waters. The trenches which surrounded, and the inundation which was now fast approaching, prevented their escaping out of the city, and it was impossible for them to remain long in it, without the extremest danger; they took measures, therefore, as well as they were able, for their own protection.

In the first place, they filled up and secured every opening and crevice in the gates with pitch and tow; then they propped and strengthened the walls with earth, stones, and wood, heaping up against them anything which was at hand. Every one was employed; women, children, and old men; for no age, no sex, ever refuses labour when it is for the preservation of their lives. They who were best able to bear fatigue were employed in digging a subterraneous and narrow passage, from the city to the enemy's mound, which work was thus conducted:

They first sunk a shaft near the walls, to the depth of five cubits; and when they had dug it below the foundations, they carried their mine on forwards towards the bulwarks with which they were inclosed, working by torchlight; those who were behind receiving, in regular order, the earth thrown out from those who were before, and depositing it at length in a vacant place in the city, formerly occupied by gardens, where they raised it into a heap.

Their intention in these operations, was to give some vent and outlet to the waters, in case they should reach the city; but the approach of the calamities which threatened them was too speedy for their endeavours to prevent it. The Nile, rolling through the channel which had been prepared for it, soon reached the trench, overflowed it everywhere, and formed a lake of the whole space between the dyke and the walls; so that an inland town seemed like an island in the midst of the sea, beaten and dashed against on all sides by the waves.

At first, and for the space of a day, the strength of the walls resisted; but the continued pressure of the waters, which were now raised to a great height, and penetrated deeply into an earth black and slimy, which was cleft in many places, from the summer's heat, sensibly undermined the walls; the bottom yielded to the pressure of the top, and wherever, owing to the fissures in the ground, a settlement took place, there the walls began to totter in several places, menacing a downfall, while they who should have defended the towers were driven from their stations by the oscillation.

Towards evening a considerable portion of the wall between the towers fell down; not so much, however, as to be even with the ground, and afford a passage to the waters, for it was still about five cubits above them; but now the danger of an inundation was imminent and most alarming.

At this sight a general cry of horror and dismay arose in the city, which might be heard even in the enemy's camp—the wretched inhabitants stretched out their hands to the gods, in whom only they had hope, and besought Oroondates to send deputies with offers of submission to Hydaspes. He, reduced to be the slave of Fortune, unwillingly listened to their entreaties; but he was entirely surrounded with water, and it being out of his power to send an officer to the enemy, he was reduced by necessity to this contrivance—he wrote down the purport of their wishes, tied it to a stone, and endeavoured, by means of a sling, to make it serve the purpose of a messenger by traversing the waters; but his design was disappointed; the stone fell short, and dropped into the water before it reached the other side. He repeated the experiment several times. The archers and slingers strained every nerve to accomplish that upon which they thought their safety and life depended; but still without success. At length, stretching out their hands to the enemy, who stood on their works spectators of their distress, the miserable citizens implored their compassion by the most piteous gestures, and endeavoured to signify what was meant by their ineffectual stones and arrows—now clasping their hands together, and holding them forwards in a suppliant manner—now putting their arms behind their backs, in token that they submitted to servitude.

Hydaspes understood their signs, and was ready to receive their submission—for great minds are easily inclined to clemency by the sight of a prostrate enemy—but he was desirous first to make trial of their intentions.

He had already prepared some river-craft, which floating down the Nile, were drawn up near the mound: he chose ten of these, and filling them with archers, he ordered them what to say to the Persians, and sent them towards the city. They set out well prepared to defend themselves, in case the enemy should attempt anything against them.

This passage of a vessel, from wall to wall, presented a novel sight—mariners sailing over an inland country and cultivated plains: war, which is wont to produce strange spectacles, seldom, perhaps, afforded a more uncommon one than this—a navy proceeding against a town, and sailors, in boats, engaged with soldiers upon the walls.

Those in the city observed the boats making for the part of the wall which had fallen down, and their spirits being sunk with their misfortunes, surrounded as they were with perils, they began to suspect and dread the designs of those who were coming for their preservation:

for, in such extremity of danger, everything is a cause of suspicion and of fear. They began, therefore, to cast their darts and to shoot their arrows towards those who were in the boats: for men, who despair of safety, think even the shortest delay of destruction as so much gained. They flung their weapons, however, in such a manner as not to inflict wounds, but only to hinder the approach of the enemy.

The Ethiopians returned the attack more in earnest, not knowing the intentions of the Persians: they wounded several of those who were upon the ramparts, some of whom tumbled over into the water. The engagement was proceeding with greater warmth, one party endeavouring merely to repulse; the other to attack, when an old man, of great authority among the Syenæans, who stood upon the wall, thus addressed his fellow-citizens:

"Infatuated men! your distresses seems to have taken away your senses. You have encouraged and besought the Ethiopians to come to your assistance; and now, when they are, beyond all your hopes, arrived, you do everything in your power to drive them away again. If they come with friendly intentions, and bring conditions of peace, they are your preservers; if they have hostile designs, you need not fear their landing; we are so numerous, that we shall easily overpower them. But if we were to destroy all these, what would it avail us, surrounded as we are by such a cloud of enemies both by land and water? Let us then receive them, and see what is their business here."

This speech was received with approbation, both by the people and the Viceroy; and withdrawing from the breached portion of the wall, they stood motionless with their arms.

When the space between the walls was thus cleared, the inhabitants signed to the Ethiopians that they might freely approach: they advanced, therefore, and when near enough, they from their boats addressed the besieged multitude as follows:

"Persians! and inhabitants of Syene! Hydaspes, King of the Eastern and Western Ethiopia, and now your sovereign also, knows how to subdue his enemies, and to spare those who supplicate his mercy—the one belongs to valour, the other to humanity: the merit of the former belongs chiefly to his soldiers; that of the latter is entirely his own. Your safety or destruction is now in his hands; but since you throw yourselves on his compassion, he releases you from the impending and unavoidable dangers which encompass you. He does not himself name the conditions of your deliverance, but leaves them to you to propose; he has no desire to tyrannize over justice—he wishes to treat the fortunes of men with equity."

To this address the inhabitants of Syene replied,—"That they threw themselves, their wives and children, upon the mercy of the Ethiopian prince, and were ready to surrender their city (if they were spared), which was now in such sore distress, that unless some god, or Hydaspes himself, very speedily interposed, there were no hopes of its preservation."

Oroondates added,—"That he was ready to yield up, and put into their hands, both the cause of the war, and its prizes—the city of Philœ, and the emerald mines: in return, he required that neither he nor his soldiers should be made prisoners of war, but that Hydaspes, as a crowning act of generosity, would permit them to retire to Elephantine upon condition of their doing injury to no one: as to himself, it was indifferent to him whether he laid down his life now, or perished hereafter, by the sentence of his master, for having lost his army; the latter alternative would indeed be the worst, for now he would undergo a common, and possibly, an easy kind of death; in the other case, he would have to suffer the refinements of cruelty and torture. He also requested them to receive two of his Persians into their boats, that they might proceed to Elephantine, professing that if they found the garrison of that city disposed to surrender to the Ethiopians, he would no longer delay to follow their example."

The delegates complied with his request; took the Persians on board, returned to the camp, and informed Hydaspes of the result of their embassy.

Hydaspes smiled at the infatuation of Oroondates, who was insisting upon terms, while his very existence hung upon another's will. "It would be foolish, however," said he, "to let so many suffer for the stupidity of one." Accordingly he permitted those whom the Viceroy had sent to proceed to Elephantine; little regarding whether the troops there yielded or resisted. He ordered his men to close up the breach which they had made in the banks of the Nile, and to make another in those of the mound or wall; so that the river being prevented from flowing in at one opening and the stagnant water retiring apace out of the other, the space between his camp and Syene might soon be dry, and practicable for his soldiers to march over.

His commands were executed. His men made a beginning of the work, but night coming on deferred its completion till the next day. Meantime they who were in the city omitted nothing which might contribute to their preservation, not despairing of preservation, though it appeared almost beyond hope.

Some carried on their mine, which they now supposed must approach near the enemy's mound; having computed, as well as they could, by means of a rope, the interval between that and their own walls. Others repaired the wall which had fallen down, working by torchlight, readily finding materials from the stones which had fallen inwards. They had, as they thought, tolerably well secured themselves for the present; but were destined to have a new alarm; in the middle of the night, a portion of the mound, in that part where the enemy had been digging on the preceding day, suddenly gave way. This was caused either by the earth which formed the foundation being moist and porous, or by the mining party having sapped the ground above them, or by the ever-increasing body of water widening the narrow breach, or perhaps it might be ascribed to divine interposition. So tremendous was the noise and the report, that the besiegers and besieged, though ignorant of the cause, imagined a great part of the city wall to have been carried away; but the Ethiopians, feeling themselves safe in their tents, deferred satisfying their curiosity till the morning.

The inhabitants of Syene, on the contrary, were, with reason, more solicitous; they immediately examined every portion of their walls, and each finding all safe in his own vicinity, concluded that the accident had happened in some other part. The approach of daylight cleared up all their doubts; the breach in the mound, and the retreat of the waters, being then visible.

And now the Ethiopians dammed up the breach in the river's bank, by fixing planks, supported by strong wooden piles, strengthening them still more with a quantity of earth and fascines, taken partly from the banks and partly brought in boats, thousands labouring at the work. In this way the water was got rid of. The space, however, between the camp and the town was, as yet, by no means passable, being very deep in mud and dirt; and though it was in some places apparently dry ground, the surface was thin, and treacherous for the feet either of horses or men.

Thus passed two or three days. The Syenæans opened their gates, and the Ethiopians discontinued all hostile movements; the truce, however, was carried on without any intercourse between the parties. Guards on either side were discontinued; and they in the city gave themselves up to pleasure and enjoyment.

It happened that this was the season for celebrating the overflowing of the Nile; a very solemn festival among the Egyptians. It falls out about the time of the summer solstice, when the river first begins to swell, and is observed with great devotion throughout the country; for the Egyptians deify the Nile, making him one of their principal gods; and equalling him to heaven; because they say, that without clouds or rain he annually waters and fertilizes their fields; this is the opinion of the vulgar. They consider it a proof of his divinity, that the union of moist and dry being the principal cause of animal life, he supplies the former, the earth the latter quality (admitting also the existence of other elements.) These opinions are promulgated among the vulgar, but they who have been initiated in the mysteries, call the earth Isis, the river Osiris, substituting words for things. The goddess, they say, rejoices when the god makes his appearance upon the plains, and grieves proportionably when he is absent, feeling indignation against his enemy, Typho.

The cause of this is, I imagine, that men skilled in divine and human knowledge, have not chosen to disclose to the vulgar the hidden significations contained under these natural appearances, but veil them under fables; being however ready to reveal them in a proper place, and with due ceremonies, to those who are desirous and worthy of being initiated. So much I may be allowed to say with permission of the deity, preserving a reverential silence as to what relates to more mystic matters.

I return now to the course of my story. The inhabitants of Syene were employed in celebrating their festival with sacrifices and other ceremonies; their bodies, indeed, worn with labour and suffering, but their minds filled with devotion towards their deity, whom they honoured as best their present circumstances would permit.

Oroondates, taking the opportunity of the dead of night, when the citizens, after their fatigues and rejoicings, were plunged in sleep, and having beforehand secretly acquainted his Persian soldiers with his intentions, and appointed them the particular hour and gate at which they were to assemble, led them out of their quarters.

An order had been issued to every corporal to leave the horses and beasts of burden behind, that they might have no impediment on their march, nor give any intimation of their design, by the tumult which the mustering them would cause. Orders were given to take their arms alone, and, together with them, a beam or plank.

As soon as they were assembled at the appointed gate, they proceeded to lay their planks across the mud, (close to one another) which were successively passed from hand to hand, by those behind, to those in front. They passed over them, as by a bridge, and the whole body reached, without accident, the firm land.

They found the Ethiopians sleeping in security, without watch or guard; and passing by them unperceived Oroondates led his men with all possible speed to Elephantine. He was readily received into the city by means of the two Persians whom he had sent before, and who, having watched, night after night, caused the gates to be opened upon the concerted watch-word being given.

When day began to dawn, the inhabitants of Syene were aware of the flight of their defenders. Every one missed the Persian whom he had lodged in his house, and the sight of the planks laid over the mud, confirmed them in their suspicions, and explained the manner of it. They were thrown into great consternation at this discovery; expecting, with reason, a severe punishment, as for a second offence, fearing they should be thought to have abused the clemency of their conqueror, and to have connived at the escape of the Persians. They determined therefore, after some consultation, to go out of the city in a body, to deliver themselves up to Hydaspes, to attest their innocence with oaths, and implore his mercy. Collecting together then all ranks and ages, with the air of suppliants, they marched in procession, over the bridge of planks. Some carried boughs of trees, others tapers and torches, the sacred ensigns and images of their gods preceding them as messengers of peace.

When they approached the camp of the Ethiopians, they fell down on their knees, raising, as with one consent, a plaintive and mournful cry; and deprecating, by the most humble gestures, the victor's wrath.

They laid their infants on the ground before them, seemingly leaving them to wander whither chance might lead; intending to pacify the wrath of the Ethiopians by the sight of their innocent and guiltless age. The poor children, frightened at the behaviour and outcries of their parents, crept (some of them) towards the adverse army; and with their tottering steps and wailing voices, presented an affecting scene, Fortune, as it were, converting them into instruments of supplication.

Hydaspes observing this uncommon spectacle, and conceiving that they were reiterating their former entreaties and imploring pardon for their crime, sent to know what they meant, and why they came alone, and without the Persians.

They related all which had happened—the flight of the Persians, their own entire ignorance of it,—the festival they had been celebrating, and the opportunity secretly taken by the garrison to leave them, when they were buried in sleep, after their feastings and fatigues; although, had they been awake, and had they seen them, it would have been out of their power, unarmed as they were, to hinder the retreat of men in arms.

Hydaspes from this relation suspected, as was really the case, that Oroondates had some secret design and stratagem against him; summoning the Egyptian priests therefore, and for the sake of greater solemnity, adoring the images of the gods which they carried with them, he inquired if they could give him any further information about the Persians. He asked whither they were gone, and what were their hopes and intentions. They replied, "That they were ignorant of their schemes; but supposed them to be gone to Elephantine," where the principal part of the army was assembled, Oroondates placing his chief confidence in his barbed cavalry. They concluded by beseeching him, if he had conceived any resentment against them to lay it aside, and to enter their city, as if it were his own.

Hydaspes did not choose to make his entry for the present, but sent two troops of soldiers to search every place where he suspected an ambush might be laid; if they found nothing of that sort, destining them as a garrison for the city. He dismissed the inhabitants of it with kindness and gracious promises, and drew out his army ready to receive the attack of the Persians, should they advance; or, to march against them himself if they delayed.

His troops were hardly formed in order of march when his scouts informed him that the Persians were advancing towards him to give battle: Oroondates had assembled an army at Elephantine, just at the time when as we have seen, he was forced, by the sudden approach of the Ethiopians, to throw himself into Syene with a few troops; being then reduced to imminent danger by the contrivance of Hydaspes; he secured the preservation of the place, and his own safety, by a method which stamped him with the deepest perfidy. The two Persians sent to Elephantine, under pretence of inquiring on what terms the troops there were willing to submit, were really dispatched with a view of informing him whether they were ready and disposed to resist and fight, if by any means he could escape, and put himself at their head.

He now proceeded to put into practice his treacherous intent, for upon his arrival at Elephantine, finding them in such a disposition as he could wish, he led them out without delay, and proceeded with all expedition against the enemy; relying chiefly for success on the hope that by the rapidity of his movements he should surprise them while unprepared. He was now in sight, attracting every eye by the Persian pomp of his host; the whole plain glistening as he moved along, with gold and silver armour. The rays of the rising sun falling directly upon the advancing Persians, shed an indiscribable brightness to the most distant parts, their own armour flashing back a rival brightness.

The right wing was composed of native Medes and Persians—the heavy armed in front—behind them the archers, unincumbered with defensive arms, that they might with more ease and readiness perform their evolutions, protected by those who were before them. The Egyptians, the Africans, and all the auxiliaries were in the left wing. To these likewise were assigned a band of light troops, slingers and archers, who were ordered to make sallies, and to discharge their weapons from the flanks. Oroondates himself was in the centre, splendidly accoutred and mounted on a scythed chariot. He was surrounded on either side by a body of troops, and in front were the barbed cavalry, his confidence in whom had principally induced him to hazard an engagement. These are the most warlike in the Persian service, and are always first opposed, like a firm wall, to the enemy. The following is the description of their armour—A man, picked out for strength and stature, puts on a helmet which fits his head and face exactly, like a mask; covered completely down to the neck with this, except a small opening left for the eyes, in his right hand he brandishes a long spear—his left remains at liberty to guide the reins—a scimitar is suspended at his side; and not his breast alone, but his whole body also, is sheathed in mail, which is composed of a number of square separate plates of brass or steel, a span in length, fitting over each other at each of the four sides, and hooked or sewn together beneath, the upper lapping over the under; the side of each over that next to it in order. Thus the whole body is inclosed in an imbricated scaly tunic, which fits it closely, yet by contraction and expansion allows ample play for all the limbs. It is sleeved, and reaches from neck to knee, the only part left unarmed being under the cuishes, necessity for the seat on horseback so requiring. The greave extends from the feet to the knee, and is connected with the coat. This defence is sufficient to turn aside all darts, and to resist the stroke of any weapon. The horse is as well protected as his rider; greaves cover his legs, and a frontal confines his head. From his back to his belly, on either side, hangs a sheet of the mail, which I have been describing, which guards his body, while its looseness does not impede his motions.

Thus accoutred and as it were fitted into his armour, this ponderous soldier sits his horse, unable to mount himself on account of his weight, but lifted on by another. When the time for charging arrives, giving the reins, and setting spurs to his horse, he is carried with all his force against the enemy, wearing the appearance of a hammer-wrought statue, or of an iron man. His long and pointed spear extends far before him, and is sustained by a rest at the horse's neck, the butt being fixed in another at his croupe. Thus the spear does not give way in the conflict, but assists the hand of the horseman, who has merely to direct the weapon, which pressing onwards with mighty power pierces every obstacle, sometimes transfixing and bearing off by its impulse two men at once.

With such a force of cavalry and in such order, Oroondates marched against the enemy, keeping the river still behind him, to prevent his being surrounded by the Ethiopians, who far exceeded him in number. Hydaspes, on the other hand, advanced to meet him. He opposed, to the Medes and Persians in the right wing, his forces from Meröe, who were well accoutred, and accustomed to close fighting. The swift and light-armed Troglodites, who were good archers, and the inhabitants of the cinnamon region, he drew up to give employment to those posted on the left. In opposition to the centre, boasting as they did of their barbed cavalry, he placed himself, with the tower-bearing elephants, the Blemmyæ, and the Seres, giving them instructions what they were to do when they came to engage. Both armies now approached near, and gave the signal for battle; the Persians with trumpets, the Ethiopians with drums and gongs. Oroondates, cheering on his men, charged with his body of horse. Hydaspes ordered his troops to advance very slowly, that they might not leave their elephants, and that the enemy's cavalry, having a longer course to take, might become exhausted before the conflict. When the Blemmyæ saw them within reach of a spear's cast, the horsemen urging on their horses for the charge, they proceeded to execute their monarch's instructions.

Leaving the Seres to guard the elephants, they sprang out of the ranks, and advanced swiftly towards the enemy. The Persians thought they had lost their senses, seeing a few foot presume to oppose themselves to so numerous and so formidable a body of horse. These latter galloped on all the faster, glad to take advantage of their rashness, and confident that they should sweep them away at the first onset. But the Blemmyæ, when now the phalanx had almost reached them, and they were all but touched by their spears, on a sudden, at a signal, threw themselves on one knee, and thrust their heads and backs under the horses, running no danger by this attempt, but that of being trampled on: this manœuvre was quite unexpected, many of the horses they wounded in the belly as they passed, so that they no longer obeyed the bridle, but became furious, and threw their riders; whom, as they lay like logs, the Blemmyæ pierced in the only vulnerable part, the Persian cuirassier being incapable of moving without help.

Those whose horses were not wounded proceeded to charge the Seres, who at their approach retired behind the elephants, as behind a wall or bulwark. Here an almost total slaughter of the cavalry took place. For the horses of the Persians, as soon as the sudden retreat of the Seres had discovered these enormous beasts, astonished at their unusual and formidable appearance, either turned short round and galloped off, or fell back upon the rest, so that the whole body was thrown into confusion. They who were stationed in the towers upon the elephants (six in number, two on either side, except towards the beast's hind quarters), discharged their arrows as from a bulwark, so continuously and with such true aim, that they appeared to the Persians like a cloud.

Fighting upon unequal terms against mailed warriors, and depending upon their skill in archery, so unfailing was their aim at the sight holes of the enemy, that you might see many galloping in confusion through the throng, with arrows projecting from their eyes.

Some, carried away by the unruliness of their horses to the elephants, were either trampled under foot or attacked by the Seres and the Blemmyæ, who rushing out as from an ambush, wounded some, and pulled others from their horses, in the melée. They who escaped unhurt retreated in disorder, not having done the smallest injury to the elephants: for these beasts are armed with mail when led out to battle, and have, besides, a natural defence in a hard and rugged skin, which will resist and turn the point of any spear.

Oroondates, when he saw the remainder routed, set the example of a shameful flight; and descending from his chariot, and mounting a Nysæan horse, galloped from the field. The Egyptians and Africans in the left wing were ignorant of this, and continued still bravely fighting, receiving, however, more injury than they inflicted, which they bore with great fortitude and perseverance; for the inhabitants of the cinnamon region, who were opposed to them, pressed and confounded them by the irregularity and activity of their attacks, flying as the Egyptians advanced, and discharging their arrows backward as they fled. When the Africans retreated, they attacked them, galling them on all the flanks, either with slings or little poisoned arrows. These they fixed around their turbans, the feathers next their heads, the points radiating outwards; and drawing them thence as from a quiver, they, after taking a sudden spring forward, shot them against the enemy, their own bodies being naked, and their only clothing this crown of arrows. These arrows require no iron point; they take a serpent's back bone, about a foot and a half in length, and after straightening it, sharpen the end into a natural point, which may perhaps account for the origin of the word arrow.

The Egyptians resisted a long time, defending themselves from the darts by interlocking shields—being naturally patient, and bravely prodigal of their lives, not merely for pay but glory; perhaps, too, dreading the punishment of runaways. But when they heard that the barbed cavalry, the strength and right hand of their army, was defeated—that the viceroy had left the field, and that the Medes and Persians, the flower of their foot, having done little against, and suffered much from, those to whom they were opposed, had followed his example, they likewise, at last, gave up the contest, turned about, and retreated. Hydaspes, from an elephant's back, as from a watch tower, was spectator of his victory; which when he saw decided, he sent messengers after the pursuers, to stop the slaughter, and to order them to take as many prisoners as they could, and particularly, were it possible, Oroondates.

Success crowned his wishes, for the Ethiopians extending their numerous lines to a great length on each side, and curving the extremities till they surrounded the Persians, left them no way to escape but to the river. Thus the stratagem which Oroondates had devised against the enemy they found turned against themselves, multitudes being forced into the river by the horses and scythed chariots, and the confusion of the crowd. The viceroy had never reflected, that by having the river in his rear he was cutting off his own means of escape. He was taken prisoner with Achæmenes the son of Cybele. This latter informed of what had happened at Memphis, and dreading the resentment of Oroondates, for having made an accusation against Arsace which he was not able to prove, (the witnesses who would have enabled him to do so being removed,) endeavoured to slay his master in the tumult. He did not, however, give him a mortal wound, and the attempt was instantly revenged, for he was transfixed with an arrow by an Ethiopian, who watched, as he had been commanded, over the safety of the viceroy; and who saw, with indignation, the treacherous attempt of one, who, having escaped the enemy, took the opportunity presented by fortune, to wreak his revenge against his commander.

Oroondates was brought before Hydaspes, faint and bleeding; but his wound was soon staunched by the remedies applied, the king being resolved, if possible, to save him, and himself giving him encouragement.

"Friend," said he, "I grant your life. I hold it honourable to overcome my enemies by my arms while they resist; and by my good offices when they are fallen: but why have you shewn such perfidy towards me?"

"Towards you, I own," replied the Persian, "I have been perfidious; but to my master I have been faithful."—"As vanquished, then," replied Hydaspes, "what punishment, think you, that you deserve?"—"The same," returned the other, "which my master would inflict upon one of your captains who had fallen into his power, after having proved his fidelity to you."—"If your master," replied the Ethiopian, "were truly royal, and not a tyrant, he would praise and reward him; and excite the emulation of his own people, by commending the good qualities of an enemy: but it seems to me, good sir, that you praise your fidelity at the expence of your prudence, after having adventured yourself against so many myriads of my troops."—"Perhaps," replied Oroondates, "in regard to myself, I have not been so imprudent as may at first appear. I knew the disposition of my sovereign—to punish cowards, rather than to reward the brave. I determined therefore to hazard every thing, and trust to Fortune, who sometimes affords unexpected and improbable successes in war. If I failed and escaped with life, I should at least have it to say, that nothing in my power had been left untried."

Hydaspes, after listening to his words, praised him, sent him to Syene, ordered his physicians to attend him, and all possible care to be taken of him. He himself soon after made his public entry into the city, with the flower of his army. The inhabitants of all ranks and ages went out in procession to meet him, strewed crowns and flowers of the Nile, in his path, greeting him with songs of victory.

He entered the city on an elephant, as on a triumphal chariot, and immediately turned his thoughts to holy matters and thanksgivings to the gods. He made inquiries concerning everything worthy of his curiosity, particularly about the origin of the feasts of the Nile. They shewed him a tank which served as a nilometer, like that which is at Memphis, lined with polished stone, and marked with degrees at the interval of every cubit. The water flows into it under ground, and the height to which it rises in the tank, shews the general excess, or deficiency, of the inundation, according as the degrees are covered or left bare. They shewed him dials, which, at a certain season of the year, cast no shade at noon; for, at the summer solstice, the sun is vertical at Syene, and darts its rays perpendicularly down, so that the water, at the bottom of the deepest wells, is light.

This, however, raised no great astonishment in Hydaspes; for the same phenomenon happens at the Ethiopian Meröe. The people of Syene loudly praised their festival and extolled the Nile, calling it Horus (the year), the fertilizer of their plains—the preserver of Upper Egypt—the father, and, in a manner, the creator of the Lower—as it brings annually new soil into it, and is from thence, possibly, called Nile, by the Greeks.

It points out, they said, the annual vicissitudes of time—summer by the increase, and autumn by the retiring of its waters—spring by the flowers which grow on it, and by the breeding of the crocodiles. The Nile then, is, they say, nothing else but the year, its very appellation confirming this, since the numeral letters which compose its name, amount to 365 units, the number of days which make up the year. They extolled also its peculiar plants and flowers, and animals, and added a thousand other encomiums. "All these praises," said Hydaspes, "belong more to Ethiopia, than to Egypt. If you esteem this river as the father of waters, and exalt it to the rank of a deity, Ethiopia ought surely to be worshipped, which is the mother of your god?"

"We do worship it," replied the priests, "both on many other accounts, and because it has sent you to us, as a preserver and a god." After recommending them to be less lavish in their praises, he retired to a tent which had been prepared for him, and devoted the rest of the day to ease and refreshment. He entertained, at his own table, his principal officers, and the priests of Syene, and encouraged all ranks to make merry. The inhabitants of Syene furnished herds of oxen, flocks of sheep, goats and swine, together with store of wine, partly by way of gift, partly for sale. The next day he mounted a lofty seat; and, ordering the spoil to be brought out, which had been collected in the city, and on the field of battle, distributed it amongst his army, in such proportions as he thought their merit deserved. When the soldier appeared who took Oroondates, "Ask what you please," said the king.—"I have no occasion to ask anything," he replied. "If you will allow me to keep what I have already taken from the Viceroy, I am sufficiently rewarded for having made him prisoner, and preserved him alive, according to your commands." And with this he shewed a sword belt, a scimitar richly jewelled of great value, and worth many talents; so that many cried out, it was a gift too precious for a private man, a treasure worthy of a monarch's acceptance. Hydaspes smilingly replied—

"What can be more kingly than that my magnanimity should be superior to this man's avarice? Besides, the captor has a right to the personal spoils of his prisoner. Let him then, receive as a gift from me, what he might easily have taken to himself, without my knowledge."

Presently those who had taken Theagenes and Chariclea appeared. "Our spoil, O king!" said they, "is not gold and jewels, things of little estimation among the Ethiopians, and which lie in heaps in the royal treasures; but we bring you a youth and a maiden, a Grecian pair, excelling all mortals in grace and beauty, except yourself, and we expect from your liberality a proportionate reward."—"You recall them seasonably to my memory," replied Hydaspes. "When I first saw them, in the hurry and confusion in which I was engaged, I took but a cursory view of them. Let some one bring them now before me, together with the rest of the captives."

An officer was immediately despatched for them to the place of their confinement, which was among the baggage, at some distance from the town. They inquired, in their way to the city, of one of their guards, whither they were being conducted. They were told that the king Hydaspes desired to see the prisoners. On hearing the name, they cried out together, with one voice—"O ye gods!" fearing till that hour lest some other might be the reigning king; and Theagenes said softly to Chariclea—"You will surely now discover to the king everything which relates to us, since you have frequently told me that Hydaspes was your father."

"Important matters," replied Chariclea, "require great preparation. Where the deity has caused intricate beginnings, there must needs be intricate unravellings. Besides, a tale like ours is not to be told in a moment; nor do I think it advisable to enter upon it in the absence of my mother Persina, upon whose support, and testimony, the foundation of our story, and the whole of our credit, must depend; and she, thanks to the gods I hear, is yet alive."

"What if we should be sacrificed," returned Theagenes; "or, presented to some one as a gift, how shall we ever get into Ethiopia?"—"Nothing is less likely," said Chariclea. "Our guards have told us that we are to be reserved as victims, to be offered to the deities of Meröe. There is no likelihood that we, who are solemnly devoted to the gods, should be destroyed, or otherwise disposed of; such a vow no religious mind would break. Were we to give way to the incautious joy with which this sudden gleam of good fortune transports us, and discover our condition, and relate our adventures, in the absence of those who alone can acknowledge us, and confirm what we say, we run the greatest risk of raising the indignation of the king; who would regard it as a mockery and insult, that we, captives and slaves as we are, should endeavour to pass ourselves off upon him, as his children."

"But the tokens," said Theagenes, "which I know you always carry about you, will give credit to our relation, and shew that we are not impostors."—"These things," replied Chariclea, "are real tokens to those who know them, and who exposed them with me; but to those who are ignorant of this, they are nothing but bracelets, and precious stones; and may possibly induce a suspicion of our having stolen them. Supposing even that Hydaspes should recollect any of these trinkets, who shall persuade him that they were presented to me by Persina, and still more, that they were the gifts of a mother to her daughter? The most incontrovertible token, my dear Theagenes, is a mother's nature, through which the parent at first sight feels affection towards her offspring,—an affection stirred up by secret sympathy. Shall we deprive ourselves, then, by our precipitation, of this most favourable opening, upon which depends the credit of all we have to say?"

Discoursing in this manner, they arrived near the tribunal of the king. Bagoas was led after them. When Hydaspes saw them, rising suddenly from his throne—"May the gods be propitious to me!" he exclaimed, and sat down again, lost in thought. They who were near him inquired the reason of this sudden emotion. Recollecting himself, he said—"Methought that I had a daughter born to me this day, who at once reached her prime, and perfectly resembled this young maiden, whom I see before me. I disregarded, and had almost forgotten my dream, when this remarkable resemblance recalled it to my memory."

His officers replied—"That it was some fancy of the mind bodying forth future events;" upon which the king, laying aside for the present any farther thought upon the subject, proceeded to examine his prisoners. He asked them—"Who, and from whence, they were?" Chariclea was silent. Theagenes replied, "That they were Grecians, and that the maiden was his sister."

"All honour to Greece," said Hydaspes—"the mother of brave and beautiful mortals, for affording us such noble victims for the celebration of our triumphal sacrifices." And turning to his attendants, he said—"Why had I not a son as well as a daughter born to me in my dream, since this youth, being the maiden's brother, ought according to your observation, to have been shadowed forth to me in my vision?"

He then directed his discourse to Chariclea, speaking in Greek; a language known and studied by the Gymnosophists, and kings of Ethiopia—"And you, O maiden," said he, "why do you make no answer to my questions?"—"At the altars of the gods," replied she, "to whom we are destined as victims, you shall know who I am, and who are my parents."

"And what part of the world do they inhabit?" said the king.—"They are present now," said she, "and will assuredly be present, when we are sacrificed." Again Hydaspes smiled.—"This dream-born daughter of mine," he observed, "is certainly herself dreaming, when she imagines that her parents are to be brought from the middle of Greece into Meröe. Let them be taken away and served with the usual care and abundance, to fit them for the sacrifices. But who is this standing near, and in person like an eunuch?"—"He is an eunuch," replied one of the bystanders; "his name is Bagoas; he was in great favour with Oroondates."

"Let him too," said the king, "follow and be kept with the Grecian pair; not as a future victim, but that he may attend upon, and watch over the virgin victim, whom it is necessary to preserve in the utmost purity for the sacrifice; and whose beauty is such, that her virtue, unguarded, may be exposed to much danger and temptation. Eunuchs are a jealous race; and fitly employed for debarring others from the enjoyments of which they are themselves deprived." He then proceeded to examine and decide the fate of the remaining prisoners, who appeared in order; distributing among his followers those who were slaves before; dismissing with liberty those who were free and noble: but he selected ten young men, and as many virgins, in the bloom of youth and beauty, whom he ordered to be preserved for the same purpose to which he had destined Theagenes and Chariclea. And having answered every complaint and application, at last he sent for Oroondates, who was brought in lying on a litter.

"I," said he to him, "now that I have obtained the object of my going to war, feel not the common passion of ambitious minds. I am not going to make my good fortune the minister of covetousness; my victory creates in me no wish to extend my empire. I am content with the limits which nature seems to have placed between Egypt and Ethiopia—the cataracts. Having recovered then what I think my right, I revere what is just and equitable, and shall return peacefully to my own dominions. Do you, if your life be spared, remain viceroy of the same province as before: and write to your master, the Persian king, to this effect, 'Thy brother Hydaspes has conquered by might of hand; but restores all through moderation of mind; he wishes to preserve thy friendship, esteeming it the most valuable of all possessions: at the same time, if desirous of renewing the contest, thou wilt not find him backward.' As to the Syenæans I remit their tribute for ten years; and command thee to do the same." Loud acclamations, both from the soldiers and citizens, followed his last words.

Oroondates crossing his hands, and inclining his body, adored him; a compliment not usual for a Persian to pay to any prince, except his own.—"O ye who hear me," said he, "I do not think that I violate the customs of my country, as to my own sovereign, in adoring the most just of kings, who has restored to me my government; who instead of putting me to death has granted me my life; who, able to act as a despotic lord, permits me to remain a viceroy. Should I recover, I pledge myself to promote a solid peace and lasting friendship between the Persians and Ethiopians, and to procure for the Syenæans that remission of tribute which has been enjoined; but should I not survive, may the gods recompense Hydaspes, his family, and remotest descendants, for all the benefits which he has conferred upon me!"

Book X

We have now said sufficient about Syene, which, from the brink of danger, was at once restored to security and happiness, by one man's clemency.

Hydaspes, having sent the greater part of his army forward, proceeded in person towards Ethiopia, followed by the applauses and blessings both of Persians and Syenæans. At first he marched along the Nile, or the parts bordering upon that river; but when he reached the cataracts, having sacrificed to the river, and to the gods of the boundaries, he turned aside, and travelled through the inland country.

When he arrived at Philœ, he rested, and refreshed his army there for two days; and then as before, sending part of it forward, together with the captives, he stayed some little time behind them, to direct the repair of the walls, and to place a garrison, and soon afterwards set out himself. He dispatched an express consisting of two troopers, who changing their horses at every station, and using all speed, were to announce his victory at Meröe.

He sent the following message to the wise men of his country, who are called Gymnosophists, and who are the assessors and privy councillors of the Ethiopian kings in affairs of moment.

"Hydaspes to the most holy Council.

"I acquaint you with my victory over the Persians. I do not boast of my success, for I know and fear the mutability of fortune; but I would greet your holy order, which I have always found wise and faithful. I invite and command your attendance at the usual place, in order that the thanksgiving sacrifices for victory, may, by your presence, be rendered more august and solemn in the sight of the Ethiopian people."

To his consort, Persina, he wrote as follows:—

"Know that I am returning a conqueror, and, what you will still more rejoice at, unhurt. Make therefore preparations for the most sumptuous processions and sacrifices, that we may give thanks to the gods, for the blessings which they have bestowed. In accordance with my letters, assist in summoning the Gymnosophists; and hasten to attend, with them, in the consecrated field before the city, which is dedicated to our country's gods—the Sun, the Moon, and Bacchus."

When this letter was delivered to Persina—"I now see," said she, "the interpretation of a dream which I had last night. Methought I was pregnant, and in labour, and that I brought forth a daughter in the full bloom of youth and beauty. I see, that by my throes, were signified the travails of war; and by my daughter, this victory."

"Go," continued she, "and fill the city with these joyful tidings." The expresses obeyed her commands; and mounting their horses, having crowned their heads with the lotus of the Nile, and waving branches of palm in their hands, rode through the principal parts of the city, disclosing by their very appearance, the joyous news.

Meröe resounded with rejoicings; night and day the inhabitants, in every family, and street, and tribe, made processions, offered sacrifices, and suspended garlands in the temples; not more out of gratitude for the victory, than for the safety of Hydaspes; whose justice and clemency, mildness and affability, had made him beloved, like a father, by his subjects. The queen, on her side, collected together from all parts, quantities of sheep and oxen, of horses and wild asses, of hippogriffs, and all sorts of animals, and sent them into the sacred field, partly to furnish a hecatomb of each, for sacrifice, partly to provide from the remainder, an entertainment for all the people.

She next visited the Gymnosophists, who inhabit the grove of Pan, and exhorted them to obey the summons of their king, as also to gratify her by adorning and sanctifying the solemnity with their presence. They, entreating her to wait a few moments, while they consulted the gods, as they are used to do on any new undertaking, entered their temple, and after a short time returned, when Sisimithres, their president, thus addressed her:—"O queen! we will attend you, the gods order us to do so; but, at the same time, they signify to us, that this sacrifice will be attended with much disturbance and tumult, which, however, will have an agreeable and happy end. A limb of your body, or a member of the state, seems to have been lost; which will be restored by fate."

"Your presence," said Persina, "will avert every threatening presage, and change it into good; I will take care to inform you when Hydaspes arrives."

"You will have no occasion to do that," replied Sisimithres: "he will arrive to-morrow, and you will presently receive letters to that effect." His prediction was fulfilled. Persina, on her return to the palace, found a messenger with letters from the king, announcing his intended arrival for the following day.

The heralds dispersed the news through the city, and at the same time, made proclamation, that the men alone should be suffered to go out and meet him, but that the women should keep within their houses; for, as the sacrifice was destined to be offered to the purest of all deities—the Sun and Moon—the presence of females was forbidden, lest the victims should acquire even an involuntary contamination.

The priestess of the Moon was the only woman suffered to attend the ceremony, and she was Persina; for by the law and custom of the country, the queens of Ethiopia are always priestesses of that divinity, as the kings are of the Sun. Chariclea, also was to be present at the ceremonial, not as a spectatress, but as a victim to the Moon.

The eagerness and curiosity of the citizens was incredible. Before they knew the appointed day, they poured in multitudes out of the city, crossed the river Astabora, some over the bridge; some who dwelt at a distance from it, in boats made of canes, many of which lay near the banks, affording an expeditious means of passage.

These little skiffs are very swift, both on account of the materials of which they are composed, and the slight burden which they carry, which never exceeds two or three men: for one cane is split in two, and each section forms a boat.

Meröe, the metropolis of Ethiopia, is situated in a sort of triangular island, formed by the confluence of three navigable rivers; the Nile, the Astabora, and the Asasoba. The former flows towards it from above, where it forms two branches; the others, flowing round it on either side, unite their waters, and hasten to mingle their stream, and lose their names, in the channel of the Nile.

This island, which is almost a continent, (being in length three thousand furlongs, in width one thousand), abounds in animals of every kind, and, among the rest, with elephants. It is especially fertile in producing trees. The palm trees rise to an unusual height, bearing dates of large size and delicious flavour. The stalks of wheat and barley are so tall, as to cover and conceal a man when mounted on a horse or camel, and they multiply their fruit three hundred fold. The canes are of the size which I have before mentioned.

All the night were the inhabitants employed in crossing the river; they met, received, and congratulated Hydaspes, extolling him as a god. They had gone a considerable way to meet him. The Gymnosophists went only a little beyond the sacred field, when, taking his hand, they kissed him. Next appeared Persina at the vestibule, and within the precincts of the temple.

After worshipping the gods, and returning thanks for his victory and safety, they left the precincts, and prepared to attend the approaching sacrifice, repairing for that purpose to a tent, which had been erected for them on the plain. Four canes, newly cut down, were fixed in the ground, one at each corner, serving as a pillar, supported the vaulted roof, which was covered with the branches of palm and other trees. Near this another tent was erected, raised considerably from the ground, in which were placed the images of the gods of the country—Memnon, Perseus, and Andromeda—whom the kings of Ethiopia boasted to be the founders of their race: under these, on a lower story, having their gods above them, sat the Gymnosophists. A large portion of the ground was surrounded by the soldiers; who in close order, and with their shields joined, kept off the multitude, and afforded a clear space sufficient for the priests to perform their sacrifice, without confusion or disturbance.

Hydaspes, after speaking briefly upon the victory which he had gained, and the advantages obtained by it to the state, commanded the sacred ministers to begin their rites.

Three lofty altars were erected, two in close proximity to the Sun and Moon; a third, at some distance, to Bacchus: to him they sacrificed animals of every kind, as being a common deity, gracious and bountiful to all. To the Sun they offered four white horses, the swiftest of animals to the swiftest of the gods; to the Moon, a yoke of oxen, consecrating to her, as being nearest the earth, their assistants in agriculture.

While these things were transacting, a loud confused murmur began to rise as among a promiscuous multitude; "Let our country's rites be performed—let the appointed sacrifice be made—let the first-fruits of war be offered to our gods."

Hydaspes understood that it was a human victim whom they demanded, which it was customary to offer from among the prisoners taken only in a foreign war. Making a motion for silence, with his hand, he intimated to them, by gestures, that they should soon have what they required, and ordered those who had the charge of the captives to bring them forward. They obeyed, and led them forth, guarded, but freed from their chains.

The generality were, as may be imagined, dejected and sorrowful. Theagenes, however, appeared much less so than the others; but the countenance of Chariclea was cheerful and elate. She fixed her eyes upon Persina with a fixed and steady glance, so as to cause in her considerable emotion; she could not help sighing, as she said—"O husband! what a maiden have you destined for sacrifice! I never remember to have seen such beauty. How noble is her presence! with what spirit and fortitude does she seem to meet her impending fate! How worthy is she of compassion, owing to the flower of her age. If my only and unfortunately lost daughter were living, she would be about the same age. O that it were possible to save this maiden from destruction; it would be a great satisfaction to me to have her in my service. She is probably Grecian, for she has not at all the air of an Egyptian."

"She is from Greece," replied Hydaspes: "who are her parents she will presently declare; shew them she cannot, though such has been her promise. To deliver her from sacrifice is impossible: were it in my power, I should be very glad to do so; for I feel, I know not why, great compassion and affection for her. But you are aware that the law requires a male to be offered to the Sun, and a female to the Moon; and she being the first captive presented to me, and having been allotted for the sacrifice, the disappointment of the people's wishes would admit of no excuse. One only chance can favour her escape, and that is, if she should be found when she ascends the pile, not to have preserved her chastity inviolate; for the law demands a pure victim to be offered to the goddess as well as to the god—the condition of those offered on the altar of Bacchus is indifferent. But should she be found unchaste, reflect whether it would be proper that she should be received into your family."

"Let her," replied Persina, "be found unchaste, provided only she be preserved. Captivity and war, absence from friends, and a wandering life, furnish an excuse for guilt, particularly in her, whose transcendent beauty must have exposed her to more than common temptations."

While she was weeping and striving to conceal her weakness from the people, Hydaspes ordered the fire-altar to be prepared, and brought out. A number of young children, collected by the officials from among the multitude, brought it from the temple (they alone being permitted to touch it), and placed it in the midst. Each of the captives was then ordered to ascend it. It was furnished with golden bars of such mystic virtue, that whenever any unchaste or perjured person placed his foot upon it, it burnt him immediately, and he was obliged to retire: the pure, on the contrary, and the uncontaminated, could mount it uninjured.

The greatest part of the prisoners failed in the trial, and were destined as victims to Bacchus, and the other gods—save two or three Grecian maidens whose virginity was found intact. Theagenes at length ascended it, and was found pure. It raised great admiration in the assembly, that with his beauty, stature, and in the flower of youth, he should be a stranger to the power of love—accordingly he was destined as an offering to the Sun. He said softly to Chariclea—"Is death then, and sacrifice, the reward which the Ethiopians bestow upon purity and integrity? But why, my dearest life, do you not discover yourself? How long will you delay? Until the sacrificer's knife is at your throat? Speak, I beseech you, and disclose your condition. Perhaps when you are known, your intercession may preserve me; but if that should not happen, you will be safe, and then I shall die with comfort and satisfaction."

"Our trial," said Chariclea, "now approaches—our fate trembles in the balance."—So saying, and without awaiting any command, she drew from out of a scrip which she had with her, and put on, her sacred Delphic robe, interwoven and glittering with rays of light. She let her hair fall dishevelled upon her shoulders, and as under the influence of inspiration, leaped upon the altar, and remained there a long time, unhurt.

Dazzling every beholder with more than ever resplendent beauty; visible to all from this elevated place, and with her peculiar dress, she resembled an image of the goddess, more than a mere mortal maiden. An inarticulate murmur of applause ran through the multitude, expressive of their surprise and admiration, that with charms so superhuman, she should have preserved her honour, enhancing her beauty by her chastity. Yet they were almost sorry that she was found a pure and fitting victim for the goddess. Notwithstanding their religious reverence they would have been glad could she by any means escape. But Persina felt more for her than all the rest. She could not help saying to Hydaspes—"How miserable and ill-fated is this poor maiden! To no purpose giving token of her purity! Receiving for her many virtues only an untimely death! Can nothing be done to save her?"

"Nothing, I fear," replied the king: "your wishes and pity are unavailable. It seems that the gods have from the beginning selected by reason of her very excellence this perfect victim for themselves." And then directing his discourse to the Gymnosophists: "Sages," said he, "since every thing is ready, why do you not begin the sacrifice?"—"Far be it from us," said Sisimithres (speaking in Greek, that the multitude might not understand him) "to assist at such rites; our eyes and ears have already been sufficiently wounded by the preparations. We will retire into the temple, abhorring ourselves the detestable offering of a human victim, and believing too that the gods do not approve it. Would that the sacrifices even of brute animals might cease; those consisting of prayers and incense being, to our mind, sufficient. Do you, however, remain; for the presence of a ruler is sometimes necessary to stay the turbulence of the multitude. Go on with this unhallowed sacrifice, since the inveterate custom of the people has made it unavoidable; remembering that when it is performed, yourself will stand in need of expiation, though perhaps, you will not need it, for I think this rite will never be brought to consummation. I judge from various divine tokens, and particularly from a kind of glory shed around these strangers, signifying that they are under the peculiar protection of the gods;"—having said this, he arose, and was about to retire with his brethren.

At this instant Chariclea leapt down from the altar; rushed towards Sisimithres, and fell at his feet. The officials would have hindered her, supposing that she was deprecating death, but she exclaimed "Stay, Sages, I beseech you! I have a cause to plead before the king and queen; you are the only judges, in such a presence; you must decide in this, the trial for my life. You will find that it is neither possible nor just that I should be sacrificed to the gods." They listened to her readily, and addressing the king, said,—"Do you hear, O king, the challenge and averment of this foreign maiden."

Hydaspes smiling, replied, "What controversy can she have with me? From what pretext, or from what right, can it arise?"—"That, her own relation will discover," said Sisimithres.—"But will it not be an indignity, rather than an act of justice," rejoined the monarch, "for a king to enter into a judicial dispute with a slave?"—"Equity regards not lofty rank," said the sage. "He is king in judgment who prevails by strength of arguments."—"But," returned Hydaspes, "your office gives you a right of deciding only when a controversy arises between the king and his own subjects, not between him and foreigners."—"Justice," said Sisimithres, "is weighed among the wise, not by mere appearances, but by facts."—"It is clear that she can have nothing serious to advance," said the king, "but some mere idle pretext to delay her fate, as is the case with those who are in fear of their lives. Let her, however, speak, since Sisimithres would have it so."

Chariclea, who had always been sanguine, in expecting her deliverance, was now inspired with additional confidence when she heard the name of Sisimithres. He was the person to whose care she had been committed ten years before, and who delivered her to Charicles at Catadupa, when he was sent ambassador to Oroondates in the matter of the emerald mines—he was then one of the ordinary

Gymnosophists: but now, he was their president. Chariclea did not call to mind his face (having been parted from him when only seven years' old), but recollected and rejoiced at hearing his name, trusting that she should find in him a support and an advocate. Stretching out then her hands towards heaven, and speaking audibly,—"O Sun!" she exclaimed, "author of my family; and you, ye gods and heroes who adorn my race! I call you to witness the truth of what I say. Be you my supporters and assistants in the trial which I am about to undergo—my cause is just, and thus I enter upon it:—Does the law, O king, command you to sacrifice natives or foreigners?"

"Foreigners only," replied Hydaspes.—"You must then seek another victim," said she, "for you will find me a native." The king seemed surprised, declaring it to be a figment. "Do you wonder at this?" said she; "you will hear much stranger things. I am not only a native, but closely allied to the royal family." This assertion was received with contempt, as so much idle speech: when she added—"Cease, my father, to despise and reject your daughter!"

By this time the king began to appear not only contemptuous, but indignant, taking the matter as a personal insult to himself. He said, therefore, to Sisimithres,—"Behold the reward of my endurance! Is not the maiden downright mad! Endeavouring with wild and incredible fictions to escape the fate awaiting her! desperately feigning herself to be my daughter, as in some sudden appearance and discovery upon the stage—mine, who was never so fortunate as to have any offspring. Once, indeed, I heard of a daughter's birth, only, however, to learn her death. Let then some one lead her away, that the sacrifice may be no longer deferred."—"No one shall lead me away," cried out Chariclea, "till the judges have given sentence. You are in this affair a party, not a judge; the law perhaps permits you to sacrifice foreigners, but to sacrifice your children, neither law nor nature allows; and the gods shall this day declare you to be my father, however unwilling you appear to own me. Every cause, O king, which comes for judgment, leans principally upon two kinds of proof, written evidence, and that of living witnesses: both these will I bring forward to prove myself your child. I shall appeal to no common witness, but to my judge himself (the consciousness of the judge is the prisoner's best ground of confidence); as to my written evidence it shall be a history of my own and your misfortunes." So saying, she loosened from her waist the fillet which had been exposed with her, unrolled, and presented it to Persina. She, as soon as it met her sight, appeared struck dumb with astonishment; she continued a considerable time casting her eyes first on the writing, then again on the maiden. A cold sweat bedewed her limbs, and convulsive tremblings shook her frame.

Her first emotions were those of joy and hope; but anxiety and doubt succeeded. Dread of the suspicions of Hydaspes followed; of his incredulity, and perhaps of his anger and vengeance.

The king observing her agitation and astonishment, said to her, "Persina! what is it which ails you? from what cause has this writing such effect upon you?"—"My king, my lord, and my husband!" she replied, "I know not what to answer you: take and read it yourself: let this fillet explain everything." She gave it him, and remained trembling, in anxious silence.

He took the fillet, and began to read it, calling to the Gymnosophists to read it with him. As he proceeded, he was struck with doubt and amazement; but Sisimithres was still more astonished: his ever-changing colour betrayed the various emotions of his mind: he fixed his eyes now on the fillet, and now on Chariclea.

At length Hydaspes, when he came to the account of the exposing of the infant, and the cause of it, broke silence, and said, "I know that I had once a daughter born to me, having been told that it died almost as soon as it was born. This writing now informs me that it was exposed: but who took it up, who preserved, who educated it? who brought it into Egypt? Was that person, whoever he were, taken captive at the same time with her? How shall I be satisfied that this is the real child that was exposed? May she not have perished? May not these tokens have fallen into the hands of some one, who takes advantage of this chance? May not some evil genius be paltering with my desire of offspring, and clothed with the person of this maiden, be endeavouring to pass off a supposititious birth as my successor,—overshadowing the truth with this fillet, as with a cloud?"

But now Sisimithres replied, "I can clear up some of your doubts; for I am the person who took her up, who educated and carried her into Egypt, when you sent me thither on an embassy. You know me too well to suspect me of asserting what is untrue. I perfectly recollect the fillet, which is inscribed with the royal characters of the kings of Ethiopia, which you cannot suspect to have been counterfeited elsewhere; for you yourself must recognize the handwriting of Persina. But there were other tokens exposed with her, which I delivered at the same time to him who received the damsel from me, who was a Grecian, and, in appearance, an honest and worthy man."

"I have preserved them likewise," said Chariclea, and immediately shewed the necklace and the bracelet. Persina was yet more affected when she saw these.

Hydaspes still inquiring what all this agitation could mean, and whether she had anything to discover which might throw light upon this matter; she answered, "that she certainly had, but it was an examination more proper to be made in private than in public."

Hydaspes was more than ever perplexed, and Chariclea proceeded— "These are the tokens of my mother; but this ring is a present of your own;" and produced the stone Pantarbè.

The king instantly recollected it as a present which he had made to his wife during the time of their betrothment; and he said, "Maiden, these tokens were certainly mine; but how does it appear that you possess them as my child, and have not obtained them by some other means? Besides, in addition to my other doubts, your complexion is totally different from that of an Ethiopian."

Here Sisimithres interposed, and said, "The child whom I took up was perfectly white: and farther, the time when I found her seems very closely to coincide with the age of the maiden, for it is just seventeen years since this happened. The colour of her eyes too occurred to me as being the same; in short, I recognize in her the general expression of her features, and in her surpassing beauty a resemblance with what I recollect of the child then exposed."

"This is all very well," replied Hydaspes, "you speak with the fervour of the advocate more than as the judge; but take care lest while you are clearing up one doubt, you do not raise another, and that a more serious one; throwing suspicions upon the virtue of my consort; as we are both Ethiopians, how could we for our offspring have a white child?"

Sisimithres, with rather a sarcastic smile, replied, "I know not why you should object to me, that I am an advocate for this maiden. He is the best judge who inclines to the side of right: may I not rather be called an advocate for you, while I am endeavouring, with the assistance of the gods, to establish your right to be called a father; and neglecting no means to restore to you, in the bloom of her youth, that daughter whom I preserved in swathing bands? However, deem of me as you please, I do not esteem it necessary to make any apology; we do not shape our lives so as to please others: we endeavour to follow the dictates of truth and virtue, and think it sufficient if we can approve our conduct to ourselves: yet, as to the doubt which you entertain concerning her complexion, the writing clears this up, explaining how Persina, from her contemplation of Andromeda, might have received an impression upon her mind agreeing with the subject of the picture. If you wish for farther proof, the original is at hand; examine the Andromeda, the likeness between the picture and the maiden will be found unmistakeably exact."

The king complied: and had the picture brought; when being placed near Chariclea, an instant cry of surprise, admiration, and joy, was raised throughout the assembly, at the striking likeness; those who were near enough to understand what was passing, spreading the intelligence among the rest.

Hydaspes could no longer doubt, and he stood for some time motionless, between wonder and pleasure. But Sisimithres added, "One thing is still necessary to complete the proof; for recollect the succession to the kingdom, and the truth itself is now in question. Bare your arm, my child; there was a black mark upon it, a little above the elbow. There is nothing unseemly in doing this, in order to establish the evidence of your birth and family." Chariclea obeyed, and uncovered her left arm, when there appeared, as it were, an ebon ring, staining the ivory of her arm.

But Persina could now no longer contain herself—she leapt from her throne, burst into tears, rushed into her daughter's embrace, and could express her transports only by an inarticulate murmur. For excess of joy will sometimes beget grief. They had nearly fainted and fallen on the ground.

Hydaspes felt for his consort, affected as she was, and a kindred emotion was gaining possession of himself; yet he gazed upon the spectacle with eyes as unmoved as though they were of iron, struggling against his tears, his mind contending between fatherly feeling and manly fortitude, and tossed to and fro as by opposing tides. At last he was overpowered by all conquering nature; he not only believed himself to be a father, but was sensible of a father's feelings. Raising Persina, he was seen to embrace his daughter, pouring over her the paternal libation of his tears.

He was not, however, driven from that propriety which the circumstances demanded. Recollecting himself a little, and observing the multitude equally affected, shedding tears of pleasure and compassion at the wonderful events which had taken place, and not heeding the voices of the heralds, who were enjoining silence, he waved his hand, and stilling the tumult, thus addressed them:—"You see me, by the favour of the gods, and beyond all my expectations, entitled at length to the name of a father. This maiden is shewn to be my daughter by proofs which are infallible: but my love for you, and for my country, is so great, that disregarding the continuance of my race, and the succession to my throne, and the new and dear appellation which I have just acquired, I am ready to sacrifice her to the gods for your advantage. I see you weep; I see you moved by the feelings of humanity; you pity the age of this maiden, immature for death; you pity my vainly cherished hope of a successor, yet even against your wills, I must obey the customs of my country, and prefer the public weal to any private feelings of my own. Whether it be the will of the gods just to shew me a daughter, and then take her away again (shewing her to me at her birth, taking her away now that she is found), I leave you to judge: I am unable to determine. As little can I decide whether they will permit her to be sacrificed, when, after driving her from her native land to the extremest ends of the earth, they have, as by a miracle, brought her back again a captive; but if it be expedient that I sacrifice her whom I slew not as an enemy, nor injured as a prisoner, at the instant when she is recognized to be my daughter I will not hesitate, nor yield to affections which might be pardonable in any other father. I will not falter nor implore your compassion to acquit me of obedience to the law, out of regard to the feelings of nature and affection, nor even suggest that it is possible the deity may be appeased and satisfied by another victim; but as I see you sympathize with me, and feel my misfortunes as your own, even so much more does it become me to prefer your good to every other consideration, little regarding this sore grief, little regarding the distress of my poor Queen, made a mother and at the same moment rendered childless. Dry then your tears, repress your ineffectual grief for ever, and prepare for this necessary sacrifice: and, thou, my daughter! (now first and now last do I address thee by this longed-for name,) beauty is to no purpose, and in vain discovered to thy parents! thou who hast found thy native land more cruel than any foreign region! who hast found a strange land thy preserver, but wilt find thy native country thy destroyer! do not thou break my heart, by mournful tears; if ever thou hast shewed a high and royal spirit, shew it now. Follow thy father, who is unable to adorn thee as a bride; who leads thee to no nuptial chamber; but who decks thee for a sacrifice; who kindles, not torch of marriage, but the altar torch, and now offers as a victim this thine unrivalled loveliness. Do you too, O ye gods! be propitious, even if anything unbecoming or disrespectful has escaped me, overcome as I am, by grief, at calling this maiden daughter, and at the same time being her destroyer!" So saying, he made a show of leading Chariclea to the pyre, with palpitating heart, and deprecating the success of the speech, which he had made in order to steal away the people's wills.

The whole multitude was strongly excited by these words—they would not suffer her to be led a step towards the altar; but loudly and with one voice cried out—"Save the maiden! Preserve the royal blood! Deliver her whom the gods evidently protect! We are satisfied; the custom has been sufficiently complied with. We acknowledge thee our king: do thou acknowledge thyself a father; may the gods pardon the seeming disobedience; we shall be much more disobedient by thwarting their will; let no one slay her who has been preserved by them. Thou who art the father of thy country, be also the father of thy family!" These, and a thousand such like exclamations, were heard from every side. At length they prepared to prevent by force the sacrifice of Chariclea, and demanded steadily that the other victims alone should be offered to the gods.

Gladly and readily did Hydaspes suffer himself to be persuaded, and to submit to this seeming violence: he heard with pleasure the cries and congratulations of the assembly, and allowed them the indulgence of their wills, waiting till the tumult should spontaneously subside.

Finding himself near Chariclea, he said:—"My dear daughter (for the tokens you have produced, the wise Sisimithres, and the benevolence of the gods declare you to be such), who is this stranger who was taken with you, and is now led out to be sacrificed? How came you to call him your brother, when you were first brought into my presence at Syene? He is not likely to be found my son, for Persina had only one child, yourself."

Chariclea, casting her eyes on the ground, blushed, and said:—"He is not, I confess, my brother: necessity extorted that fiction from me. Who he is, he will better explain than I can."

Hydaspes not readily comprehending what she meant, replied:— "Forgive me, my child, if I have asked a question concerning this young man which it seems to hurt your maiden modesty to answer. Go into the tent to your mother, cause her more rejoicing now, than you caused her pain when she gave you birth; add to her present enjoyment, by relating every particular about yourself. Meanwhile, we will proceed with the sacrifice, selecting, if possible, a victim worthy to be offered with this youth instead of you."

Chariclea was nearly shrieking at mention of sacrificing the young man; hardly could she for ultimate advantage, check her frenzied feelings, so as to wind her way covertly towards the end she had in view. "Sire," said she, "perhaps there needs not to seek out another maiden, since the people remitted in my person the sacrifice of any female victim? But if they insist that a pair of either sex should be sacrified, see if it be not necessary for you to find out another youth, as well as another maiden; or, if that be not done, whether I must not still be offered."

"The gods forbid!" replied Hydaspes; "but why should you say this?"

"Because," said she, "the gods have decreed that he is to live with me, or die with me."

"I commend your humanity," replied the king, "in that having so hardly escaped yourself, you are desirous of saving a foreigner, a Greek, a fellow-prisoner, and of the same age, with whom, from a communion in misfortunes, you must have contracted some degree of familiarity and friendship: but he cannot be exempted from the sacrifice; religion will not permit our country's custom to be in everything curtailed, neither would the people suffer it, who have with difficulty been persuaded by the goodness of the deities to spare you."

"O king!" said Chariclea, "for perhaps I may not presume to call you father, since the mercy of the gods has saved my body, let me implore their and your clemency to preserve my soul: they know with how much justice I call him so, since they have so closely interwoven the web of my destiny with his. But if his fate is irretrievably determined; as if a foreigner he must necessarily suffer, I ask only one favour—Let me with my own hand perform the sacrifice; let me grasp the sword—even like a precious treasure—and signalize my fortitude before the Ethiopians."

Hydaspes was astonished and confounded at this strange request. "I know not what to make," said he, "of this sudden change in your disposition: but a moment ago you were anxious to save this stranger, and now you desire permission to destroy him as an enemy with your own hands; but there is nothing either honourable or becoming your sex or age in such a deed: granting that there were, it is impossible; it is an office exclusively belonging to the priests and priestesses of the Sun and Moon, the one must be a husband; the other is required to be a wife; so that even the fact of your virginity would be sufficient to preclude this unaccountable request."

"There need be no obstacle here," rejoined Chariclea, blushing, and whispering her mother, she said, "give but your consent and I already have one who answers to the name of husband."—"We will consent," replied Persina, smiling, "and will bestow your hand at once, if we can find a match worthy of yourself and us."—"Then," said Chariclea, raising her voice, "your search need not be long, it is already found."

She was proceeding (for the imminent danger of Theagenes made her bold, and caused her to break through the restraints of maiden modesty), when Hydaspes, becoming impatient, said—"How do ye, O gods, mingle blessings and misfortunes! and mar the happiness ye have bestowed upon me! ye restore, beyond all my hopes, a daughter, but ye restore her frenzy-stricken! for is not her mind frenzied when she utters such inconsistencies? She first calls this stranger her brother, who is no such thing; next, when asked who the stranger is, she says she knows not; then she is very anxious to preserve him, as a friend, from suffering; and, failing in this, appears desirous of sacrificing him with her own hands; and when we tell her that none but one who is wedded can lawfully perform this office, then she declares herself a wife but does not name her husband. How can she indeed? She whom the altar proves never to have had a husband; unless the unfailing ordeal of chastity among the Ethiopians has, in her case only, proved fallacious, dismissing her unscathed, and bestowing upon her the spurious reputation of virginity; upon her, who with one breath calls the same person her friend and enemy, and invents a brother and a husband who have no existence? Do you, then, my Queen, retire into your tent, and endeavour to recall this maiden to her senses: for either she is frenzied by the deity, who is approaching the sacrifices, or else she is distraught through her unexpected preservation. I will have search made for the victim, due to the gods, as an offering in her stead; meanwhile I will give audience to the ambassadors of the different nations, and will receive the presents brought in congratulation of my victory." So saying, he seated himself in a conspicuous place near the tent, and commanded the ambassadors to be introduced, and to bring what gifts they had to offer.

Harmonias, the lord in waiting, inquired whether they should all approach without distinction, or a few selected from every nation; or whether he should introduce each separately.

"Let them come separately in turn," said the king, "that each may be questioned according to his deserts."

"Your nephew, then, Mercœbus," said Harmonias, "must first appear; he is just arrived, and is waiting outside the troops for his introduction."

"You silly, stupid fellow," replied Hydaspes, "why did you not announce him instantly? Do you not know that he is not a mere ambassador, but a king, the son of my own brother (not long deceased), placed by me on his father's throne, and adopted by me as my own son?"

"I was aware of it, my lord," replied Harmonias; "but I considered that the duty of a lord in waiting required him above all things, to observe a proper time and season. Pardon me, therefore, if when I saw you speaking with the royal ladies, I felt averse to drawing your attention from matters of such delight."

"Let him enter now, then," replied the king. The master of the ceremonies hastened out, and soon returned with him.

Mercœbus was a handsome youth, just past the season of boyhood, his age being about seventeen; but he exceeded in stature almost all those who surrounded him, and his suite was splendid and numerous. The Ethiopian guards opened on either side to let him pass, and regarded him with wonder and respect.

Hydaspes himself rose from his throne to meet him, embraced him with fatherly affection, placed him by his side, and taking him by the hand said, "Nephew, you are come very seasonably both to assist at a triumphal sacrifice, and a nuptial ceremony; for the gods, the authors and protectors of our family, have restored to me a daughter, and provided, as it seems, for you a wife. The particulars you shall hear hereafter; at present if you have any business relating to the nation which you govern, make me acquainted with it."

The youth, at the mention of a wife, was seen to blush through his dark complexion from mingled pleasure and modesty (the red rushing, as it were, to the surface of the black). After an interval he said, "The other ambassadors, my Father, in honour of your splendid victory, bring you the choicest productions of their several countries: I, as a suitable compliment to a brave and first-rate warrior, make you an offering after your own heart, a champion who is invincible; not to be matched either in wrestling, or boxing, or in the race;" and so, saying, he motioned to the man alluded to, to advance.

He came forward and made his adoration to Hydaspes. So vast and "old world" was his stature, that when kissing the king's knees, his head nearly equalled those who sat on raised seats above him; and, without waiting for any orders, he stripped and challenged any one to engage with him, either with skill of arms, or with strength of hands. And when, after many proclamations made, no antagonist appeared to oppose him—"You shall have," said Hydaspes, "a reward quite in character;" and he ordered an old and very bulky elephant to be brought out and given to him.

The man was pleased with, and vain of the present; but the people burst into a shout of laughter; delighted at the humour of the king; consoling themselves by their derision of his boastfulness, for the inferiority which they had virtually expressed.

The ambassadors of the Seres came next. They brought spun and woven garments, both white and purple; the materials of which were the produce of an insect, which is bred in their country. These gifts being accepted, they begged and obtained the release of certain prisoners who had been condemned.

After them, the envoys from Arabia the Happy approached. They presented many talents worth of fragrant leaves, lavender, cinnamon, and other productions, with which that land of perfume abounds; all which filled the air around with an agreeable odour.

Then appeared the Troglodites. They brought gold dust (which is turned up by the ant-eater), also a pair of hippogriffs guided by golden reins.

The ambassadors of the Blemmyæ offered bows and arrows, formed of serpents' bones, and disposed into the form of a crown.

"These our presents," said they, "in value fall far behind those of others; nevertheless, they did good service against the Persians, at the river, as you yourself can testify."

"They are of more value," said Hydaspes, "than other costly gifts, and are the cause of my now receiving other presents;"—at the same time he bid them declare their wishes. They requested some diminution of their tributes, and obtained a full remission of them for ten years. When almost all the ambassadors had been admitted, and had been presented, some with rewards equal to their gifts, others with such as were far greater, at last the ambassadors of the Axiomitæ appeared. These were not tributaries, but allies: they came to express their satisfaction at the king's success, and brought with them their presents; and among the rest there was an animal of a very uncommon and wonderful kind: his size approached to that of a camel! his skin was marked over with florid spots: his hind-quarters were low and lionshaped: but his fore legs, his shoulders, and breast, were far higher in proportion than his other parts; his neck was slender, towering up from his large body into a swanlike throat, and his head, like that of a camel, was about twice as large as that of a Lybian ostrich; his eyes were very bright and rolled with a fierce expression; his manner of moving was different from that of every other land or water animal; he did not use his legs alternately, one on each side at once, but moved both those on the right together, and then, in like manner, both those on the left; one side at a time being raised before the other; and yet so docile in movement and gentle in disposition was he, that his keeper led him by a thin cord fastened round his neck; his master's will having over him the influence of an irresistible chain. At the appearance of this animal the multitude were astonished; and extemporising his name from the principal features in his figure, they called him a camelopard. He was, however, the occasion of no small confusion in the assembly. There happened to stand near the altar of the Moon a pair of bulls, and by that of the Sun four white horses, prepared for sacrifice. At the sudden sight of this strange outlandish beast, seen for the first time, terrified as if they had beheld some phantom, one of the bulls, and two of the horses, bursting from the ropes of those who held them, galloped wildly away. They were unable to break through the circle of the soldiery, fortified as it was with a wall of locked shields; but running in wild disorder through the middle space, they overturned vessels and victims—everything, in short, that came in their way; so that mingled cries arose, some of fear in those towards whom the animals were making; some of mirth for the accidents which happened to others whom they saw fallen and trampled upon. Persina and her daughter, upon this, could not remain quiet in their tent; but gently drawing aside the curtain they became spectators of what was done.

But now Theagenes, whether excited by his own courageous spirit, or by the inspiration of the gods, observing the keepers who were placed around him dispersed in the tumult, rose from his knees, in which which posture he had placed himself before the altar, awaiting his approaching sacrifice; and seizing a piece of cleft wood, many of which lay prepared for the ceremony, he leaped upon one of the horses who had not burst his bands; and grasping the mane with one hand, and using it for a bridle, with his heel (as with a spur) and the billet he urged on the courser, and pursued, on full speed, one of the flying bulls.

At first, those present supposed it an attempt of Theagenes to escape in the confusion, and called out not to let him pass the ring of soldiers; but they soon had reason to be convinced that it was not the effect of fear or dread of being sacrificed. He quickly overtook the bull and followed him for some time close behind, fatiguing him, and urging on his course, pursuing him in all his doublings, and if he endeavoured to turn and make at him, avoiding him with wonderful dexterity. When he had made the animal a little familiar with his presence and his movements, he galloped up close by his side, actually touching him, mingling the breath and sweat of both animals, and so equalizing their courses, that they who were at a distance might imagine their heads had grown together. Every one extolled Theagenes who had found means to join together this strange hippotaurine pair. While the multitude was intent upon, and diverted with this spectacle, Chariclea was agitated, and trembled. She knew not what was the object of Theagenes; should he fall and be wounded it would be death to her; her emotion, in short, was such that it could not escape the observation of Persina.

"My child," said she, "what is the matter with you? You seem very anxious about this stranger. I feel some concern for him myself, and pity his youth. I hope he will escape the danger to which he has exposed himself, and be preserved for the sacrifice; lest all the honours which we meant to pay the gods, should be found failing and deficient."

"Yours is strange compassion," replied Chariclea, "to wish that he may avoid one death, in order that he may suffer a worse. But if it be possible, O my mother! save this young man for my sake."

Persina not understanding the real case, but suspecting that love had some share in it, said, "This is impossible; but let me know the nature of your connection with this youth, in whom you seem to take so great an interest. Open your mind with freedom and confidence, and recollect that you are speaking to a mother. Even if giving way to any youthful weakness, you have felt more for this stranger than perhaps a maiden ought to own, a parent knows how to excuse the failings of a daughter; and a woman can throw a cloak over the frailties of her sex."

"This too is my additional misfortune," replied Chariclea; "I am speaking to those of understanding, yet I am not understood. While speaking of my own misfortunes, I am not supposed to speak of them. I must enter then upon a 'plain unvarnished' accusation of myself." She was preparing to declare everything which related to her situation and connections, when she was interrupted by a sudden and loud shout from the multitude; for Theagenes, after urging his horse at its swiftest speed and getting even with the bull's head, suddenly leaping from the animal (which he allowed to run loose) threw himself on the bull's neck. He placed his face between his horns, closely embraced his forehead with his arms (as with a chaplet), clasped his fingers in front, and letting his body fall on the beast's right shoulder, sustained his bounds, and shocks with little hurt. When he perceived him to be fatigued with his weight, and that his muscles began to be relaxed and yield, just as he passed by the place where Hydaspes sat, he shifted his body to the front, entangled his legs with those of the bull, continuously kicking him and hindering his progress. The beast being thus impeded, and borne down at the same time by the weight and force of the youth, trips and tumbles upon his head, rolls upon his back, and there lies supine, his horns deeply imbedded in the ground, and his legs quivering in the air, testifying to his defeat. Theagenes kept him down with his left hand, and waved his right towards Hydaspes and the multitude, inviting them, with a smiling and cheerful countenance, to take part in his rejoicing, while the bellowings of the bull served instead of a trumpet to celebrate his triumph. The applause of the multitude was expressed not so much by articulate words, as by a shout, giving open-mouthed token of their wonderment, and with its sounds extolling him to the very skies. By order of Hydaspes, Theagenes was brought before him, and the bull, by a rope tied over his horns, was led back weak and dispirited towards the altar, where they again fastened him, together with the horse which had escaped. The king was preparing to speak to Theagenes, when the multitude, interested in him from the first, and now delighted with this instance of his strength and courage, but still more moved with jealousy towards the foreign wrestler, called out with one voice—"Let him be matched with Marœbus's champion. Let him who has received the elephant contend, if he dare, with him who has subdued the bull." They pressed and insisted on this so long, till at length they extorted the consent of Hydaspes. The fellow was called out: he advanced, casting around fierce and contemptuous looks, stepping haughtily, dilating his chest, and swinging his arms with insolent defiance. When he came near the royal tent, Hydaspes looking at Theagenes, said to him in Greek—"The people are desirous that you should engage with this man, you must therefore do so."

"Be it as they please," replied Theagenes. "But what is to be the nature of the contest?"—"Wrestling," said the king.—"Why not with swords, and in armour?" returned the other, "that either by my fall or by my victory I may satisfy Chariclea, who persists in concealing everything which relates to our connection, or perhaps at last has cast me off."

"Why you thus bring in the name of Chariclea," replied Hydaspes, "you best know; but you must wrestle, and not fight with swords, for no blood must be shed on this day, but at the altar." Theagenes perceived the king's apprehension lest he should fall before the sacrifice, and said,

"You do well, O king, to reserve me for the gods; they too, you may be assured, will watch over my preservation." So saying, taking up a handful of dust, he sprinkled it over his limbs, already dripping with sweat, from his exertions in pursuit of the bull. He shook off all which did not adhere; and stretching out his arms, planting his feet firmly, bending his knees a little, rounding his back and shoulders, throwing back his neck, and contracting all his muscles, he stood anxiously waiting the gripe of his antagonist. The Ethiopian seeing him, grimly smiled, and by his contemptuous gestures seemed to slight his adversary.

Making a rush he let fall his arm, like some mighty bar, upon the neck of Theagenes—at the echo which it made the braggart laughed exultingly. Theagenes, trained in the wrestling-school tricks from his youth, and familiar with all the tricks of the Mercurial art, determined to give ground at first, and having made trial of his adversary, not to stand up against such tremendous weight and savage ferocity, but to elude his undisciplined strength by skill and subtlety. Staggering back, then, a little from his place he affected to suffer more than he really did, and exposed the other side of his neck to his opponent's blow; and when the African planted another hit in that quarter, purposely giving way, he pretended almost to be falling upon his face. But when waxing stronger in contempt and confidence, his antagonist was now a third time, unguardedly rushing on, and about to let fall his upraised arm, Theagenes got within his guard, eluding his blow by a sudden twist, and with his right elbow struck up the other's left arm, and dashed him to the earth, already impelled downwards by the sway of his own missed blow; then slipping his hand under his armpits, he got upon his back, and with difficulty spanning his brawny waist, incessantly kicked his feet and ancles, and compelled him to rise upon his knees, strode over him, pressed him in the groin with his legs, struck from under him the support of his hands, and twining his arms about his temples, dragged his head back upon his shoulders, and so stretched him with his belly on the ground.

An universal shout of applause, greater than before, now burst from the multitude; nor could the king contain himself, but springing from his throne—"O hateful necessity," he cried, "what a hero of a man are we compelled to sacrifice!" and calling him to him he said, "Young man, it now remains for you to be crowned for the altar, according to our custom. You have deserved a crown too for your glorious but useless victory, and transitory triumph; and though it be out of my power, however willing I may be, to preserve your life, whatever I can do for you I will. If therefore there is any thing you wish to have done, either before or after your death, ask it freely." So saying he took a crown of gold, set with precious stones, and put it on his head; and, while he placed it there, was seen to shed tears.

"I have but one thing to ask," said Theagenes, "and this I earnestly beseech you that I may obtain. If it be impossible for me to avoid being sacrificed, grant that I may suffer by the hands of this your newly recovered daughter."

Hydaspes was annoyed at this reply, and called to mind the conformity of this request to that made just before by Chariclea; but, as the time pressed, he did not think it necessary to inquire particularly into the reasons of it, and only said, "Whatever is possible, Stranger! I encouraged you to ask, and promised that you should obtain; but she, who performs the sacrifice the law distinctly declares, must be one who has a husband, not a maiden."

"Chariclea has a husband," said Theagenes.—"These are the words," replied Hydaspes, "of one who trifles and is about to die. The altar has declared her unmarried and a virgin—unless indeed you call this Merœbus her husband (having somehow heard the rumour); he however is not yet her husband—he is yet in accordance with my will, only her intended."

"Nor will he ever be her husband," said Theagenes, "if I know aught of Chariclea's sentiments; and, if being a victim, credit is due to me as inspired by prophecy."—"But, fair Sir," said Merœbus, "it is not living but slaughtered victims which afford knowledge to the Seers. You are right, Sire, in saying that the stranger talks folly, and like one just about to die. Command, therefore, that he be led to the altar; and when you shall have finished all your business, begin the rites, I pray you."

Theagenes was being led away; and Chariclea, who had breathed again when he was victorious, was once more plunged into grief, when she saw it had profited him nothing. Persina observed her tears, and feeling for her affliction, said—"It is possible I may yet have power to save this Grecian, if you will explain more clearly all the particulars relating to yourself."

Chariclea, who saw that there was not a moment to be lost, was a second time preparing to own everything; when Hydaspes inquiring from the lord in waiting whether any ambassadors remained who had not had audience, was told only those from Syene, who were that instant arrived, with letters from Oroondates, and presents. "Let them too approach, and execute their commission," said the monarch. They were introduced, and delivered letters to this effect:—

"Oroondates, Viceroy of the Great King, to Hydaspes, the king of Ethiopia.

"Since conqueror in fight, you are yet more conqueror in magnanimity, in restoring to me a viceroyalty unasked, I have little doubt that I shall obtain a slight request. A young maiden who was being conducted from Memphis to my camp, became involved in the perils of war, and as I am informed, was sent by you into Ethiopia. This I have learnt from those who were with her and who escaped: I beg she may be sent to me, both on account of the maiden herself, as well as for her father's sake, who, after having wandered over half the globe, in search of his daughter, came at last to Elephantine, and was taken prisoner by the garrison. When reviewing those of my soldiers who survived, I saw him and he earnestly desired to be sent to your clemency. He is among the ambassadors, his manners and bearing show him to be of noble birth, and his very countenance and looks speak strongly in his favour. Dismiss him then, O king, I beseech you, happy and contented from your presence. Send back to me one who is a father not merely in name but in reality."

Hydaspes, having read the letter, inquired who it was, who was come in quest of his daughter. When he was pointed out to him, he said, "I am ready, stranger, to do every thing which Oroondates requests of me. Out of the ten captive maidens whom we have brought hither, one assuredly is not your daughter; examine the rest, and if she be found among them take her."

The old man, falling down, kissed his feet. The maidens were brought, and passed in review before him; but when he saw not her whom he sought, he said sorrowfully—"None of these, O king, is my daughter."—"You have my good will in your behalf," replied Hydaspes. "You must blame Fortune if you have not discovered your child. It is in your power to search, if you will, through the camp; and to ascertain that none else has been brought hither besides these."

The old man smote his forehead, and wept; and, then after raising his eyes, and looking round him, he suddenly sprang forward, like one distracted; and upon coming to the altar, he twisted the end of his long robe into the form of a halter, threw it over the neck of Theagenes, and pulled him towards him, crying out—"I have found you, my enemy! I have found you, man of blood, detested wretch!"—The guards interposed, and endeavoured to resist and pull him away, but keeping a firm hold and clinging closely to him, he succeeded in bringing him before Hydaspes and the council.

"This, O king," said he, "is the man who stole away my daughter. This is he who has rendered my house childless and desolate; who, after ravishing away my daughter from the midst of Apollo's altar, now sits as though he were holy beside the altars of the gods."

The assembly was thrown into commotion at what was taking place. They did not understand what he said, but wondered at what they saw him do; and Hydaspes commanded him to explain himself more plainly, and say what he would have; when the old man (it was Charicles), concealing the true circumstances of the birth and exposure of Chariclea, lest, if she should have perished in her flight or journey, he might come into some collision with her real parents, explained briefly such matters as could produce ηo ill results.

"I had a daughter, O king! and had you seen her various and uncommon perfections, both of mind and person, you would say I have good cause for speaking as I do. She lived the life of a virgin, a priestess of Diana, in the temple at Delphi. This noble Thessalian, forsooth, who was sent by his country to preside over a solemn embassy and sacrifice to be celebrated in our holy city, stole her away from the very shrine, I say, of Apollo.

"Justly may he be considered to have insulted you by profaning your national deity Apollo and his temple, Apollo being identical with the Sun. His assistant in this impious outrage was a pretended priest of Memphis. In my pursuit, I came to Thessaly; and the Thessalians offered to give him up should he be found as one accursed and deserving death. Thinking it probable that Calasiris might have chosen Memphis as a place of refuge, I hastened thither. Calasiris, I found, was dead; but I learnt all particulars concerning my daughter from his son Thyamis, who told me that she had been sent to Oroondates at Syene. After being disappointed at not finding the latter at Syene, and having been myself detained prisoner at Elephantis, I now appear before you as a suppliant, to seek my child. You will, then, deeply oblige me, a man of many griefs, and will also gratify your own self, by not disregarding the Viceroy's intercession." He ceased, and burst into tears.

The king asked Theagenes what reply he had to make to all this. "The whole charge," said he, "is true. To this man I have been a ravisher, unjust, and violent; but to you I have been a benefactor."—"Restore, then, another's daughter," said Hydaspes. "You have been dedicated to the gods; let your death be a holy and glorious sacrifice—not the just punishment of crime."

"Not he who committed the violence," said Theagenes; "but he who reaps the fruits of it, is bound to make restitution. Do you then restore Chariclea, for she is in your possession. The old man, you shall see, will own your daughter to be her whom he seeks."

None could repress their emotion: all were in confusion. But Sisimithres, who had hitherto kept silence, though long since understanding all that was being said and done, yet waiting till the circumstances should become yet clearer, now ran up and embraced Charicles. "Your adopted child," said he, "she whom I formerly delivered into your hands, is safe: she is, and has been acknowledged to be, the daughter of those whom you know."

Upon this Chariclea rushed out of the tent, and overlooking all restraints of sex or maidenly reserve, flung herself at the feet of Charicles, and cried out, "O my father! O not less revered than the authors of my birth, punish me, your cruel and ungrateful daughter, as you think fit, regardless of my only excuse, that what has been done was ordained by the irresistible will and appointment of the gods." Persina, on the other side, threw her arms round Hydaspes, and said, "My dear husband, be assured that all this is truth, and that this stranger Greek is her betrothed." The people, on the other hand, leaped and danced for joy; every age and condition were, without exception, delighted—not understanding, indeed, the greater part of what was said, but conjecturing the facts from what had taken place with Chariclea. Perhaps, too, they were brought to a comprehension of the truth by some secret influence of the deity, who had ordered all these events so dramatically, producing out of the greatest discords the most perfect harmony: joy out of grief; smiles from tears; out of a stern spectacle a gladsome feast; laughter from weeping; rejoicing out of mourning; the finding of those who were not sought; the losing of those who were in imagination found; in one word, a holy sacrifice out of an anticipated slaughter.

At length Hydaspes said to Sisimithres, "O sage! what are we to do? To defraud the gods of their victims is not pious; to sacrifice those who appear to be preserved and restored by their providence is impious. It needs that some expedient be found out."

Sisimithres, speaking, not in the Grecian, but in the Ethiopian tongue, so as to be heard by the greatest part of the assembly, replied: "O king! the wisest among men, as it appears, often have the understanding clouded through excess of joy, else, before this time, you would have discovered that the gods regard not with favour the sacrifice which you have been preparing for them. First they, from the very altar, declared the all-blessed Chariclea to be your daughter; next they brought her foster-father most wonderfully from the midst of Greece to this spot; they struck panic and terror into the horses and oxen which were being prepared for sacrifice, indicating, perhaps, by that event, that those whom custom considered as the more perfect and fitting victims were to be rejected. Now, as the consummation of all good, as the perfection of the piece, they show this Grecian youth to be the betrothed husband of the maiden. Let us give credence to these proofs of the divine and wonder-working will; let us be fellow workers with this will; let us have recourse to holier offerings; let us abolish, for ever, these detested human sacrifices."

When Sisimithres had uttered this, in a loud voice, Hydaspes, speaking also in the Ethiopian tongue, and taking Theagenes and Chariclea by the hand, thus proceeded:—

"Ye who are this day assembled! since these things have been thus brought to pass by the will of the deities, to oppose them would be impious. Wherefore, calling to witness those who have woven these events into the web of destiny, and you whose minds appear to be in concert with them, I sanction the joining together of this pair in wedlock and procreative union. If you approve, let a sacrifice confirm this resolution, and then proceed we with the sacred rites."

The assembly signified their approval by a shout, and clapped their hands, in token of the nuptials being ratified. Hydaspes approached the altar, and, in act to begin the ceremony, said, "O lordly Sun and queenly Moon! since by your wills Theagenes and Chariclea have been declared man and wife, they may now lawfully be your ministers." So saying, he took off his own and Persina's mitre, the symbol of the priesthood, and placed his own upon the head of the youth, that of his consort upon the maiden's head.

Upon this Charicles called to mind the oracle which had been given to them in the temple before their flight from Delphi, and acknowledged its fulfilment.

In regions torrid shall arrive at last,
There shall the gods reward their pious vows,
And snowy chaplets bind their dusky brows.

The youthful pair then, crowned by Hydaspes with white mitres, and invested with the dignity of priesthood, sacrificed under propitious omens; and, accompanied by lighted torches and the sounds of pipes and flutes, Theagenes and Hydaspes, Charicles and Sisimithres, in chariots drawn by horses, Persina and Chariclea, in one drawn by milk white oxen, were escorted, into Meröe (amidst shouts, clapping of hands, and dances), there to celebrate with greater magnificence the more mystic portions of the nuptial rites.

Thus ends the Romance of the "Ethiopics," or Adventures of Theagenes and Chariclea, written by a Phœnician of Emesa, in Phœnicia, of the race of the Sun—Heliodorus, the son of Theodosius.

A Note About the Author

Heliodorus of Emesa (c. 3rd–4th century C.E.) was a Greek novelist and possibly an early Christian bishop. Born in Emesa, modern day Syria, Heliodorus is known for writing *Aethiopica*, the most complete extant novel in the ancient world. Also referred to as *The Adventures of Theagenes and Chariclea*, the novel is an ancient Greek romance that was rediscovered in manuscript form in the city of Buda in 1526. It has since been translated and republished countless times, and further codices copying the text of the novel have been discovered. Although not much is known about Heliodorus, it is believed that his father's name was Theodosius and that the family came from a line of solar priests. Some scholars, including Socrates of Constantinople in the 5th century and Nikephoros Kallistos Xanthopoulos in the 14th century, have claimed that Heliodorus of Emesa converted to Christianity and became bishop of Trikka before being pressured to resign from the role, but his identity and religious background remain uncertain.

A Note from the Publisher

Spanning many genres, from non-fiction essays to literature classics to children's books and lyric poetry, Mint Edition books showcase the master works of our time in a modern new package. The text is freshly typeset, is clean and easy to read, and features a new note about the author in each volume. Many books also include exclusive new introductory material. Every book boasts a striking new cover, which makes it as appropriate for collecting as it is for gift giving. Mint Edition books are only printed when a reader orders them, so natural resources are not wasted. We're proud that our books are never manufactured in excess and exist only in the exact quantity they need to be read and enjoyed.

Discover more of your favorite classics with Bookfinity™.

- Track your reading with custom book lists.
- Get great book recommendations for your personalized Reader Type.
- Add reviews for your favorite books.
- AND MUCH MORE!

Visit **bookfinity.com** and take the fun Reader Type quiz to get started.

Enjoy our classic and modern companion pairings!